Raven's Rise

World on Fire, Book III

by

Lincoln Cole

Published by Lincoln Cole, Columbus, 2017
admin@lincolncole.net
www.LincolnCole.net

Cover Design by M.N. Arzu
www.mnarzuauthor.com

Table of Contents

This one is for four people: my Mom, Crazy Kateen, Alan, and Mike.

"Not necessity, not desire—no, the love of power is the demon of men. Let them have everything—health, food, a place to live, entertainment—they are and remain unhappy and low-spirited: for the demon waits and waits and will be satisfied."

Friedrich Nietzsche

Prologue

As soon as Matt Walker stepped inside his quiet little church in the center of Phnom Penh, something felt terribly wrong. The lights remained off, just as he expected, but he could feel the presence of someone else hiding in the room.

The mere fact that they hid from him filled him with concern. He couldn't see anyone but could tell they hid there.

"Hello?" he called out in Khmer. "Who's there?"

No response. He tried English as well, but still, no answer came. Probably kids hiding away from their mothers. He'd experienced situations like this many times in the past, finding children avoiding their schoolwork or chores, though not usually this late in the day.

No doubt, they hid from him as well, hoping he wouldn't return them to their angry parents.

However, something about the situation made him worry, and even though wayward children seemed the likeliest scenario, something told him that this case differed.

Matt walked across the hardwood floor toward the front of the church and to the light switch. Wary and uncomfortable, he felt unsure what might be afoot but also afraid he would miss his dinner appointment.

He used the light spilling in through the open doorway to navigate between the wooden pews toward the front, keeping his eyes open for any trespassers.

He made it to the far side of the room and felt around for the switch. It took a few seconds for his fingers to find it in the darkness, and then he flicked it on.

Nothing happened. The room remained dark.

Suddenly, the door behind him swung closed with a crash, casting him into complete darkness.

A shiver danced across his spine, and he backed up against the wall, willing his eyes to adjust to the darkness. Someone stood inside the room with him, and a tinge of panic rushed through his body.

"Who's there?" he asked in Khmer. "Come out where I can see you."

"Why would I do that?" a woman asked in English from across the room. She sounded young, with a sultry voice.

"Who are you? Why are you in my church?"

"Maybe I came here looking for God."

She sounded closer this time as if she'd moved across the room toward him. He listened but couldn't hear any footsteps tapping across the wooden floor.

"He *does* hide in the most unexpected places," the woman said.

"What do you want?"

"I want *you*, Matthew. You have no idea how much you mean to me."

"Me?"

"Yes, you. You make the last piece of my puzzle. The light at the end of my tunnel. Matthew. I like your name. So Biblical."

He backed away slowly, one hand on the wall. He aimed to move away from the approaching voice and head for a door at the back of the cathedral. One he kept locked normally, and that exited into a back alleyway.

His eyes still hadn't adjusted to the darkness, and he bumped into a pew while he scrambled through the church, knocking it sideways to scrape across the floor.

"Where do you think you're going?" she asked, a few steps to his left. "Our fun has only just begun."

"Stay away from me."

"I couldn't stay apart from you any more than a moth can from a flame."

Suddenly, the door to the church blasted open, pouring bright sunlight in once more. A wretched-looking woman stood in front of him, maybe two meters away. She appeared of Indian descent, though pale. Pockmarks and rashes covering her skin and face gave her a sickly appearance.

The woman turned toward the door and let out a laugh when the light came in.

"I wondered when you would show up."

Matt glanced over. Another person stood the doorway. This one silhouetted by the sunlight, which made it impossible to make out the features or see the face.

"Matt, run!" the person in the doorway—a woman—yelled.

The newcomer's arm flew up, and a thunderous roar of gunshots filled his tiny church. On reflex, he covered his ears and stumbled backward, trying to get away from the sound.

He glanced back at the first woman, the scarred and sickly one. She dodged back and shifted behind one of the pillars that held up the roof. Gunshots thudded into the area around her.

The woman moved with unnatural speed, gliding as much as moving. Matt watched her in awe, not even sure if she qualified as human. More rounds blasted into the church. They buried into the pillar behind which she hid, shattering off huge wooden fragments that went flying through the air.

She turned, looked at him, and let out a hissing sound.

"Run, Matt!" the newcomer screamed from the open doorway before firing off more rounds at the Indian woman. "Get out of here!"

Matt ran.

Chapter 1

Haatim clutched the gun in his hands. They shook, and he worried that he might lose his grip and drop it onto the floor. He stood in the loading area of the hotel in Switzerland, where the Council had resided over the last few months, and aimed the pistol at his father.

He had found the weapon on the floor near his father, who looked to have a broken leg and had trouble moving. Aram looked at him with an expression of sadness and terror, which should have made it harder for Haatim to want to hurt him.

It didn't.

"I should shoot you," he whispered, the words barely audible. "I should pull the trigger and end this."

"Haatim, please. I'm your father."

"Is that supposed to make everything better? Should that absolve you of your crimes?"

"I love you, son. I never wanted any of this to happen. Please, don't do this."

The sheer insanity of the situation washed over Haatim and made him feel dizzy. A year ago, he had known nothing about the Council of Chaldea or the Hunters who served them by stopping supernatural and demonic threats. He'd had no idea that his father was anything except a religious figure in his community who went on a lot of business trips on behalf of his congregation.

Now, here he stood, trying to wrap his mind around the fact that he might actually pull the trigger. He might end his father's life, the man who'd raised and protected and taken care of him. The man who'd taught him right from wrong.

The man who'd gotten it wrong.

Nausea gripped Haatim, and everything about this situation felt surreal as if he watched all of this happen from outside his body rather than as an active participant. His mind numb, and hands sweaty, he couldn't think straight.

"Why would you do this?" he asked. Then he shook his head. "No. I don't want to know. Nothing you say could absolve you for your crimes."

Abigail dead. The Council betrayed and murdered. The hotel a devastated wreck out in the middle of nowhere. And all caused by the man cowering on the ground before him. Haatim couldn't remember ever getting so angry in his entire life. He felt furious at the betrayal, the manipulations, the hypocrisy, everything.

At the same time, an empty pit of grief also filled his heart. The sheer finality of what had happened sank in for him, albeit slowly. There could be no going back. This part of his life had finished, and he would never look at his father the same way again.

It seemed like he was closing out a chapter of his life and losing a part of him that he could never get back. He had never imagined that his father could keep so much from him.

Aram whimpered on the floor in front of him, leg broken and battered. The man held his left hand in the air between the two of them with an expression of confused fear. Mixed in with that fear, though, Haatim saw resignation. It looked as though he'd already decided that Haatim would pull the trigger and end his life.

Maybe he should.

"Haatim, please ..."

Haatim didn't want answers, but he needed them.

"How could you do this?" he asked his father. "All of these people are dead because of you."

"Let me explain."

"Explain what? Nida? Betraying the Council? What could you possibly say to justify *this*?"

"I did it for us."

The words hit like a punch to Haatim's gut, a lie so brazen it took his breath away. Haatim's hands tightened on the grip of his gun, and he narrowed his eyes. Could his father have become so deluded that he believed his words true?

"You did it for *you*. All of this, you did for your own selfish reasons and nothing else. Don't you dare try to bring me into this."

"When Nida got sick, your mother—"

"Not her, either. My mother had nothing to do with this."

"You don't understand ..."

"I understand perfectly. You made a deal with the devil to get back your daughter, and now everyone else has paid the price for your crimes."

"It isn't that simple."

"No. It is. You are a coward and a traitor."

"Haatim."

Haatim ignored him. "Right now, I'm just trying to decide if I should shoot you, or let Frieda decide what to do with you."

Aram blinked. "Frieda is still alive?"

"Does that surprise you? Did that not form part of your bargain with The Ninth Circle?"

Aram winced. "No, it isn't that. I just ... she was all Nida wanted. She promised me ... I didn't think ..."

"You didn't think what?"

Aram took a deep breath. "Nida promised to take only Frieda and leave

14

everyone else. No one should even have known of her presence until Frieda had gone."

"Oh, so you only tried to betray and murder *one* person. Is that supposed to make me feel all rosy inside?"

"No. No ... I just ... who else survived?"

Haatim didn't reply immediately. He felt unsure if he should withhold any information from his father, considering what had happened. Not because he thought his father might use it against them or betray them further.

The thing was, he didn't doubt his father's sincerity; at least, not in how things had played out. Aram seemed genuinely distraught by what had happened here, and it was clear that none of this had been in his original plan.

He had simply tried to play with fire and learned the hard way that it's easy to get burned.

No, Haatim considered withholding the information because his father didn't deserve to know. He had betrayed them and caused all of this to happen, and Aram found it painful not to know how badly everything had turned out. Part of Haatim wanted to keep him in the dark about it and torture him further.

But that part of himself, he didn't want to give rise to. He felt furious, and the more he tapped into that anger, the angrier he became. No matter what happened, he didn't want to become that kind of person. At length, he could see nothing to be gained by withholding the information.

"Dominick," Haatim said.

A moment passed. "Is that all?"

"Yes."

"You said I got *her* killed a few moments ago," Aram said. "Who did you mean?"

Haatim's hands shook again while emotion coursed through his body. He couldn't find the words to speak, only rage.

"Abigail," Aram finished, face turning pale. "Oh, son, I'm so sorry."

"Don't say her name," Haatim said in an anguished whisper. Then, with more anger, "You have no right."

"You have no idea how much I regret what happened."

"Your regrets mean nothing. Only actions, and *your* actions got her killed."

"Then, do it. Please. Pull the trigger. I'm guilty. I confess. I deserve this."

"I know you're guilty. But I need to know *everything*. I need to know what else you've done."

"You know it all."

"I need you to say it."

"I worked with The Ninth Circle. I thought I could manipulate them, but clearly, they manipulated me."

"What else?"

"Nothing."

"Don't lie."

"I'm not. I have nothing to hide. I've lost everything in my life, everything that mattered to me, and without you, I have nothing; I can see it in your eyes:

I've lost you too. Pull the trigger and end it, Haatim. You're right, I'm guilty, and I should pay for my crimes."

Haatim's hands shook some more. With his finger, he could feel the cool, curved metal of the trigger. He wanted to squeeze it in the hopes that it might offer a solution to the pain and misery coursing through his soul. Silent, jaw clenched and eyes hard, he prayed that it would give a balm against the agonizing loss and despair that smothered him.

However, killing Aram wouldn't bring a solution to his problems or the way he felt. It wouldn't make anything better, and if anything, would serve to make things worse.

Haatim lowered the gun to his side and let out a shuddering breath.

"Abigail is dead," he said, the words spilling forth. Even as he spoke, he had trouble admitting them as true. The words sounded hollow and unreal, like a sentence he wasn't supposed to say aloud. "You got her killed."

"I'm sorry; I never—"

"Yes, you did. You got your wish. She died saving Frieda's life."

"How?"

"A train wreck and explosion. We couldn't even find her body."

"Haatim, I ..."

"Maybe, I *should* execute you." Haatim ignored the man on the ground in front of him. "A part of me knows it would be the right thing to do. I know you deserve to pay, the same as I know that all the people you betrayed didn't deserve it."

Aram stared up at him, bottom lip trembling.

"But I won't kill you."

"Thank you, Haatim."

He shook his head. "Not because I shouldn't kill you, but because I *want* to. A large part of me wants to kill you, but for vengeance. Not justice. Then, I would be just as bad as you. I refuse to sink to that level."

Aram didn't reply, but Haatim could tell by his father's face that the words had stung him.

"Also, I won't forgive you. Ever. I'm done with you, and I never want to see you again for the rest of my life. Do you understand?"

"Haatim."

"Do you understand?" He gave his father a hard stare. "We're done."

Aram remained silent for a long moment, letting the finality of the words sink in. Finally, he looked away, unable to meet his son's gaze. "I understand."

Haatim nodded. "This is the last time you'll ever speak to me. Goodbye, Aram."

Haatim turned and strode out of the room before his father could respond. He headed back out into the cold night air outside the loading bay of the hotel. The wind washed over him, chilling the sweat on his skin and making him shiver.

For a long while, he stood there, listening to the wind and watching the snow swirl around him. Emotion and energy drained out of him, leaving him a husk standing in the cold Switzerland air, alone and broken.

Haatim couldn't believe how close he'd come to murdering his father, but he also couldn't believe that a part of him still wanted to go back in and finish the job. Lost and confused, he didn't have any clue what he should do.

This world, he didn't know. This world, he didn't belong in. This life seemed too brutal, too evil, and he felt unready to spend his entire future balancing on a knife's edge between life and death.

This wasn't his world.

Chapter 2

Haatim walked aimlessly around the outside of the destroyed and broken down hotel toward the lobby. Lost in his thoughts, exhausted and bitter, he ought to hurry back to Frieda and Dominick to let them know that he'd found a survivor, but right now, he didn't want to talk to anyone.

The moisture around his eyes froze against his cheeks. He made it to the outer fence and perimeter of the enclosure around the property. Here, the Council had holed up for Frieda's trial, and now it had turned into the place in which they had all died.

The fence hung damaged and broken, and near the breach, Haatim found dozens of piled bodies. Dead men and women, some of them servants of the cult who'd broken in, and others the mercenaries hired to protect the Council against just such an incursion.

So many dead. It looked like a warzone. It *was* a warzone. Only in movies had Haatim seen brutality and death like this, and he'd never imagined how much worse it could prove in person. The smell of blood hung in the air and a metallic taste like copper on the tip of his tongue.

The snow lay drenched in it. Haatim turned and looked back at the hotel, broken and destroyed in the middle of the storm. He tried to remember what it had looked like only a few days earlier, before any of this had happened, but couldn't.

Only these ruins remained.

He found Frieda inside the destroyed lobby of the hotel with Dominick. They looked like they ran on fumes alone, barely able to stay on their feet. They all needed a break, a chance to recover and catch up with everything that had happened. They wouldn't get that anytime soon.

The warm air from the slow-burning fires spread throughout the building washed over him when he walked inside, thawing him out, but he barely felt it.

"I checked the first floor," Dominick said to Frieda, and then glanced over at him when he entered. "No survivors."

"Keep looking," Frieda said. "I refuse to believe that everyone is gone."

"I will." Dominick turned back toward the stairs. He hesitated. "I don't know what we'll find."

"We have to check."

"I know, but we won't have a lot of time. Once the storm clears, rescue teams and police will come out here to find out what happened, and they'll ask a lot of questions. We can't be here when that happens."

"We won't be."

"They could be on their way already."

"I know."

"Then, don't you think we should—?"

"We have to keep looking," Frieda said. The expression on her face remained unreadable. She looked exhausted but had the same poise and grace about her that Haatim had come to expect from his time spent traveling with her. She always stayed calm and collected, no matter the situation. "We won't leave until we've combed every inch."

Dominick hesitated and then nodded. Frieda had been hurt badly in the train incident, and of the three of them, she was the worst off. They had patched her up in the helicopter before landing, but she would need medical attention soon. If she was willing to press on, then they knew they couldn't object.

He glanced over at Haatim, expression grim, and then headed to the stairs. Haatim watched him go: he couldn't remember a time since first meeting Dominick a few months earlier that he'd seen the man this serious. Dominick always joked and laughed; optimistic to an almost annoying degree.

It appeared as if that optimism had gone.

Bullet holes riddled the walls of the lobby, and the casings covered the floor. Shards of broken wood surrounded them, and three bodies in military garb lay in here. All of them had gotten stacked into the corner hastily, forgotten and dismissed.

When, finally, Haatim looked over at Frieda, she sat staring at him, studying him. From the look on her face, she had been gazing his way for some time. He met her eyes, frowning.

Frieda asked, "What's wrong?"

"Nothing."

She tilted her head to the side, curious. "What did you find?"

Eerie how easily she could always read him.

"I found my father," he said, the words mechanical. "Down in the loading bay."

"Aram? Alive?"

"Yes." Haatim nodded.

"Is he injured? Why didn't you bring him up? Does he need a stretcher?"

Haatim didn't reply straight away. "He *is* injured."

"But alive?"

"For now."

Realization dawned on Frieda's face. "He did this."

"Yes."

"How? What happened?"

"He betrayed everyone. He has the responsibility for all of this, including what happened to you."

"What?"

"He made a deal with the Ninth Circle to get back my sister, but they didn't exactly hold up their end of the bargain. Whatever lives inside her, it isn't Nida. Not anymore."

Frieda blinked. "Nida. That's what happened to her? I thought it a cruel joke by the demon, using her body like that after her sickness. I never thought ..."

"Everyone died because of him." Haatim shook his head. "We lost everything."

"Not everything," Dominick called down. He had returned and now stood at the top of the stairs. "I found Jun in his room. He's injured and has lost a lot of blood but managed to patch himself up fairly well. I think he'll make it."

Frieda let out a sigh of relief. "Thank God."

"He's a stubborn old bastard. Haatim, come help get him to the helicopter. We need to get him to a hospital."

Haatim followed Dominick up the stairs to the third floor of the hotel. They made their way down the hallway toward Jun's room. This section hadn't gotten as badly damaged as some of the others, though it did have a desolate feel that made Haatim's skin crawl.

The lights flickered under the power of the weakening backup generators as they ran out of power. The two men went silently, not even glancing at each other. Haatim considered telling Dominick about his father, and then changed his mind. He didn't want to talk about it. Frieda could fill him in on it if she wanted, but Haatim had done with giving that man any of his attention.

They passed a few dead people on this floor: the body of one of the Council's guards lay near an open doorway. It looked like the man had gotten caught off-duty and unprepared. Someone had executed him with a bullet in his forehead, and he lay in a pool of drying blood. Haatim felt sick to his stomach while he helped Dominick drag the man out of the way, trying to come to terms with what his last moments must have felt like while Nida and her army poured into the hotel and took it by force.

It must have been horrible. Men had tied up Haatim in a hotel room with his unconscious mother, but if he had been here, he would have ended up like this man: just another body mixed in with the dead.

"What are you wondering about?"

Dominick's words pulled Haatim back to reality. He realized he had stood unmoving for the last several moments, lost in his thoughts.

He shook the concerns away and focused on the task at hand. "Just ... we weren't here."

Dominick nodded. "I know. I keep thinking ... what if I had been here. Could I have helped? Could I have stopped this?"

"I doubt it." Haatim shook his head. "The Council got completely outnumbered and overrun."

"I know." Dominick nodded. "They would have killed me too. It still makes me wonder. So many people dead. Why did they spare us?"

Haatim didn't have a good answer for him. Subdued, they headed back out into the hallway and down to Jun's room.

Jun lay on the floor, covered in blood and leaning against the hotel bed. Pale and barely conscious, he had a bullet wound in his side. He'd managed to wrap one of the white linen sheets around the wound to staunch the bleeding, but it bloomed with a giant ring of blood where it had seeped through.

"Don't worry," Dominick said softly, gathering up the blankets from the bed. "We'll get you some help, Jun. Just hang on."

"Worry?" Jun blinked his eyes open and panted. He looked unfocused and in pain, but Haatim could see the strength of will that had kept the old man alive despite everything. "Why would I worry? I mean, it's not like you're taking your sweet time with this rescue effort or anything."

Dominick chuckled. "We can come back if you aren't ready to go."

"At the rate this hotel charges? Not a chance."

"How's your side? Want me to check it?"

"Sure. Let's spend another ten minutes here while you see if I bandaged myself okay."

"Did you know that you get sarcastic when you're in pain?"

"Did you know that you move at a snail's pace when you're trying to save people? I'm just going to chalk it up to laziness."

Dominick handed Haatim one end of the blanket he'd retrieved from the bed, ignoring the old man. "Help me get him onto this, and we'll use it to carry him down."

After some wrangling, they managed to get Jun Lee onto the comforter. Each time they moved him, he let out a grunt of pain but didn't complain anymore. He held on by a thread and had lost a lot of blood. If he survived this, it would make something of a miracle.

When they lifted him to carry him out to the helicopter, it surprised Haatim at how light Jun seemed. He hadn't looked like a small man when Haatim had first met him, but he proved thin and frail underneath his clothing. Haatim hadn't spent a lot of time with him but had considered Jun one of the older and wiser members of the Council: someone who kept others in check.

They carried him as carefully as they could down the stairs. Frieda had disappeared from the lobby when they got Jun down. Where had she gone? With Jun so badly off, they needed to get him to help.

"Where's Frieda?" Dominick glanced around.

"I don't know," Haatim said. "Probably checking for more survivors."

"We don't have much time," Dominick said. "Jun doesn't have much left."

"No, I reckon not," Jun said. He still panted and gasped, clearly in pain while the blanket weaved up and down with him. It made for a terrible gurney, Haatim knew, but better than nothing.

They brought Jun out through the lobby door and into the winter landscape beyond. It had begun snowing again, though not as heavy as earlier. They carried him out to the helicopter and set him down in the back, resting him on the hard metal floor.

"No gurney?" Haatim asked.

"I didn't think to grab one since landing in Switzerland. This isn't your regular life-flight equipped ride. I wasn't exactly prepared for something like today to happen."

Haatim let out a sigh. He could fully understand their lack of preparation.

Even after his months of training with Frieda and Dominick, he couldn't imagine how they might have prepared for something like what Nida had done to them.

"I do have a first-aid kit and some supplies. I'll get Jun patched up with a new bandage. I don't have much pain medication, though, past Tylenol and Advil."

"I'll be fine," Jun said, gritting his teeth. "This is nothing I haven't experienced before."

"What do we do now?" Haatim asked.

"We need to get airborne." Dominick glanced over at him and stepped away from Jun. He spoke softly so that the old man couldn't hear. "Jun won't last long unless we can get him to a hospital. Even then, it's hard to say. He got hit pretty hard and won't have a lot of time left if we don't get him to a real doctor."

"I'll go get Frieda."

"Hurry," Dominick said. "Two minutes. If you don't see her, then just get back here."

"We can't leave her here."

"We can't let Jun die, either. Worst case scenario, Frieda has to take care of herself, which she can. Jun can't last another hour without help."

Haatim hesitated, then nodded. "All right."

"Go get Frieda. Sweep the building to make sure no one else remains alive, and then get back here. I'll prep for takeoff."

"Where do you think she'll be?"

"Check the library. She mentioned that she wanted to look for something."

"Okay." Haatim rushed back through the deep snow and into the lobby of the hotel. His entire body had grown cold from spending so much time outside, but it didn't bother him nearly as much as it might have a few years ago. Dominick had taught him how to deal with the pain and push it somewhere else. He knew how much his body could tolerate.

In the lobby, he saw no sign of Frieda, so he shouted for her, but got no answer. Then he ran up the stairs, shouting as he went to get her attention and see if anyone else might respond. No replies came, though, from her or anyone else.

Though Dominick felt in a hurry, Haatim didn't want to leave Frieda behind if they didn't have to. The authorities wouldn't take long about getting out here, and leaving Frieda meant that she would have a difficult time of getting back to the city.

He headed straight for the small makeshift library that the Council had put together shortly after coming here. It lived on the third floor, an old sitting room that they'd converted with shelving space. The extent of the Council's library proved, basically, nothing more than a single bookshelf and a collection of old tomes that they had gathered through the years that had importance to their Order. Historical accounts, mostly, detailing their origins and everything that had happened through recent centuries.

He found Frieda sitting at one of the tables in the room, staring at the ground with her hands folded in front of her. Her shoulders sagged, and she wore a defeated expression that he'd never seen on her.

Around her lay the scattered remains of all of the Council's books, many of which Nida's mercenary army had destroyed. The books lay with pages torn asunder and ripped up, and many of them had gotten burned.

The history of the Council lay scattered around the room, mimicking the Council itself in the surrounding hotel.

The woman didn't even seem to notice him come into the room.

"Frieda." He spoke softly, worried that he might startle her. She didn't move, so he raised his voice. "Frieda!"

She glanced up at him. "Yes?"

"You okay?"

She shook her head. "I apologize. I went somewhere ... else."

"We need to leave. We can't stay here, and Jun needs serious medical attention."

"All of this." Frieda shook her head. She barely seemed to hear him or understand what he wanted. With her eyes dull, she held up a few torn pages. "We lost everything today. So much death. I—I never thought ..."

"We need to go," Haatim said. "Jun won't last much longer, and we need to fly him out of here."

Frieda stared at him for a long few seconds, and then, finally, nodded. She stood slowly, surveying the carnage around her. "I know. I'm sorry."

"Let's go."

"Check upstairs one last time, please. Make sure no one else is alive."

"We don't have time."

"Please, Haatim. It's our last chance."

He thought to object, since Dominick had insisted on hurrying, but he doubted they would make it back out here before the police arrived. If anyone remained alive that needed their help, it would be their last chance of saving them.

"All right," he said. "Tell Dominick I'll come right out."

Haatim sprinted up to the fifth floor and ran through another cursory sweep. He didn't want to accept the fact that no one else had lived through the attack. Over a hundred people had lived in this hotel, and the idea that all of them had died seemed unthinkable. He ran down the hallway, passing the carnage and looking around for survivors.

As expected, he didn't find any. Most of the rooms stood empty. The doors hung broken from forced entries, and holes and blood riddled the few that housed people. He found two people, but both of them had long since expired.

On the way down, he glanced at the other floors and called out, but received no response. It looked like all of the luck had run out. Jun became the only survivor of the attack.

Jun, and Haatim's father.

When he made it back outside to the helicopter, Frieda had found her way outside and waited for him. She must have heard the chopper turning on and come out to find them.

Dominick had the helicopter started up and idling, and he glanced down at Haatim from the cockpit. "Find anyone else?"

"No. Empty."

"We need to leave now."

Haatim turned toward Frieda, who climbed into the back and then offered him her hand to help him get in. He made it halfway and then froze, staring at the passenger seat behind her.

Aram sat there, eyes closed and making pained gasping noises.

"What in God's name is he doing here?" He gestured with his arm, angry.

Aram's eyes popped open, and he looked at his son guiltily.

"We can't leave him," Frieda said.

"Like hell, we can't."

"The police will get here soon—"

"We should just hand him over to them."

"—and we can't let them have him or any of us. They'll ask too many questions."

Though Frieda had it right, Haatim still couldn't stifle the rage running through his body as he looked at the man who used to be his father.

"He betrayed everyone. All of these people died because of him."

"We can't just leave him."

"We should drop him in the woods," Haatim said.

"We won't just let him die, either."

Haatim stared directly at Aram. "Why not?"

Frieda didn't reply for a few seconds. "It isn't our way."

Dominick shouted, "Close the damn door. We need to get up in the air. Haatim, get up here. You're my copilot."

Haatim hesitated another second, and then climbed the rest of the way in. He slammed the door behind him. It proved difficult to move through the helicopter, but he made it to the front and put on his headgear. Dominick pointed at the helmet and microphone, and Haatim flipped it on so that they could communicate.

"Haatim, I promise, it wasn't my idea. Frieda was adamant."

"Did she tell you what happened?"

"I got the gist."

They rose into the air, snow swirling all around. Haatim stared out through the window, struggling to control his raging emotions.

"So, that's where Frieda went while I checked the upper floors. To rescue my father. I shouldn't have told her about him."

"What's done is done. Don't waste time worrying about it. I promise you; no one will let Aram off easy. Especially Frieda."

"There isn't a punishment terrible enough for what he did."

"No," Dominick said. "There isn't."

Frieda spent a few minutes tending to Jun in the back of the helicopter, making sure he got comfortable, and then took the seat next to Aram. Haatim glanced back at her. She still had the defeated look on her face as she flipped on her headset.

"Everyone all right?" she asked.

"Fine," Dominick said. "What's left of us."

Everyone fell silent for a long moment.

Then Frieda said, "I know."

"Thank God it's over," Dominick said.

"It isn't." Frieda shook her head. "This is only the beginning."

"What do you mean?"

"Nida took one of the books with her, and now I know what she came after."

"What?"

"The original seven." Frieda pursed her lips. "She intends to release Surgat."

Chapter 3

"Who—or what—is Surgat?" Haatim asked. "And what do you mean by 'the original seven'?"

Frieda didn't respond to his question. Instead, she stared out of the window, lost in thought and with a worried look on her face. Haatim watched her for a long second and then faced back to Dominick.

"Any idea?"

He shook his head. "I've heard of the original seven. They founded the Council. I think back in the thirteenth century, though I'm not sure. History isn't really my thing. Surgat, though, I've never heard of."

"A demon?"

Dominick shrugged. "No clue."

"I've heard of Surgat from the Great Grimoire of Honorius. He's bad business."

"Like Belphegor?"

"Worse," Haatim said. "Like, by a lot."

"That doesn't sound promising."

"What did you learn about the original seven?"

"Not much. My uncle didn't know much, either, and he didn't think that would help keep me alive, so he kind of breezed over it. All I know is that of those original founding families, Frieda makes for the only one left from their bloodlines who serves on the Council. The rest sort of ... fell out over the centuries."

"I see."

They flew back toward the city. The storm had died down almost completely overtop the buildings and streets by now, and it proved a quick flight to get to the hospital. Absently, Haatim watched the landscape and lights flit past, wondering what Frieda might have meant. Release Surgat? Release him from what?

He didn't worry about that for long, though; he had other more immediate concerns. It concerned him much more about what would happen next to all of them. Particularly with his father. What would Frieda do to him, as one of the last members of the Council, to punish him for his crimes?

Dominick radioed ahead to the hospital to alert them to the incoming flight and received clearance to land. He explained that they carried two injured and would need one gurney. The helipad lay up on the roof, and by the time they got there, the hospital had cleaned it off and turned on all the searchlights to make the landing as easy as possible.

A crew of nurses and doctors waited for them on the roof as they touched down. A trauma team, it looked like, ready to go.

"This will be interesting," Dominick said.

"What do you mean?"

"We have contingencies for a situation like this. I've just never seen them enacted on this kind of scale."

"Contingencies?"

Dominick didn't answer since they'd reached the roof now. As soon as they touched down, the staff rushed forward and pulled open the helicopter doors. Gently, the team helped Frieda climb out, and then moved Jun onto a stretcher. The old man looked pale and weak, barely able to keep his eyes open, but still alive.

Haatim watched while the staff wheeled him into the hospital. Hopefully, Jun would make it. He sent out a silent prayer for the tough old man.

Another nurse climbed into the helicopter and helped Aram step out of the back and into a wheelchair. Her gentleness with him annoyed Haatim. His father had a difficult time moving around and, clearly, had a lot of pain, but Haatim held no sympathy for him.

The nurse wheeled Aram toward the doorway of the hospital to follow after Jun Lee, though much slower than the last group. Near the entryway, Aram glanced back at the helicopter. Haatim could feel his father's gaze on him but refused to look in his direction or make eye contact.

Right now, he wanted nothing less in life than to speak with his father.

On the helipad, Frieda glanced back at them. She waved at Dominick and held up two fingers. He nodded back at her, took off his helmet, and then climbed through the seats into the back of the helicopter. Frieda turned and disappeared into the hospital.

"What was that?" Haatim had to shout so that Dominick could hear him.

Dominick grabbed Frieda's helmet and put it on. "What?"

"I asked what that gesture meant. What did Frieda try to say?"

"She'll be back in two minutes. Not sign language, exactly. I need to find the paperwork."

"What paperwork?"

Dominick didn't respond. He tossed his helmet back onto the chair and dug through the supplies. Haatim watched him with curiosity while he tossed things around until he finally found what he wanted. It looked like an organizer for folders, packed full of paper.

Dominick flipped through it, pulled out a manila folder, and handed it to Haatim, and then flipped again until he found a second. They had numbers on them, and it looked like some sort of identification code.

A few minutes later, the door to the hospital opened once more. Frieda came walking out, accompanied by three stern-looking men. One wore a business suit, and the other two had the garb and collars of ordained priests.

They stopped well short of the helicopter, and Frieda came over to Dominick. He handed her the two manila folders. She flipped through them, nodded, and then took them over to the three men. She handed both to the elder of the two priests.

He scanned through them, nodded, and handed them over to the businessman.

The businessman shook Frieda's hand, and then tucked the folders under his arm and walked off toward the hospital. The priests spoke to Frieda, looking annoyed and distressed, and then rushed off after the man.

Frieda watched them go, and then hurried to the helicopter. She climbed in, closed the door, and beckoned for Dominick to get back to his seat up front.

Dominick climbed through, put on his helmet, and cycled the controls to prepare for takeoff.

"Time to go," Dominick said, once the sound came on again.

"Already? We won't stay with Jun to make sure he's all right?"

"We have more pressing issues."

"What happens if he doesn't make it?" Haatim asked.

Frieda answered, "We'll give him a glorious funeral. But, until then, we have work to do."

They lifted off the helipad and headed east, in the direction of the airport. Haatim's adrenaline wore thin, and his entire body ached with soreness and exhaustion.

"What was that?" Haatim asked as they flew. "The thing Frieda gave to them?"

"Full medical history," Dominick said. "That man you saw owns the hospital."

"And the priests?"

"They're keeping us out of jail. It could get back to the Catholic Church if we got arrested, so they pulled some strings. From the looks on their faces, though, they didn't feel too happy about it." This statement, he directed at Frieda, but she didn't respond.

"They let us go, just like that?" Haatim asked.

"Contingencies," Dominick said. "The Church pays handsomely and doesn't ask any questions."

"Does this happen often?"

"It depends. We have plans for all of our agents, as well as full authorization for medical procedures and payment systems in place to handle issues like this, just not on this scale. They have a lot of bodies to clean up, and the Church will stay busy for a long while keeping what happened at the Hotel out of the press. That's why we need to keep moving."

"You have files like that on everyone in the Council?"

"And the Order of Hunters," Dominick said. "We have one for you, too."

Haatim hesitated. "You do?"

"Yep."

"Don't you need my consent for something like that?"

Dominick laughed. "With what we deal with, consent for medical treatments is the least of your concerns."

"We need to get to the airport," Frieda said. "I'll call ahead and prepare our flights."

"Flights?" Haatim shook his head. The whole thing overwhelmed him. He had barely caught up with the events at the Council building, and everything seemed to be happening so fast. "What do you mean?"

Luckily, Frieda and Dominick didn't feel as overwhelmed as he did. "Dominick is going stateside to find and secure an asset. Haatim, you'll go to the Vatican."

"The Vatican?" That caught him off-guard. "Why would I go there?"

"You are studied up on Catholicism, right? It formed part of your education?"

"Yes, but—"

"I need you to retrieve something and find information. A book. It might prove difficult to get hold of, but I have an old friend that should be able to help you out. Father Paladina."

"Paladina's still alive?" Dominick's eyes widened.

Frieda ignored him. "I shall have him meet you, and he will help you retrieve the relevant information from the Vatican Libraries."

"What book?"

"One of our histories. The original copy is stored at the Vatican. They only allow us to have an abridged version. You will only need that one, not the original."

"Abridged?" Haatim asked, confused. "Why? It's the history of the Council, right? Why not get the full version?"

Frieda hesitated. "It doesn't matter. This is the same text that Nida stole when she broke through our defenses. Mostly, it's just a historical accounting of our origins, but it also contains a list of very important family names."

"Names of who?"

"My distant relative, for one. The family bloodlines of the original council members. I know of most of the family names on the list, but not where they reside today. Now, Nida knows all of them, and so she has a head start on us."

"The original council?" Dominick asked from beside Haatim, glancing back at Frieda. "What could she want with them?"

Frieda stayed silent for a moment, as though weighing her response. "When the Council got founded, it came in the aftermath of a terrible event."

"What event?"

"An awakening. A terrible evil came into the world several hundred years ago."

"A demon?" Haatim asked.

She nodded. "A demon, but so much more. They called it Surgat, but that's just a name humans gave to it. A group of seven managed to stop it and lock the demon away in one of the coldest and darkest corners of hell, but doing so had consequences. Forever bound to the creature, their blood, and the bloodline of their lineage, would become the key to setting it free once more."

"Your blood."

"Yes. Mine, and many others. Nida only needs to locate one person from each line to set Surgat free. We need to keep that from happening."

"And how, exactly, will we do that?"

"We'll find out where she's headed and stop her before she manages to acquire all the blood. I don't think she knew any of the names on the list beyond mine, which was why she sought to retrieve the book from the Council; so, at least, we know we will have time while she tries to track down living descendants. Luckily, I know of one of them in Pennsylvania without any living relatives."

"So, if we keep that person safe, we know Nida won't manage to complete her ritual."

"Exactly. If we keep Jill Reinfer safe, then Nida won't have enough to finish it."

"What happens if we can't keep her safe?" Dominick asked. "Do we have a backup plan?"

"Yes," Frieda said. "We kill her."

✳✳✳

"Please, tell me you're joking," Dominick said.

"I wish I was," Frieda replied. "If we can't stop Nida from collecting the bloodline, then we need to make it impossible for her to complete this task. That remains of the utmost importance. We must find every living member before Nida can get to them."

"Frieda, that's insane."

She sighed. "I know. But, we don't have any alternatives right now. Things are desperate, but they're about to get a lot worse. We have weeks, maybe only days, to stop this from happening. If Nida succeeds, then everything we've ever worked and stood for all these years will come to an end."

✳✳✳

Once they made it to the airport, Frieda slipped away from Dominick and Haatim to make a phone call. Hopefully, the man still held some sway with the Church.

Niccolo answered on the third ring. "Hello?"

"It's me," she said.

The priest remained silent for a minute. "Frieda, what have you done?"

"We don't have a lot of time, Niccolo. What does the Church have planned?"

"I can't discuss—"

"Please. This is important."

A pause. "They don't know much."

"Will the order go through?"

"It looks like it will."

"Can you stall them?"

"Frieda—"

"Only for a few days. I just need some time to get things sorted out."

"We need answers."

"What if I give you Aram?"

"You would turn him over?"

"If that buys us time."

Father Paladina let out a sigh. He sounded quite old at the moment that he spoke, "Yes. They're still debating, and I believe I can stall the decisions. But I hold little influence, and they will overrule me."

"I know," Frieda said. "I just need some time."

"We need to talk," the priest said. "You owe me that."

"We will," Frieda said. "After all of this is over."

Father Paladina didn't like that answer, but she hoped he trusted her enough to accept it. She'd put him in a terrible position, asking for favors this large. It could jeopardize his career and maybe even his life.

"Fine," he said.

"One more favor," she said. "Haatim isn't one of mine. He's a bystander."

"He knows a lot."

"Do they have him on the list?"

"No," Paladina said. "But if he's hard to find, they might reconsider."

"He'll be easy to find," she said. "I'm sending him to you."

"What?"

"Keep him out of this, and keep him safe."

"All right," he said. "The further he is from you, the safer he will be."

"I know. I need to go. Take care of yourself, Niccolo."

"You too, Frieda. Until we meet again."

She hung up, wondering if she would ever see Father Niccolo Paladina again.

✳✳✳

Only a few hours later, Haatim found himself on a private jet headed for Italy. Despite his overwhelming exhaustion, he found it utterly impossible to fall asleep. His mind refused to settle down and kept running at a million miles an hour, trying to piece his new reality together.

The plan ordained that he would land in Rome and then get dropped off at a hotel just outside Vatican City. He would arrive late at night, and so would have time to settle in and fight off his jet lag before entering the Holy City and meeting Father Paladina in the morning.

Frieda had made some phone calls at the airport when they'd landed. After that, it had only taken a few hours to get him onto this private jet— something he'd never before experienced.

Even when he'd traveled with Frieda all around the world during his initiation, they'd flown on commercial flights, albeit first class. Haatim had grown used to cushioned seats and little beverages and peanuts for in-flight refreshments.

This jet, however, had only enough seats for four passengers and a full-service bar and flight attendant. The attendant, a man named Richard, proved entirely too cheerful for Haatim's liking.

Richard offered to prepare for his sole passenger any variety of alcoholic and non-alcoholic beverages and bragged that he could cook any of twenty five-star menu options for the in-flight meal.

However, Haatim didn't feel hungry. Though his body needed nourishment, he found the simple idea of eating food entirely unappealing. He didn't even answer Richard during his initial introductions, and after a few prompts, the flight attendant realized that Haatim didn't want to talk and disappeared into the kitchen at the back and closed the door.

At some point, he must have returned because Haatim found a granola bar and bottle of water lying on the seat next to him, but he didn't remember seeing the attendant come forward.

Haatim traveled in silence, completely numb to the expensive furnishings and decorations surrounding him. The cabin had wooden décor with earthy colors. Oblivious, he got lost in his thoughts, worries, and apprehensions, and struggled to understand how his father could have betrayed him so completely and utterly.

Just when he'd thought that he could trust his father again, the man had ripped out his very soul. Gradually, they had come to terms with their new reality, and nothing could have clued him into this as their possible future. Finally, things had started to look up.

The worst part was that, at the core of it, a part of him truly sympathized with what his father had done. He missed his sister dearly, and the thought of having Nida back—the real Nida, not the demon controlling her—seemed incredibly pleasant. Had he been in his father's position, might he have made the same choice?

However, sympathizing with the man and forgiving him for what he had done presented as two entirely different things, and none of it changed the fact that his father had betrayed them, nor did it make it all right. His father became a traitor to them all and had gotten dozens of people killed.

Aram also released a terrible evil out into the world. Worse still, that evil wore the body of his departed sister like a set of used clothing and seemed to have some horrible plan to bring an even greater ancient evil back into the world.

How could this day get any worse?

Haatim forced himself to eat the granola bar and drink the water. He couldn't allow for his body or mind to weaken. In all probability, he would have a brutal next couple of days, and he needed to stay at his best.

At some point later in the flight, he must have nodded off because the next thing he knew, Richard stood tapping him on the shoulder to wake him.

The man frowned down at him, a concerned expression on his face. "Are you all right?"

"What?"

"You were mumbling in your sleep."

Haatim rubbed his face and groaned. "Yes. I'm fine."

"We will land soon, and I would ask that you, please, fasten your seatbelt during the descent."

Haatim mumbled a reply, though even he felt unsure what he tried to say, and fastened himself in with haste. Richard disappeared again, and Haatim rested back in the seat with a terrible headache and sinuses feeling dry and uncomfortable. The plane tipped forward at a slight angle, and vertigo settled over him.

He hated flying and the way it seemed to dry him out and make him feel miserable. Unfortunately, he'd done more of it these last few months than in his entire previous life.

Not only the amount of flying he did had changed in his life. Everything had ended up different, down to how he made decisions, his priorities, and the way he operated in his daily life. There had come, he knew, a single pivotal event that rearranged everything about him.

Everything centered on when he'd met Abigail.

Abigail ...

✳✳✳

When he thought of her, his stomach sank. When the train had crashed in the mountains, and she'd disappeared with it into the water, he'd felt a part of himself get ripped out along with her.

The hardest part for Haatim to fathom was exactly *why* he had such strong feelings for the woman. Never had he considered himself much of a romantic, but just thinking about Abigail and the idea that he would never see her again hit him with a feeling of such loss and longing that he could barely wrap his head around it.

Consciously, he knew that she represented his foundation during a moment of great change in his life. She'd rescued him and opened his eyes to a new world. Unconsciously, though, things grew less clear. Abigail embodied everything that he considered important in a person: brave, selfless, caring, and intelligent.

And, he couldn't help but add, she had great beauty. Not in a cover-girl way with a perfect body, but in her own way, completely unique to her.

He'd barely known her outside of those days they'd spent together, leading up to Raven's Peak, and in the months after, as he'd learned more about this world and his new existence, but it felt like he'd known her his entire life.

At least the parts that mattered.

The plane landed a short while later, touching down on a private airfield and taxying over to a large hangar. The flight crew ran a metal staircase up next to the plane for him to disembark, and already, a silver car waited nearby on the tarmac for him.

It felt like something out of a movie, and if things hadn't seemed so dire, and he didn't feel so exhausted, he might have thought it an awesome experience. As it was, however, all he wanted to do was curl up into a ball and pass out.

The driver didn't speak to him, but rather opened the door for him and then took him to the hotel. They drove down the road, past ancient buildings full of culture and history. This made for his first time in Italy, and the entire place gave off an air of culture and history like he'd stepped into an older world that had gotten lost to the ages.

The hotel appeared small and quaint, and he barely remembered walking inside. Once he retrieved his key at the front desk, he headed over to the elevators. Dominick had forbidden him from riding in elevators, but he decided that this made an exception.

Haatim dropped his meager luggage to the floor and collapsed onto the bed without even taking off his shoes. He couldn't remember ever feeling so exhausted in his entire life.

He fell asleep in only seconds.

Chapter 4

Desperation and worry settled over Frieda as soon as both Dominick and Haatim got on their flights out of Switzerland. It worried her that they might get stopped and their passports confiscated, but luckily, they had made it through all right.

She had contingency plans and passports for all of them that the Church didn't know about, but she remained grateful that she didn't have to go that route yet. With any luck, Paladina would manage to hold up his promise and keep them safe, but she didn't have any huge expectations.

It felt like a rope hanging around her neck. Helplessness crept into Frieda, and she could see the writing on the wall: they were all in trouble as soon as the Catholic Church decided they'd outlived their usefulness.

Seated in the small chapel in the hospital in Switzerland, she bided her time and tried not to think about Jun Lee and his condition. She hadn't had time to shower or change clothes and felt grimy and disgusting. Situated in one of the pews, hands folded in front of her, she attempted to think about nothing.

Of course, it didn't work.

Haatim had gotten on a flight to the Vatican, where he would be safe. Father Paladina had explained that the Church wasn't looking for him and that they had no reason to. Haatim had no part in this, and no fault lay with him. As long as she distanced herself from him, he would remain safe. However, she couldn't tell him that. He could behave quite stubbornly.

Dominick, on the other hand ...

Frieda hated to lie to him. A good man, he didn't deserve it, but some roads she felt unwilling to go down. Not yet. Instead, she would keep him occupied and out of the way. Right now, he made his way to protect a woman that she loathed.

Everything had crumbled around her, and she'd never felt so alone. She was truly on her own, and had been ever since Arthur had fallen and gotten shoved into that prison.

How had things gone so wrong so quickly? Utterly overcome with fear and worry, Frieda dreaded the future in ways she had never even imagined.

She missed Arthur. Desperately. He always stayed so calm and collected in the face of danger and strife. He would know how to handle this situation. At the very least, he would tell her not to worry and that things would work out all right in the way that only he could.

It would have been a lie, though. For certain, everything most certainly would *not* work out all right. But, right now, she could use a little baseless encouragement.

✳✳✳

Things had turned desperate so fast, and Frieda had gotten completely blindsided by all of it. She had expected something to happen—had for years—but not on this scale. The Council had weakened, and carefully-wrought bonds had frayed at the edges. What caught her most off-guard, though, was just how deep the betrayal went.

She had known Aram as her personal enemy but had never imagined him capable of something as horrendous as this. She'd assumed he would continue to work against her and try to have her ousted from the Council. Instead, he had sold out the Council to their mortal enemy and single-handedly brought the multi-generational Organization to its knees.

So many dead. Jun remained alive, but only just, and the next few days would prove critical. Not a young man anymore, the doctors had promised he would need multiple surgeries to survive this. To lose him would feel akin to losing her real father, and she dreaded the moment a doctor told her that Jun had passed on.

Despite everything that had happened, and the helplessness she felt, she couldn't afford to stop and grieve. Nor could she take the time to catch her breath and absorb her new reality. At such a critical moment, she couldn't rest. Things had become as desperate as they had ever been, and she didn't know what might happen next.

What she *did* know was that if they wanted to stop Nida and keep her from releasing Surgat out into the world, they would need to act fast and get everything locked down.

Frieda had called in the favor that Father Niccolo Paladina owed her. Or, more specifically, the favor he owed Arthur. She felt certain it would prove the last time they would speak in a long time and doubted he would manage to buy her much time, even after she held up her end of the bargain and turned Aram over to the Church.

Father Paladina remained one of the last friends she had that she could call upon for help, and even then, he had limitations in what he could offer. He had promised, however, to keep Haatim out of it, and that felt good enough for her.

✳✳✳

Her sending Dominick to Pennsylvania would be a shot in the dark. On the off-chance that Nida went after Jill Reinfer, they might head her off and stop her completely.

That, of course, assumed that Jill had become the next target. For all Frieda knew, Nida might have gotten to the woman already. Or, maybe Nida knew about another living relative that would serve as a replacement for Jill; in which case, she'd wasted one of her most valuable assets protecting a woman who didn't want her help.

It also assumed, of course, that if Nida did go after Jill in her Pennsylvania home, that Dominick would manage to stop her. Frieda had a lot of faith in Dominick, and he made for one of her most loyal allies and Hunters, but she had seen Nida up close and at her best. In total honesty with herself ...

Dominick didn't stand a chance.

At times like this, she would turn to her assistant Martha to bounce ideas from. Martha had remained a loyal friend and ally, helping her plan and think through all of the problems that she faced on a daily basis. At the thought that her assistant probably hadn't survived the attack, an aching pain settled in her heart.

Frieda hadn't found Martha's body at the Council building, but she hadn't had time to do a more thorough search. When things quieted down enough to begin recovering the bodies, she would make sure that Martha received the special burial she deserved.

Right now, though, she simply had no time.

Yet another person for whom she didn't have the opportunity to cry. Once all of this had finished, she would need to honor and pray for all of the friends that she'd lost. She would need to grieve and bury the dead.

That, of course, depended on her not becoming one of them.

***

Frieda waited in the chapel as long as she could before returning to the room where Jun lay recovering. They didn't allow her in right away, though. Instead, they directed her to the lobby and told her they would contact her momentarily.

Doctors flitted in and out of Jun's room but wouldn't let her inside. The lobby stood mostly empty: a pair of nurses sat at a desk, an old television played soap operas that she didn't recognize, and a coffee machine with burnt coffee rested in the corner.

Apart from her, a garbed priest who watched her with careful eyes made for the only other person in the lobby. He wore loose-fitting robes and seemed calm but dangerous. He waited just like she did. Father Paladina had assured her that they wouldn't come here for her ... not if she gave him what he needed.

Aram, the traitor.

She paced back and forth, waiting for news of Jun's condition. Frieda prayed for the best and feared the worst. No one came out to talk to her, and she didn't know if that meant a good thing or bad.

Frieda wanted to speak with the doctors to find out what they expected in Jun's recovery and how optimistic they felt about his chances. She wanted to find out because she hated not knowing and didn't have a lot of time before she had to get on a flight to meet Dominick out in Pennsylvania.

Also, she wanted to speak with Aram because this would, likely, offer the last chance she ever had. Or, rather, she felt that she *needed* to speak with him to try and come to terms with what had happened over the last few months before handing him over to the Catholic Church for questioning.

It would have satisfied her to go through her entire life without seeing the man again, but if there remained even a slight chance that he might have information that could prove beneficial to her, then she had to at least check. Right now, she felt willing to grasp any straw that might keep them alive.

The priest waited calmly in the corner, watching her in an unsettling way that made her skin crawl. After another hour, she decided she had waited long enough and needed answers. Needed them now. Determined, she went down the hall to Jun's room.

She found the door closed, though could see Jun through the window. He lay alone in the room, sleeping and hooked up to a plethora of medical monitoring equipment. He seemed small and frail in the bed and gown—a weak old man wholly unlike the powerful figure she'd come to know and respect through the years.

She prayed he would make it.

For a moment, she considered just barging in. No one stood watching the door, and the hallways lay empty. This late at night, nearly midnight, most of the other rooms in this wing remained vacant. She decided not to, however, as it worried her that it would draw undue attention or possibly harm his chances of survival. Instead, she went looking for someone who could offer her information.

It took a little searching before she found a nurses' station. A tired-looking young woman sat there, typing slowly into a computer and reading from a clipboard. She used two fingers, which irked Frieda.

"Excuse me?" Frieda cleared her throat to get the woman's attention.

The woman looked up at her and offered a weary smile. Her eyes, though, made it clear that she didn't appreciate the interruption. "Yes? Can I help you?"

"I hoped to ask about the patient in room three-oh-four. Jun Lee. Has there been any status change since his arrival this morning?"

The woman hesitated. "I'm sorry, are you family?"

"No," Frieda said. "But if you look up his account, you'll find me on his listed exceptions list."

The woman typed into the computer, and Frieda passed her an identity card. It didn't use her real name, or any actual information about her, but it did give her full access to Jun Lee and all the other Council members, as well as her Hunters, in case of emergencies like this. It was government issued.

The woman checked over the information on the file and then the card. Finally, she nodded before handing back the ID.

"He remains in stable condition. He had surgery this morning, but the doctor said he couldn't remove all the damaged tissue. Mr. Lee is scheduled to go back into surgery in a few hours for another minor fix. They found a lot of internal damage and bleeding, but the doctor seems optimistic that he'll make an almost full recovery."

Frieda nodded, breathing an internal sigh of relief. Thank God something had, finally, gone right on this terrible day. Though she had no way of telling how Jun's body would react to the surgery, at least he'd cleared the first major hurdle. Frieda could breathe again, and it felt like a humungous weight had lifted off her chest.

"Do you have any idea when he might be well enough to have visitors?"

"Definitely not today."

"I didn't expect to see him so soon. I just wondered when I should come back. Maybe by tomorrow?"

She didn't like the idea of postponing her flight out of the country, but the encouragement that Jun might survive made her want to see him alive and well that much more. Dominick would need her help, but she might manage to spare an extra day or two to make sure her old friend recovered well.

"Most likely the day after that, provided everything goes well with this next surgery. It will be worth calling ahead, though, so you don't end up wasting a trip down here for nothing."

Frieda nodded. "Thank you."

"Will that be all?"

Frieda hesitated, glancing over at the corner of the room where the robed priest sat. He watched her, a blank expression on his face, and Frieda knew what he wanted. It made her feel sick to her stomach, but it was best not to delay.

"Actually," Frieda said. "I'd hoped to check on the status of another patient. They brought him in with a broken leg. Last name is Malhotra. First name, Aram."

The woman typed into the computer, scanning through the records. She pressed her finger to the screen, trailing it across the list of names.

"I don't have anyone here by that name."

The paperwork shouldn't have included an alias for him. It would have been preferred, but they hadn't had time to put something like that together.

She frowned. "Can you check again?"

The woman gave her a sour look but did return to the keyboard and type some more. After a moment, the nurse glanced up at her. "He came in here earlier but checked out a while ago."

"What?" Frieda asked, surprised. "He wasn't supposed to be allowed to check himself out."

The woman typed some more, frowning. "Ah. I see that note in his file, but it looks like his nurse didn't notice and discharged him."

"How the hell does that happen?" A burst of anger and panic hit Frieda. "Do you even bother to check the records when you discharge people?"

The woman frowned deeper. "Ma'am, I am sorry for the inconvenience this has caused you. I know it's frustrating, but *I* didn't check him out. We *are* quite busy."

41

Frieda looked around at the empty lobby and thought about the fact that she hadn't seen more than a few patients all day. However, the prudent thing to do would be not to bring that up.

"So, he's gone?"

"I'm sorry, but it looks that way. All of his discharge paperwork has been filed, and him released. He checked out about an hour ago."

"Damn it," Frieda said.

"Is that all you need?"

This time, Frieda didn't reply. Instead, she turned and rushed away from the station. In the corner of the room, the priest stood and shadowed her, following her toward the exit.

Frieda had an idea of where Aram might go. She just hoped she'd guessed right.

***

Luckily, Aram didn't go far. Frieda went to the hotel where his wife had stayed these past few weeks while in Switzerland. Would Aram try and run? If so, he might well try to collect his spouse before fleeing.

When she arrived at the hotel in the center of the city, however, she saw Aram sitting on a stool at the restaurant bar, sipping a drink. The long bar hosted only a handful of people. Soft music played in the background, classical and upbeat, and the opposite of how Frieda felt.

Aram had a giant cast on his leg that went up all the way to his thigh, and two crutches leaned next to him. Frieda walked toward him, and then a soft voice came from behind.

"If you don't do it, I will."

She turned and saw the bald head of the priest walking away from her. He had followed her from the church, though she hadn't known he'd gotten so close to her. He moved so silently it terrified her.

With a steadying breath, she faced back toward Aram. Whatever had happened to him back at the Council must have proven painful. With the cast on, he sat awkwardly on the stool, half hanging off the edge. He looked distant, thoughts far away, and barely noticed when Frieda sat down at the bar next to him.

They sat in silence for a moment.

"Want a drink?" he asked.

"I thought you didn't imbibe alcohol?"

"Just started." He took a sip. "Thought I'd give it a try."

The bartender glanced over at her, but she waved him off. "Terrible time to start."

"Great time." He shook his head. "What the hell else do I have?"

Frieda didn't have a good answer.

"I came here to check on my wife. I wanted to make sure she was okay and not too freaked out by everything going on. Whatever drugs Nida gave her, though, she's still unconscious."

"Does she know what happened?"

He shook his head again. "No. She'll feel confused and disoriented when she wakes but won't remember anything."

"Probably for the best."

He took another sip and didn't reply.

"You came here just to check on her?"

"I don't plan to run." He stared down at his drink. "If that's what you think. Where the hell would I go?"

"You know what happens next."

"Yeah. You can do whatever you want to me. I won't fight back. Just one last time, I wanted to see my wife."

"Do you want to wait until she wakes?"

Aram thought about it, and then shook his head. "Better this way. I'd rather leave her wondering than tell her the truth."

He turned to Frieda, and on his face, she saw the look of a thoroughly defeated man.

"After what I've done, I couldn't possibly ask forgiveness."

"What you did ...?" Frieda trailed off. Unable even to think of the words to justify how furious and betrayed she felt.

Part of her wanted to grab a bottle, smash it on the counter, and then use it to stab Aram until he stopped moving. She should pay him back for everything he'd done and all the people he'd gotten killed.

"I know," he said. "I thought ... I thought I had it all under control. That I'd stayed in charge and things happened because of me. I didn't know they—"

"Used you?" Frieda raised her brows.

Aram nodded and stared down at the bar. "I had no clue that I was just a pawn in their game until Nida showed up. I did this. I destroyed everything we built for my selfish reasons. I can't hide from that. And now my daughter is dead, my son hates me, and I can no longer face my wife as the man she believes me to be."

"If you expect sympathy, you won't find any here."

"I don't," he said. "All our friends have died except for you, me, and Jun, and it's my fault."

"I should kill you."

Frieda clenched and unclenched her fists, trying to decide her next course of action. She stared at Aram, knowing that the proper punishment for what he had done, as dictated by both the decrees of the Council and the way she felt right now, could only be death.

That felt wrong, though. There seemed something inherently perverse about punishing a man for these crimes by killing him. Hadn't enough people died already?

Honestly, she didn't know. Never in her entire life had she felt so confused and conflicted as she did at this moment. Her entire world had fallen and now showed to be a sham. Everything she had worked for and believed in had gone, and all that remained ...

Emptiness.

"I won't do it." Frieda shook her head. "Honestly, part of me thinks I should thank you."

"Thank me?"

"I've waited for this day to come for a long time. I've expected it and felt terrified of it for long enough. At least now, I don't have that shadow looming over me."

"What?" Aram glanced up and coughed.

Frieda ignored his reaction. "She's as prepared as she'll ever be. After what happened in Raven's Peak, I had my doubts, but now we've simply run out of time. Arthur believed this day would come."

"What are you talking about?"

Frieda fell silent. Finally, she turned to Aram, "You had it right. You always had it right about her. The best thing we could have done was kill her on the day we found her. I knew how bad things could get, and still, I let Arthur talk me into all of this. Now, we're committed."

Aram stared at her, a confused expression on his face. "Kill who?"

She didn't answer. Instead, she stood and bundled back up in her coat. "For what it's worth, Aram. I'm sorry. I hope they end it quickly."

"End what quick?"

Again, she didn't reply.

Realization dawned on his face. "I thought you wouldn't kill me?"

"I won't. The Church will, though. They'll hunt us all down and kill us for what you did. You're only the first."

While she spoke, the garbed priest walked out of the hotel lobby and into the bar area. He saw Aram and looked at her in question. Frieda nodded and walked at a slow pace toward the exit.

"If it's any consolation," she said, turning back around to face Aram one last time. "Your death bought us space."

Aram turned and spotted the priest. His eyes widened. Clumsily, he reached over and grabbed Frieda by the wrist.

"No. Please! I'll do anything. Don't turn me over to them."

She eyed him for a second, feeling just an iota of pity. Finally, she shook her arm loose. "Goodbye, Aram. I hope you can find peace in your next life."

Then, she left the bar. A week. Father Paladina had promised to get her seven days for turning over Aram to the Church. Not much time.

Next, they would come after her.

Chapter 5

Early the next morning, when his flight landed at the John Glenn International Airport, Dominick felt exhausted. Though still dark outside, it promised to become a dreary day. He rented a car and headed away from the airport, struggling to stay awake.

Dominick now ran on fumes and needed a real bed to sleep in to recharge his batteries. He felt sure he could sleep for a week at least. And though he'd managed to zonk out for a few hours during the flight, if anything, he felt worse from it and not better. The seats on his international flight had seemed some of the least comfortable in which he'd ever sat.

Or maybe that just came down to the exhaustion talking. Either way, he didn't care.

Frieda had asked him to check in on Arthur's brother, Mitchell, before hopping over to Pennsylvania and guarding Jill Reinfer. He had never met Jill before, but her reputation as a spoiled rich brat with no common sense appeared legendary. All of the Hunters disliked her, and he'd never heard anyone say anything nice about her. Wealthy, she liked people to know it. In her mind, it made her better than everyone else.

That proved a fairly normal attitude that Dominick had experienced from rich people, but hers went a step further. She had served on the Council many years earlier, but only for a few months before opting out. And had only done it to appease her father, who'd felt she didn't take her life seriously. She had no interest in the day-to-day monotony of the work and could care less about protecting people from the demonic underworld. All she cared about was money.

Which meant she felt willing to risk the lives of the Hunters for completely meaningless reasons if it benefitted her. Dominick could deal with her being a spoiled rich brat, but not someone who risked the lives of others for no reason.

Mitchell Vangeest, on the other hand, and an old acquaintance but not necessarily someone Dominick would call friend, he got along with just fine. He could check on him fairly easily but doubted that Nida would have gone after him. Mitchell, not exactly the sharpest tool in the shed, rarely kept up-to-date with Council events.

To check on him would just prove a shot in the dark. Neither he nor Frieda had any idea what Nida planned to do next, which meant that, basically, everything they did would end up a shot in the dark. The problem was that they lagged four or five steps behind her already, and didn't feel sure where she would go next or what might be her overall agenda.

Dominick didn't know if she intended to go after any more of the Order of Hunters. A few out there hadn't been at the Council when it got attacked, which meant they could be at risk. He doubted that would be her next move, though. The damage she had done would cripple the Council for years, if not end the organization entirely. Whatever endgame Nida played at, it went beyond just damaging the Council.

He just wished he knew what it was.

✳✳✳

Dominick didn't have any better ideas of what they should do than what Frieda offered. And checking on and protecting Mitchell and Jill for Frieda gave a productive way for him to spend his time; something he could use right about now. To have spare moments to sit around and think offered the last thing he wanted.

He hadn't found the courage to call his husband yet because he felt petrified of what he would say. How could he explain any of this without telling Marvin the truth? A truth he had withheld from his partner for years. He'd grown used to lying to his husband on a daily basis about the true nature of his work, but right now, all of the other lies seemed tiny by comparison.

Often, he justified the mistruths he fed to his spouse by telling himself that he did it for the greater good of humanity and that keeping Marvin in the dark kept him safe. This, however, had become something else entirely, and those justifications seemed flimsy.

The thing was, he knew the job as risky, but now that risk had jumped to an entirely new level. He only remained alive through a sheer turn of luck that he'd gone away with Haatim when the attack came.

To keep the secret while he believed in his survivability proved one thing, but how could he maintain the lie now that all his illusions had gotten stripped away?

Worse, what if he had put Marvin at risk? Did Nida know about his relationship and family? Would she use such information against him?

Dominick had no clue. He also had no clue about what he would do if that ever came to pass. If he had to pick between the Council and his husband ...

He honestly didn't know what would happen.

So, instead of facing the problem, he simply avoided it. Marvin still expected for him to stay away for the next several days on a business trip, which meant he could push off the problem for now. But, eventually, he would run out of time and have to confront the issue head on.

✳✳✳

Dominick headed out of Columbus, traveling east on the freeway. Already, the rain fell, and the roads had grown slick, but it stayed early enough that not a lot of traffic used the route.

He reached about an hour away from Mitchell's shop, and about two hours away from the Reinfer estate. He'd known Mitchell casually over the years as a fixer for the Council: the kind of guy good at tracking things down that seemed impossible to find. Not a Hunter or a member of the Council, he had only a loose affiliation.

Dominick doubted that Nida would go after him unless he had something she needed. For Mitchell's sake, Dominick hoped he didn't.

Mitchell also being a notorious user of various illegal narcotics and other substances gave one of the reasons the Council kept him at arm's length. They only used his services occasionally, and almost three years had elapsed since Dominick had last seen him.

That didn't make for the only reason the Council had stopped requesting his services, though: rumor had it that Mitchell and Arthur had had something of a falling out several years ago. That happened before Arthur lost control and got put into the underground black-site prison.

After the falling out, the Council had shunted Mitchell to the side. They wouldn't risk jeopardizing the feelings of one of their deadliest and most dangerous Hunters for the sake of his pothead brother.

Dominick drove through the cold rain, listening to the pattering and forcing himself to stay awake. It sounded soothing and relaxing, and he considered pulling over and taking a short nap just in case. He didn't, though, because he needed to keep moving and get to Jill Reinfer's residence by late afternoon.

It took him a little over an hour and a few breaks for coffee before he reached Mitchell's shop. The store was an old rented establishment, part of a strip mall, and it had tinted windows out front and a dirty welcome sign hanging in the door. The sort of place that might have been a tattoo parlor in another life.

The sign on the door said "open," but he felt unconvinced. The place looked empty, almost abandoned, and had fallen into serious disrepair over the last few years. Though the sign lay flipped to "open," that didn't mean too much. If he hadn't known Mitchell lived here, he would have driven right past without even noticing the place.

At first, he thought Mitchell might have moved shop sometime in the last year or so, but he soon dismissed that idea. If he had, he would have notified them as part of protocol. Mitchell hadn't seemed much for taking care of the place before, anyway, so there could have been any number of reasons for its current state.

The parking lot stood barren, and the entire strip mall quiet. No sign came from just looking at the property that Nida had come here, but he couldn't be certain. Dominick climbed out of the car. The rain pattered on his skin, cold as it ran down his hair and onto his back. To be safe, he slipped his gun free and chambered a round, and then he tested the door handle.

Unlocked. Gently, he slid it open and stepped inside, gun ready just in case any threat waited for him. The interior looked dark and smelled of too many incense sticks burning. His husband loved incense, and it had become one of Dominick's pet peeves and a constant point of contention in their marriage. He hated everything about it: the way it smelled, the smoke, and the way it lingered.

Mitchell Vangeest, on the other hand, loved it, too. He always seemed to have a couple of sticks burning in his shop.

The main storefront proved empty. The shelves lay in disarray; items discarded and lying haphazardly on the floor or completely out of place on the shelves. None of the products seemed to have a theme, and it appeared as if a grocery store had smashed against a flea market: canned goods alongside antique jewelry; candles up against vinyl records. No rhyme or reason to any of it.

It looked like the place had gotten tossed, as though someone had come through here searching for something. Of course, maybe that just came down to Mitchell's unconventional way of sorting things, but Dominick doubted it.

Either way, he felt unwilling to take any chances where Nida was concerned. Maybe she did need something here, after all, something that Mitchell had hung onto or could get for her.

She must have come out here to take it from him.

Which meant the odds of finding Mitchell alive had just grown slim.

A half-finished burrito and multiple candy bar wrappers covered the front register, and the door to the backroom stood open. The food looked old like it had lain there for days. He listened at the doorway and thought he heard movement in the back.

Maybe Mitchell, maybe not. It could be that Nida remained here, continuing her search. If she did, that would prove lucky for him: then he could end this now, once and for all.

He slid open the door and crept into the storage room, careful not to step on anything or make noise. It looked dark in here, with only a small amount of light filtering through a window. Further in, lay a couple of rooms. On the left was the break room, where Mitchell hung out and got high, and on the right was another small storage place, where Mitchell kept his prized possessions, the things of true value, and a curtain of beads blocked his way.

The noise came from there—a shuffling of footsteps. Slowly, Dominick raised his pistol and slid the curtain aside.

Mitchell stood there, spray bottle in hand, as he surveyed a small tray of short green plants. He bent and eyed each one of them critically.

He had headphones on and bobbed his head, taking little footsteps. A desk lamp stood nearby, aiming down at them with a soft grow light to keep the plants alive and fortified while indoors.

In the middle of winter, Dominick felt pretty sure those weren't tomatoes.

Off to Mitchell's right lay the small hidden cubby from where he'd slid the tray. Built right into the wall, a heavy shelf that he'd dragged out of the way hid it.

Dominick lowered his gun and rubbed the bridge of his nose with his free hand. "You've gotta be kidding me."

Mitchell kept bobbing with his music, completely unaware that Dominick stood right behind him.

"Mitchell. Hey, Mitchell!"

No response. Dominick let out a sigh before sliding his gun away. He stepped forward and tapped Mitchell on the shoulder.

"Earth to Mitchell. Come on, man."

Mitchell let out a little half-groan, half-scream, and then stumbled to the side away from where Dominick had touched him. His foot caught on a rolled up rug, and he tripped. Hastily, he tried to pull the cords out of his ears and managed to wrap his arms up in them instead.

To save himself, he clutched the edge of his tray of little green plants, but it wasn't braced and couldn't support his weight. Dominick watched as Mitchell fell back in seemingly slow-motion, eyes wide, as the tray slid across the table toward him. He flailed his arms wildly, and then pulled it off, sending his little plants and dirt flying everywhere around and on top of him.

Dominick bit back a chuckle and folded his arms. He looked down at Mitchell, frowning. "Seriously?"

Mitchell took out his headphones and brushed dirt from his face. "Jesus Christ, you scared the crap out of me."

"I thought you were dead."

"Do I look dead?"

"I mean in general. The shop's empty, and the lights are off. I figured someone came here to kill you."

"I keep the lights off to conserve energy. Do you know how much electric costs out here? Who would want to kill me?"

"I'm sure we could find someone if we looked hard enough."

Dominick held out his hand to help Mitchell stand. The man grabbed it, and Dominick jerked him to his feet. He stumbled, off-balance, and hit his hip hard against the table. The opposite of graceful, which proved painful to watch.

"I haven't done anything particularly stupid in a while. Why would they want to kill me now?"

"The place looks like crap, too. When I came inside, you weren't out front, so I didn't know what might have happened. The place looks like it's been tossed."

"Oh, that? Just doing some spring cleaning."

"It isn't even spring."

Mitchell shrugged. "Winter cleaning, then."

"How do you consider *that* cleaning?"

"I just started," Mitchell said, and then straightened his spine in a defensive posture. "And I needed a break."

"To water your crop?"

Mitchell frowned and looked down at the ground around him. He wore a look of immeasurable sadness while he surveyed the plants. "I'll have to re-pot all of them, and I'm sure some of them will die because of this."

"Trust me, that's the least of your concerns."

"Are you kidding me? These are a special strain. Cost me a fortune. I should bill the Council for this."

Dominick stayed silent for a moment. "Good luck with that."

Mitchell's entire demeanor changed. "What's wrong? What happened?"

Slowly, Dominick shook his head. "Mitchell ... you need to answer your damn phone. Frieda tried calling you several times, and you didn't pick up."

"The battery died yesterday, I think. Might have happened the day before. I plugged it in to charge but forgot about it and left it at home. Why? What's so important that you need to talk to me?"

"The Council has gone."

Mitchell stood perfectly still for a second, mouth hanging open, and then he burst out laughing.

"Oh, you almost got me. Very convincing, Dominick."

Dominick didn't respond except to stare at him.

Slowly, the smile on Mitchell's face faded. "Holy crap. You're serious."

"We got attacked. Only a handful of people survived. The rest all died."

"Died? Like dead-dead?"

"All of them."

Mitchell looked like a gust of wind could have blown him over at that moment.

"Holy mother of God. Is Frieda all right?"

"She got injured but will be fine. Jun Lee survived as well."

"Abigail?"

Dominick didn't respond, but Mitchell could read the look on his face.

Mitchell's face fell. "Damn it. I think I need to sit down."

He walked across the hall to the back room of the shop, and Dominick followed. Mitchell sat on an ugly red giant couch, and Dominick lowered himself into the beanbag chair opposite. The place reeked of recently smoked marijuana.

A few minutes passed while they just stared at each other. Dominick waited, letting the information sink in for Mitchell.

"What happened?" he asked, finally.

"We got attacked. Aram Malhotra betrayed us, and the entire Council got murdered."

"Damn. I knew things had gone bad but never expected anything like this."

"No one did," Dominick said. "It gets worse."

"What do you mean?"

"The demon who attacked us had control of Nida's body and plans something else ... some sort of summoning ritual."

"To bring back the creature the Council locked away?"

"You know about that?"

Mitchell nodded. "I found out everything I could about the Council when they first approached me. I like to know who I'm about to get in bed with, so to speak, but that was a long time ago. Most of the rumors came out of the Catholic Church, and apparently, the original seven members of the Council locked away some horrible creature a long time ago, and their reward came in the guise of getting formed into the Council on behalf of the Church and receiving support and funding."

"But they didn't want to serve the Church directly," Dominick said. His uncle had told him much the same story when he first joined the Order of Hunters, minus the part about locking away an evil creature. "So, instead, they looked for funding from other sources and stayed mostly autonomous. That's why we're multi-religious. Do you know what they locked up? A demon?"

"From what I heard, something worse. An integration of sorts."

"Integration?"

"When demon and host bond completely, we call it integration. It's incredibly rare, and barely ever actually works. The host has to invite the demon in, and they become one and the same. And even then, it proves rare to find a truly powerful demon willing to integrate with a host because the host gains some sort of symbiotic benefit from the demon."

"So, not possession?"

"With possession, the demon wears the human like a set of clothing. They have control, but it comes with a built-in lag time and safety network whereby the body slowly dies and falls apart. They are *inside* the host, like a parasite, but gradually, the host dies as the demon poisons and corrupts it. With integration, they *are* the host, and the host becomes them. It's way worse."

"So, the Council stopped one of these a long time ago, and their bloodline locked it away?"

"In the deepest pits of hell." Mitchell nodded. "So the story goes. Not sure how much I believe of it. I've seen possession, and I've heard about forms of integration, but whatever this was, it sounds way worse."

"Well, I guess at least some of it holds truth. The demon is after the blood of the descendants from the original Council. It captured Frieda and took vials of her blood. We aren't sure, but we think it might have gotten another few of the bloodlines it needs before it attacked the Council, so we're running out of time to stop Nida."

Mitchell fell silent while he thought through the consequences. "Even if the demon got all of the blood it needed, it would still need to perform an actual ritual to make this a reality. Something like that isn't simple to do."

"Frieda said there's a stolen book that the demon could use for that purpose when it invaded the Council. Something with the history of the Council and all of the surnames she would need to find living descendants. We're up against the clock and out of options. We need to find some way to stop the demon from gathering up all of the blood and completing the ritual before it's too late."

"What do you need from me?"

"Nothing," Dominick said. "Frieda just wanted me to check on you to make sure you still lived. You didn't answer your phone, and I'd already come to the neighborhood, so it made just a short jaunt out of my way."

"Ah, so I wasn't a top priority?"

"Not exactly."

"How reassuring."

"I'm on my way to Pennsylvania. One of the descendants Frieda knows lives there."

"Who?" Dominick asked, then his eyes widened, and he groaned. "You can't mean Jill Reinfer."

"The one and only. She's on the list of people we need to keep track of."

"That woman is a witch."

"I'm not a fan, either. But, if keeping her safe stops Nida from whatever she plans to do, then I'm fine with it."

"Yeah. I guess so."

"Frieda thinks she might be one of the targets, so I need to get there and make sure she's still alive."

"So, you're just going to leave me here? What am I supposed to do if this crazed demon woman comes after me?"

"You're welcome to travel with me if you think that's better?"

"To Pennsylvania? No, thanks. I'll take my chances."

Dominick laughed. "Suit yourself. But look, if anything suspicious happens at all, you let me know, all right?"

"All right."

"And turn on your damn phone. I don't want to have to make another trip out here to see if you're still alive."

"Fine."

Dominick stood and headed back out through the shop. He chuckled to himself as he passed the spilled tray of little marijuana plants.

"And clean this damn place up," he shouted back at the room. "It looks like a tornado came through here."

"Yeah, yeah," Mitchell shouted back.

Dominick headed back outside, grabbing a candle on the way. Marvin loved candles, and it might serve as a peace offering when all of this ended. He glanced at the label: Eucalyptus and mint; Marvin's favorite.

It remained cloudy and overcast outside, but at least it had stopped raining. The wind made it feel a lot colder than the temperature. Dominick hadn't been to Ohio many times in the past few months, but he didn't much like it in winter. Too many people packed closely together, and too variable weather. He would take California over Ohio any day.

Of course, Pennsylvania didn't rank much better. He had gone to Portsmouth only once and hated the way the entire city smelled. Jill Reinfer lived in that city, which made it his next stop.

Chapter 6

Jill Reinfer had worked as a member of the Council about ten years ago, though she had only lasted a few months. Just until her father died, and she had inherited his vast fortune. George Reinfer had been a good man. His daughter, not so much.

She had left around the time Dominick's uncle first initiated him into the Order of Hunters, and so he'd never known her personally. He'd heard a lot about her and the fact that she considered herself above and better than others, especially the Hunters. Though not that old, only in her mid-fifties, she didn't want to stay a part of the underground world any longer.

The thing was, even though he disliked her, Dominick couldn't blame her for wanting out. The life of the Council members, like the Hunters, got spent in the shadows, and one had to look over one's shoulder constantly. Continually lying and playing things close to the chest.

Dominick envied her a little for wanting to escape and managing to. Sometimes, he wished he could just drop everything, return to Marvin, and start their life anew.

However, his position as a Hunter lasted for life.

Jill had had importance on the Council, much like Frieda. They were descendants of the original Council members from hundreds of years ago. Until a few days ago, that hadn't meant much to Dominick, but now, it had taken on a whole new meaning.

He arrived at her estate late in the day. The gate out front looked ornate and tall, and a buzzer and screen sat out front. Dominick drove up to it, rolled down his window, and clicked the button. A moment later, the screen flashed to life.

"Hello," he said.

On the screen, a middle-aged and bored-looking man appeared.

"Name and business?"

"Dominick Cupertino. Here to speak with Jill Reinfer about an important matter."

The man yawned. "I apologize, but she isn't receiving guests right now. You'll need to schedule an appointment."

"Could you, please, just tell her Dominick is here on Council business? It's urgent that I speak with her."

The man remained silent for a minute, just staring at Dominick through the camera. Finally, the screen went dark.

He sat there in his car, unsure what to expect from the conversation. Would the man speak with Jill, or had he just dismissed Dominick summarily?

Just when he considered how he might break onto the premises, a clanking noise sounded. The gate swung open, clearing the path for him to drive up to the manor. With a sigh of relief, Dominick put the car back into gear and continued up the driveway.

Jill lived on a mammoth estate, large enough to house a few-dozen families and still have rooms to spare. Her father had grown rich in the Fabricated Metal Industry and diversified his assets when that industry stagnated. The brilliant businessman grew vast fortunes out of nothing.

He also became a firm believer in the work the Council did. Proud of his family line and the legacy of the Reinfer family, for years, he invested a substantial amount of money into the Council of Chaldea. At least while he lived, though he never served on the Council himself since he remained too busy with his business. It offered a source of pride for him, doing his part by helping pay the Council's bills.

Jill, on the other hand, hated the Council and her heritage. Born to wealth and privilege, as such, she felt that the Council and Order of Hunters were an outdated relic, a staple from another time, and that they abused their power. She only served on the Council to appease her father, and she quit and left the moment he passed on.

Maybe she had it right that they had become an outdated relic. Her opinion certainly got validated when Arthur fell from grace and killed innocents, but Arthur made the exception rather than the rule. He'd held too much responsibility on his shoulders, and at a certain point, he had just snapped.

By Dominick's estimation, Jill had never seen the world for what it was. She knew nothing about what the Hunters actually dealt with, and judged them without understanding what they came up against and just how dangerous their world was.

He drove his car around an enormous stone fountain and up to the front door of the property. Two men stood there, wearing expensive suits and sunglasses. Both looked armed and watched Dominick carefully.

He climbed out of the rental, and one of the men beckoned for him to follow. Silently, the guards turned and walked into the building. Inside, a double staircase wrapped around to the second floor, and an antechamber led off to the right, left, and straight ahead deeper into the manor. This antechamber stood three stories high with a vaulted ceiling. Gorgeous rugs ran from the front entrance and up the stairs.

The décor, maroon and smooth, contained rich tapestries that decorated the walls. The guards led him up to the second floor, down a hall, and to a sitting room where Jill sat waiting. An overweight and soft woman, she wore an expensive gown that did little to hide her many folds.

Jill had a scowl on her face and looked mildly constipated while she sized up Dominick. He hadn't managed to shower in the last couple of days, and looked rough from the road. He didn't like the feeling that she judged him because, in her estimation, he was rabble.

The two guards flanked him when he walked into the room, hands folded near their waists. Well-trained, they looked quite capable as bodyguards.

"Frieda sent you," Jill said, finally.

"She did." Dominick nodded. "She wanted me to check up on you and make sure you were safe."

Jill laughed. An ugly laugh. "Frieda? Are we talking about the same woman? Frieda could care less about my well-being."

"Things have changed."

"Yes, they have. I heard about what happened in Switzerland. A shame."

Dominick bit back of a flash of anger. He could hardly believe she would so casually dismiss what had happened. So many of his friends had gotten murdered in the attack.

But, even though callous, she wasn't at fault for what had happened. Dominick had a job to do, even if one he didn't particularly like.

"Frieda sent me because she thinks you might be at risk."

"So, this isn't over?"

"No."

Jill let out a disgusted sigh. "I thought I'd freed myself from that life. Why? Was my name on one of their stupid lists?"

"It ..." Dominick hesitated. He glanced back and forth between the two men flanking him.

Annoyed, Jill waved her hand, dismissing the two guards. Wordlessly, they slid out of the room and closed the door behind them. Dominick waited until they had gone and then turned back to Jill.

"It's your lineage," he said. "Your bloodline. The demon is trying to resurrect an ancient evil, and it needs you to complete it."

"Me?"

"It's only a possibility. The demon might go after one of your relatives instead if she knows about them. However, Frieda thinks it might come for you out of spite since you used to serve on the Council."

"What does it want with me?"

"Your blood."

Jill frowned. "That's all? Maybe it should just call ahead. I can have my doctor draw a few vials and hand them over."

"I'm serious."

"So am I. We have no love lost between me and your silly Council, and if a few pints of blood will get rid of this mess, then I will gladly pencil in the appointment."

"We can't allow you to do that."

Jill narrowed her eyes. "And you think you could stop me?"

Dominick stayed silent for a moment. He'd heard stories but never imagined just how cold and heartless Jill was.

"You do understand that if the demon is successful, a lot of people will die."

"A lot of people will die no matter what I do. However, I do not intend to become one of them."

"In any case, I doubt the demon will ask politely for your blood. From everything we've seen so far, it intends to kill everyone in its path to accomplish this task. It won't spare anyone."

Jill softened up a tiny bit. "I know. A shame, but demons aren't the most reasonable of creatures."

"I'm here to make sure that if you *are* on the demon's list that it will never get your blood."

"My security team can handle my protection."

"They have experience with demons?"

"They have faced things you can't even imagine, boy."

"Either way, I'm staying," Dominick said.

He didn't add that it went against his better judgment and objection, but he couldn't afford to let her hand over her blood to Nida. He'd assumed he would come here to protect her from Nida, not the other way around.

"Are you, now?"

He nodded. "So, this can either be easy-peasy, where you give me access to your premises, or difficult, where no one ends up happy."

Jill studied him for a few seconds from her cushioned seat. Finally, she nodded. "Very well. Talk to Trent, outside. He is my head of security and will set you up with clearance. I'll tell him you work for a rival company, and I hired you for a security check. That should keep him on his toes."

Dominick nodded. "I promise not to get in your way. It'll be like I never came here at all."

"It better be."

✳✳✳

Trent glowered—annoyed—when Dominick exited the sitting room. The big man looked burly and muscular, and not the kind of bloke who took too well to getting dismissed.

He wore the air of someone who had worked at this household guarding Ms. Reinfer for a long time, which meant he would feel completely averse to Dominick stepping in as a rival and competitor. An outsider stepping on his toes and watching his back would give an affront to his pride. Which meant Dominick would need to tread lightly.

Dominick didn't want to piss off anyone; he just wanted to make sure that their security systems came up to par with Nida's capabilities. After what had happened to the Council, the stakes had raised incredibly high.

Trent showed him to a security office on the first floor. Two men sat manning the cameras, of which he estimated dozens, if not hundreds, on the premises. Trent ignored the two men and went to a computer station nearby.

Dominick handed him his passport—the mostly legit one, as already, he'd given them his real name—and then waited while Trent typed into the computer.

"This will get you into many rooms in the estate," Trent said, finally, handing Dominick a keycard. "But not all. It also has a GPS locator in it, so keep it with you at all times."

"Okay."

"I'll let my men know that you're on site and not to harass you. Ms. Reinfer said you were doing a security check for an outside firm? What firm?"

"Cupertino Consulting," Dominick said. "She asked me to look over everything and make sure it's all up to snuff."

Trent scowled. "Our equipment is all top of the line. We have facial recognition, motion sensors, heat sensors, and ultraviolet sensors at all points of ingress, as well as regular randomized patrol teams."

"How do you randomize the system?"

"We use a Bar-Link time scheduler with global randomization. In addition, a top of the line firewall locks down all of our internet connections, and we do regular auditing of the logs to check for unauthorized access even from admin accounts."

Dominick nodded. "That sounds good. How many guards do you have?"

"Six in rotation, another six on call for events, and two techs."

An expensive operation. Not that it surprised him, though; Jill could afford it and knew about the dangerous underworld and what it could offer.

"Equipment?"

"A fully stocked armory, two armored Jeeps, and easy access to any heavier equipment we might need."

Dominick nodded again. "Excellent. Do you have a map for external sensors so that I can look it over? I'd hoped to do a perimeter sweep."

"We have a map but won't supply it to you. It's locked down, and we don't allow outsiders access."

"Ms. Reinfer hired me—"

"Ms. Reinfer pays *us* to keep her safe, and that includes from herself. You're welcome to tour the grounds, check the equipment, and do whatever you like while you're here. But, please, don't think for a second that we'll give you access to any sensitive information."

Again, no surprise there. Dominick just hoped that he hadn't overstepped. He didn't want to annoy Trent too much. At least, not yet. "Of course. I understand."

"Besides, if you're good enough to think you can win *our* contract, you won't need a map anyway."

Trent said it with a little smirk that made Dominick want to punch him in the face. "What about accommodations?"

"I'll have the staff prepare you a guest room and set you up with meals. We've logged your phone number into the system, so you'll get a text when it's ready."

Dominick nodded. He slid the keycard into his pocket and headed out of the security room. Exhausted, he didn't have time to deal with Trent just now. The security chief perceived that Dominick threatened his cushy job and lifestyle and saw him as an enemy, and Dominick could do nothing to prove to him that they worked on the same side.

At least, not until Nida attacked.

He had access now, though, which meant a good thing. He could move about the premises freely and look over the security systems. Although, he doubted he would find weaknesses in their system. They seemed well prepared; at least, to handle human intrusions.

To be honest, right now he looked forward more to having a nice place to sleep and a good warm meal. It had proven too long since he'd last managed just to clean up and relax. He could do his perimeter search later, once he'd rested. Besides, he had no telling of when—or if—Nida would attack.

Now, he could only wait.

Chapter 7

Haatim arrived at St. Peter's Basilica Cathedral early the next morning. A car waited for him when he awoke and drove him from the hotel and across the border into Vatican City. He had a headache and remained exhausted from the last couple of days, but the sheer fact that he'd come to the Vatican kept him awake and made him curious beyond his greatest expectations.

Previous research told him that while not difficult to get into the Vatican as a tourist, much of the city stayed locked away and nearly impossible to visit without prior authorization from the Church.

However, the people who picked him up had all the paperwork necessary for him to get inside and meet with Father Niccolo Paladina. Normally, such paperwork should have taken weeks, if not months, to procure and, honestly, he might never have received permission.

The driver barely spoke to him during the drive, which he didn't mind: he felt overwhelmed at seeing the scenery and the holiest of cities—a place he had only imagined visiting in his wildest dreams. Beautiful, it held an aura of awe-inspiring authority and power.

The Cathedral looked amazing as well, and completely beyond anything he'd experienced. The pictures of it that he'd seen in books and online didn't do it justice, and the feelings that overwhelmed him, in addition to feeling so tired that he could barely walk, made him feel closer to God. The placed seemed to have a spiritual connection. The building loomed overhead, enormous, and carried with it an air of grandiosity that made him stop and just stare at the intricate décor on the outside.

His excitement overtook him, and he allowed himself to bask for just a few moments in the realization that he stood truly within Vatican City and before the heart of the Catholic Church.

For many years, while studying religion at the University in Arizona, he had dreamed of coming here. Back when he had thought religious study as just a fun thing he could do at school to keep his parents happy. Back when he knew nothing about this life. Back when he didn't have a care in the world.

Haatim enjoyed studying Eastern religion, and Buddhism as well, but Western Religion had become the focus of his education since he'd taken courses in a Western School. Nothing quite embodied the *idea* of Western Religion the way the Vatican City did, and it had made it onto his bucket list of things to do before he died.

To remain perfectly honest, he'd never expected to complete any of the items from his bucket list while he remained so young.

And, the more he thought about it, the closer he realized he'd come to dying young.

A sobering thought.

"Quite magnificent, isn't it?" a voice asked from nearby.

Haatim turned. An Italian man stood a few feet away, watching him. He had olive skin, jet black hair, piercing eyes, and had the collar of an ordained priest around his neck. The man looked to be in his late sixties, maybe older.

He wore a half-smile on his face as he studied Haatim, looking over his wide-rimmed oval glasses the way one might stare at a book. It took Haatim a moment to recognize him from the photos Frieda had given him, and he realized the photos must have been taken when the man was quite a bit younger.

"Father Paladina?"

"One and the same," the man said, nodding.

"Ah, Frieda sent me here to find you."

The Father didn't reply. Instead, he turned and looked over at the Basilica Cathedral.

"I always wish I could see it the same way the tourists do. The way *you* do once again, as though seeing it for the first time."

"It's beautiful."

Father Paladina nodded. "I can appreciate the beauty and sheer majestic quality of it still, but it simply doesn't *affect* me any longer. I long with nostalgia for the emotions that coursed through my body when first I beheld it."

"How old were you?"

"Merely a child. Seven years was all I had in this world when I first got brought to the city. After a while, it ceased to seem amazing and simply became home."

A moment passed in silence. Finally, Haatim spoke, "I apologize for being rash, but Frieda sent me here to meet with you." Haatim turned to face the priest once more. "She said you could help me locate a book? Something about the history of the Council of Chaldea that the Vatican holds."

Father Paladina smiled. "Right to the point."

"I don't have much time, and it's incredibly important. Life or death. I'm in a hurry."

"I know of the burden placed upon you," Father Paladina said. "But, sometimes, it's important to stop and take note of our surroundings, lest we fall out of touch. Occasionally, in our rush to get somewhere, we need to slow down and take stock of where we are, or else we might never get where we need to go."

"I can appreciate the beauty of this place some other time."

Father Paladina frowned at him. "How can you ever feel sure that there will come some other time?"

"I can't," Haatim said. "But, right now, I *really* need to find that book."

Father Paladina nodded. "You remind me of someone I once knew from a long time ago. He behaved in a brash and impatient way, too. Don't fret; already, I have pulled the book that Frieda requested from the library and will give you all of the access to it that you require."

"You have? That's great."

"Actually, for the last few weeks, I've looked into the issue the same as Frieda has."

"Oh? Why?"

"Because," Father Paladina said. "I'm afraid things are a lot worse than she thinks."

✳✳✳

"What do you mean?" Haatim asked.

Father Paladina gestured for Haatim to follow him and walked away from the Basilica and toward a waiting car. The sleek BMW had tinted windows and looked much like a government issued vehicle.

"Things like this are best not discussed in public."

Haatim followed him across the parking lot, weaving through tourists and traffic. Father Paladina walked quickly, with purpose, and Haatim had to struggle to keep up.

He waited until they'd settled comfortably inside the car before speaking once more.

"There. Much better. I have spent too much time on my butt these past years and have grown unaccustomed to standing so much."

"What were you saying?" Haatim asked. "What do you mean that it's worse than Frieda thought?"

The driver glanced at them in the rearview mirror. Father Paladina waved his hand at him, and the driver rolled up the divider to separate them and provide privacy. Slowly, they rolled away from the Cathedral and onto the street, heading deeper into the city.

Father Paladina sat for a moment in silence, staring out of the window. "When Frieda called, she said you would come here to search for a list of names. She also mentioned that it could prove important."

"Yes, she sent me here to research the original Council and look for any descendants."

"For a few months now, I've investigated that same list."

"What? Why?"

"Because those descendants have developed a bad habit of turning up dead."

"What do you mean?"

"We have certain contingencies in place to track coincidences and happenstance because what seems like one rarely is. Four people turned up dead in the last three months, and all of them descendants of the original founders of the Council of Chaldea."

"Four?" The news shocked Haatim.

Father Paladina nodded. "Four. And when I spoke to Frieda earlier, she said that her blood got taken as well. That means that only two bloodlines remain unaccounted for of the original seven."

"We need to tell Frieda," Haatim said.

"No." Father Paladina shook his head.

"This could become critical information. What do you mean by 'no'?"

"Frieda refuses to tell me what's going on, and until she opens up to me, I shan't open up to her. There remain only two bloodlines unaccounted for, but she won't tell me what the blood is for?"

Haatim understood that the priest had tried to prompt him by turning the last into a question. "I need to inform Frieda," he said, finally. "She needs to know about this."

"I won't stop you, and I understand fully. I just want to be clear that I dislike being kept in the dark. How can I help when you keep me at arm's length?"

Haatim didn't know whether or not Frieda had a good reason to withhold information from Father Paladina, and he hadn't known the priest for more than a couple of minutes, but he could think of no good reason to withhold information from him. After all, Frieda had sent him here to find help.

"It's related to an ancient evil. Something the Council locked away long ago. My sis—the demon that attacks us—is trying to release it."

Father Paladina frowned. "Surgat?"

"You know about it?"

"Only stories. Not anything conclusive. I've seen mention of him in some older texts, but only in passing. I believe that the Church has withheld and protected most of the information, though I cannot be certain why."

"Well, there you go. That's why these people are getting killed. For their blood so that the demon can release Surgat."

"What demon is this who attempts to release Surgat? Do you know its true name?"

Haatim shook his head. "No. It possesses my sister, though; and, unfortunately, we don't know what demon it is or how powerful it might be."

"Names are power. If we can find out which demon lives inside her, then we can—maybe—find a weakness and put an end to this."

That thought hadn't occurred to Haatim. "Makes sense."

"More to research. However, it sounds like we have our work cut out for us."

"If four of the bloodline have gone missing in the last few months already, why didn't you warn anybody?"

"I did. Or tried to, but only in passing."

"In passing? This seems like more than an 'in passing' problem. We might have gotten better prepared if we'd known something like this had happened."

Father Paladina shrugged. "A regrettable mistake. Hindsight makes for a cruel mistress. Things like this have happened before, and it usually comes to nothing. As I said, I've investigated it. Things always seem much clearer when looking backward, but you need to understand that my information came from all over the world and proved vague in nature. In no way could I have known that something like *this* would happen."

"You should have reached out to the Council."

"I did. Multiple times, but with the trial of Frieda Gotlieb commencing, they became wholly focused inward and unwilling to look out at the world around them. The Council isn't what it once was and has suffered under hubris for years. When I worked with them, a long time ago, it operated like a completely different organization."

"You worked for the Council?"

"*With*," the Father said. "I worked alongside Arthur Vangeest a few times, though that happened many years ago, back when the Order of Hunters numbered in the hundreds. Back then, I thought them just vigilante murderers killing people who *might* have a touch of corruption in them."

"What do you think now?"

Father Paladina hesitated. "The same. Only now, I think that a lot less of them exist."

Chapter 8

Dominick spent most of his time in the lounge on the second floor of the estate and tried not to think about just how much money someone had to have that their estate would have multiple lounges inside the same building.

Four lounges, to be exact. Every single one of them big enough for him and his husband to live in comfortably, and each filled with grandiose and expensive items that lent an ostentatious feel. The second-floor one seemed the least pretentious he could find. It also made for one of the only ones stocked with a full bar.

Jill Reinfer liked to collect expensive items and antiques, apparently, and so Dominick found himself constantly surrounded by things that he couldn't afford.

He had stayed here for two days so far and felt seriously like a useless third wheel. When he'd first arrived, he had felt like his presence might prove necessary and that he could help the security team in closing up any defensive holes they might have.

After all, they didn't expect a supernatural threat or anything dangerous to happen, and so he would be able to keep their employer safe from threats that her security team couldn't even imagine.

However, he had done a full sweep of the entire estate, inside and out, and come to the conclusion that he could do little to augment what they had already. The estate worked like a well-oiled machine with good security—drum tight—and he couldn't find any weaknesses in it.

Worse, they *knew* their security setup as good. The head of security, Trent Dopper, took extreme offense to Dominick coming here, and even with the good graces of the lady of the estate, he showed Dominick no courtesy. It ended up like a constant pissing contest, and the more time that went by, the less willing Trent became to help him with anything.

Which didn't surprise Dominick at all, but it did make him feel more than a little useless. He couldn't come out and explain that he wanted to keep Jill Reinfer safe from a demonic threat, which meant that, basically, he just sat around twiddling his thumbs and waiting for something to go wrong.

So, while waiting, he poured himself a tall glass of scotch and rested in an armchair. He needed to call Marvin and let him know things remained okay and that he might be gone a few extra days, but he couldn't bring himself to pick up the phone. He felt torn between hoping the demon would attack to get it over with and dread that it might actually happen.

And getting a chance to slow down and take a breath proved welcome if not necessarily a good thing. Also, having time to recover meant that he had time to think, and that meant worrying about the attack on the Council and how easily they had gotten destroyed.

Never had he believed that something like that could happen, let alone with such efficiency. They hadn't even known an attack loomed imminent until the army showed up at their doorstep. This had been planned for a long time, and even with Aram's help, the attack bespoke years of planning.

It made Dominick feel paranoid in a way he'd never before felt. Always, he had assumed relative safety, or at least, not living in the dark about what might happen. He'd believed in the strength of the Council, and now, he saw that he'd misplaced his belief.

They hadn't even imagined that The Ninth Circle could have resources enough to hire a mercenary army, let alone plan something like this. Well-trained mercenaries at that, which wouldn't have come cheap. They had launched an all-out war on the Council, a surprise attack, and it had proven completely effective. Now, nothing endured. Except for Frieda, a few scattered Hunters, and a kid who remained something of an infant where this world was concerned.

They'd become the last hope of stopping Nida and saving the world.

✳✳✳

His vigil at the Reinfer estate continued while his boredom intensified. The next morning started much like the previous day had ended, and already, everything blended together. He had breakfast and did his morning exercises, and then just kicked back in his lounge and relaxed.

Too early for a drink, he decided, after a lengthy internal debate. After a few hours, he went out for a walk around the grounds, hoping to meet some new and—with any luck—less hostile people.

He managed to speak with one of the guards on the southern side of the estate, but the man's coldness and hostility kept him from striking up a meaningful conversation. Evidently, someone had warned him about Dominick.

Instead, he kept walking and did another full outer sweep of the fences surrounding the estate. He did it to distract himself, but the excuse he offered himself was to do another perimeter check. After all, he might have missed something the first several times around. He knew he hadn't, but at least he could keep busy.

Most of the security team gave him dirty looks whenever they saw him. He had been here for several long days now, but he still hadn't managed to break through their animosity and win over any of them. They proved a tight-knit team, incredibly loyal to Trent and their employer, and he a simple outsider.

All fine with him. He understood tight-knit communities and families. The Hunters worked like that ... or, at least, they used to. For years, they'd all looked up to Arthur as a father figure of the organization. They held him up as what they all aspired to become.

He supposed that Arthur's fall from grace had given the catalyst for all of this. It had brought an ominous foreboding of dark times to come. The Order of Hunters had fractured, some denouncing Arthur and everything he had stood for, and others remaining loyal to what he had lived as and represented. Their split opinion on what had happened did considerable damage to their morale. Loyalties separated.

No one had stepped up and taken on the mantle of leadership after Arthur got locked away in prison. They had become disorganized and unfocused, and that had, no doubt, contributed to the fall of the Council.

Just as he made it outside into the courtyard, his phone rang. Frieda. He answered, "Hello?"

"Dominick? Where are you?"

"At the Reinfer estate. Why?"

"I'll be flying in sometime in the next couple of days."

"How's Jun?"

"Better," she said. "I think he'll make it."

"What about Aram?"

Frieda didn't answer. A moment passed. "Stay prepared. I have reason to suspect an attack imminent."

"Why?"

"I just received word from Haatim. I got it wrong. Nida has already acquired the blood of five descendants. There only remain two families unaccounted for."

"Only two?"

"Yes. And Jill Reinfer makes for one of them."

He mulled over her words. "And the other one?"

"Haatim and Father Paladina are looking into it, but so far, we don't have any concrete names. Nida will, no doubt, come for this bloodline soon, though."

"Jill has living relatives. Shouldn't we protect them as well?"

"Jill takes priority, as the only one who knows about the Council's existence."

"She also has a full security team and state-of-the-art tech keeping her safe. Nida would be a fool to attack this holdout when she has easier targets."

"She should have been a fool to attack us. Look at us now."

"Still, I should go track down the other relatives and keep them safe, too."

"No. Father Paladina has dispatched Church officials to check in on the others, but for now, *our* priority must stay on Jill."

Dominick thought to argue further—he doubted Nida would be foolish enough to attack this estate—but decided against it. After all, it wasn't his place to object.

Moreover, the biggest reason he wanted to go out and check on the other members of the bloodline came down to simple boredom. He hated sitting around here and feeling useless.

"All right," he said, finally. "I'll stay here."

"Keep her safe," Frieda said. "She's one of the last pieces the demon needs to make this ritual a reality. I'll get there soon to help."

"Sure."

He hung up and slid the phone into his pocket, frowning. With the estate so secure, it would prove almost impossible to break into, but Frieda seemed certain that this had become a target. Why would the demon break into such a heavily fortified position?

That said, he would have thought the same thing about the Council building. Frieda had called it right: it would prove unwise to underestimate her. They had hired and withdrawn an army of soldiers to keep the Council safe, and Nida had still destroyed it in under an hour. It might seem foolish to attack such a fortified position, maybe even arrogant, but he wouldn't put anything past the demon.

If Frieda felt concerned, then he should too.

It had gone way past the time that he went to have a talk with Trent.

✳✳✳

He found Trent in the security office with the two members of his technical team. One sat watching the bank of camera feeds, and the other looked at one of the computers alongside Trent.

The security head's expression soured when Dominick entered. "Can I help you?"

"I'd hoped to get a couple of minutes of your time. We need to talk."

"We've talked. What else do you need?"

"In private," Dominick said.

Trent frowned but, finally, nodded. "Sure. Ten minutes. I'll meet you in the lounge where you've been hiding out."

Dominick took the insult in stride, nodded, and then headed back upstairs to the second floor. He checked his watch. Enough time had passed now. It had reached afternoon, albeit by only a couple of minutes. He poured himself a drink, poured one out for Trent, and then took a seat to wait.

Trent took about twenty minutes to show but came in at length. He stopped in the doorway, glancing over at Dominick, and made no move to sit.

"Can you shut the door?" Dominick stood and offered Trent the extra drink. The chief waved away the glass but did close the door. Dominick gestured toward the seat opposite him, and after a moment, Trent dropped onto the chair.

"What?" Trent folded his arms across his chest. "What do you need to talk about?"

"Ms. Reinfer never hired me to look into the security system."

Trent frowned further. "No?"

Dominick shook his head. "We used to work together, Ms. Reinfer and myself. Years ago. I did security for her, though not like this. More of a ... targeted operation. I have reason to believe that there is a credible threat planned on her life."

Trent continued frowning at him for a second. Finally, he rocked his head back and laughed. Not a real laugh, but just an exaggerated facsimile. "You're kidding?"

"Nope."

"You've seen our security. You can't, honestly, think someone would try to break in here."

"I have reason to believe that they will, and soon."

"Who is this fictional group that you believe will try and murder Ms. Reinfer?"

"You wouldn't understand."

"Try me."

"A cult."

Taken aback, Trent's jaw slackened. "Like Satanists?"

"Nothing like Satanists as you would picture them. This group is the real deal. What these people have planned is violent and dangerous."

Trent stayed silent for a moment, studying Dominick. "You never served."

"Excuse me?"

"In the military," he said. "You never served in any branch of the military, did you? I looked you up and found no records."

"No. I didn't serve."

"The men I hire, all of them served. Mostly Rangers."

"Your point?"

"These men stand ready for *anything*. They've fought in war zones and hostile locations all their lives. They've gone to hell and back, and they live and breathe ready to handle any situation in which they find themselves. So, when some little jackoff comes in here and tries to tell me that *my* men aren't ready, I don't take too kindly to it."

"I'm not saying they aren't ready for most things. They just aren't ready for *this.*"

"They *are* ready for *anything*." Trent stood and crossed his arms. "I don't know what game you and Ms. Reinfer have going on, but I've gotten just about sick of it. From this point forward, you can deal directly with her. Stay away from my men."

Trent headed for the door.

Dominick watched him go. "What do you have against me?"

Trent paused, midstride, and looked back at him. "What?"

"I didn't come here to threaten your job. I didn't come here to challenge your masculinity or your livelihood. What the hell do you have against me?"

"I don't know you."

"No, you don't, so stop acting like you do. You think me weak because I didn't serve?"

"I know you are."

"You think because I wasn't in the military that I'm a coward and haven't dealt with any tough situations in my life. You think that since you did serve in the military that you have a monopoly on dangerous situations."

Trent turned and faced him, narrowing his eyes. "You look in good shape, and I'm sure you can handle yourself in a fight, but the men I hire are trained killers. They would eat you alive."

"You honestly believe that?"

"I don't believe it. I know it."

Dominick eyed him for a second, and then stood. He took off his coat and dropped it on the seat behind him.

"Then, I'll enjoy proving you wrong."

"What? You think you can take on one of my guys? If you do this, know that I'll pick one of my best."

"Go ahead and pick two." Dominick grinned. "Let's make this interesting."

Chapter 9

Father Paladina and Haatim arrived at an old building in an older district of the city early the next morning. The previous day, Father Paladina had given him a tour of the city, explaining that nothing ever happened fast in Vatican City and that Haatim would need to stay patient.

Haatim believed that the priest had employed delaying tactics but didn't know the man well enough to feel certain. In either case, the tour proved a lot of fun, and they had a relaxing dinner at an outdoor restaurant.

Now, they made their way to a not-oft-used library. Not one of the Vatican libraries (secured and impossible for either of them to get into without months of waiting—and even then it remained doubtful that Haatim would ever get approved to enter), but a library where they could work in privacy without fear of intrusion.

Dim inside, it had a high-vaulted ceiling and rows and rows of tables running down the center. At least fifty. Each table held a small lamp for reading, and the room itself didn't look at all well-lit. Most of the lamps sat turned off, and the building lay almost empty.

Around the outer walls of the central chamber stood bookshelves filled to the brim with old tomes, most of which looked ancient but well-tended. It all left Haatim impressed, which must have shown on his face because, when he glanced over at Father Paladina, the man smirked at him.

"You should see the Vatican Libraries. They put this and the others like it to shame."

"You've been?"

"A few times. At least three Church officials always accompany visitors to make sure they don't harm any of the books, and they still won't let me anywhere near the important texts despite my many years of service to the Church. The one that you require, I've pulled out for extended use. The actual text gets stored in the archives, so when I need it, a senior librarian has to retrieve it for me and make copies."

"The archives?"

"Where we keep the important books. Very few people have access to those."

Haatim nodded. "You said others. You have more libraries like this?"

"Several. The Church has some of the largest and most complete collections of ancient texts anywhere in the world, and many of them duplicated for safety."

"Not digitized?"

Father Paladina laughed. "Where, exactly, do you think we are?"

He led Haatim over to one of the librarians' desks, where a middle-aged woman sat. She looked unpleasant, peering at them through glasses that sat at the end of her nose. She wore a vaguely hawkish expression while she sized up and summarily dismissed Haatim.

She spoke to Father Paladina in Italian, completely ignoring the fact that Haatim stood beside him.

Father Paladina answered her easily, and after a few minutes of pleasant conversation and a few laughs, she retrieved a binder from under the desk and handed it to him. She did give one last, untrusting look at Haatim before releasing the book, but Father Paladina won her over.

He thanked her and tucked the tome under his arm. Then, nodding to Haatim, they walked over to one of the tables and flipped on the light.

"Not that secure if you ask me," Haatim said. "She kept that under her desk?"

"The relevant pages that I managed to copy aren't deemed important enough by the Church to protect. And, this building is rather secure with cameras, guards, and modern security in case anyone tries any foolishness."

"Ah," Haatim said. "I thought you said they weren't up-to-date in the digital world?"

"They have state-of-the-art security. I'm not allowed to take the documents outside the building, but they do allow me to keep them here, on occasion, for easy access when I might need them. As I said, I've spent time looking into this rather frequently of late, so our friend over there looked after the copies for me."

"From what did you take the documents?"

"*A History of the Council of Chaldea.* A rather simple name if you ask me. It is the original text that recounts the founding of the Council."

"And the Order of Hunters?"

"That came later. A few hundred years, I believe. No, this is simply in reference to the Council itself."

"The Catholic Church has the only copy?"

"One of the last ones. A few others remain unaccounted for."

"You think that several exist?"

Father Paladina shrugged. "No idea, but Arthur told me once that Frieda had an original copy as well."

"You knew Arthur?"

"Yes. At one time, long ago."

"What was he like? Frieda has told me a little, and Abigail told me some, but they stayed short with the details."

"He was arrogant and overzealous," the priest said. "Nonetheless, he was also a good man. He believed in what he did, and he saved my life on more than one occasion."

They sat down at the table, and Father Paladina slid the folder across the top to Haatim.

"But, those tales can wait for another day. Right now, we have work to do."

Haatim opened up the folder, which held only a handful of pages. They showed photocopies of what looked to be an ancient text, and one that proved difficult to read.

Each of the pages held a family tree, detailing the lineage lines of various families. The first two pages expanded wildly, following a prolific growth pattern that would result in countless living descendants.

The other bloodlines appeared slightly less prolific but still entailed quite a few people who might share the blood, provided none of the lines ended. Haatim only recognized the names of Gotlieb and Reinfer.

The Gotlieb and Reinfer lines looked considerably less expansive, and the spouses or partners didn't get documented at all if they didn't share the bloodline directly.

Someone had circled some of the names and left others alone, and the entire list began around the thirteenth century and continued up through the sixteenth.

"They stopped tracking there," Father Paladina said, seeing the question on Haatim's face before he could even ask.

"You have no records beyond this?"

"Not from after they ceased to maintain the records. However, I've managed to find the links to pick up where those records left off in certain cases, using online tools and registries."

"These are the founding families?"

"Their lineages, yes. The original seven. The Church tracked them for just such an eventuality, but the more time that passed, the less likely it seemed that what is happening today would ever come to pass. We grew lax."

"A little shortsighted if you ask me."

Father Paladina chuckled. "You try maintaining records that span centuries without complete information."

Haatim looked over the names. "Why are some circled and some not?"

"The sons," Father Paladina said, a hint of distaste in his voice. "More ignorant times, as though the blood of their daughters held less validity."

"So many names," Haatim said, scanning the list. "How are we supposed to track down all the living descendants?"

Father Paladina sighed. "As I said, four of the bloodlines are already compromised and not worth our time."

He reached across the table and filtered through the pages, removing four of them. "And Frieda's blood got taken as well."

Then the priest pulled loose the Gotlieb page, leaving only two.

"Two left," Haatim said.

One of them showed the Reinfer line, and the other, Otolan. Neither of them seemed as expansive as some of the others but still would result in quite a few descendants.

"Yes."

"Still a lot of people to look up."

"I've been looking into it for weeks now. Of the Reinfer line, I can only be sure of one true descendent, and that is Jill Reinfer, who served on the Council. I've found a few others who might match the criteria, but if I had to guess, I would say that Jill would seem likeliest."

"Why?"

Father Paladina frowned. "What happened in Switzerland feels distinctly personal. Jill served on the Council, albeit briefly. And targeting her would make a powerful statement, much like targeting Frieda rather than one of her relatives."

Haatim hesitated. "But, now the demon knows we're onto it."

"True. I might have it wrong. In either case, the Otolan bloodline proves most interesting."

"Why?"

Father Paladina pulled out the sheet and pointed toward the point where the families no longer tracked. "Around this point, nearly all of them died."

"What? Over sixty people? How did they all die?"

"They got hunted."

"By whom?"

Father Paladina stayed silent for a long time. "Us."

✳✳✳

A stunned silence hung in the air.

"You're saying the Catholic Church hunted down and killed all of these people?"

"Every single one; at least, as far as I can tell."

"Why? There are dozens of people here."

"So this ritual could not be completed. If all of them died, we surmised, then the ritual could never take place."

"That's ..." Haatim couldn't think of the words to describe it.

Father Paladina nodded. "I know. Barbaric. Genocidal. Darker times, Haatim."

"Why then? What happened to make them do it?"

"If I had to guess, someone tried to do what the demon is doing today. Someone tried to release Surgat. The Church officials theorized that if one of the bloodlines got eliminated completely, then Surgat would stay trapped in hell forever."

Haatim fell silent while he thought through the ramifications. "Then, all of this is for nothing. If they murdered everyone involved, then the ritual can't get completed, right?"

"If that were the case, I doubt the demon would bother at all. The demon must know something we don't."

"So the purge happened for nothing?"

Father Paladina shook his head. "They didn't get them all. They thought they had, but one of the children survived, and his bloodline continued. The only problem is, I can't follow it past the mid-nineteen-twenties, so I don't know who or where the descendants might be today."

"And you think the demon does?"

"We have to assume so. If there remains even the slightest chance that the demon can find out what living descendent might have the necessary blood, then we need to find that person first."

Haatim tapped his chin, thinking. It made sense, though he had no clue where to start looking to try and figure this out. He would need a computer, a lot of time, and a general idea of where he should begin.

If what Father Paladina said proved true, then he estimated that there could be no more than ten or twelve living descendants if each generation had the normal number of children. That meant that only ten or twelve people lived out in the world that Nida could use to complete her ritual and ...

After a few moments, he felt Father Paladina's eyes boring into him.

"You have it, don't you?"

"Excuse me?"

"Frieda didn't tell me that when she told me of you. Quite interesting."

"What are you talking about?"

"The Gift. The Touch. The Curse. Whatever you want to call it. You can channel, can't you? I can sense it inside you. How many times have you done it?"

The hairs rose on the back of Haatim's neck. "I have no idea what you're on about."

"Yes, you do. You know exactly to what I refer. Maybe that made for one of the reasons Frieda sent you here to me. She asked me to keep you safe, which I thought strange. Of all the places she could have sent you, she chose here. But, now it makes sense."

"What are you talking about? What do you mean that Frieda asked you to keep me safe?"

"Come with me."

Father Paladina stood, sliding the papers back into the file. He walked quickly over to the counter, spoke to the woman, and handed her the folder. She slipped it back out of sight, and then the priest rushed toward the exit.

Haatim struggled to keep up, not sure what was going on. What did the priest mean by "keep him safe?" Frieda had sent him here to find information, right?

Keep him safe from what?

They slipped back out of the dark library and into the sun, headed for the car. Father Paladina spoke at speed to the driver in Italian and then gestured for Haatim to climb in the back seat.

"Where are we going?"

"One last stop, then I will drop you off at your hotel for the rest of the day."

"Stop where?"

"Please, Haatim, just get in the car."

Haatim hesitated, and then nodded. He climbed into the back, and

Father Paladina stepped in after him. The driver put the car into motion, and they got back on the road in only moments.

They traveled in silence, and Father Paladina wouldn't even look at him as they went. The drive took about fifteen minutes, and as they went, the buildings grew less impressive and more rundown. They'd entered the slums.

Finally, they stopped in front of a nondescript older building with no identification or markers. It stood in a residential district that appeared incredibly quiet, with brick roadways and numerous arches segregating the areas.

"Where are we?"

"A training ground, of sorts."

"Training for what?"

The priest didn't answer. Instead, he opened the door and climbed out, and without looking back, walked into the building. Haatim glanced at the driver but found no help there. Finally, he unbuckled and followed.

Dark inside, the building felt ancient. It had a low ceiling and smelled dank and dusty.

It reminded him, just for a second, of when he had gone with Abigail into the caves in the forest outside of Raven's Peak, where they'd found the knife; though they hadn't known it at the time. That also made the first time he'd seen Nida, albeit only her feet through a tunnel. This building made him feel just as claustrophobic as crawling through those narrow holes deep underground.

Father Paladina had gone already, walking further into the building. Somewhere up ahead, a door closed.

"Hello?" Haatim asked. "Where did you go?"

No answer. He waited a second, wondering where the priest had gone, but the room remained silent and empty. A hallway stretched off in front of him, heading deeper into the building, but it seemed quiet.

He waited a full five minutes, but the priest didn't return. Finally, hesitantly, he walked to the hallway and peered inside. It had no windows or lights, but he could see a faint glow somewhere further down. A faint sound came from the distance—like whistling wind or exhaled breath—but nothing else.

"Hello?" he tried one more time. Again, he received no response.

Haatim steeled his nerves and edged down the hallway, peering into the rooms on his right and left. They looked like cells in a prison, though with no attached doors or windows with views of the outside world. They seemed like empty boxes, roughhewn and uncomfortable.

The deeper he went into the building, the heavier the air felt and the worse it all smelled. He came to the end of the hallway, where it turned to the right to a staircase leading down. The windy noise sounded louder now, but no more discernable than a few moments ago.

Briefly, Haatim considered his options, sighed, and then started down the staircase. It went down into the darkness for a long way, with the stairs cut into the rock of the ground. It proved narrow and offered no handrail. The small steps, broken in places, made it difficult to navigate. If he tripped, it wouldn't end well for him.

He stepped off the final stair what felt like four floors deep into the ground, maybe more. Though still dark, just enough light filtered in from up ahead that he could see and move.

He walked, one hand touching the cold and unforgiving wall until he came to another doorway. This one opened into a large chamber, and he could hear that windy/breathy sound coming from inside.

His eyes had adjusted to the thick gloom, but he couldn't see the far wall of the room. Had Father Paladina gone this way? Why on Earth had they come here? It all felt extremely eerie, and Haatim hesitated.

"Father Paladina, are you in here?"

No response. He thought to turn back and head for the car. Maybe the priest hadn't come this way at all. Whatever was going on, it felt clear that Father Paladina wanted to mess with him, maybe even scare him.

If that was the case, then it had worked.

Haatim turned back toward the stairs, but then a shuffling sound came from the chamber behind. He glanced back. A form stood a few meters away, shrouded in the darkness.

"Father Paladina?"

Haatim pulled out his phone, flicking it to turn on the flashlight. The shuffling sound moved closer, and then came a metallic clanking sound too.

Something felt wrong. The eeriness had gone, replaced by fear. He sweated and panted as he backed out of the room. Finally, Haatim managed to swipe his phone and get the flashlight activated.

He held up the light.

It shone onto a torn and ragged face in front of him, only a meter away and with a collar around its neck.

It tried to jerk forward, face in a twisted grimace, but reached the end of its slack. It made a snarling sound at Haatim, and he saw rotten teeth and gums.

A chained demon.

Locked in the basement of this building.

"What the hell?"

The demon lunged at him, and he stumbled back. It couldn't reach him but still scared the crap out of him. His foot caught on the rough ground, and he fell backward, landing hard on his tailbone with a grunt.

"This is where we train new exorcists." Father Paladina's voice came from off to the right.

Haatim turned on his light. The old Priest sat on a wooden stool in the corner of the room, watching him solemnly. "We give them their first taste of what they will have to deal with."

"What?"

Father Paladina glanced over at him. "Most don't even make it to this point. A few don't make it past that. When you see something like this, it changes you. For the longest time, I knew nothing of this world. But then, my eyes were opened."

"You're an exorcist?"

"A scholar and teacher. My duty was to survey situations to determine where a true exorcist would be needed. We have so few, and their services remain in constant demand. In my lifetime, I've only known a few true exorcists. That's how I could sense your gift. It's tangible, otherworldly, and once you see it ... well, you can't forget it."

"What do you mean?"

Father Paladina shook his head. "When did you first channel? How many times?"

Haatim hesitated. "Raven's Peak. The first and only time. Frieda told me not to talk about it."

The priest nodded. "She told you right. Your gift could get corrupted as easily as harnessed. She should have sent you directly to us when she realized, but I can understand her reluctance. I haven't felt anyone quite like you before. Most people only get a touch if anything at all, but you ..."

"What is the gift?"

"The real power. The essence of how you can affect the world around you. It is divinity incarnate."

"And you think I have it?"

"I know you do. What happened that first time?"

"I ..." Haatim frowned, climbed back to his feet, and rubbed his tailbone. It hurt, a lot. "I walked through a volley of flying objects and came out unharmed."

"Do you remember how you did it?"

"I didn't do anything. I just knew they wouldn't hurt me."

Father Paladina nodded, then turned and gestured toward the chained demon.

In the light, Haatim could see that it lay dead already, skin rotting off the corpse. It looked to have lain here for a long time.

The priest said, "Expel this creature."

"Excuse me?"

"Command this creature to leave and return to hell."

Haatim stared at the priest.

All of a sudden, the demon lunged forward, reaching for Haatim, who staggered back out into the hallway. It snarled, at the end of its chain.

"What is wrong with it?"

"It has been trapped here for a long time. The body died, and it lost the ability to communicate."

"You mean you've been torturing it?"

Father Paladina frowned but didn't answer. "It is a creature from hell. Send it back there."

"I can't do that."

"Yes, you can. You just don't know how. Yet."

"Can you teach me?"

Father Paladina shook his head. "I can guide you, but it isn't something

I've ever experienced personally. It remains an incredibly rare thing. Less than one percent of one percent of the population has it, and even then, very few ever learn how to use it even a little bit. You have the gift, and you have a lot of it."

"But you can't teach me how to use it?"

"Practice. That's the only way I know."

Father Paladina stood from his stool and walked toward Haatim. Then he went into the hallway and headed back toward the staircase.

"You will return here daily. Learn how to control your powers. How to use them. Because they can make a weapon for good."

"We need to figure out who the demon in my sister has gone after," Haatim said. "We can't waste time on other things."

"This will not prove a waste. You will find it incredibly necessary, and it could prove vital."

"Why?"

"I offer no exaggeration. When you can control your abilities, you can send these creatures back from whence they came. You can command and control them."

"I thought I needed to know their names."

"The name gives power, but you won't need it. With your gift, you can send demons home without it."

Haatim frowned. "That still doesn't help me with the 'how' of what you're talking about."

Father Paladina laughed. "Hence the practice. Over the coming days, you will get to know *this* demon very well."

Chapter 10

Dominick told himself that he did this for the sake of what Frieda wanted him to do. After all, he couldn't do his job if the security team wouldn't let him. Trent seemed the kind of guy only impressed by strength and courage, and the surest way to win him over would come through respect. And taking on his guys and winning would do that, so it appeared practical.

But, to be honest, Dominick did it because it just sounded fun.

Though sure these guys would prove tough opponents, that didn't worry him too much. Win or lose, he felt confident he could make his point. Filled with pent-up energy and frustration, he needed to blow off some steam. He'd stayed cooped up for too many days now, waiting for something to happen, and had grown anxious.

Plus, he could use the workout.

Trent set up the fight on the west lawn, an open space with soft grass and firm soil. Only an hour after Dominick had thrown down the gauntlet, four men stood out there, already, waiting for him.

Jill Reinfer turned up as well, scowling at Dominick when he walked across the lawn with Trent. She wore an expensive gown and sat in a white lawn chair that looked enormous. A butler stood just behind her right-hand side, watching everything and unmoving.

"Is this truly necessary?" Jill asked.

"Just trying to keep you safe."

"By picking a fight with my security force?"

"Only fists. It'll give good practice all around."

"It'll waste all our time. I could call off this fight if I so chose."

"But you won't," Dominick said, half-smiling at her. "Because you think I'll lose."

Jill continued frowning at him, but he could see her bemusement. She waved her hand, beckoning for them to get on with it.

Trent nodded and turned to Dominick. "Last chance. I'd hate to see you hurt that pretty face."

Dominick glanced at him. "Don't worry. I'll take it easy on them."

Trent smiled the tiniest bit and nodded. "Patrick, Greg."

The two called men stepped forward from the group. They wore their expensive suits, but at a nod from their boss, they removed their coats, ties, and shirts.

Both burly and ripped, they had the mirthless eyes of men who had experienced and done terrible things. They also presented precisely what Dominick had expected, and they would underestimate him. Patrick, the bigger one, had a long scar under his right armpit that looked many years old.

Dominick stripped off his shirt. He had several scars of his own, collected through the years. They belied one of the more interesting parts of his life before his husband and became something that he explained away as his younger and more boisterous life before their marriage.

Not a far stretch: he'd behaved like a hellion as a teenager and twenty-something, prone to getting into fights. When he told Marvin the stories, he just left out that a lot of those fights involved demons.

"How we doing this?" he asked. "First blood?"

"Until you yield."

Dominick laughed. "Or they do. Stakes?"

"You lose, you get the hell out of here."

Dominick nodded. "I win, you call in all of your reserve forces to bolster security and actually listen to me."

Trent studied him for a moment, and then nodded. "Deal."

They shook hands, and then Trent walked over toward the center of the lawn, about ten meters from Ms. Reinfer. Dominick and the two men followed, standing about two meters apart and eyeing each other.

"Keep it over here. You come too close to Ms. Reinfer, and I'll have to get involved. Got it?"

Dominick nodded, as did the other two. They stood eyeing him, sizing him up and summarily dismissing him. They thought this would all be over soon, and that he'd jumped in over his head.

Maybe he had. Though confident in his hand-to-hand skills, maybe he *had* underestimated his opponents. They'd trained as soldiers, after all, which meant they would prove well-trained in hand-to-hand combat as well, and that they had seen action overseas if Trent could be believed.

"Do you think they have ice packs in the freezer for us after all this?" he asked.

The men just stared at him.

He shrugged. "Guess we'll find out."

"Ready?" Trent asked the two men. Patrick nodded, never taking his eyes from Dominick.

Trent turned to him. "What about you?"

"I'm good."

"All right."

Trent turned and walked back toward Ms. Reinfer. About halfway there, glancing over his shoulder, he said, "Begin."

✳✳✳

Patrick—to Dominick, he looked like a charging buffalo—came running in at him. His partner, Lobster—on account of his flushed red face—circled around, trying to flank Dominick and surprise attack him.

He danced backward, shifting his stance and ducking under a punch from Buffalo. He didn't fight back yet, just moved and shifted and sized up the two men. Buffalo got impatient, launching attack after attack and not defending himself properly.

Lobster stayed more patient, watching Dominick and searching for a weakness. He waited for Dominick to engage Buffalo before launching strikes.

Happily, after only a few punches and kicks, Buffalo grew winded. He mustn't have spent as much time at the gym as he should have, or at least less than his boss knew. That would make a factor in Dominick's favor, and the longer the fight went on, the less dangerous Buffalo would become.

A few seconds later, however, Dominick found out that Buffalo remained quite dangerous right now. He launched a feint that Dominick missed while making sure Lobster didn't attack, and Buffalo followed it up with a sucker punch that caught Dominick in the jaw. He only managed to clip him, but it gave enough force to stagger him to the side.

He rolled with the blow, shifting his weight and quick stepping to keep his feet. As expected, Lobster chose that as his time to strike, coming from the side with a series of punches. Dominick blocked the first two with his arms, ducked a third, and shifted his body to put Lobster between him and Buffalo. His best option would be to face them one at a time.

Lobster's hits didn't come that heavily but they came fast. Dominick couldn't avoid them so easily, but he also didn't fear them as much as his oversized partner. He deflected one, then launched a counter.

His hit landed, and he knocked Lobster back and to the ground, but before he could follow through, Buffalo waded back in, forcing him to backpedal and maintain distance.

They separated and circled. Lobster shook his head, dazed, and climbed to his feet. Surprise and respect settled on the two men's faces. They grew more cautious now, astonished at how difficult this had turned out.

Dominick didn't give them long to wonder about that before wading back in. He didn't want to give Buffalo time to catch his breath. To that end, he kicked out at Lobster, forcing him back a few steps, and then weaved under a punch from Buffalo before stepping in close.

From that position, he launched a series of heavy rib punches, and he could tell from the sharp intake of breath that his hits had the desired effect. His flurry didn't come without cost, though, and a second later, a kidney punch landed on his right side.

Dominick staggered, and Lobster got another quick kick to the back of his knee before he could roll away, dropping him down to the ground. The man followed this with a kick aimed at his face, but he dipped and rolled under the attack, coming to his feet a few steps away.

Buffalo clutched his heaving side and winced in pain. Lobster glanced at his friend, concerned, and then back at Dominick.

"Not bad."

"Not bad, yourself."

"You done?"

"Nope," Dominick said. "I can do this all day."

Though pain flared up his side, Dominick refused to wince. Lobster got him good. He'd grown used to fighting through pain, but it would limit his mobility.

"You guys had enough?" he asked, stretching up his arm.

They didn't answer. Buffalo tapped his friend on the shoulder, and they split apart to flank Dominick. They could tell that he hurt, and he couldn't afford to let their confidence build.

He charged in at Buffalo, deflected a punch, and then hit him once in the chest. It proved a feint, though, and as expected, Lobster came at him from behind a second later.

This time, he stood ready.

He spun, knocking Lobster's punch wide, and then lashed out and hit him, hard, in the throat with his knuckles. The man's windpipe collapsed under his hit, and Lobster clutched at his neck and spun away.

Dominick waded in, circling to put distance between himself and Buffalo, and then landed another three solid hits, two to the man's stomach and one to his jaw. Lobster staggered off balance, trying to defend himself, but the hits landed hard.

He went down, rolling into a fetal position to defend his weak points. Dominick moved to pursue, planning on taking him out of the fight, but Buffalo didn't give him the chance. Grabbed from behind, Dominick got yanked sideways and thrown.

Not thrown just a little. He flew two meters before touching the ground. On landing, he hit and rolled, sliding up to his knee. Buffalo came charging after him, focused, and forced Dominick to backpedal and give ground.

He ducked and dodged, struggling to catch his balance, but his luck ran out. He took a hit to the temple—a hard one. It rang his bell, and he became too disoriented to block or deflect the next one that came in at his jaw.

Once again, Dominick fell back, hitting the ground, and forced himself to roll and dodge. A kick to his side clipped him, and the wind got knocked out of his lungs.

Dazed, he struggled to his feet and backpedaled. Buffalo came after him, landing heavy blow after blow. Dominick could taste blood, and he shook his head to regain his concentration.

His opponent's breathing came hard, and his attacks had slowed, but the longer he waited, the more likely that Lobster would get back in the fight. Then it would be over, and Dominick would end up done for.

In an evasive move, he ducked an attack and slid in across the grass on his knee, wrapping the man's legs up. He'd used a wrestling move; one for which he hoped his opponent hadn't readied. Buffalo sprawled, but Dominick had him around the knees and didn't let go.

He lifted, picking up the huge man onto his shoulder, and then came down hard, slamming him back to the ground. He slid forward, pinning Buffalo's arm, and then used his free hand to whale on the man's face with his closed fist.

Though not heavy punches, enough of them could do serious damage. Buffalo squirmed and rolled, trying to get loose, but Dominick stayed with him, keeping him pinned.

"Yield," he shouted. He tasted blood, and then spat it to the side.

Buffalo kicked and thrashed, trying to break free. Dominick rolled and kneed him hard in the face, and then grabbed his arm, shifted it between his legs, and lay back, extending the arm out straight.

"Yield," he said. "Or I'll break your arm."

Buffalo stopped moving, laying still and panting. Dominick held the arm extended and kept steady pressure on the joint.

"Fine. I yield," Buffalo called, dazed and clearly annoyed.

Dominick let go of his arm, and the man yanked it free. They rolled apart, and Dominick staggered to his feet.

Lobster had found his feet and headed toward them, face flushed and angry, but a quick shake of the head from Buffalo stopped him.

"It's over."

Clearly, Lobster didn't like that but didn't object.

Dominick felt grateful because he could barely stand. His sides ached, his jaw hurt, and he saw double from the exertion and hits to his face. His left temple throbbed, and he felt positive he'd popped a blood vessel. When he took a step, walking proved hard with messed up equilibrium, but he wouldn't give them the satisfaction of knowing they'd hurt him seriously.

Instead, he went slowly over toward where Trent and Jill sat waiting. They watched him, Trent with respect and Jill with annoyance. He wanted to clutch at his side, and thought he might vomit, but held himself steady.

"Done."

"Fine. I'll call in all my men. For how long?"

"A few days," Dominick said. "And I have some other things I would like to discuss."

"Like what?"

"Not yet," Dominick said. He rubbed his mouth. Blood coated his arm. "Let me get cleaned up, and then we'll talk."

✳✳✳

In the kitchen, he found the ice without much problem. Most of the staff remained absent for now, prepping for dinner, but the room held a huge walk-in freezer, fully stocked. He made himself several bags of ice, then went back to the room where he stayed and poured it into the bathtub, which he then filled with cold water and slipped into.

Everything hurt, and he felt dizzy and disoriented. But, honestly, the pain didn't bother him too much. The feelings of worry and anxiety had seemed worse than this pain, and it gave a kind of relief to spend his time distracted by the pain and not the other problems he faced.

And, at least he'd won the fight. It hadn't looked good for a minute there, and if Lobster and Buffalo hadn't underestimated him, he wouldn't have stood a chance. That wouldn't prove an advantage he would get a second time, but it had paid off.

However, that made the name of the game: in the end, fights like that became as much games of the mind as the body. Neither of those two buffoons had much in the way of that.

Trent, on the other hand.

Maybe he could become reasonable.

Dominick climbed out of the tub after a long soak, wrapped himself in a towel, and collapsed onto his bed. He'd grown hungry and would need to go out foraging for food sometime soon. The kitchen didn't lay too far away, and usually, would contain someone who could put together a good meal for him. They might even have finished up dinner by then. But, for now, just lying on the bed in pain felt good enough.

After about an hour, a knock came at the door. He tossed on a pair of pants and a shirt and went to answer.

Trent stood there, sizing him up. He frowned at Dominic. "You good?"

Dominick nodded. "Yeah."

Trent turned and headed down the hall. "Come with me."

Dominick thought to grab some more clothes, and then changed his mind. He followed Trent through the estate to the security room. Inside, the two technicians sat waiting for him next to one of the screens. On it, he saw a frozen image of the front of the estate; an image taken by one of the cameras of the roadway.

"What's this?"

"Started about a week ago," Trent said. "We have someone casing the place."

Trent nodded to one of the techs, and the guy hit play on the computer. The video started rolling, and a few seconds later, a gray sedan drove by. It moved fairly slowly, but from the angle, he couldn't see the driver.

"That car has shown up for the last week or so at different times throughout the day. In the last two days, it has happened around the time of our shift change."

"Who is it?"

Trent hesitated. "For a while, we thought it was you. Maybe one of your people screwing with us or trying to make us look bad."

"What? That has nothing to do with me."

"You sure?"

Dominick narrowed his eyes. "I told you, I don't even work for a security company. I'm just here to help."

Trent seemed to consider that. Finally, he nodded. "That's not the only thing. Last couple of nights, we've also had some alarms triggered. Motion sensor, infrared. Stuff like that. When we go to check it out, nothing is there. It's like—"

"Someone is testing your security."

"Yep, and we know it wasn't you."

"Yeah, you have a camera in my room."

Trent looked surprised. "You knew?"

Dominick shrugged. "You didn't put it there the first night because you knew I would do a sweep, but it showed up the second. Your guys didn't hide it too well."

"So, then who's testing our security? You seem to know something about this."

"You wouldn't believe me if I told you."

"Try me."

"An assassin after your employer, but this one has allies. When she comes, she's going to do it hard and fast."

"She? Does she have a name?"

"Nida. A dangerous and unstable foe. I won the fight, so you need to call in more men."

"I already did," Trent said. "Yesterday. I called in all my reserves and hired four more contractors."

Dominick tilted his head in confusion. "You could have just said that earlier. Then, the fight? What the hell was that for?"

Trent shrugged. "I didn't think you would win, and we don't need you stepping on our toes. You provoked it, remember?"

Dominick sighed and rubbed his jaw. It still hurt to talk. "Yeah. Sure."

"In any case, Fred and Kenny here are at your disposal. They'll show you the schematics and floor plans and where we have the alarms situated. You know more than you're saying, and that's fine, but I want you to check it and make sure we don't have any weak spots."

This proved way more of an olive branch than Dominick could have hoped for.

He nodded. "Sure."

"Let me know if you find anything. The rest of the crew should show up in a couple of hours, and I plan to reset our patrols and make sure we don't have any weak points in the coverage. You think that if we get hit, it'll happen soon?"

"If it comes, it'll come the next week or so."

"Good. I don't want to waste money. Let me know if you find anything."

Trent headed out of the security office. Dominick watched him leave, and then turned back to the two technicians, Kenny and Fred. They both looked at him, waiting to see what he would need.

Food—he needed food.

"Which one of you is better with these computers?"

They exchanged a glance, and then—tentatively—the guy on the left raised his hand. He wore a badge, which identified him as Kenny. A skinny guy with thinning hair and a long face.

Fred appeared a little bigger with huge glasses that covered half of his head. Dominick pointed at him. "Fred, you're on delivery. Go out and buy three of the biggest pizzas you can find, and load them with everything."

"Even anchovies?"

"Especially anchovies."

"I hate anchovies."

"Fine. One without anchovies. Then pick up a couple of gallons of coffee."

"I hate coffee."

"Jesus, Fred. Then pick up some energy drinks." He waved his hand as though sweeping Fred to the door. "Now go. Hurry."

"All right."

Just before he reached the door, Dominick added, "And donuts. Also, some candy. It'll be a long night."

Fred didn't reply, disappearing outside the security room. Dominick rubbed his hands together and turned to Kenny.

"Okay, then. Let's get to work."

✳✳✳

It took about eight hours to go over all of the estate defenses and floor plans. He'd worked with the team who designed the Council defenses for a lot of different buildings, so he knew a good security system when he saw one.

This one was good. Damn good. Trent had every point of ingress covered by between two and five separate security systems to watch for different things. They also had in-depth reaction plans that the team drilled in case of just about any form of attack.

Not a thing for demon attacks, though.

By the end of the night, he had a list of about twenty suggestions for Trent about improvements. Some of them felt like overkill, but that made for the entire point. Move a camera here, adjust a sensor there.

His only complaint came from the system being technology heavy, but they had multiple backup generators linked together and spread throughout the estate in case the power got cut. It would prove nearly impossible to get them all without triggering at least a few external alarms.

By the time he finally submitted the information to Trent, he felt exhausted and didn't stick around to hear the man's response. In any case, most of the suggestions wouldn't be super necessary, so if Trent just ignored them, he wouldn't mind too much. Dominick just felt glad he'd gotten a chance to see the security system for himself, and it satisfied him that it had proven about as good as possible.

To be honest, now he wondered whether or not Nida would show up at all. The security system remained effective even with only a handful of guards, but bringing in an extra ten would make it nearly impossible to gain access. On top of that, they had tested the local police and riot team response times for the area, and from the first breach to a heavily armed police team on site, it completed in under ten minutes.

To attack this estate would be to take an unnecessary risk. Hell, if he'd met Trent before, he might have taken him to the Council and offered him a job. Trent might have said no, but it would have been worth the shot.

Dominick called Frieda, who answered right away, "What is it? What's wrong?"

"Nothing," he said. "I looked over the security. It's good. Found nothing we can do to help."

"Any sign of Nida?"

He hesitated. Thought to tell her the truth. However, she didn't need more things about which to worry. Not knowing if Jun would make it ate at her inside.

"None. You should stay with Jun."

"I should come and assist—"

"I've got this," he said. "It's more important that you make sure Jun's all right. He's important to you, and you should be there when he wakes up."

She stayed silent for a moment. "You sure? I could delay a few days, but if you think you'll need me, I can come tonight."

"I've got this," he said. "Take care of Jun."

"All right," Frieda said. "Thank you, Dominick. I'll schedule my flight in a couple of days."

"Sounds good."

He hung up and then spent some time stretching to loosen up his body. Every inch hurt, but he couldn't let his muscles tighten. Dominick went to bed that night in pain but slept better than he had since the attack.

✳✳✳

Four days went by without anything out of the usual, and Dominick believed that nothing would happen. The testing of the defenses still happened at night, but the car had stopped showing up, and things had mostly gone quiet. Nida wouldn't attack them: not after she'd tested the defenses and realized them so secure.

Still recovering from the fight, he had some bruises but had almost gotten back to normal. After finishing his morning exercises, he sat relaxing in his room. The phone rang.

A glance showed Mitchell's caller ID, from his shop back in Ohio. No doubt Mitchell had become paranoid and wanted to make sure no one planned to come after him.

Dominick let out a sigh and answered, "Hey, Mitchell."

"Dominick." The tone of voice gave Dominick pause, and he realized this call held much more seriousness than he'd anticipated. "We need to talk."

"What's up?"

"I ... I think I found something."

"What? Tell me."

"Not over the phone. How soon can you get here?"

"I'm busy right now. Is it urgent?"

"Very."

"I'll see if I can swing by. Let me give Frieda a call and—"

"No," Mitchell said, breathless. "Not Frieda. Don't talk to her right now. I just need you to get here."

Dominick hesitated. "Mitchell, what are you talking about?"

"Look, just trust me. I need you to come to my shop so that I can show you this, but you can't bring Frieda in on it."

Dominick stayed silent for a long moment, thinking. It sounded like a trap, and maybe Mitchell had gotten compromised. The man sounded worried, or maybe scared.

Had they found Mitchell and his ties to the Council? Had Nida used this as an excuse to get Dominick out of the picture?

He had no idea. The only thing he did know was that Mitchell was Arthur's family. If he faced danger, then Dominick shouldn't abandon him.

Why didn't he want him to tell Frieda, though? She should fly in sometime in the next day or so. Did Mitchell have something *on* Frieda? That didn't make sense.

Dominick almost said no because he'd come here to keep Jill Reinfer safe, but at the last second, he changed his mind. The security team didn't need him with their level of security, and he felt stir crazy again and didn't mind checking in on Mitchell to make sure he remained okay.

And, if it proved a trap, at least he would know Nida's location.

"I'm on my way."

Chapter 11

Haatim clicked through the various websites somewhat absently, sleepiness creeping in. He had trawled through the information for days and had a mind-numbing headache from spending so much time in front of a computer. Yet, still, had only managed to track down a few of the possible targets Nida might go after.

Four days had passed since he'd started coming to the library with Father Paladina, and the more time he spent working on this problem, the more insurmountable it became.

The trouble was, for most of the possible ancestors, too many possible descendants existed to narrow down anything. A quick search through ancestry related websites showed innumerable possibilities of people Nida could track down to acquire the blood she needed.

And that came from looking to defend only one bloodline from her attack. Worse, that bloodline they believed to have become extinct hundreds of years ago, which meant the records proved nearly impossible to parse through. No way could they possibly keep all of them out of Nida's grip.

In addition, most of them probably weren't related, and their blood wouldn't suffice for the ritual she wanted to accomplish. Most of them dead-ended, but verifying that became almost impossible. And protecting them all didn't make an option, either. They couldn't put guards on all the potential descendants of the Otolan bloodline, and no way could Haatim predict with any accuracy how his demon-sister would pick her targets.

No, he needed to narrow down the list to the most likely candidates, but that meant a lot of searching, cross-referencing, and guessing. Haatim hated that it proved so difficult to attain accuracy, and his mind felt numb from the work.

But, he couldn't afford to stop. Father Paladina had gone out as well, chasing down leads and trying to find out if anyone knew more about the extinct-but-not-extinct bloodline. So far, that had turned into a dead end, too.

He hadn't heard from Frieda in a couple of days but knew she could be en route to help Dominick protect Jill Reinfer in Pennsylvania. The last report he'd received had said that Jun would be all right, but it would take a long while before he got well enough to leave the hospital.

From the sounds of it, the woman that Dominick had gone to protect seemed a likely target for one of these last two bloodlines, so Frieda wanted Haatim to focus solely on the Otolan line.

To that end, he stayed there scrolling through articles and websites, looking for any clue that might help narrow down his list of two-hundred possible targets. He felt fairly certain that he could cross half of them off the list, but he didn't want to make any broad-stroke decisions that could bite him in the butt later.

The whole thing seemed like a waste of time but better than the alternative of worrying about what would happen now with the Council destroyed. The more occupied he became with menial tasks, then the better.

The idea that Nida had five of the seven bloodlines already and had come close to releasing Surgat proved terrifying. When Haatim got initiated into this world, he had viewed the Council as an ancient organization, powerful and all-knowing. What a silly idea—the more he thought about it—but he had believed them untouchable.

First hand, he had watched while Nida and her team murdered and destroyed them, and now almost nothing remained. He wished he could have done something to help; to keep the attack from happening or being so successful.

Of course, maybe, he could have. If Father Paladina were to be believed.

✳✳✳

As well as searching for names from the Otolan bloodline, Haatim also looked for information about what Father Paladina had told him about himself and people like him.

Each morning when he got up and finished eating and getting dressed, a car picked him up out front. Father Paladina met him at the empty building in the Vatican slums with the demon in the basement. There, he would confront the demon, face it, and face his fears.

For the first couple of days, nothing happened, and it felt like a waste of time. They would spend hours in that dank basement, face-to-face with a dead man rotting in front of their very eyes. It seemed hopeless, and it annoyed him that Father Paladina insisted they spend so much time there. Time that he could better spend trying to solve their other problems.

But, then, he felt something. It happened all at once on the third day. A sort of heat in his chest, which imbued him with a sense of purpose and *rightness*. It gave him a clear knowledge that the demon would not be allowed to hurt him if he didn't allow it himself.

It seemed like tapping into something, an essence inside him but normally unreachable. And touching it that first time felt like a light-bulb moment, and once he knew where to look, he could do it over and over again. It seemed like a switch had gotten thrown.

Still, though, he couldn't control the power. It came in waves; there one moment and gone the next, but he could *feel* it. The idea that he could recreate the power that had happened at Raven's Peak struck him as awe-inspiring.

Father Paladina made an excellent teacher, spending hours with him in the room facing the demon, and letting him learn in a controlled environment made it much easier to deal with.

So far, he couldn't actually *do* anything, but Father Paladina said that it would just take time. He could cross over, as the priest described it, and that made for the hardest part. With practice, everything else would just come.

Of course, they didn't have a lot of time to spare. The old priest had also given him numerous ancient texts to look into, which explained the abilities— old documents that described the power and great things people had done with it.

Detailed accounts of different periods in history when seemingly ordinary people had performed "miracles" filled the documents. Things like walking out of crashes or accidents unscathed to surviving terrible injuries. They even held accounts of healing people with only a single touch.

In the stories—or historical accounts; Haatim couldn't decide if he believed them or not—such people could use the power to go so far as dragging demons directly out of hosts and dismissing them back to hell.

A few years ago, he would have dismissed all of this as simply fantastical information spread by the Church; rumors they created to encourage the lay people to believe more firmly in divinity. But now, he knew that anything was possible. The world had become a lot bigger and more complex than he'd ever imagined. He'd witnessed demons, rituals, and any number of terrible occurrences in these last few months, including the possession of his sister.

A few passages of the tomes stuck out to him in particular, along the lines of what Father Paladina had described to him as a form of *channeling*— something that exorcists practiced and used on behalf of the Catholic Church while dealing with a demonic presence, whereby they could willingly become an instrument of God's will.

Or, at least that was how the accounts described such. If Father Paladina could be believed, less than one percent of all operating exorcists in the world could even manifest such abilities at all, and those made for a minuscule population of self-selected priests out of the larger population of the world. The overall impact of such an "ability" would prove negligible within the greater society, and even those that did have it could rarely do anything influential with it.

To Haatim, it sounded like even if this were possible, it probably had little to do with the Catholic Church or the Abrahamic God at all. Maybe it did come from God as a form of divinity, but not in the sense of any particular religion. Much like the demons: they became easy to describe through the lens of Christianity but existed beyond it.

In fact, when he searched around on the internet, he discovered similar accounts from all over the world and by people from every background imaginable. People from many different countries and religions described similar amazing feats that could be prescribed to what he sat learning about channeling.

Same powers, different lens.

If he believed one version of the abilities, he decided, then he might as well believe in them all.

A few hours later, while he still sat browsing down the rabbit hole of *channeling*, Father Paladina returned to the library. He looked weary when he sat down in the chair next to Haatim.

Haatim leaned back in his seat and rubbed his face. "That bad, huh?"

"I spoke to my colleagues," Father Paladina said. "But no one knows anything about the Otolan bloodline, and I've been unable to verify any of the names on our list."

"I have had no more luck than you, I'm afraid."

"We could defend a few of them, but I'll not send anyone out while our list remains this long. It would prove a complete waste of resources."

"I know," Haatim said. "Any word from Frieda?"

"She's meeting with Dominick to defend the Reinfer residence. Currently, she's in flight over the ocean."

"No attack yet?"

"No. But if something is to happen, she believes it will be soon. Dominick reported the all quiet, but Frieda feels that doesn't indicate safety. Something will happen."

"Unless Nida has blood from the Reinfer bloodline already, and this is just a misdirection."

"True."

"I should be there helping."

"You're helping here."

Haatim sighed. "Barely. We haven't found anything useful, and I still can't channel consistently."

"It takes time."

"We don't have time."

Father Paladina frowned but didn't respond. They sat in silence for a moment, staring at the laptop in front of Haatim.

"Have you looked over the book I gave you?"

Haatim hesitated. "I'm still not convinced."

"That it's real?"

"That I can do it," Haatim said. "You told me I had more of a gift than most, but when I reach out, I barely feel anything."

"You've felt it, though. It's like an unused muscle. The more you use it, the more you can call upon it to aid you."

"So, it's like energy. I'm tapping into my energy to do it."

"In a sense."

"What happens when I run out?"

Father Paladina stayed quiet for a moment. "Bad things."

"What do you mean?"

"It's more akin to tapping into your soul. When you deplete it ..."

Haatim paused, then said, "Point taken."

"In any case, now that you can do it, you will grow stronger in a short time. Already, you've felt the essence, and now it is simply about directing it."

"I felt something, but the accounts in this book describe some crazy things happening."

"Not all of them are real. Some of them, the Church fabricated, and it's difficult to tell them apart. I didn't expect you to believe all the accounts. I only believe a handful. However, I have seen powers before, similar to what you described, and I can sense them in you. You remind me of someone I knew long ago, and he had the abilities."

"Who?"

"A man named Father Reynolds."

"What happened to him?"

"He passed away."

"How?"

"It isn't important." Father Paladina pursed his lips. "He was a dear friend."

Clearly, he didn't want to discuss this topic, so Haatim changed the subject, "These seven families we've been tracking down ... why are they so important? What's the demon trying to do?"

"Frieda hasn't told me."

"But you have some idea," Haatim said. The more time he spent with the man, the more he realized that Father Paladina put on an unassuming air while knowing everything going on. "I know you do."

The priest frowned. "They were the original seven from the Council of Chaldea. The founding group. Most of them went their separate ways over the years, but the ritual linked their blood."

"What ritual?"

"The binding ritual the demon wants to undo."

"Everyone keeps saying that, but you won't tell me what they bound. Frieda said it is a demon named Surgat."

Father Paladina nodded. "Except, not only Surgat. The demon was bound into a human, a vessel he attached himself with, and the vessel got trapped as well."

"So, they sent a human to hell?"

"More or less. I know little else. Surgat has been accounted for throughout history, but from what I've gathered, no one has learned the demon's true name. From all accounts, what the Council stopped was a *true* integration, the type only experienced a few times in history."

"So, something bad."

The priest chuckled. "Yes, something bad."

They sat in silence. After a moment, Haatim reached forward and closed his laptop. He turned to face Father Paladina. "Why did Frieda send me here?"

"So you could find the next target of the demon."

"No, the real reason."

"What do you mean?"

"She sidelined me. I should be out there, helping Dominick keep Ms. Reinfer safe, but instead, she's got me here with you. Why?"

"I don't know."

"Yes, you do. You don't have to tell me, but at least stop lying to me. You've watched out for me since I arrived and made sure I don't try to leave."

The old priest studied Haatim for a while before standing, "Come with me."

"Where are we going?"

Father Paladina didn't reply. Instead, he turned and headed toward the exit of the library. Haatim slid his laptop away into his bag and then followed, rushing after the old priest. He followed him out into the afternoon sun, blinking as his eyes adjusted from the dim library.

They went across the street to where the car sat parked and climbed in. The driver looked at them in the rearview mirror.

"Take a break, Mason," Father Paladina said.

The driver nodded, opened the door, and slipped out of the car. Haatim, through the front windshield, watched him walk down the street and disappear around a corner.

"What are we doing?"

"Some things are best discussed in private."

"What things?"

Father Paladina glanced over him, "Frieda did ask me to keep you here. She asked me to keep you safe."

"From who?"

"The Church."

✳✳✳

"What?"

"Frieda doesn't want me to tell you this, but you have a right to know. Assassins are, after all, surviving members of the Order and Council, including Frieda and Dominick. You are *not* a member of either organization, and thus not a likely target, but Frieda felt afraid that you might get targeted by association if you stayed out there with them."

"Wait. Back up. What do you mean that they're after Frieda and Dominick? Church assassins?"

"Yes."

Haatim gasped. "Why?"

"I don't know the full details. After the Council got attacked, an order went out. I stalled it for a few days to give Frieda time. That's what I've been doing these last few days. Now, I've reached the end of what I can help with. She's on her own."

Haatim shook his head. "That doesn't make sense. Why would the Church want to kill the Council? *We* were the ones that got attacked."

"*They,* not you," Father Paladina said. "I wish I knew. Frieda knows, I believe, but she refused to elaborate when I asked her."

"So, she sent me here?"

"And I'm not supposed to let you leave until this finishes," Father Paladina said.

"So, basically, you can't tell me anything else?"

"No. I'm sorry. That's the extent of what I know."

Haatim let out a sigh. "Then, what *can* you tell me?"

"What can you tell *me?*" Father Paladina asked. "I know little about what happened out in Switzerland."

"I wasn't there, but when the demon controlling my sister came through, she spared no one. They killed everyone except for Jun Lee."

"Did you confront the demon?"

"No," Haatim said. "Will I be able to?"

"Maybe, eventually, but not yet."

Haatim sat in thought. "But, you mean I will be able to banish the demon. I could send it back to hell, and then my sister ..."

He didn't finish the thought, seeing the frown on the old priest's face. "No, Haatim. I'm sorry. Your sister is gone."

Haatim felt a surge of hope at the prospect, and he didn't quite believe the priest. The thing was, from everything he'd read in the accounts, if he banished the demon, the host would manage to recover and go back to normal. It had even been reported to happen with people thought to be dead.

Maybe, he could rescue Nida.

"Haatim, if the demon completes the unbinding and lets loose Surgat, things will go very badly very fast."

"Why isn't the Church trying to stop all of this? Shouldn't they *help* Frieda stop this instead of hunting her and Dominick?"

"We *are* trying to stop it, but through different avenues."

"What do you mean?"

Father Paladina rubbed his eyes. "The odds of Frieda and Dominick succeeding at keeping Jill Reinfer safe from the demon look slim at best. We have agents trying to locate the demon instead and stop it from doing this. Some of our best operatives are dealing with this threat directly."

"By hunting down the demon?"

Father Paladina nodded. "I apologize if that offends. I know it has possession of your sister."

Haatim lied, "It doesn't offend me. I came to terms with that a while ago. Now, I just want to put her to rest again. Do you know her location?"

Father Paladina hesitated and didn't reply. From the look on his face, Haatim could tell that he hid something.

"What? You know?"

"Maybe."

"But you don't want to tell me?"

"Frieda asked me not to. In any case, we're not certain that the demon is there."

"I'm getting sick of Frieda deciding what I should and shouldn't know. Tell me, please."

Father Paladina nodded. "I understand. We aren't sure, exactly, where

Nida is, but the feeling of the Church is that it will be where we find the person hunting her, and our last report places that person on a flight into Cambodia at the Capital, Phnom Penh."

"Cambodia?" he asked, shaking his head. "Why? What's in Cambodia?"

Father Paladina shrugged. "I have no idea."

Haatim froze. "Wait, you said the person hunting her is the one you're after. Who's that?"

"That's what Frieda asked me not to tell you. She doesn't want you to know our other target."

"What do you mean? Who is it? Who is your target?"

"Abigail Dressler."

✳✳✳

At that moment, a gentle breeze could have knocked over Haatim. His jaw dropped open, and he almost fell out of his seat.

"Abigail?"

"Yes."

"She's alive?"

"Yes. Frieda didn't want you to know for the same reason she wants to keep you here."

"Because you're hunting her."

Paladina nodded. "Yes. We have operatives on their way there to deal with her now."

"What?" Haatim pushed back his chair. "Why would you kill her?"

Father Paladina shook his head and looked at the floor. "I'm sorry. You knew her?"

"She was—is—my friend, and she's saved my life countless times. I ... I thought she'd died."

"So did the Church. Until recently. After the attack on the Council, we took Frieda at her word that Abigail had perished in the train wreck, but recently, we stumbled upon evidence to the contrary. Abigail remains alive, and what's more, we believe that she's hunting Nida."

"Did Frieda know?"

"I don't believe so. I told her a few moments ago, and she seemed genuinely surprised by the information. She forbade me to tell you."

"Yet, you told me."

"You have a right to know," he said.

Haatim took a moment to digest the information. Abigail alive? He'd felt certain that she'd died in the crash. How could she have survived?

And, if she did survive, why didn't she come back to them and let them know she was okay? Why didn't she call or contact them in some way?

Was she safe? Was something wrong?

The questions flooded through Haatim's mind, but he already knew the answer: she didn't want them to know she lived.

She didn't want *him* to know she lived.

"Why did you tell me?" Haatim asked. "You have to have some other motive to break your promise to Frieda."

"First off, I never promised," the priest said. "But, you are correct, I do have an ulterior motive."

"Which is?"

"I'm not one of the people who agree with the Church's decision to exterminate the Council. We have operatives in place to deal with Abigail, but I believe there exists a better way of handling all of this."

"What way?"

"You could bring her back here."

"What? If I bring her here, they'll kill her."

"I believe that if she turns herself in, I can keep the Church from executing her. At least, not without a formal trial. But, if they catch her outside the Vatican, they won't hesitate."

"Her last trial didn't end well."

The priest ignored him. "Will she trust you?"

Haatim hesitated. "I don't know."

"Well, let's hope she does because you offer the only chance she has of staying alive."

Chapter 12

Dominick made it to Mitchell's shop later that afternoon after a few hours of driving, still unclear exactly why he'd headed out there. He had left the Reinfer estate after giving Trent a vague explanation of where needed to go.

Trent seemed surprised at his leaving but didn't object; he promised to notify Dominick if anything changed at the manor.

Neither of them expected an attack now, not after the security had increased. Trent had enacted almost all of the changes that Dominick had asked for, as well as a few of his own to ramp up their defenses. Moreover, all of his guards carried rifles now and wore Kevlar vests. Nida would have to be a complete psycho to attack the estate at this point.

Of course, Dominick fully understood the danger of underestimating Nida, so he stayed ready to head back at a moment's notice, and at least before Frieda got there. After the vague call from Mitchell, he'd considered not going because Mitchell wasn't exactly known as a level-headed individual.

He should have demanded more information about what Mitchell wanted to tell him, especially as he risked pissing off Frieda and putting Jill Reinfer at risk to go check on a nut-job.

Probably, this would prove just another of his wild conspiracies. Mitchell, a conspiracy theorist, liked to talk about wild and crazy events that had, supposedly, happened in the world. Although, he did have the benefit that many of the conspiracies he blabbed about had occurred, in actual fact. That didn't change the fact that he remained prone to overreaction and exaggeration.

The shop stood closed up and dark when he pulled into the empty lot. This time, the door sign hung flipped to "closed." Did Mitchell ever have any customers at all? Dominick couldn't remember ever seeing one.

The door stood locked. He knocked on the glass window, and Mitchell answered almost immediately.

"You came alone?" He peered around the corner, and then looked out past Dominick, scanning the area behind him. A look of genuine fear clouded his features.

"Yeah," Dominick said. "I'm alone."

"You sure?"

"That's what you asked for on the phone," Dominick said, a little annoyed. "Just me."

"Come in." Mitchell beckoned him through the doorway but only opened it a small bit. He locked it behind them, double bolted it, and then led Dominick through the shop toward the back.

With the lights off, the place looked gloomy and in just as much disarray as it had the last time Dominick stopped by.

"I thought I told you to clean this place," Dominick said with a grin.

The look on Mitchell's face made it clear that the mirth came unappreciated.

Dominick sobered up slightly, wondering what had spooked the man so much.

"I didn't know who to call when I translated the information in the text because I wasn't sure who I could trust with what was going on. Still, after everything that happened, I thought it important that I talk to someone and—"

"Mitchell," Dominick said in a soothing tone. "You're rambling."

Mitchell frowned, and then took a deep and steadying breath. "You've been marked."

"What?" Dominick asked. "What do you mean?"

"The Catholic Church has marked you for death. Frieda too."

Dominick shook his head. "What do you mean? Why?"

"I have no idea," Mitchell said. "At least, nothing I can verify. I found out from one of my contacts, but you and Frieda have become the Church's secondary targets."

"Who do they have as the primary?"

"Abigail."

"She's alive?"

"I guess so. At least, the Church thinks so, and they've gone after her."

"Why?"

Mitchell scratched his chin and frowned. "That's the scary thing and the reason I called *you*. I *might* know the answer to that question."

✳✳✳

Dominick studied Mitchell. "What are you talking about?"

Mitchell met his eyes and let out a heavy sigh. "Keep in mind that if Frieda knew what I'm about to tell you, she would get so mad, to say the least."

"Just tell me."

"Okay. Here goes. Many years ago, I helped Arthur and Frieda perform a ritual. Like, one of the bad ones that the Council forbids."

Shock hit Dominick. "You what? A ritual?"

"Yes. It was supposed to help Abigail control whatever dark thing the cult had done to her as a little girl. Over time, something happened to her, and she changed, and Arthur wanted to stop it from happening and protect her from it."

"So, Frieda did a ritual?"

Mitchell nodded. "Yes. We performed it here."

Dominick shook his head, a slow back and forth, trying to come to terms with that idea. The Council had firm policies against performing any sort of rituals, or spells, which meant that what Mitchell had admitted to proved tantamount to treason against the Council.

Worse, he'd also stated that Frieda formed a part of it, as well as Arthur. They, more than anyone, should have understood the risks of such an action, as well as what the punishment would be if they got caught. Arthur had, personally, executed many people for that precise crime.

"Why have you told me this?" he asked, suspicious. "Guilt? Are you just trying to get it off your chest and confide in someone?"

It made sense. After all, with the Council and Order essentially destroyed, the possibility of repercussions against Mitchell remained minute.

"I wish, but that's not all," Mitchell said. "The ritual made a binding. We linked Abigail's soul to Arthur's so that at least some of the corruption that affected her would affect him instead. We meant it to protect her and let her grow up with a normal life, but instead, it corrupted and destroyed Arthur, gradually."

A pit of worry formed in Dominick's stomach when realization crept in. "That's why he ..."

Dominick couldn't finish the thought.

Mitchell nodded. "Yes. That's why Arthur killed those families. By the end when he got locked up, Arthur couldn't even tell the difference between right and wrong."

It explained Arthur's slow fall from grace into the pariah he had become. Right then, everything clicked into place for Dominick, and not in a good way. It also explained what had happened to Abigail once Arthur had gone.

"Then, that's why things went bad for Abigail so fast after Arthur went. Arthur was no longer there to absorb whatever evil thing lay inside of her."

"Yes."

"You said Frieda had a part in this?"

Frieda loved Arthur, though she'd never admitted her feelings to him, but it remained hard to believe that she could go against the Council like that. Always fiercely loyal to the Council and the world she'd sworn to protect, the idea that she could become a part of something like this seemed unthinkable.

"Frieda performed the ritual. We helped and made sure everything worked as expected."

"Holy crap."

"I know," Mitchell said.

"And you think that's why the Church now hunts us? How would they know?"

"No," Mitchell said. "At least, not entirely. I'm sure they have ways of knowing, but that's not why. When Frieda and Arthur came here all those years ago, she brought some texts with her; photocopies out of some old book. A history of the Council."

"The Council has a copy," Dominick said, nodding. "Or had. But not a complete version, and the Church archived most of it. We only had certain sections that they copied."

"Well, this copy *was* complete."

"What?"

Mitchell ignored the question. "I felt that the text seemed odd when she first brought it here, but I never thought about why. After all, the ritual worked, and Abigail went back to normal, and then Arthur kept and stored the book at his home, locked in his safe."

"So, Frieda performed a ritual against the wishes of the Council?"

"Yeah, but that's not why I called you. Keep up."

"It gets worse?"

"A lot. You might want to sit down."

✳✳✳

"Abigail came to see me a few weeks ago. Before she went to turn herself in at the Council. She brought the text with her from Arthur's home."

"Why?"

"She wanted me to look into it and find out anything I could about the ritual Frieda performed. She wanted to see if something else might prove useful; some way to stall, or perhaps control, what was happening to her and keep her from losing control."

"Did you?"

He shook his head. "No. But I found something way worse. While going through the papers, I found a *lot* more rituals mentioned there than just what I'd seen originally. And, these aren't normal rituals, but demon summoning and binding ones. The kind that are seriously off limits."

"You mean like the Ninth Circle type of rituals?" Dominick asked.

"Yes."

"That doesn't make any sense. Why would those be in a book about the history of the Council?"

"That's the thing. I don't think it is just a history of the Council. I think it is a history of The Ninth Circle, too."

"What do you mean? You think Frieda brought the wrong book?"

He shook his head. "No. I think them one and the same."

✳✳✳

Dominick coughed. "What?"

"From everything I can gather from this book: the original Seven that formed the Council had operated as leaders from The Ninth Circle first. When the Cult performed a ritual to summon and integrate Surgat with one of their own, the Seven realized they had gone too far. They turned against the cult and

104

helped the Church stop Surgat."

Dominick just stood in stunned silence, trying to wrap his head around Mitchell's words.

"You can't be serious."

"Completely. For that sole reason, the Catholic Church keeps the document locked in their vaults. I don't believe that Frieda ever thought I would translate this."

"Frieda knew?"

"She had to have."

"Did Arthur?"

"I don't reckon so. But, maybe. He had a limited understanding of Latin and trusted Frieda implicitly, and so I doubt he would have looked into this. Honestly, though, I don't know."

"This ... this ..."

"I know," Mitchell said. "I think that's why the Church has set about hunting all of you down. Us down. One of the conditions of the Church allowing the original seven to continue living depended upon nothing like this ever happening again. The Church wants to tie up loose ends."

"You said us. You think they'll come after you, too?"

"I don't know. That's why I called you. I have no idea what to do now."

"And why you didn't call Frieda?"

Mitchell nodded. "Because she knew. She had to. The book belonged to her, and she could read the Latin. If she could keep something like *this* from us, what else might she hide?"

A scary thought. He'd never imagined Frieda keeping secrets from him, but this proved something else entirely.

The idea that their legacy came from a cult, and that the Church only allowed them to live because they had turned against their own ...

The idea that their war against The Ninth Circle for all these centuries came down, essentially, to nothing more than a long-running civil war ...

His phone beeped and startled him. He shook his head to clear his thoughts and glanced at it. A message had come from Trent: *When will you get back? Something happened. Need to talk.*

He texted back that he was on his way, and then glanced up at Mitchell. "I don't think they'll come after you. You aren't one of us."

"I hope not."

"But, look, we can't just avoid Frieda. You're right; she has a lot to explain from this, but we have bigger fish to fry right now. She'll get here in about twelve hours and plans to meet up here."

"Here?" A flash of fear lit Mitchell's face.

"Don't worry. I'll come back before she arrives. We can confront her together; but, I'm telling you, she has a good explanation for all of this. You'll see. I'll head back to the Reinfer estate but will return soon."

"Okay. Well, hurry."

"I will," Dominick said. "Don't worry; everything will work out fine."

Mitchell frowned. "I hope so."

Dominick headed for the door, unbolted it, and headed outside to his car. Once he got out of earshot and stood alone, he let out a deep sigh.

Things just kept getting worse.

Chapter 13

"Focus, Haatim."

"I *am* focusing." He shook his head in annoyance. "Why wouldn't I?"

"You need to look *at* the creature but also see *into* it."

"How would you know? You can't even do this."

Father Paladina didn't reply except to purse his lips and stare at Haatim.

"I'm sorry," Haatim said. "That was uncalled for."

"I understand your frustration, but you need to use that energy to your advantage. Focus on what lays inside you."

They stood in the dark basement beneath the old abandoned prison. Or, at least, Haatim assumed it a prison: Father Paladina still hadn't told him what the building used to be.

Haatim stood only a meter from the demon in front of him. Chained to the wall, it had a leather collar around its neck and stared at him with dead eyes. Haatim had looked into those eyes and the soul of this demon enough for the rest of his life, and yet they still spent six to eight hours a day down here.

Heat marks and scabs, as well as sections of rotten flesh falling off, covered the man's body, which the demon possessed. The beast panted and clawed at the air to reach Haatim. Though stretched to the end of the chain around its neck, it didn't seem to notice. Like a chained dog, it tested its boundaries continually.

"Hard to focus with it staring at me like this."

"You need to push everything else away," Father Paladina said. "Only you and the creature. Think not of what happens anywhere else in the world, or anything around us. Focus only inward and find the power there."

"I am focusing, but there's nothing *there*."

"We've only been at this for a few days, Haatim. Don't grow frustrated."

"It's kind of hard knowing that we don't have any more time. I need to get to Abigail and stop her. I shouldn't be here."

"You cannot leave here until you grow ready."

"Why not?"

"What if you get attacked?"

"By Abigail?" Haatim asked, incredulous. She hadn't told him she remained alive after Switzerland, but that made a far stretch from her wanting to hurt him. "Not a chance."

"Your sister," the priest said. "Our agents believe she chases Nida."

"But Frieda thinks Nida has gone to Pennsylvania. Basically, the opposite side of the world. She can't occupy two places at the same time."

"Exactly. We don't know her whereabouts, which means we have to assume the worst could happen. If she confronts you, you will find yourself wholly unprepared if you cannot control your abilities."

"I'm as ready as I'll ever be," Haatim said. He stepped back from the creature and turned to face Father Paladina. "You said you could get me a flight to Cambodia to help Abigail. If that's the case, then why do I remain here?"

"I can," Father Paladina said, frowning. "You have a flight tomorrow morning. But, you *need* to focus. I can feel the power, Haatim. You just need to channel it."

"Last time I did it in Raven's Peak, it just happened," Haatim said. "Maybe I can't do it when it isn't necessary."

"That isn't how this works. You just need to learn how to control it. Once you manage it one time when you intend to, you will change forever."

Haatim sighed and nodded. He couldn't complain because Father Paladina *had* gotten him a flight to Cambodia to try and help Abigail. Moreover, he had agreed not to tell Frieda about it until he'd set on his way. She would feel furious with both of them, but right now, Haatim didn't care.

Abigail remained alive, and if even the slightest chance of saving her existed, he felt willing to do anything.

Unfortunately, the Church had sent two assassins to kill her in Phnom Penh, which meant he worked on a short timetable. He had to get to Abigail before they did. Haatim prayed that he wouldn't reach her too late, which meant these little lessons wasted precious time.

However, he wanted to get out there for another reason, and not one he felt willing to admit to the old priest: part of him hoped that he *would* see Nida out there.

Maybe, now that he expected to see her, he could reach past the demon and communicate with his sister. Perhaps, he could help her break free of the demon's hold and cast it out. Nida had enough strength to break free of the demon, and it would prove a simple matter of managing to talk to her.

Not that he'd admit that to Father Paladina. Heck, he didn't believe it would happen anyway. Much more likely that Nida had gone to Pennsylvania than out to Cambodia.

He asked the priest, "Do you know why Abigail has gone to Cambodia?"

Father Paladina shook his head. "Still nothing. The agents haven't located her yet, but they know an area where someone spotted her."

"Where?"

"One of the smaller districts on the south side of Phnom Penh. Where we first received reports about her and where our agents now look."

"What's around there?"

"Nothing major," the priest said. "Shops, restaurants, a few Buddhist temples, and a church."

Haatim frowned. "Do you think she went looking for the last bloodline?"

"No clue. Would she even know about the bloodlines? I suppose it remains a possibility. You'll need to go soon, though, because the agents are on their way."

"Can't you call off the assassins? Buy me some time, like you did for Frieda."

"I have no control over this anymore. I've been here for a long time, so I have a lot of friends and contacts but little power. I have little more worth than a messenger."

"I appreciate everything you've done for me," Haatim said. "I know it isn't what Frieda wants, so I'm glad that you've given me this chance."

Father Paladina stayed silent for a moment. "My debt lays not to Frieda but Arthur, and the thing he loved more than anything else in this world was his adopted daughter. If you can convince her to turn herself in, I think I can convince the right people that she isn't worth killing."

Haatim let out a sigh. "No pressure."

The old priest smiled. "None at all."

Haatim turned back to the chained up demon. It shook at the end of its chain, much like a dog might do when tied up in the yard. It even bared its teeth at him.

He could sympathize with it, to an extent. It had lain trapped here for weeks, at least, with no contact to the outside world except for the people manipulating it or, like Haatim, trying to harm it.

He would feel angry, too, in such a situation. How much of that anger stemmed from the demon's treatment? And how much came inherent to its existence? Did an enormous difference exist between them, or had this mistreatment made it hate to begin with?

Did it even matter?

"I'll make sure your travel plans are in order. When you finish here, give me a call, and I will send the driver to bring you to your hotel."

"I won't be ready in time," Haatim said. "I won't be able to channel by the end of the day."

"You will," the priest said. "Because you need to."

Then he left, leaving Haatim alone in the darkness with the demon. Haatim watched the priest go, and then turned back to face the creature.

He could feel the essence of the demon like an energy emanating from the body. Then he realized that it had always had a presence, but his mind just didn't feel ready to interact with it yet.

He wished he could test this connection to the demonic essence on other beings. Maybe he could use this to sense similar creatures. However, he couldn't feel sure if it proved unique to this creature or might be something other demons would share, and he didn't remember feeling anything like this in Raven's Peak.

"Okay," he said, talking as much to himself as the creature. "So, I can *see* the thing inside of you, but how am I supposed to get it out?"

It gave him a puzzle, and he missed a lot of the pieces. This felt like the kind of thing that would take months to learn, maybe even years, but he'd only had a little over a week. A crash course from hell, and the harder he pushed for it to happen, the more difficult it became.

In fact, he'd felt more confident in himself and his abilities when he'd first arrived in Vatican City than right now. This had seemed like a more achievable plan when he first experienced the connection, as if something he could actually do, and his lack of progress left him frustrated and disoriented.

A few hours later, he left the building, thoroughly defeated and depressed about his lack of progress. Father Paladina had it wrong, and no way could he recreate what had happened in Raven's Peak, let alone do something entirely new. Not in the timeframe he had to work with, at least.

But, he couldn't tell the old priest that. Even if he couldn't use this ability, he still needed to get to Phnom Penh and find Abigail. If she stayed alive and needed help, then no way would he sit here and do nothing.

✳✳✳

Haatim woke early the next morning to make sure he had all of his stuff packed. He didn't have a lot of belongings in the hotel, having only brought a few outfits and supplies with him to Rome in the first place. Already anxious, the closer he got to leaving for Cambodia, the worse it grew.

Desperate to see Abigail, he needed to make sure she remained okay. After everything that had happened, he wanted more than anything to talk to her and find out how she had survived the train crash and what she had done in the days since.

Part of him also felt anxious about the possibility of running into his sister. Or, what remained of her. Such an encounter seemed unlikely, though, and he should try to avoid her per Father Paladina, but he might have a slim chance of seeing her. He dreaded that moment but also dreamed about sending the demon home and freeing his sister from its clutches.

When he exited the lobby, Father Paladina waited for him in a black car out front. He looked anxious as well as tired. Haatim tossed his luggage into the trunk, climbed in the back of the car, and expected the old priest to give him a rundown of anything new he'd found out during the previous night.

Instead, he looked away when Haatim climbed into the backseat next to him. The driver looked at Haatim in the mirror, and then shifted the car into gear, pulling slowly away from the hotel.

"Any news?"

Father Paladina shook his head but didn't reply. They rode in silence for a while, and then Haatim realized that they hadn't headed for the airport. They'd gone deeper into the city.

"Where are we going?"

Still, Paladina didn't reply. It didn't take Haatim long to realize that they headed toward the old building with the demon.

"Why here? I thought we'd done with this?"

"Nearly."

After a few more minutes of driving, they pulled up in front.

Haatim frowned. "Shouldn't we be going to the airport?"

"We will."

"Then, why come here?"

"More training."

"Do we have enough time?"

"We need to make time," the priest said, opening the door and stepping out of the car. It had turned out a sunny and beautiful day, with not a cloud in the sky.

"I plan on avoiding Nida, remember? I'll just go after Abigail. Nida shouldn't even be there."

"And what if she is? What happens if you run into her? What happens if she doesn't spare you like last time?"

Haatim didn't reply. He didn't have a good answer to the question.

"I'm still going," he said, finally. "I can't control the powers yet, but I'll not leave Abigail out there alone."

"I won't ask you to stay," Father Paladina said, heading into the building and walking down the hallway. Haatim followed hesitantly. "I only insist that you spend every possible second preparing in case something goes wrong."

Haatim sighed. "Fine."

Father Paladina gestured for Haatim to go first. He stepped by the priest and went down the stairs, moving deeper into the old building.

They descended into the darkness of the catacombs beneath. Haatim still felt uncomfortable making the descent, even though he had done it a dozen times in the last few weeks. The hallway seemed too narrow, the ceiling too low.

"Besides," the priest said. "Up until now, we've focused solely on attack, not defense. Your abilities can do both when you can control them. So, now, we will practice a little bit of defense."

"You mean like in Raven's Peak when I avoided the demon's attacks?"

"Exactly so."

"I think that was just a fluke," Haatim said. The door to the room with the demon chained up stood closed, which seemed odd. Usually, they left it open for airflow so that the demon didn't suffocate with poor ventilation. "I hadn't readied for it that time, and it just sort of ... happened."

He gripped the handle and yanked open the door. Heavy, it needed a good application of oil.

"Yes," Father Paladina said. "We need to recreate that sensation of risk so that you can learn how to harness your abilities."

Haatim hesitated in the doorway, turning back toward the priest. All at once, he felt wary. "Uh ... what?"

A snarling sound came from the room behind him, and then something grabbed hold of the back of his shirt and jerked him backward into the dark depths.

✳✳✳

He hit his left arm against the doorframe, hard, and then staggered sideways onto his knees. Wholly unprepared, he felt disoriented from the first few seconds of realizing he'd come under attack.

He willed his mind to process the situation: the demon had gotten free, and it felt pissed and stood only a meter away. The chain hung loose on the far wall, removed, and the leather collar lay on the ground, and now they'd opened the door.

This situation had never even crossed his mind as a possibility, and he cursed his trusting nature. Father Paladina stood in the doorway, a gun in his hand, watching everything unfold inside the room with great care. He had a curious expression on his face as he watched the demon throw Haatim to the floor.

And, Haatim realized a second later, the demon hadn't done. It lashed out, punching him in the face. He tried to roll with the blow, but in the darkness, found it hard to get his bearings. Stars shot across his vision, and a sharp pain lanced the side of his face.

"What the ...?"

The demon charged in at him and forced Haatim to roll out of the way. His training kicked in from the months spent with Dominick, and he blocked the next attack from the demon while he found his way to his feet.

He gave ground, backing up deeper into the darkness of the room, away from the door. The demon hissed at him, hitting with heavy punches, but clearly, it didn't know how to fight.

Haatim blocked another attack, ducked under a wild swing, and then tripped the creature. It fell to the ground, landing on its back, and then rolled back to its feet. Haatim edged away, catching his breath, and looked over at the door.

Father Paladina stared at him, expression blank, unsurprised by events.

"You let it loose."

"I felt it necessary."

"You could have warned me."

"That would have defeated the purpose."

The demon came charging in, and Haatim blocked and dodged a series of punches and wild kicks. He responded with strikes of his own, landing two hits on the creature's chest and then kicking it in the knee. The kick staggered it, but if it even noticed the punches, it didn't show it.

The man this creature inhabited proved neither large nor strong, and after months of captivity, his muscles had atrophied. Yet when the demon lashed out at Haatim, the attacks had quite a bit of unexpected power behind them. Already, Haatim's forearms ached from blocking, and the creature continued, relentless.

"What do you expect me to do?"

"Reach out to the creature. Channel."

"I can't."

"Then deal with it some other way," Father Paladina said. "Show me that you can defend yourself."

"Other way?"

The priest fell silent for an interminable moment. Then, "Kill it."

The man who the demon inhabited had died already, and his soul had long since vacated the body, but a part of Haatim still felt wrong about the idea. The demon made for his enemy, not the man it possessed, and killing the body to get the demon just felt wrong.

Of course, that offered the lesser of his two problems. The bigger issue came down to how the hell was he supposed to kill it?

He didn't have any weapons with him. He'd expected to go to the airport today, not back down here, and carrying weapons through airport security always made a bad idea. Even a knife would have proven too much to bring along, which meant that his hands and feet gave him the only things he could use to fight.

Father Paladina offered no help at all. The old priest just watched, standing in the doorway and waiting to see what would happen. He looked as though he stood watching a prize fight, studying the opponents to decide on which one to put his money.

From the look on his face, he didn't have a bet on Haatim.

The demon came charging in, grabbing Haatim around the waist. It drove him backward and slammed him against the wall, knocking the air out of his lungs. Haatim elbowed down, hitting it around the ribcage as hard as he could, but the demon didn't relent.

It had him locked in a tight bear hug, refusing to let up even a little. Then it jerked away from the wall and slammed him again. Not a smooth wall, but rather rough-cut and uneven stone, parts of it proved sharp and stuck into his back painfully. Spots of wetness bloomed where the wall pierced his skin and cut him.

He grabbed the demon under the armpits, twisted, and threw it sideways. It didn't let go, at first, but when he wrenched it to an odd angle, the move forced the demon to let go and stumble away.

"You won't beat it that way," the old priest said. "Turn inward."

Haatim staggered forward, away from the wall. Bursts of pain shot up his back, and he tried to stretch it out.

"The gun would help."

"Focus, Haatim. Channel your abilities."

"I *can't.*"

"You just need to focus."

"This is useless. Help me."

The demon stood and turned to face him once again. It walked toward him, stopped, and then turned to the doorway, instead, where Father Paladina stood.

"You're on your own." The priest stepped back into the hallway and grabbed the door handle. "One of you will walk out of here."

"Wait!"

"I'm sorry."

The demon charged toward the door. Father Paladina swung it shut, slamming and bolting it only seconds before the demon arrived.

It hit the door with its shoulder and bounced off, then pounded on it. It did that for a full ten seconds before desisting and backing away.

Slowly, it turned around to face Haatim.

He gulped.

Chapter 14

The demon had seemed far less intimidating while chained up and he could take the luxury of just looking at it. Scary, yeah, but not that threatening. Haatim had almost forgotten what they were capable of while it stayed pacified, focusing only on what he could do to it and not the other way around.

It seemed a lot like a dangerous animal someone might see in a zoo: harmless enough while in its enclosure, but once it got out ...

Now, however, he stood trapped in a room with it with no exit. The priest had bolted the door from the outside, and Father Paladina had no intentions to let him out.

Cautious, the demon moved toward him, not in much of a hurry anymore. It seemed to size him up, taking things slowly. A word came to mind, *Savoring,* but Haatim pushed it away.

After training with Dominick, he could handle himself in a fight and could protect himself from this demon. But, for how long? Already, he'd grown sore and tired, and they had only been at this for a few minutes, maybe less.

The demon, on the other hand, would never get tired and could keep pursuing him all day. It didn't need to rest or take breaks, and eventually, it would wear him down enough to overpower and crush him.

He needed a strategy to win this fast, but nothing came to mind. The problem was that he had enough strength to hold his own against the demon, but not enough to do much more than that.

Maybe he could chain it up again. Father Paladina had removed the collar, but it still hung on the wall, open and ready. If he could get the demon close enough, he might manage to get it around its neck and chain it up once more. Then he would be able to move to one of the corners, out of its reach.

It wouldn't solve the problem of finding himself locked in the room with it, but he could address that later when he didn't have a raging demon chasing after him.

He eyed the creature, backing away from it slowly, and then took off running across the room toward the collar. The demon sprang forward as well, trying to cut him off. It seemed to know what he planned to do and didn't want to let him get close.

It dove forward at him, catching him around the shoulders in an awkward hug, and then tried to pull him back and off-balance. He threw his elbow, dipped his shoulder, and rolled away from the demon in an escape maneuver that Dominick had taught him.

Then he reached the chain. He picked it up, and the rattling sound seemed to fill the entire room and bounce off the walls. Haatim tried to get hold of the metal neck collar. He fumbled for it, and then the demon hit him from behind. It threw him into the wall, and he hit hard enough to daze him.

He managed, however, to get hold of the collar. Then he spun, lunging at the demon and getting inside its reach. In a split second, he wrapped his arm around its neck, pulled up the harness, and snapped it closed.

Victory.

Short lived.

The demon bit him just under the armpit, and he cried out in pain, jerking loose. It let him go, and then pummeled him instead. Haatim held up his hands, trying to protect his face from the blows, but he grew further dazed when it lashed out at him.

The demon stood caught, and all he had to do was get away. Enough separation and it wouldn't be able to get to him. Haatim ducked and ran under its arm, coming up behind the demon and heading toward the closed door.

He thought he'd ran clear, all up until he saw the chain fly over his head and catch him around the throat. The demon yanked him back, and he stumbled off-balance, and then it looped the chain a second time, tying it like a noose.

Haatim reached up for his neck, trying to grab the chain and pull it loose, but already, the beast had pulled it tight. The cold links dug into his neck, biting at the tender flesh, and the pain seemed nearly unbearable. In only seconds, he developed tunnel vision and could feel his pulse throbbing painfully in his temples.

The demon stood close behind him, pulling the chain tighter and tighter. Haatim gasped, or tried to, but couldn't draw in any air.

Not thinking, he reached back and grabbed the demon's hand where it clenched the chain. His first impulse encouraged him to try and pry the fingers loose, but he didn't do that.

Instead, he reached *inside* the hand, feeling for the demonic presence within. It felt like a white-hot energy, throbbing with rage. He crawled his way up that energy, like a tendril, until he could feel the presence of the demon. It appeared as a swirling mass in the man's chest, like an intangible cancerous growth.

He gripped that mass, mentally clenching it, and it recoiled in surprise. A burst of terror mixed in with the demon's rage. Terror and realization.

Haatim refused to let go, though. Mentally, he squeezed, tightening his grip on the demonic presence. It fought back, but it proved of no use. Even as Haatim's body weakened from the pain and lack of oxygen, the demon writhed in terror under his mental grip.

He kept squeezing and squeezing, and with each passing second, the demon became more panicked and desperate. Things slipped out of focus, and Haatim could no longer see or think straight, but still, he kept squeezing.

And then the world disappeared.

116

✳✳✳

When Haatim woke up, he had the worst headache of his life. Someone tapped on his shoulder, and when consciousness set in, the first thing he did was cry out in agony.

Or, at least, he tried to. Barely audible, what came out sounded more like a pathetic gasp than anything.

His neck hurt like nothing he'd ever experienced and felt like it had gotten torn open and set on fire. He opened his eyes. Father Paladina stood above him, a concerned expression on his face.

"Wow, he did a real number on you, didn't he?"

Haatim reached up to touch his neck, and the old priest caught his hand.

"Wait a second. I wouldn't do that just yet. It'll hurt like hell later."

It did already, but when he tried to open his mouth to speak, nothing came out. He just shook his head and looked at the priest.

"Yeah, you probably won't be able to talk for a little while, but I don't think you've got any permanent damage. I mean, I'm not a doctor or anything, but I think you'll be fine."

Haatim frowned.

"Don't give me that look. It worked."

He gestured with his hand toward the limp body lying on the ground next to them. The demon, or what remained of it, now resembled a decomposing corpse, lifeless and empty.

The presence of the demon had gone as well, completely snuffed out.

Had he done that? He recalled going after the demon and trying to crush it, but he didn't remember exactly what had happened before he had passed out.

Father Paladina seemed to recognize the look on his face. "Yes. You banished and sent it away. It's gone back to hell. My plan worked."

Haatim gave him a sour look.

"Well, it mostly worked," Father Paladina said, frowning, as he studied Haatim's neck. He stood and reached out, helping Haatim to his feet. "I rescheduled your flight for a few hours to give you time to recover and, hopefully, get your voice back. I know you're none too happy with me, but no way would I let you go out of the city if you couldn't defend yourself; so, you can get mad at me later."

Haatim reached up and, tenderly, touched the flesh around his neck. Lines marked it, and it felt painful to the touch. He winced but felt glad that the wounds hadn't gone any deeper than they had.

"Yeah, those will go away," Father Paladina said. Then he shrugged. "Eventually. In the meantime, how do you feel about scarves?"

Chapter 15

Haatim had thought the flight to the Vatican long and uncomfortable, but the series of flights to get him from Rome to Phnom Penh in Cambodia proved far worse. He felt like he had passed through the ringer with this trip.

Of course, it didn't help that his neck glistened in sweaty agony from wearing a stupid scarf, and his entire body ached from what had happened back in the basement. Part of him felt furious with Father Paladina for putting him in that situation and risking his life, but another part experienced elation. Or, at least, it did when the pain wore off a bit, and he got his voice back.

He had managed to expel a demon from a human host. Had reached out, grabbed it with his mind, and sent it back to whatever hellish place from which it had crawled out. He had won.

The idea that he had managed to do it filled him with hope for the future that he hadn't felt since the attack on the Council, but it amounted to more than that. It gave a vindication as well, and confidence in himself that he might manage to save his sister.

He'd never felt so pleased or relieved in his entire life. Father Paladina's methods seemed questionable, but the results proved more than he ever could have imagined.

The thought that he might be able to do the same thing to the demon inside of Nida filled him with a happiness he hadn't felt in a long time. Father Paladina had warned him that nothing had changed, and that under no circumstances should he face Nida by himself.

If the Church found out she lurked in the area, his orders told him to leave immediately and get on the next flight back to Rome. He'd come here to find Abigail and convince her to turn herself in and nothing more.

But, on the off-chance that he did run into his sister, he fully intended to practice his new skill and send that horrible demon packing. He wanted to repay it for what it had done to his family, his friends, and mostly, to his sister.

That was, of course, provided he survived the stupid flight there.

Each flight on its own didn't feel that bad, and to be honest, the last plane he'd flown in to get into Cambodia from Thailand had turned out quite comfortable. They even had a humidification system in the ceiling to keep the air from getting dry and stale feeling, and they served trays of fresh and delicious fruit.

Unfortunately, he had to spend so much time waiting between each flight in one airport after another. Over a day and a half, he'd jumped on four different flights, landing in various cities, rushing to the next terminal, and then waiting for hours for the next plane to take off.

Plus, the constant up and down of altitude got to him. His ears hurt, he had a constant headache, and he fought down nausea from the takeoff and landing routines. He couldn't imagine how jet-setters did it when they had to move about the world constantly.

The humidity and heat, he noticed first when stepping off the plane. The air felt swampy and difficult to breathe, and it took him a few minutes just to acclimate to the heavy air.

The airport didn't seem that large, and certainly, didn't have air conditioning. Haatim hadn't grown up with air conditioning in his family home but had spent the last several years with it on a regular basis. It only took him a few minutes to break out into a sweat. He felt overdressed in a t-shirt and shorts.

Tired, sweaty, and grumpy, he retrieved his luggage and stepped outside into the hot afternoon sun. Father Paladina had organized a car to take him to a nearby hotel and rented out a room for him over the next couple of days. The driver, a local, would—hopefully—help him locate Abigail in Phnom Penh.

A line of vehicles sat parked outside the airport entrance, along with a cabal of drivers waiting for their passengers. His driver, a man named Savin, had a description as a short and thin man. That didn't help at all, though, because all of them looked extremely thin, and none particularly tall.

One of them seemed to recognize him, however, and waved him over. Haatim adjusted his luggage and made his way to the vehicle. A beat-up old BMW in need of a good washing. The driver had a huge grin on his face.

"Savin?" Haatim asked.

The man nodded. "Yes, hello, great to meet you." The man bowed and offered his hand for Haatim to shake. He had a thick accent and only partially pronounced a few letters, but Haatim found him easy to understand.

Immediately, the man grabbed Haatim's luggage and rushed around to the trunk, opening it up. He tossed it in, not particularly gently, and then hurried over to open Haatim's door.

"Nice to meet you, too," Haatim said.

The man gestured for Haatim to climb in, and so he did. Savin slammed the door shut and ran around to the far side of the car. He seemed impatient and in a hurry to do everything fast.

The heat made Haatim sleepy and exhausted but didn't seem to have any effect on Savin. He moved with endless energy, climbing into the driver's seat and turning on the car.

After only seconds, they glided out of the parking lot toward the main road outside the airport. Savin pulled up to the exit, performed a cursory glance both ways, and then drove right out into the middle of heavy traffic.

Cars swerved around them, narrowly missing them, and horns honked as angry drivers shouted out of their windows at them. Savin barely seemed to notice any of it. One car came only centimeters from clipping them, and the driver yelled and slammed his hand on his door, but Savin ignored the man completely.

He turned, instead, to Haatim. "First time to Cambodia?"

"Yes," Haatim said, clutching his seat with one hand and the seatbelt with the other. His muscles tensed, and he couldn't help but wince when they almost hit another car. "First time to Southeast Asia, too."

"Welcome," Savin said, grinning even more widely. "My English, you can understand?"

"Yes. Quite well."

"I practice a lot. I am English teacher."

"That's great," Haatim said.

Absently, Savin weaved through traffic, narrowly dodging countless accidents. The rules of the road didn't seem to apply, and everyone cut each other off.

At least their brakes seemed good.

"You are cold?"

"What? No, it's too hot."

Savin glanced at the scarf around his neck. He'd worn it all day and almost forgotten he had it on. An ugly yellow thing, made of cheap material, it had proved the only one Father Paladina could find on such short notice, and it looked completely out of place with the rest of his ensemble.

"No," he said. "I'm not cold."

"Why do you wear that, then?"

"To protect my neck from the sun," Haatim said, and then winced at the unsophisticated lie. It seemed like a plausible excuse, but Savin looked unconvinced. He didn't follow up with his questions, however, and instead, moved on to the next subject.

"You are Christian?" Savin asked.

The query caught Haatim off guard, but he realized it shouldn't have. Father Paladina had organized this, and so it made sense that he would live a Christian life.

"No," he said. "Not really."

"Hindu?"

Haatim shook his head. "I don't attribute myself to any particular religion. I study philosophy, so I like to try and understand *all* religions."

Savin glanced at him, a curious and confused look on his face. "Not religious?"

"I consider myself spiritual but not religious."

"Oh," Savin said, but clearly, he didn't understand.

"What about you?" Haatim asked, trying for politeness.

"I am Buddhist."

"Ah," Haatim said. "Theravada, correct?"

Savin nodded, surprised that Haatim knew. Theravada seemed a much more hardline form of Buddhism than Mahayana or Vajrayana. The country had temples all around, and many monks would live in them, on the path to escaping the cycle of life and death and achieving Nirvana.

Not necessarily a declining form of Buddhism around the world, it didn't grow as fast as other forms friendlier to newcomers and outsiders and less restrictive. That, in Haatim's estimation, echoed the way of the world: people expected for things to be streamlined and have easier access to keep up with the frantic pace of modernity.

"It's so hot here," Haatim said after another couple of minutes on the road. "Hotter than where I grew up, for sure."

Savin looked at him sideways. "This is the cold season. Today isn't hot."

"It's hot to me," Haatim said with a laugh. "I'm not used to this."

Savin nodded, incredibly formal, and rolled down his window. The smell of the city seemed worse here, and it made Haatim gag when the wind pushed it into the car. Almost like a sewage smell, though faint. He opened his mouth to ask what it came from but decided that would appear impolite and changed his mind.

A moment later, he had his answer. They drove alongside a deep-cut body of water flowing in a ravine about thirty meters down. At first, he thought it only a river, and then recognized it as a sewer.

An open sewer that flowed through the middle of town. Savin didn't even seem to notice, and Haatim assumed most people simply grew used to it over time.

"Where does that go?"

"It flows into the Mekong River and out of the city."

"Ah."

He didn't particularly want to get used to the smell. After a moment, their path led away, farther from the sewage, and the smell dissipated a little.

"You are from America?" Savin sounded a tad surprised.

Haatim nodded. "For the last several years. I grew up in India. My father was a religious figure where I'm from, which is probably why I decided to study religion. He was important."

Savin nodded. "Sounds like a great man."

"He was. Or, at least, I thought so. Now, I don't feel so sure."

Savin looked at him, expecting for him to elaborate. Haatim didn't, having no desire to talk about his father. Instead, he turned and looked out through his window at the passing buildings. The city had an old feel to it, but a lot of newer structures stood mixed in with a more modern appearance. They drove past countless restaurants, and all of the signs showed both Khmer and English.

They even passed a handful of fast-food restaurants, though none of them had names he could recognize or a brand that existed outside Southeast Asia. How closely would they match up to American fast-food establishments? That seemed something they tried to emulate.

As they drove, the one thing he noticed, in particular, was how young the entire population appeared. While people walked down the streets, he barely spotted anyone over the age of forty.

Father Paladina had explained the Khmer Rouge to him prior to this trip and the bloody way in which the country had fallen into civil war. So many people had died, the country had starved, and a huge proportion of elderly people hadn't survived.

As such, the entire nation remained young, rebuilding from scratch to regain what they had lost in their civil war. The scars of that conflict lay everywhere, a testament to the brutality of humanity, much the same as the French Revolution, though much more recent.

Haatim couldn't even begin to imagine why Abigail had come out here. For what did she search? Did she simply want to hide away from everything?

The Church assassins hunted for her and had done so for a few days. So far, they hadn't managed to locate her, but Father Paladina insisted it would only take a matter of time.

Abigail played everything close to the chest, but that didn't make the hurt go away. The knowledge that she hadn't trusted him enough to tell him she still lived stung him to the core.

The fact that she didn't care enough hurt even more.

"We're here."

Haatim glanced up, dazed, and realized they'd reached another section of Phnom Penh. This part seemed a bit classier, more upscale, and they'd parked in front of an expensive-looking four-story hotel.

"Ah," Haatim said, stepping out of the car.

Savin hopped out as well, but let the engine run. He popped open the trunk.

"Here, let me carry them in for you."

Haatim intercepted him and picked up his bags. "No, I've got it."

"You sure?"

"Yes."

Savin shrugged. "Okay. When do you want me to pick you up?"

"A few hours," Haatim said. "I just want to rest some, and then we can go. Have you found any sign of her?"

"No. But I'll ask my friends. Tourists are usually fairly easy to find."

Haatim nodded. A number of tourists occupied the city from what he had seen, but they tended to stick out.

Still, it seemed a big enough city, so he had no idea how long it might take to track down Abigail. His job—as far as Savin knew—was identifying her if they did locate her.

He thanked Savin, grabbed his luggage, and headed into the hotel. Savin climbed back into his car and jerked back out into the street, heralded by another wave of honks and shouts.

A cool wave of cold air hit Haatim when he stepped inside the lobby, and he took a moment to bask in it and breathe, eyes closed.

"Can I help you?"

A young woman stood behind the counter, watching him suspiciously.

"Yes," he said. "Sorry. I have a reservation."

She nodded, and after a short back and forth, presented him with a keycard to his room. It lay on the second floor, and they didn't have any elevators.

At one time, that might have bothered him, but now it just reminded him of his time with Dominick at the Council building. He still dreaded stairs, but now, they'd become the sort of evil he could understand.

He made it into his room, dropped his luggage on the floor, cranked up the AC to max, and then collapsed onto his bed.

Though not comfortable, right now, it felt like heaven. Exhausted, he fell fast asleep after only a few moments.

Chapter 16

The drive back to the Reinfer estate felt as if it took no time at all. Dominick, absorbed in his thoughts, tried to come to terms with what Mitchell had told him, and so barely even noticed the scenery flitting past. Each time he thought he had come to terms with the new information, the sheer insanity of it would overwhelm him.

The idea that their legacy was that of a cult ...

It seemed impossible to fathom and went against everything he'd been taught. They didn't come from the cult; they were the ones *hunting* the cult. The good guys, right?

Right?

He could fully understand Frieda keeping such a huge secret from them. What a horrible thing to learn about their history, and it went completely against everything for which they stood. Technically, he knew, it didn't change anything because he remained the same person. Yet, that logic proved hard to cling to: it didn't change the fact that everything he'd thought true had become a lie. Nothing was how it appeared.

Dominick pulled into the driveway of the Reinfer estate and waited for the gate to open. He felt so distracted, it took him a few minutes to realize that nothing had happened and that the screen looked dead. Trent had given him a badge for situations like this, but when he waved it over the reader, again nothing happened.

The power must be off.

Something had gone wrong.

Instantly, Dominick's mind shifted into high gear, and all worries about the Council or Frieda vanished. He came back to the present and assessed the situation.

The front gate appeared untouched, but without power, it might as well have been a brick wall keeping him out. He could see the driveway leading up to the estate through shrubbery and trees, but no patrolling guards on the roadway or in his line of sight from the parked car.

He climbed out of his vehicle and flipped on his phone. He called Trent, but it rang through to voicemail without an answer.

Had someone attacked in his absence? Certainly not at the front gate, but maybe Nida and her team had breached from somewhere else on the estate.

Maybe it came down to something more mundane, but not likely. The fact that the power went out meant that multiple points of failure had become compromised and all the backup generators had gone offline. Either they had run out of power—they should have been able to last a day, so not likely—or someone had destroyed them.

Either way, he would know soon enough.

He walked up to the gate and climbed his way to the corner. Two cameras watched him do it, but he doubted they had power either. He reached the top and dropped onto the roadway on the other side. By now, alarms should have sounded throughout the property, and a security team should have converged on his position.

Instead, only silence.

He drew his pistol and moved up the driveway. It meant about a half-kilometer hike to reach the actual estate, and as he got closer, his sense of wrongness intensified. No patrols, no warnings, nothing. Just empty lawns and complete stillness throughout the entire place.

Not until he reached the front of the manor and the circular turnaround did he see signs that something had most definitely gone wrong. The double entry doors looked broken and hung open, and next to them pooled a puddle of blood on the front steps. It had begun to dry but remained a little wet, so whatever had happened, must have done so in the last few hours.

Dominick walked into the antechamber of the estate, raising his pistol and keeping his eyes peeled for any signs of movement. Inside the main entryway, more bloodstains and signs of violence met him: a broken chair, bullet holes, and tears in the carpeting.

But, aside from that, he identified nothing in the main place. No bodies of guards, butlers, or enemies. He took a few more steps into the estate, and then froze.

From off to his left, in the dining hall, came a chewing and slurping sound, like someone eating noisily. He moved through the foyer toward the slurping sounds, padding quietly across the floor and with his gun held ready.

Slowly, he rounded the corner, gun leading the way, and stared into the dining hall. A man sat at the center of a long table, hunched over. Though dressed in a guard's outfit, it looked like blood covered it. The noises came from him, and it appeared as if he sat gnawing on a turkey leg.

The room seemed relatively untouched, otherwise. Dominick took a step further into the room and saw that a body lay on the ground behind him. It looked like one of the butlers, and he lay there, definitely dead. He had a missing ...

Dominick looked back at the seated guard: no, not a turkey leg but the upper arm of the butler lying on the floor. It dripped blood while the man shoved his face into it, ripping off huge mouthfuls of flesh and eating as fast as he could.

Dominick had seen some disgusting stuff in his life, but this made for one of the worst. Dominick fought down his gag reflex and backed slowly out of the dining hall and back into the antechamber. The man remained too invested in his meal even to notice.

He crept back to the double staircase, leading to the second floor, and headed up. Part of him wanted just to leave, knowing that searching the building wouldn't net anything positive. The odds of Jill Reinfer remaining alive seemed incredibly small, but he needed to find out, nonetheless.

The head of security, Trent Dopper, hadn't sent any texts after that first, which meant that whatever had happened, it must have happened fast. It only took a two-hour drive to get here from Mitchell's shop, which meant the attack had occurred within that timeframe.

Dominick felt so frustrated with himself for leaving. He'd promised Frieda he would stay here to protect Jill and keep her safe, and he'd failed at that. Still, right now, he had bigger concerns.

Like, did the attacker remain here? With such a short timeframe, the possibility existed that whoever had invaded the estate still hid in the building. If that were Nida, then he would need to prepare.

It caught him a little off-guard at just how still the building felt. After the last few weeks of near constant activity and sound, the house seemed a lot less inviting this empty.

He found most of the guards and an explanation of what had gone on a few moments later when he reached Jill Reinfer's personal quarters. The guards, he found in the entry room, laid around in various positions in the room and clearly dead. A layer of blood and dismembered body parts covered the flooring.

The blood looked fresher than what he'd seen outside, and the air still smelled of gunpowder, which meant the fight had only ended in the last half-hour or so.

Many of the guards had been dismembered and sliced apart with sharp blades, though he couldn't tell if they'd received their wounds pre or post-mortem. Whatever weapon the attacker had used, it had a jagged and curved blade, and when Dominick inspected the cuts, he found them ripped as much by force as by cut.

Which meant the blades must be dull, and if the slices proved pre-mortem, they would also have proven incredibly painful. The entire floor felt slippery, making it difficult to move through without sliding on the slick ground.

Every fiber in his being told him to turn back now. In this room, he found more than eight dead people, and all of them trained and skilled combatants. He felt certain of what he would find in the next room: no way had Jill Reinfer survived.

But, he couldn't turn back. He had to know for sure.

With a steadying breath, Dominick peeked around the corner into Jill Reinfer's bedroom. She lay on the sheets, and at first glance, he took them as red sheets. Then he realized that they had once glowed brilliant white, and only showed red because her blood stained the fabric.

An odd and grotesque statue stood beside her bed, some sort of alien creature. She had weird tastes in culture, but that took it to a new extreme.

He let out a breath of air and lowered his gun, allowing a moment of pity for the lady of the estate. He hadn't much liked her, but no person deserved what had happened to her. It appeared as though Jill had gotten ripped apart on her bed, with bloody limbs scattered around and tossed against the walls. Her face showed a mask of horror and pain.

Bits of her dress, the same one she'd worn at his fight on the lawn a few nights ago, lay strewn about on the floor and—

Dominick hesitated, turning his gaze back to beside her bed and the alien statue standing there.

That was no statue.

It looked almost insect-like as it stood perfectly still. The skin on it looked gray and rough, almost like an outer shell of concrete, and it had four arms that ended in long and jagged talons. Something had caught his eye, but he couldn't tell for sure what. It didn't move and looked locked in place. What had he noticed?

Suddenly, it hit him.

The talons dripped blood.

"What the hell ...?" he muttered, raising his gun.

The statue turned to face him and opened its eyes. Blood-red eyes, filled with hunger and desperation.

Dominick raised his pistol and fired. He shot off three rounds at the thing, the first two thudding into its chest and the third clipping its head.

If the shots even hurt it, though, he couldn't tell. For certain, they didn't stop it. Slowly, the creature raised itself to its full three-meter height and turned to face Dominick.

"Uh-oh," he muttered.

A high-pitched shriek filled the room and forced Dominick to cover his ears with his hands. Then he looked up.

The creature charged at him.

Time to run.

✳✳✳

He stumbled back, nearly losing his balance and slipping on the puddles of blood in the room behind him. He caught himself on an armchair and pushed himself back across the floor, heading for the second-floor hallway.

As he ran, he saw that one of the dead soldiers had dropped his assault rifle. He reached down while he ran, picked it up, and ducked into the hallway just as the creature entered the room.

It had to bend to get through the doorway, and as it came into the entry area, it swung its bladed talons in wide arcs and let out another horrible screeching sound.

Dominick turned, raised the rifle, and then pulled the trigger. He hoped it didn't prove empty, and grinned savagely a second later when the reassuring roar of rounds firing reached his ears.

They hit the monster in the chest—or carapace; he couldn't be sure—and the creature staggered back. However, it didn't stop coming. It let out another screech and rushed forward, swiping the blades at him.

Dominick ducked just in time to keep his head, and the talons sunk deep into the doorframe beside him. The creature seemed strong, and a single hit from one of those blades would mean lights out for him just like it had for the soldiers.

He fired off more rounds into the creature's chest while he backpedaled down the hallway. It jerked its arm, trying to get it free, and managed to pull it loose on the second try. Dominick didn't wait, but instead, turned and sprinted toward the staircase leading downward, the monster in hot pursuit.

Dominick didn't try to run around the outer railing to reach the top of the staircase; instead, he jumped over the barrier and landed about four meters down on the stairs, tumbling the rest of the way in a controlled roll. It hurt like hell but bought him some time.

Or so he thought.

The creature smashed into the railing above, bursting through and staggering onto the staircase behind him. It lost its balance and slid down the stairs. Dominick sprinted away from it to the right, toward the dining hall.

The man he'd seen earlier, chowing down, had heard the commotion and came out to investigate. Dominick dashed right past him and into the hall, turning and heading for the kitchen.

He glanced back. The man came after him, but the creature came faster. It didn't stop either, but instead, just swung a talon down and stabbed the blades into the guard's back. It swung the other arm in as well, punching the blades through the man's chest, and then pulled the arms apart.

The man split into shreds, and it seemed like watching a water balloon pop. Dominick winced, and then looked forward as he rushed into the kitchen.

He made it inside a few steps ahead of the creature and slid forward onto his knees, leaning his upper body back and gliding underneath the long metal table in the center of the kitchen.

A huge crashing sound erupted when the creature slammed one of its talons onto the table above his head, but it didn't have strength enough to burst through. It stumbled into hanging pots and pans while it maneuvered through the room to try and reach him, but he had at least a few seconds' head start on it.

To run didn't seem an option, nor did fighting. He needed a distraction and safe place to get to. Brain calculating, he glanced over at the freezer. Could the creature open the door?

Hopefully not.

Dominick rushed over to the stove. It had eight burners, and all of them gas. Quickly, he turned them all to the maximum position without igniting any. He'd just flipped to the last one when the creature rounded the table and swung its talon at him.

He ducked and twisted backward, stepping away from the stove, and the beast came forward again. This time, he reached out and yanked a huge cast-iron skillet down from the ceiling. He dodged one attack, sidestepped a second, and then held up the skillet to block the third.

However, he'd underestimated the monster's strength.

It blasted the skillet back into his chest, hard, and the impact threw him back across the room. He hit the wall, and pain split his chest where the skillet had hit. Thank God it had rounded sides and not sharp ones, but he still thought it might have cracked a rib.

Luckily, the creature stood in the position he needed it to. In pain, Dominick sucked in a ragged breath of air, and then fished his lighter out of his pocket. He snapped it open, flicked it against his pants to ignite it, and then tossed it at the creature.

He didn't wait to see what happened, but turned, instead, and ran toward the freezer. A whooshing sound came from behind when the flames ignited, and then he yanked the door open and dove inside, jerking it shut behind him.

He doubted the flame had killed the monster, but hopefully, it had at least hurt or distracted it. His fear that it remained alive and well got confirmed a moment later, though, when an enormous thudding smacked against the door from the outside. It came heavy enough to rock the entire room. Then scratching sounds reached him, as the beast tried to manipulate the door handle, but it didn't seem able to get a grip.

Dominick let out a sigh of relief when it banged against the metal once more. The metal door stood thick enough that it couldn't break through—he prayed.

It whaled on the door for a solid ten minutes, though, before things quieted back down, finally. Dominick found a box of frozen goods to sit on and waited in the cold, shivering and rubbing his chest where the skillet had hit him.

He waited a few hours, and nothing changed. No longer could he hear the creature or anything else outside. Dominick checked his phone, but inside the metal freezer, he couldn't get a signal.

For good measure, he waited an extra hour. The creature must have left. He could imagine it, though, standing as still as a statue outside, waiting for him to step out so that it could cut him into pieces.

Either way, he didn't have a lot of choices. He didn't have on heavy clothes and couldn't stay in here forever. The cold got to him. Also, he needed to get in touch with Frieda.

As well as finding out what had happened, he needed to let her know that Nida had—most likely—gotten Jill's blood.

With a steadying sigh to calm his nerves, he opened the freezer door, cringing at the thought of the creature's blade waiting for him just outside.

Instead, he found nothing. The creature had gone, as had any sign of fire or otherwise. The burner switches remained on, but no gas came out. No doubt, a suppression system sat in place, which had taken care of shutting off the valves.

Dominick crept through the kitchen, pistol ready, and moved into the foyer. Again, he found nothing. He went to the security office. Empty. However, the computers had their own generator and had stayed online. When he went to one, he saw the bank of security cameras around the property.

Still jittery, he took a seat and went through them, trying to find out what had happened. It didn't take him long to figure it out.

The cannibal guard must have come in as a Trojan horse, taken over by a demon to help bring the rest inside. The huge monster had attacked at the outer gates, but at the same time, the other guard had gone through the building and disabled the backup generators and alarm systems.

The guards had tried to respond, falling back to Jill's quarters, but it proved of no use. The monster had walked through a hail of bullets and cut each one of them down before shredding Jill. Another couple of men had come onto the estate behind the monster and followed it into the room, gathering the woman's blood into vials before leaving.

The feed cut out when the last generator got turned off, but Dominick knew what he needed to know: Nida had Jill's blood now. That didn't bring the only problem, though.

Nida hadn't come here.

Slow and cautious, he made his way outside. The premises remained quiet, and Dominick felt confident the monster had gone. He flipped open his phone and called Frieda.

She didn't answer, though, and he assumed her still on her flight stateside to meet him.

Instead, he called Mitchell.

"Hey, Dominick. You on your way? Frieda should be here in a couple of hours."

"Jill's dead."

"What?"

"And something ..."

He didn't even know how to continue that train of thought. How could he ever describe the monster that had attacked him? It had killed the entire security team without assistance and would have had no trouble cutting him down if he'd stuck around to face it.

"What is it?" Mitchell asked. "What were you going to say?"

"Never mind." Dominick shook his head. "Don't worry; I'm on my way."

Chapter 17

He awoke to banging on his hotel door. Groggy, Haatim sat up and rubbed his eyes. What time was it? It proved impossible to tell because his body felt completely out of sync. Not yet that awake, he staggered across the room to the door and threw it open.

Savin stood there, grinning widely. "Are you ready?"

Had a few hours passed already? He yawned. "Sure. Hang on; let me get changed."

He moved to close the door, but Savin stepped past him and into the room. "You like cold air?"

Haatim nodded. "Yeah. I turned up the air conditioning."

Savin nodded solemnly and went over to the AC unit by the window. He stood next to it, holding his hands over the vents as though studying them.

Haatim hesitated. "You, uh ... going to wait downstairs?"

Savin turned, tilting his head to the side. "No, why?"

"So I can change?"

"You *can* change." Savin turned back to the AC. "I can wait. It is no problem."

Haatim opened his mouth to object, changed his mind, and headed over to the restroom. Though small and cramped, he managed to put on some fresh clothes in only a couple of minutes. He left the bathroom door cracked open, though, because the tiny room got too hot when he closed it.

Dressed, he unwrapped the scarf from around his neck. He hated scarves, even in winter, and it felt almost like peeling off a Band-Aid on his tender skin. It still looked red and swollen but had started to heal a little. The chain marks remained visible, but they too had faded.

The bathroom door pushed open all of a sudden and almost knocked him aside. Savin stood there, smiling. "Ready?"

"Yeah," Haatim said, hastily wrapping the scarf back around his neck.

Savin's expression changed to concern. "What happened?"

"Nothing major," Haatim said. "Just an accident."

Savin didn't seem convinced but didn't say anything. Instead, he turned and headed for the exit, and Haatim followed.

As soon as they got outside the room, the heat set in again, and Haatim found himself struggling to breathe once more. Time spent in the air conditioning felt like resetting, and his body had to adjust again.

The air had cooled, though, and even though only five o'clock in local time, the sun had dropped already.

Father Paladina had set up Savin to take him around the city and act as his guide, and apparently, Savin knew their intended destination. They headed out to the street, and the car sat parked in the hotel's turn around, right next to a sign that warned that it was a tow away zone.

Savin climbed in, and then he reached across and opened the door for Haatim. Less formal now, which Haatim appreciated.

"Let's go."

Haatim shrugged and then got in. "Where to?"

"Market."

"What's at the market?"

"Food," Savin said.

He put the car into gear, jerked out into traffic, and they were off. Haatim found himself clutching the doorframe again, and in the twilight of the sun disappearing, the Cambodian's wild driving seemed even more terrifying.

"Hungry?"

"What? Yeah."

"I know good food," Savin said.

They drove the rest of the way in silence for about another ten minutes, weaving through traffic and down narrow streets until they, finally, came to a stop in front of an open-air corner restaurant.

Haatim took a few steadying breaths. His hands shook and had turned red from holding onto the car so tightly, and he sweated copious amounts once more.

"We're here."

Haatim nodded and climbed out of the car. The restaurant looked small and deep, an open establishment with ceiling fans spinning lazily overhead.

It had about ten tables inside. All of them empty except for two occupied by diners. A woman greeted them at the door, speaking quickly to Savin in Khmer, and then she led them over to one of the empty tables. Savin beckoned for Haatim to follow.

"Good food," he said.

The woman smiled at them both, set down a pair of menus, and then disappeared. Haatim picked up the menu, took one glance at it, and then looked at Savin. "I can't read any of this."

Savin nodded. "I know. I'll choose for you."

That didn't sound too encouraging. Haatim didn't consider himself a picky eater, but for definite, he didn't like having other people pick out food for him.

Still, he couldn't recognize any of the words on the page, or even the alphabet, so he sat there, sort of helpless.

The waitress returned, and Savin ordered in Khmer, speaking quickly and gesturing his hand toward Haatim. The woman nodded along and then disappeared once more into the kitchen.

"What did you order for me?"

"Chicken and rice."

That surprised Haatim because it sounded quite a bit tamer than he'd expected. By the time the food arrived, he felt starved and chowed down on it at speed, devouring the whole plateful. The food—a bed of rice—came with a dish of soupy stew that he poured over the grain as he ate. It tasted spicy and flavorful.

The kitchen had chopped up the chicken into little pieces, bone and all, and Haatim had to eat the pieces slowly to make sure he didn't swallow any little chips of the bone.

Savin had ordered himself a bowl of what looked like intestine, but Haatim couldn't make it out for sure. He'd eaten intestine before, but not in a long while, and he hadn't become a fan of the texture.

They didn't talk while they ate, focusing on the food, and Savin finished eating everything in only minutes. Haatim considered himself a fast eater, but he'd barely gotten halfway done when Savin pushed away his plate. Then, he just stared at Haatim while he chewed.

It got awkward, fast, and Haatim tried to strike up a conversation to make it less so. "Have you seen the woman we're looking for?"

Savin nodded. "Yes. The black woman."

"Where?"

"Here," he said. "That's why we came. It was a few nights ago."

"Here?"

Haatim couldn't help but look around, hoping he might spot Abigail sitting somewhere in the restaurant. Though not here, of course, he couldn't help but feel a little let down.

Still, it gave him hope that they'd come to the same area where she was last seen.

"Yes. She came here."

"Have you seen her anywhere else?"

Savin shrugged. "I have seen her around the city. In the market."

Not the most helpful of guides.

Haatim finished eating just as the waitress brought over the bill. She set it on the table and then stood next to it, staring at him. It took him a second to realize that Savin also sat staring at him.

"Oh," he said, fishing out his wallet.

He glanced at the bill but couldn't understand it. Basically, it just looked like a garbled mess of numbers, and he had no idea of the exchange rate.

Father Paladina had given him a fair amount of cash and told him the rate when he first left, but he'd forgotten—something like three or four thousand to one. With a shrug, he pulled out a twenty and handed it to the woman.

She smiled, picked up the bill, and disappeared. A few minutes passed, and then Haatim glanced over at Savin.

"I won't get change, will I?"

Savin shook his head, still grinning. "No."

Haatim sighed and stood. "What now? Should we check out the market and see if we spot her?"

"Yes."

"Okay."

Savin stood, too, and headed outside. Haatim followed. The marketplace appeared mostly empty, and it looked like many of the vendors worked at closing up. They went into a huge auditorium type of building and saw countless vendor stands littering the area. Packed close together, they formed narrow walkways that proved difficult to navigate.

Savin weaved through the crowd gracefully, but Haatim found himself stumbling into people every couple of steps. He kept an eye out as they walked, looking for Abigail, but didn't see any sign of her.

They kept walking for about an hour, moving to another marketplace that seemed to have been an old military building crammed with walls to section off individual stores. One child ran up to him, holding up bracelets and speaking quickly, and another appeared a few minutes later, offering sunglasses.

Haatim waved away both of them, gesturing that he couldn't understand them, and they seemed to get the idea. One of them tried the same thing on Savin, who yelled at him.

"Like rats," Savin said, shaking his head.

Haatim couldn't think of a good response, so they continued walking in silence. He didn't see any sign of Abigail, but he noticed a pair of foreigners that earned a double glance from him. One of them, a skinny man, had sallow skin and a shaved head, and the other had darker skin and dead eyes.

They looked out of place sitting in an outdoor restaurant, and what caught Haatim's attention most was that while he and Savin walked through the marketplace, they'd passed the same place twice about an hour apart, and the men hadn't moved. They sat watching the crowd studiously, searching for someone.

Father Paladina hadn't managed to supply him with pictures of who the Church had sent to deal with Abigail, but he'd said it was two men and gave descriptions of them. These two matched up almost perfectly.

Finally, they gave up the search that night when most of the shops had closed down, and the streets stood empty. Savin drove Haatim back to his hotel and dropped him off. His driving didn't seem as insane with fewer vehicles on the road, and to be honest, Haatim felt too tired to care anymore. His legs hurt. His neck hurt. And he just wanted to get cleaned up and go to bed.

He kicked off his shoes and took a quick shower before climbing under the sheets. The staff had shut off the AC while he'd gone out, so he flipped that on again. Worry crept through his head because if the assassins found Abigail before he could, then it would make it difficult to get her to surrender. Now that he had seen the two men, the danger of the situation seemed more present.

It would prove nearly impossible to talk to her even if he found her, though. What would he say? *Hey, I know you don't want to talk to me, but I'm here to try and save you from Church assassins?*

Hey, I know you don't care about me, but I care about you and want to keep you safe.

136

Still, he had to try.

His biggest doubt, however, came from wondering what he would do if the Church found Abigail while he met with her. If he couldn't convince her to turn herself in, then he would be forced to try and protect her, which seemed like a dangerous and risky prospect. The exact opposite of what Frieda wanted for him. The Church didn't hunt him right now, but if he did that, he would certainly get added to their list.

But, the more he thought about it, the more all right he felt with that possibility. In any case, he wouldn't abandon Abigail to her fate, no matter what she decided or how she had treated him. Even angry with her, he cared about her more than he wanted to admit.

With so much to worry about, Haatim felt unsure if he would ever fall asleep. Naturally, he went out cold after only minutes.

Chapter 18

Life can turn on a dime. One minute, everything seems as normal as can be, and the next, it all changes. Today had begun in a mundane enough way for expat, Matt Walker. Later, on the run and terrified, he lamented that he couldn't have stolen just a bit of hindsight and transmuted that gold-dust into just a touch of foresight. Yes, it had all seemed normal enough ...

"Do you speak English?"

It took Matt a few seconds to realize that the young woman had addressed her question to him. He stood on the street corner, waiting for the light to change, and the question caught him off-guard.

In hindsight, though, he shouldn't have felt so surprised: living in Cambodia as a Caucasian man, he made a complete minority and stuck out like a sore thumb, being one of the few permanent outsiders in Phnom Penh.

"Yes," he said, turning to face the woman. She looked petite and mousy with black hair and eyes. Like him, she stuck out with her fair skin; though, unlike him, she had the deer-and-headlights look of a typical lost tourist. "I speak English."

"Oh, thank God," she said, letting out a tremendous sigh. "I've been trying to get back to my hotel for *ages* now, but I seem to have gotten turned around and have no idea where I am."

"Which hotel?"

"I don't remember the name. It's near the elephant enclosure, though. I rode out here with some friends earlier today, and they went back without me while I went shopping. I haven't managed to find a tuk-tuk driver who speaks English, and I'm desperate."

Matt could tell. She looked terrified and exhausted from all of the time spent in the hot sun. He imagined that he had looked much the same when he'd first come to Cambodia four years earlier, though now, he'd gotten used to the heat and adapted.

Not able to speak Khmer out in this section of town would bring a nightmare because, even though many people living here were multi-lingual, they spoke many other languages like French and Chinese before English.

It made communication difficult at the best of times, and even generic pronunciation dictionaries proved useless when trying to communicate with a frantic tuk-tuk driver and explain where one needed to go.

"You need to go about twenty minutes that way to get there. Do you have any money?"

"Plenty," she said. "Money isn't a problem."

He laughed. "All right. Let me flag down a driver for you."

"That would be fantastic."

Matt walked over to the street and waved down one of the motorists passing by that didn't currently have passengers. They made for the cheapest form of transportation.

He managed to flag down a middle-aged driver, who pulled his motorcycle up next to Matt. The driver sized him up, and then asked very slowly, in broken English, where Matt wanted to go.

Matt spoke fluent Khmer. Maybe not perfect, but enough to get by in almost any situation. He told the man exactly where the woman needed to go. The look of shock on the man's face that he could speak their language came as nothing more than Matt had expected, and he had grown numb to it while living here.

He looked like a tourist, so when they found out he wasn't, they got surprised ... and, usually, also frustrated. The man quoted Matt a price more than five times what the trip should cost, which most tourists would pay without a second of hesitation. Matt, on the other hand, knew the game. After a quick argument, the man lowered the price to only twice what it should cost.

Though pricier than Matt had hoped for, it still cost far less than what the driver had planned to make when he pulled over. A good compromise meant both parties would leave unhappy.

He asked the driver to wait, and then walked back over to the woman. "It is set," he said. "The trip will cost you a dollar."

"A dollar?" she asked, mouth hanging open. "The trip out here cost ten."

"For your group?"

"For me."

Matt laughed. "Then, you got ripped off."

"I suppose so," she said, sighing. "But right now, I could care less. All I want to do is get back to the hotel and my friends."

"I can sympathize. I was just on my way home, actually."

"Oh, where?"

"Not too far from your hotel. I live in an apartment above the church."

"Would you like to come with?"

"Oh, no," he said. "I wouldn't want to impose. Besides, it's too costly for my blood to ride a tuk-tuk all the time, and I enjoy the walk."

"Nonsense," she said. "You already saved me a fortune on the trip. I'll pay for you as well. I would appreciate the company."

Matt smiled. "All right, then."

They climbed into the tuk-tuk carriage, and after only a few moments, they traveled on the road, weaving in and out of traffic. People didn't follow the rules of the road too well in Phnom Penh, which meant driving throughout Cambodia proved incredibly dangerous.

Matt refused to drive in the city for that reason. Motorcycles weaved in and out of the lanes, cars and tuk-tuks swerved around each other, and it all seemed rather hectic.

Matt barely noticed the chaos anymore, but he could tell that the woman had a much more difficult time of things. She gripped the edges of the carriage and looked terrified as she watched the cars weave around them.

"I'm Matt," he said, hoping conversation would distract her.

"Carla." She let go of the seat long enough to shake his hand, and then grabbed it again immediately. Her knuckles turned white.

"Where do you come from?"

"California," she said. "San Jose. Came up here with some friends on vacation. Do they always drive like this?"

"Always. Off to the beach?"

She nodded. "In a couple of days. We just got back from Siem Reap."

"Ah, did you visit Angkor Wat?"

"Yes. Incredible."

"Awe-inspiring." He nodded. "It blew me away, the first time I saw it."

"You live here?"

"Yeah. I have for three years, and before that, I lived in Banteay Meanchey. It's a northern province not too far from Siem Reap."

"That's interesting," she said, though he could tell she didn't much like the prospect of living in Cambodia.

It didn't surprise him. Many tourists came here because it made for a cheap tourist destination, and they could make their money stretch a lot further. A lot of them, especially the ones who grew up pampered in their home countries, found much of what they saw here as distasteful, and at the very least, nothing like they had expected.

Matt had been one of those pampered individuals, growing up in London. It hadn't begun that way. His parents died in a plane crash when he was young, and he got adopted by a couple who couldn't have children of their own.

His adoptive parents, though not rich, made good money and got him anything he wanted, including a solid education and a chance to visit the world.

He had come to Cambodia as part of a mission trip with his Protestant friends years ago. They operated a church far to the north, outside Banteay Meanchey. The people he'd come with had gotten a little dismayed by the lack of interest from the local populace in Catholicism, but it still pleased them to help by donating supplies and teaching English to the Cambodian people.

Matt, on the other hand, had fallen in love with the country. He saw it as an unpolished gem, full of beautiful and friendly citizens and vast untapped potential. After the mission trip, he had stuck around, quitting his job back in London and taking a post at the church.

After only a few months, he ran the local church and all community outreach efforts in the surrounding provinces. Few people he met spoke English, and none fluently, so that had forced him to learn the local language fast.

It hadn't taken long for this to become his permanent home. He'd built up a small congregation in the north, and then moved to Phnom Penh to live in a more bustling area and opened a church here as well. It reminded him more of his home back in England and had all of the amenities he missed.

Occasionally, he considered moving back home to get nearer to his family, which his adoptive parents had wanted for a long time, but each time, he decided to extend his stay for a little while longer. All of his friends lived here now, and if he went home, then coming back to Cambodia in the future would prove considerably more difficult.

So, he stayed, ran his churches, and lived a quiet life in the first real place he could call home.

"How do you like things here so far?" he asked.

"It's nice," his companion replied. "The bus rides, though, ... I thought we would never make it back to the city."

He smiled. "I know, right? Fifteen hours to take a five-hour bus ride."

"The driver stopped every ten minutes for a pee break."

"And I bet he just jumped outside and used a tree, didn't he?"

She laughed. "You know it."

"I took a trip a few years ago where the driver knew someone along the way. He stopped the bus at the guy's house. He stayed there drinking for almost five hours out in the middle of nowhere."

"Really?"

"Yeah, we had, like, thirty people on the bus, too. We all just sat there, waiting for the guy to come back. When he did, he'd gotten completely drunk and just kept right on driving."

"That's insane."

"I've seen crazier things."

"Name one."

"I saw a mother driving her motorcycle to the grocery store with a five-month-old baby on the seat behind her, clinging to her."

"Get out of here. No way."

"I'm serious. She rode on the road and everything, going at least forty kilometers per hour in heavy traffic."

"That's ridiculous. What was her plan when the baby fell off?"

"Babies have strong survival instincts. It held on. You know they don't use diapers here?"

"They don't?"

"Not much, at least. Children get potty-trained before their second birthday."

"What?"

"Yeah, it basically boils down to expectations. When you expect more out of babies, you usually get it."

"So, they adapt. That's crazy."

He nodded. "It is. What about food? What's the craziest thing you've eaten since you came out here?"

This gave another easy topic for tourists, he knew. Though nothing seemed strange to him anymore, the local cuisine freaked people out more often than not.

"Oh, no," she said. "I don't eat strange stuff. If I don't know what it is, it doesn't go near my mouth. But, my friends tried fish heads."

"Oh?"

"They hated it. I did try a chicken thing, but it surprised me how much bone it had in it. I almost choked."

"It does take some getting used to. They do tend to leave in the bone. Meat gets used more for flavor here than as the star of the dish."

"What about you? Craziest thing you've eaten."

"Balut," he said.

"What's that?"

"It translates to, basically, duck embryos in English."

"Like duck fetus?"

"Yeah," he said.

She scrunched up her face, and he had to admit she looked quite cute when she did it. He said, "They boil them like an egg. It comes out like a hardboiled egg with a chicken nugget inside when it's done."

"That sounds disgusting."

He shrugged. "Maybe. Does take some getting used to, and they love them here. Quite the delicacy."

"What else have you eaten?"

"Bug stew," he said. "And dog."

"Dog? You ate dog?"

"Yeah. Once. I went out with a friend, and we got fairly drunk."

"Do they eat a lot of dog here?"

"No. They eat black dogs for good luck, but in general, they frown upon such things. Eating dog would be like eating fast food where you live."

She laughed. "So, no one admits to it."

"Nope."

The tuk-tuk pulled to a stop at the corner that Matt had directed them to. He had to admit, getting a ride with Carla had saved him a lot of time on his trip home. He enjoyed walking, but it had turned into a hotter than usual day, and he looked forward to getting back to his apartment and relaxing.

Above his church, it proved one of the more expensive ones in the neighborhood. Unlike most residences, his had many Western amenities, including a sit-down toilet instead of a squat one. He didn't mind squatting, but sitting down just seemed more relaxing.

"We're here," he said, climbing out of the tuk-tuk.

"Thank God. At least I recognize this!"

He offered his hand to help Carla down, and then she fished her wallet out of her pocket.

"You said two dollars for both of us?" she asked. Matt nodded. Carla fished a five out of her wallet and handed it to the driver. "Can I get change—?"

The driver stuffed the five into his shirt pocket, mumbled something in

Khmer, and then drove off before she could even finish her statement. She watched, flabbergasted, and then burst out laughing.

"I guess not," she said to no one in particular.

"It happens."

"Considering how the rest of my day has gone, I just feel thrilled to have gotten home. Thank you so much."

"Glad I could help."

"Speaking of which ... all of this talk of food has made me hungry. I mean, not for duck fetuses or anything, but I haven't eaten all day. Let me buy you dinner?"

"Oh, no, I couldn't—"

"I insist," she said. "And I won't take no for an answer. My friends and I had planned to go to a little restaurant up the road from here. The one with the red sign and purple letters."

"Romdeng," he said. "I love that place."

"Good, then it's settled." She clapped her hands. "I'll go round up my friends, and we'll meet you back here. Say half an hour?"

"Sure."

Carla smiled at him, and then headed down the road toward her hotel. He watched her disappear, chuckling to himself. For definite, he hadn't expected his day to go this way, but it gave him a pleasant surprise, all the same.

It gave a nice distraction. As a rule, he avoided tourists. He'd met his fair share of criminals out here, hiding from their past or trying to find some way to satisfy their unsettling urges. Most people he'd met that came here either arrived completely clueless about what they had gotten themselves into or they knew exactly what they were doing and fell into the less savory category of individuals.

Plus, he liked to keep to himself. Carla seemed like a genuinely friendly person, though, and someone he could get along with. And, for certain, she didn't fall into his oversimplified categories of tourists.

Her friends, though, he felt less sure about. He doubted all of them would prove as friendly or outgoing as Carla. Still, he didn't put himself above giving them the chance to prove him wrong, and he did love eating at Romdeng.

The establishment offered a sort of cook-your-own-food deal with a little dome pan with holes in it where you could cook your meat and vegetables. His favorite part was putting a nice little piece of beef fat on top and letting it sit there until it turned burnt and crispy.

It cost a lot, though, and usually fell outside his price range. This would, certainly, give a nice treat.

Matt walked down the street toward his apartment with an extra bounce in his step. This had, supposedly, started out as a laid-back day for him, just heading to the market to keep busy, but now he would go and get a nice dinner and some Western company. Of young women, too.

He had just turned thirty, and estimated these girls to be a few years younger than himself if they proved the same age as Carla. He admitted to himself, at least partially, how excited he felt to see young women not native to Cambodia. He thought Cambodian women beautiful, but he just found something pleasant about seeing something exotic.

He laughed at himself: he'd stayed here long enough that Caucasian women seemed exotic, now.

Matt would check in on his church after getting ready for dinner. He would only need a couple of minutes to prepare. A fresh shirt and some cologne and he would be ready for just about anything.

The church almost always stood empty this time of day, and he probably wouldn't see anyone passing through until the weekend service.

Sometimes, Matt handled the service himself—though not a priest, he practiced as a Deacon back home at his family church and knew enough scripture to handle some short services—and, occasionally, he managed to entice priests to come visit the country for a few weeks or months and take over the parish.

A few months usually proved all he could get, and the turnout never seemed tremendous. Often, priests would come for a while and then go on their way. Only he got left living here.

He felt distracted as he walked down the road, and a man bumped into him, nearly knocking him over. The man had olive skin and a shaved head. He wore loose-fitting black clothes and had a plain face.

"I'm so sorry," the man said, reaching out and catching Matt before he could fall. "Are you all right?"

"Yeah," Matt said, a little annoyed that he'd let himself get so distracted. "Thanks."

"No problem."

The man nodded at him, and then headed down the street. He had something a little unsettling about him, but Matt brushed it off. Right away, this man fell into Matt's less savory category of tourists.

He brushed the encounter away and, instead, focused on Carla and dinner. He headed down the road toward his home with a renewed bounce in his step.

Chapter 19

Haatim felt considerably more refreshed when he woke up the next morning. This time, he'd dressed and stood ready to go before Savin managed to come up to his room. Instead, he met him downstairs in the lobby.

The hotel served a continental breakfast with hard-boiled eggs and toast, but Savin told him to skip it. Instead, he took him to another hole-in-the-wall restaurant for breakfast. They ordered soup, and it tasted delicious with leafy vegetables and huge chunks of ham. One of the best soups Haatim had ever had, and it surprised him to find out that it made for a regular breakfast item around the city.

When talking with Savin, he learned that most locals ate all of their daily meals outside the home. The idea of a home-cooked meal seemed rare, and as such, numerous small restaurants sat on every street corner, served a single menu item, and only opened for one mealtime a day. It appeared a thriving business in the city; much more than he'd experienced in Arizona. People back home ate out a lot, but not nearly as much as here.

They also, generally, ate the same food for each meal, something Haatim hadn't experienced since growing up in India. In Arizona, he'd gotten introduced to a new culinary world where he could eat any number of different foods anytime he wanted, including dishes from just about every culture in the world that had gotten transformed into American cuisine.

He loved that open-ended approach, but he also liked the idea of having a steady and consistent meal. It removed a lot of the guesswork and fretting about deciding what to eat and made it just a normal daily routine. It also went easier on the stomach and intestines.

They got back to the market by around nine in the morning, doing their rounds and searching for Abigail. Savin took him to every location at which he'd seen Abigail and seemed to have an eidetic memory.

Haatim also found out from speaking with him that Savin did this for a living. He watched tourists, and then helped people track them. He did this, he said, on behalf of governments, as a rule. For example, when known pedophiles hid out from charges in their home countries, he aided in their capture so that they could get extradited.

He knew of twenty regulars who lived in his area of the city, as well as fourteen newcomers and tourists that hadn't been here for more than a few days. Hell, he even knew the regular routines of each of these outsiders.

Abigail's schedule and routine had changed, Haatim discovered, when the other two men had shown up. The bald man and his friend had only arrived a couple of days ago, and almost always loitered at a high-traffic location, watching the passersby.

Since they had turned up, Abigail had fallen off the grid, and Savin thought she might have shifted to another part of town that he didn't frequent. Haatim hoped that didn't turn out as the case. If she had left this part of town, then he would lose his only chance of finding her before the Church did.

They stopped to get lunch a few hours later in one of the outdoor restaurants. He had a stew similar to the previous night, only this time a vegetarian one with a lot of chewy vegetables. Not nearly as tasty, it still didn't seem bad.

"Did you see her anywhere else before she disappeared?"

"Outside the market," Savin said.

Haatim had tried to eat as fast as possible, but still, Savin had finished long before him. "Where?"

Savin shrugged and pointed. "Over that way."

"What's over there?"

"Nothing," Savin said. "It is near the elephant enclosure, and has a few shops and a Buddhist temple, but nothing else."

"What did she get closest to?"

"The elephants," Savin said. "And a church."

Haatim frowned. "A church?"

"Yes."

"What denomination?"

"Christian," Savin said, making it clear he thought it a dumb question.

"I mean, Catholic, Protestant, or something else?"

Savin only stared at him. Father Paladina hadn't told him anything about a Catholic Church in the area, but maybe he just hadn't thought about it.

"Who runs it?"

"Matt Walker. He lives here. Not a tourist."

"Can you take me there?"

"Yes," Savin said. "Let's go."

Just as they made to leave, Haatim received a call from Father Paladina. He answered, stepping away from Savin for privacy. "Hello?"

"Haatim, you need to leave, now."

"What? Why?"

"I spoke to Frieda. Jill Reinfer is dead, but Nida didn't go there like they anticipated."

"Where is she?"

"We have no idea, but it is possible that she went to Cambodia. You must return to the airport and fly out."

"What about Abigail?"

The priest stayed silent. "Our agents have reported in."

"Did they find her?"

"Not yet, but they believe they know what she went after. A local, and they

148

hope that tracking him will find her."

"Who?"

"Haatim, just leave."

"You said he was a local? A Cambodian?"

"No," the priest said. "An expat."

"His name?"

Father Paladina didn't answer the question. "I've set up a flight for two hours away. I expect you to get on it."

"I shan't leave."

"If you don't, I'll send agents to gather you, and then it will turn bad for both of us."

Haatim hesitated, and then sighed. "Fine. I'll get on the flight. Two hours?"

"Yes."

"Okay."

Haatim hung up, and then turned back to Savin. "You said Matt Walker was an expat?"

"A what?"

"Not from around here," Haatim said.

"Yes. A white man."

What were the odds that Matt had become the Church's target? Probably not great, but, for certain, not enormous with so few permanent outsiders.

"Take me to that church."

Savin nodded and led him away from the restaurant. It proved a short walk to get to the church, which seemed little more than a little wooden building set on a street between a couple of shops.

They passed one of the huge fences of an outdoor enclosure, and Haatim could see a group of enormous elephants inside. The fences ran right along the side of the road, which seemed strange to Haatim. It didn't look like a zoo, just an enclosure with elephants and trees in the center of the city.

The church appeared quiet and locked up when they arrived.

"You're sure you saw her near here a few days ago?"

"Yes," Savin said. "Matt will most likely have gone out to the market right now."

"Should we wait?"

"We should go find him."

Haatim frowned. "What if he comes back? Matt might have seen Abigail and know where she went or what she's doing here."

Savin shrugged. "You stay here. I will go find him and bring him back."

"All right."

Savin walked back toward town, leaving Haatim standing on the side of the road. Maybe Abigail had gone looking for Matt, especially if the Church had targeted him to track. Why, though? It didn't make any sense for Abigail to go after him. Did they know each other? Old friends, perhaps? Or something else?

Maybe old lovers?

He pushed the thought away. Definitely not something that interested him in worrying about, and none of his business anyway. He bit back his jealousy and looked around the area.

The market stood only a ways off, but this area didn't have a lot of foot traffic. He glanced around but couldn't see any good places to sit and wait.

Instead, he'd do a circle around the block. If Abigail waited in this area and watched out for Matt, then he might spot her. He set off walking, and once he felt confident that no people came too near, he took off his scarf. It chafed his neck, and he liked to let the skin breathe, but so far, anyone who had seen the scars on his neck had grown horrified at the marks.

He stepped into an alley behind the church and rubbed at the tender flesh. It had healed quickly but still felt painful to the touch. It had also peeled, and he figured he would shed quite a bit before all got said and done.

"Hello, Haatim."

The words froze him in place, hand on his neck, and a chill ran down his spine. The voice came from behind him, deeper in the alley, and he recognized it instantly. However, Abigail hadn't addressed him.

Nida had.

✳✳✳

He turned, slowly, spine tingling.

Nida stood behind him in the mouth of the alley.

She wore the same long clothing that the locals wore, plus a shawl to cover her head, which she had pulled aside.

It chilled him more that she stood smiling at him.

He might have thought her just another Cambodian woman in those clothes, except for her face, which looked scarred and torn and covered in pock marks and heat rashes. All of which made it almost impossible for him to make out his sister's features.

She looked wretched. The demon's time spent inside of her had taken a serious toll, making her just about unrecognizable. She studied him with piercing eyes, standing calmly and watching him.

He should run. Just sprint back to the street and keep going. This made for the precise confrontation that Father Paladina had worried about and prayed wouldn't happen. Haatim found himself shaking in terror, his only option to try and get away.

However, he didn't run.

"You aren't Nida."

"No, not anymore," the demon said, smiling. "Not anymore. But, I can access her memories, and I know everything she knew about you. Have you come here for me?"

Haatim stayed silent.

"No? I must admit, I feel a hint of jealousy. But, if you didn't come here for me, why did you come?"

He tried to find an answer, but facing off with his sister took away his ability to think straight.

She studied him for a second, and then smiled. "My shadow," she said. "You came here for Abigail."

"Where is she?"

"Around. We've played something of a cat-and-mouse game, but sadly, our game draws to an end. I came here for business."

"What business?"

"None of your concern."

His hands shook. The demonic presence inside his sister's body felt strong, like with the other demon in the Vatican basement, but this one seemed different. More tangible, more real, less in control. When he reached out for it mentally, it felt like touching a powder keg.

The demon seemed to sense him, too, and her eyes fluttered for a second in surprise. "Ah, Haatim, you are so much more special than I anticipated. You will prove tremendously useful to me in the future."

"I could send you back to hell."

"You're welcome to try."

Haatim hesitated. He wanted to reach out like he had before, but something about the situation told him it would prove a bad idea. This felt anything but the same thing he'd experienced before, and he knew in only seconds that he hadn't readied enough for something like that.

Instead, he decided to appeal to his sister. She had strength enough to push out the demon if she only knew she could.

"Nida," he said. "Please. Nida, I know you're in there."

"Nida has gone. Just us chickens, Haatim."

"No, I refuse to believe that." He took a step back toward the mouth of the alley. "Nida, please. If you can hear me, give me some sign. Fight back. Take control."

The demon laughed, pursuing him slowly. "Ah, foolish and ignorant man, always clinging to your silly optimism. Your sister died. She served her purpose, and now she just gives rags for me to wear. Just like your father. So much meat and gristle."

Haatim hesitated. "What?"

"You didn't know? Your father is dead, murdered by the Church."

Haatim felt a burst of confusion and pain as he took another step back. "What?"

"They didn't tell you?"

"You lie."

"You know otherwise. They found your father in Switzerland and butchered him like an animal. All in the name of the Church. After what he did, can you blame them? I'm sure you would have killed him, too."

Haatim pushed away what she said as best he could, trying to focus on events in the here and now, but part of him still attempted to reconcile the thought that his father had died.

True? Could it be so? Had the Church hunted his father down after what happened at the Council?

He had seen him get off the helicopter and go into the hospital in Switzerland but hadn't tried reaching out to him since. Still, even then, he knew that Frieda would keep him safe.

Wouldn't she?

Maybe the demon had told the truth. It also remained equally possible that the demon had lied to him, trying to get under his skin, but that reassurance didn't give him enough to dispel the concern completely. He couldn't help but worry that, maybe, the Church did kill his father and had withheld the information from him.

Which, he knew, brought him to just what the demon wanted him to worry about. Whether or not it proved true, it didn't matter. The demon wanted him distracted and weak. But, no, he wouldn't give the beast that opportunity. He could worry about his father later.

"Nida, don't give up."

He closed his eyes and focused, trying his best to remember the sensation that had overcome him in the basement with the demon. He had reached out, not physically but emotionally and mentally, toward the demon. Though barely conscious when it had happened, he did remember the sensation. He tried his best to recreate that moment.

With a steadying breath, he grabbed the demon mentally and started to crush it the same way he had the creature he'd faced in the Vatican basement.

Within seconds, it became clear that he had made a grievous error.

The essence of the demon compressed when he squeezed it, but the sensation got almost immediately replaced with something else, something akin to rage. Not an emotion but rather felt like a tangible object. It felt odd, at first, and difficult to understand.

Then the demon lashed back, attacking him. It came like a mental blow that staggered him and blasted him away, and it landed with such force that it wrecked his concentration. Dazed and disoriented, it felt like he went out of his body. However, he could sense his body and its safety nearby, and so he moved toward it.

The demon got to him first. Its presence surrounded him and clung.

It constricted to crush him.

Haatim felt shock, first, but a pure and primal terror unlike anything he'd ever felt before soon replaced it. The demon didn't just want to kill him, it also prepared to snuff him out of existence. It attacked his psyche and toyed with his soul like a dog might a bone.

He tried to break free. However, the creature had complete dominance over him. He couldn't touch it at all, and it could do anything it wanted to him. If it so chose, it could destroy him and abolish his entire identity out of existence.

But, the worst thing—he realized in those seconds—it had tricked him. It couldn't create this connection to his soul and get him out of his body. Only he could do that through his special gifts. Had Father Paladina felt afraid of just such an occurrence?

The idea that the demon could crush his soul and snuff him out of existence seemed bad enough, but the idea that he had created the bridge for it to do so felt even worse. It hit him as so much more terrifying than what Father Paladina had warned him about.

Haatim collapsed to his knees and fought back with desperation. The world flitted in and out of existence while the demon attacked his soul. He pushed it back, tried to force it away and get back into his body, but he might as well have attempted to lift a collapsing building with his bare hands.

The demon used him like a plaything, and he could feel its amusement. Time ceased to exist while the demon pummeled him mentally, and his mind stopped answering to his commands. He couldn't do anything except thrash around in this outside state and try to regain some semblance of control, but his struggle proved futile.

Madness crept in. A sure and clear understanding that if the demon continued this for much longer, he would lose himself. The demon wouldn't even need to destroy him, it simply needed to leave him in this state of brokenness for a while longer, and he would destroy himself.

"You thought you could come here and challenge me?" the demon asked. "But you are just a weak and pathetic little boy. You are nothing, and you *have* nothing. You, Haatim Arison, are worthy of nothing."

The words struck him to his core.

The demon slipped off him, releasing him. He felt confused and disoriented. Though he could sense his body nearby, Haatim didn't have the strength to go toward it. Broken and weak, the end had come.

He would die here, alone in the alleyway.

He would watch himself expire.

He had completely and utterly failed.

The worst possible situation to find himself in.

If he could get to his body, he would find safety, but it might as well have lain a million kilometers away instead of a few meters.

He glanced to the side.

Nida walked up next to him, and then knelt and put her mouth close to his ear. "I'll come back for you, dear brother," she whispered. "Don't go anywhere."

Chapter 20

As soon as Matt Walker stepped inside his quiet little church in the center of Phnom Penh, something felt terribly wrong. The lights remained off, just as he expected, but he could feel the presence of someone else hiding in the room.

The mere fact that they hid from him filled him with concern. He couldn't see anyone but could tell they hid there.

"Hello?" he called out in Khmer. "Who's there?"

No response. He tried English as well, but still, no answer came. Probably kids hiding away from their mothers. He'd experienced situations like this many times in the past, finding children avoiding their schoolwork or chores, though not usually this late in the day.

No doubt, they hid from him as well, hoping he wouldn't return them to their angry parents.

However, something about the situation made him worry, and even though wayward children seemed the likeliest scenario, something told him that this case differed.

Matt walked across the hardwood floor toward the front of the church and to the light switch. Wary and uncomfortable, he felt unsure what might be afoot but also afraid he would miss his dinner appointment.

He used the light spilling in through the open doorway to navigate between the wooden pews toward the front, keeping his eyes open for any trespassers.

He made it to the far side of the room and felt around for the switch. It took a few seconds for his fingers to find it in the darkness, and then he flicked it on.

Nothing happened. The room remained dark.

Suddenly, the door behind him swung closed with a crash, casting him into complete darkness.

A shiver danced across his spine, and he backed up against the wall, willing his eyes to adjust to the darkness. Someone stood inside the room with him, and a tinge of panic rushed through his body.

"Who's there?" he asked in Khmer. "Come out where I can see you."

"Why would I do that?" a woman asked in English from across the room. She sounded young, with a sultry voice.

"Who are you? Why are you in my church?"

"Maybe I came here looking for God."

She sounded closer this time as if she'd moved across the room toward him. He listened but couldn't hear any footsteps tapping across the wooden floor.

"He *does* hide in the most unexpected places," the woman said.

"What do you want?"

"I want *you*, Matthew. You have no idea how much you mean to me."

"Me?"

"Yes, you. You make the last piece of my puzzle. The light at the end of my tunnel. Matthew. I like your name. So Biblical."

He backed away slowly, one hand on the wall. He aimed to move away from the approaching voice and head for a door at the back of the cathedral. One he kept locked normally, and that exited into a back alleyway.

His eyes still hadn't adjusted to the darkness, and he bumped into a pew while he scrambled through the church, knocking it sideways to scrape across the floor.

"Where do you think you're going?" she asked, a few steps to his left. "Our fun has only just begun."

"Stay away from me."

"I couldn't stay apart from you any more than a moth can from a flame."

Suddenly, the door to the church blasted open, pouring bright sunlight in once more. A wretched-looking woman stood in front of him, maybe two meters away. She appeared of Indian descent, though pale. Pockmarks and rashes covering her skin and face gave her a sickly appearance.

The woman turned toward the door and let out a laugh when the light came in.

"I wondered when you would show up."

Matt glanced over. Another person stood the doorway. This one silhouetted by the sunlight, which made it impossible to make out the features or see the face.

"Matt, run!" the person in the doorway—a woman—yelled.

The newcomer's arm flew up, and a thunderous roar of gunshots filled his tiny church. On reflex, he covered his ears and stumbled backward, trying to get away from the sound.

He glanced back at the first woman, the scarred and sickly one. She dodged back and shifted behind one of the pillars that held up the roof. Gunshots thudded into the area around her.

The woman moved with unnatural speed, gliding as much as moving. Matt watched her in awe, not even sure if she qualified as human. More rounds blasted into the church. They buried into the pillar behind which she hid, shattering off huge wooden fragments that went flying through the air.

She turned, looked at him, and let out a hissing sound.

"Run, Matt!" the newcomer screamed from the open doorway before firing off more rounds at the Indian woman. "Get out of here!"

Matt ran.

Chapter 21

Matt felt unsure where he needed to head when he burst out of his church and into the back alleyway behind it. The only thing he knew? He needed to get away from the Indian woman who'd come after him.

He also felt the keen need to get away from the other woman because he had no idea who she was or why she had come to his aid just in the nick of time. Could he trust either of them?

His heart pounded out of his chest, and his terror made him nauseous. In the alleyway, he almost stumbled over a man lying on the ground. The guy looked injured and made gasping noises in his throat.

He looked to be of Indian descent like the woman who'd attacked him and had odd bruises on and around his neck. His eyes fluttered while he lay there.

Matt's first instinct prompted him to check on the man and make sure he was okay, but quickly, he pushed that plan out of his mind. No time to wait, even if the man seemed about to die, because if he did, then *he* would probably die too. Matt had to keep moving, to get away from here as quickly as possible.

If he made it out of this alive, then he could come back and check on this man, but right now, he had to run.

The alleyway proved narrow, and he rushed out of it and onto the streets of Phnom Penh. He stumbled forward, off-balance, and barely caught himself before falling into the road. A motorcycle zoomed past, followed by a car that narrowly missed him as it swerved to the side.

The driver honked his horn and shouted at Matt, but he hardly noticed. He ignored the driver, trying to figure out what to do. The central market of the district stood off to his left, most likely brimful with people this time of day as they prepared for dinner.

The area to his right led to the outskirts of the city, toward the elephant enclosure and residential districts beyond. Though people would still be about, that district would hold far fewer than in the market, and they would prove more scattered.

So, the question: Should he run toward more people and try to disappear into the crowd? Or, should he run away from them to keep innocents out of harm's way? Would the woman chasing him shoot through civilians to get him?

He didn't have any answers. He did, however, know his way around the market like the back of his hand, whereas he rarely traveled to the city's outskirts and didn't know that section of Phnom Penh nearly as well.

In the end, he made his decision purely on impulse, hoping that he could disappear into a large group of people and find a good hiding place if he went deeper into the market. It might put more civilians at risk, but it seemed the likeliest way for him to stay alive.

That, he had to admit, made for his top priority right now. He had to get away and find somewhere safe as fast as he could. Plus, he remembered that a police station sat on the other side of the market, and from there, he might find help in dealing with this threat.

It would take a long run for him to get to that station, and he would have to cross many dangerous intersections, but he couldn't see a good alternative, and it helped to justify his decision to endanger others.

Matt turned and sprinted down the sidewalk toward his left, heading into the market. He dodged through the crowds of walking pedestrians, eliciting quite a few insults and expletives in Khmer from the people he bumped into, and kept running along the road.

After a few minutes, he reached the first intersection and lights that he would need to cross. An enormous group of pedestrians stood waiting for the light to change, and in the roadway, cars, motorcycles, and tuk-tuks zipped past in both directions. He lay a good ways away from the church now, and the people out here didn't seem to have heard the gunshots over the sounds of the traffic, and so hadn't panicked.

Not yet, at least.

He considered making a run for it and trying to weave through the hectic traffic but then changed his mind. Drivers in Cambodia proved notoriously careless, and everyone drove far faster than what he would have considered a safe speed for the amount of traffic. Even if they saw him and tried to brake, he doubted they would manage to in time.

Luckily, it looked as though the light was about to change. Matt waited at the intersection, glancing behind to see if anyone had followed. The image of the woman's face, covered in scars and pockmarks, had burned into his memory.

What did she have wrong with her to make her look like that? Did she have some sort of disease? A contagious sickness?

Why had she chased after him? She'd said he had importance to her, but he'd never before met her. How could he have importance to someone he'd never met? Matt doubted that she'd meant important like she wanted to ask him questions or something like that. No, the look on her face had made it clear that what she wanted would prove considerably more dangerous for him.

What the hell was going on?

He turned back to face forward just as the light changed. The group of pedestrians moved as one to cross the street while cars came to a stop just short of the intersection.

He tried to forget his conspicuousness in the crowd, the lone white guy in a sea of Cambodians. Used to sticking out like a sore thumb, usually it didn't bother him as much as it did right now. To live in Cambodia echoed living in a fish bowl, but normally without a hook dangling nearby to grab him.

Halfway across the street, he glanced back.

Behind him, sprinting down the sidewalk, came the Indian woman, who rushed his way. Her eyes glowed red, and she stared at him directly, barreling through the pedestrians and closing the distance between them at speed.

"Uh-oh," he muttered.

Matt turned and tried to push his way through the crowd to hurry across the street.

Outside, now in the light of day, the woman appeared even more broken and scarred than he'd first thought. The burn marks and rashes looked more pronounced, and it seemed as if sections of her face had peeled away.

She ran with a limp, and struck him as almost ghastly; she looked so pale.

People shouted at him in confusion and anger when he forced his way through the crowd, but he disregarded them completely. He needed to get loose and run so that she didn't catch up to him. Those eyes promised that terrible things would happen to him if she did.

Suddenly, a motorcycle came whipping out from between two cars and swerved to a stop in front of the group of pedestrians, straddling the crosswalk and cutting everyone off. A young black woman rode it, and she had high cheekbones and attractive features. She gestured toward the rear of the bike, looking at Matt. "Get on."

"Who are you? What's going on?"

"I'll explain later; come on."

He hesitated, glancing behind him once more.

The woman pursuing him had seen the motorcycle and rider. Matt watched as the Indian woman ran directly into the road. Smoothly, she stepped past a car and into the path of an approaching motorist.

It had to be doing at least forty kilometers an hour. Matt watched in horror when she stuck out her arm and clotheslined the driver. He fell back from the impact, landing hard on the pavement, and the bike skidded to a stop a few meters away. The man's chest had to have hit her arm hard, but she seemed unfazed by it.

She turned back and moved quickly to the now-free motorcycle.

That gave all the convincing he needed. He turned back, gulped, and then climbed on the motorcycle behind the black woman.

She kicked it into gear and raced off down the road, heading west. Matt clung to her, shivering while they weaved through the traffic. Either she had supreme confidence in her abilities, supreme recklessness, or both. Most likely both. Narrowly, they swerved around parked cars, between a pair of trucks, and even up onto the sidewalk to get past a road jam.

"Where are we going?" he shouted, but his voice couldn't get over the wind.

She drove at triple the speed he could have considered reasonable, and he closed his eyes and gritted his teeth as they went.

The woman took them toward the center of Phnom Penh. The roads widened, and traffic intensified, but she showed no signs of slowing. He clung to the woman with his hands wrapped around her waist.

A glance behind showed that the Indian woman still pursued. And she drove just as recklessly and gained ground.

The motorcycle jerked to the left, and Matt clung to the woman. They swerved narrowly between two cars, and then made a sharp right turn, heading down a side street.

The maneuver didn't trip up their pursuer, who gained ground. His driver and the motorcycle shifted, and then she twisted and swung her arm back over his shoulder.

He leaned to the side, glancing up at her arm, and realized that she held a gun. The woman aimed it down the road behind and pulled the trigger.

"What the hell are you doing?" he screamed, staring past her body and down the road. He had no clue how, but she managed to keep the bike straight while she shot.

The percussion of three shots reached him, and then the woman swung around, facing forward just in time to swerve away from oncoming traffic and turn down another side street. They'd moved away from the central market now, heading for the Mekong River and outside town.

Matt's teeth chattered, and he kept thinking, *this is crazy,* over and over again. What the hell had just happened? Who were these women? And why had one tried to kill him? He remained just as afraid of the one he clung onto for dear life as the one chasing him.

They swerved down another street, and then sharply, she drove into an old shopping building filled with the carts of street peddlers. Pedestrians dove out of the way when they zipped through, heading around side shops and past food stands. They drove so close to the shoppers that he felt his clothes brush up against them.

His driver turned westward about halfway through the building and headed for a long staircase that led out of the shopping center and down to another street, which ran along the river. It took a second to realize what was about to happen, and then he panicked.

"Oh, no, no, no!" he screamed, but too late.

They reached the staircase, dipped over the top, and rolled down. Matt screamed, and his entire body vibrated painfully while they bounced down the steep stairs to the bottom, narrowly avoiding shoppers trying to climb to reach the center.

He closed his eyes, clutched the woman's stomach, and let himself scream. It felt like they would never reach the bottom.

Then, suddenly, things smoothed out, and they reached level ground once more. She turned a sharp right down a sidewalk, and they exited the building, and then swung the bike around to face the other direction and came to a complete stop a few meters from the door.

She raised the gun in front of her, aimed it at the doorway, and waited.

"Why did we stop?"

"Quiet."

"We need to go! She's still coming."

This time, she didn't answer. He could hear the motor from inside the staircase as the other motorcycle came after them, and it grew louder. Matt thought to jump off the bike and make a run for it but felt too scared.

Suddenly, the second motorcycle came bursting out of the building. The woman driving his bike fired her pistol at their pursuer. She kept firing rounds at the Indian woman, and a few might have hit.

The other woman dove off the bike when the shots started coming and sprinted behind a parked car. She ran at an unnatural speed, and it seemed eerie to watch her, like seeing someone perform an inhuman feat of strength or bend their arm in an unnatural direction. It seemed just ... wrong.

His driver turned and fired her remaining rounds into the discarded motorcycle, flattening the tires. Then she swung the motorcycle around and took off, heading into traffic.

Horns honked, but she weaved around the vehicles cleanly, turned down another side street, and then floored it. They came up to a bridge across the Mekong River, and then they reached the city outskirts and open terrain.

He glanced back but didn't see anything behind. They turned another street, then another, and still, he couldn't see any pursuit. Once they got out of the city, he would find a good hiding place for them so that he could figure out what the heck was going on.

"I think we're clear," he shouted.

She nodded and slowed. "Did she touch you?" she shouted over her shoulder.

"No," he said. "Why? What would that matter? What the hell is going on?"

"I'll explain later. We need to get to a safe place."

"Why did she come after me?"

"She wants your blood. Do you know somewhere we can go?"

"I have a few friends in the area. Cross the bridge up ahead, and then go about two kilometers."

"We need somewhere she wouldn't know about."

"Don't worry; I haven't spoken to Pol in months. No way could she know about him." He reached into his pocket, trying to grab his phone. "Let me give him a call."

"No, no calls. I don't know if she's tapped your phone or can trace you. Toss it."

"What?"

"Toss it somewhere. You won't need it."

He fished in his pocket and found his wallet, as well as something else. It felt like a little tack in his pocket. Frowning, he pulled it out and glanced at it.

The small rounded box appeared about the size of a thumbnail, and a tiny LED blinked a green light from within. It sure as hell didn't belong to him, and he couldn't identify the object.

He tried to think of where it might have come from, but nothing came to mind. Maybe when the man had bumped into him outside his church, he had put it there. But, why would someone put something into his pocket instead of taking his wallet? It didn't make any sense.

"What's this?" He leaned forward so that the woman could see.

She tensed. "Crap."

"What?"

She opened her mouth to respond but didn't get the chance. Suddenly, a car came swerving out of a cross street and side-swiped them.

The pain felt intense and sharp, and Matt flew through the air. The world flitted past, impossible for his mind to interpret, and then he hit the ground with force.

Over the next few seconds, the world faded in and out of focus, and he tried to sit up. His motorcycle companion lay on the ground next to him, and then managed to stagger to her feet while shaking her head to clear it. She looked dazed and disoriented but otherwise okay.

A car door slammed shut, and shouting came from behind. He rolled over. Feet rushed toward him. Then came gunshots and shouts, but Matt couldn't wrap his head around events.

Was it the woman from before? He didn't think so. This seemed someone new.

Matt rolled over onto his back and looked up. Someone stood over him. The man he'd seen earlier in the market—the bald one, who had brushed up against him. He knelt and fired at someone overtop the hood of a silver car.

Matt let out a groaning sound, reaching out and grabbing the man's leg. "Help!"

Or, at least, he tried to cry for assistance. Neither his arm nor his mouth would answer the call of his brain, and when he looked over to the side, he saw that his right arm had twisted backward at an odd angle, bent and covered in blood. A bone protruded, and it took him a second to realize that the bone belonged to him.

"Uhhg," he said, shifting again and letting out a sharp whimper of pain.

The man looked down at him, an angry grimace on his face. He looked disgusted, aiming his gun down, directly at his face.

"No," Matt mumbled.

He didn't even hear the gunshot.

Chapter 22

As soon as Matt Walker had held up the tracking device for her to see, Abigail knew she was in trouble. She recognized it. The device came from the Church officials that hunted after her.

She had become aware that the Catholic Church had put out a search for her for several days, she just hadn't imagined that they could catch up to her like *this*. They'd caught her off-guard completely, as well as unprepared when they rammed her bike, and she felt fairly certain she'd broken an ankle in the subsequent crash.

Matt appeared worse off, but that didn't last long, as the Church assassin finished him with a bullet to the face. Not kidding around, they seriously wanted her dead. Civilian casualties, clearly, posed no problem.

Abigail forced herself up from the ground; she couldn't waste even a second. The passenger had already gotten out of the car and attempted to get a bead on her, but his partner hadn't managed to extricate himself from the seat.

She drew her pistol and staggered toward the driver's side door. A tall man with a sharp face sat looking at her and trying to get out of the seat. He'd buckled himself in, but it had gotten damaged in the crash and had stuck. It wouldn't let him loose.

The man reached over and attempted to draw a gun from between the seats.

Abigail didn't give him the chance, but instead, aimed through the front window and fired into the car, putting a bullet between the man's eyes.

His partner came around the front of the car with his gun raised and ready to shoot. He fired at Abigail, but she'd dove out of the way already, and the bullet went over her head.

She scrambled along the back of the car, staying low, and then rounded the back to behind the trunk. She could feel as much as hear the assassin pursuing her, firing off rounds, and then one clipped her in the hip.

A flare of pain shot up her side, and she staggered, landing on her knees behind the trunk of the silver car. She forced herself to keep going, picking herself up and testing her balance. It hurt, a lot, but she could still move.

The assassin, right behind her, came in fast. Out of bullets, he had drawn a knife as he rushed around the car at her. She ducked low, dodging his first attack, and then punched him in the chest.

She remained dazed from the crash and disoriented, and her opponent knew it. No way would he let her clear her head. Sure enough, he kept pushing hard, looking for an opening, and forced Abigail to retreat and give ground. She ducked and dodged away, raising her gun to fire at him. He stepped in close to her, shoving her arm wide, as she pulled the trigger, and then grabbed her wrist.

She jerked her arm, trying to extricate herself, but the man proved too strong. He pulled her in close and stabbed with his blade. It sank into her stomach, and the blade plunged deep into her tender flesh.

She sucked in air and winced, but instead of trying to get away, she forced herself in closer to her opponent. The blade went deeper into her stomach, but she couldn't worry about that right now.

The move caught the assassin off-guard, and he tried to pull back from her to stab her again. She quick-stepped, ducked, and then grabbed his leg. Next, she yanked, tripping him up, and he fell onto his back. He landed with a hard thud on the pavement.

His arm went wide, and she stepped in and kicked the knife out of his hand. It went flying, skidding across the pavement, and landed several feet away.

The blade had severed her intestines and, maybe, punctured multiple organs, but she would have to worry about that later. The assassin rolled to his feet but proved too slow. Abigail raised her gun, hand shaking, and pulled the trigger.

Her first shot missed, and he dove behind the front of the car, out of her line of sight. In pain, she staggered after him, using one hand to hold her torn stomach and her other to aim the gun. Her body trembled, going into shock, but she didn't have time to take care of it just then.

With gritted teeth, she staggered around the side of the car but didn't see the assassin. He must have kept moving. She could see Matt, though, and realized he hadn't died yet. He lay in a pool of blood, twitching slightly and making gasping noises. She rushed over to him, seeing a wound in his head. The assassin had shot him, but it seemed only a grazing hit. Still, without treatment, he wouldn't last long. She needed to get him to help.

However, she didn't get the chance. The assassin rushed at her from behind while she knelt in front of Matt. She heard him coming and turned, raising her gun. Though she fired, he'd come too close already. He punched her in the wrist, knocking the gun away, and then kicked her hard, aiming his foot for where the knife had cut her.

The hit landed, and her body exploded in pain. She let out a gasp and tried to back away from him. He kept coming, though. Abigail couldn't win.

They'd come close to the water's edge on the bridge, and it looked about a twelve-meter drop down to the river below.

Abigail tried to defend herself, but the assassin moved too fast, and the wound on her side and the gunshot to her hip both slowed her down. She blocked one attack and punched the assassin in the kidney, but he landed a solid hit to her jaw that completely disoriented her.

She fell to the side, landing hard on her torn stomach, and then looked up at the man. He grimaced at her, cracking his knuckles, and then kicked her in the chest, knocking the air out of her lungs.

Then, he turned and walked toward her discarded gun. Barely clinging to consciousness, she could see no salvaging of this fight. She had lost. And, though she didn't know if she could survive the water, let alone the fall, she'd run out of options.

With a groan, she shifted and rolled, pushing herself backward into the open air under the bridge railing and toward the water below.

✳✳✳

Matt faded in and out of consciousness, staring up at the sky and gasping for breath. He could only see out of one eye, and the sky looked red. There one second, he'd gone the next.

At some point, a face appeared above him, looking down. It belonged to the bald man, the same one that had shot him ... he felt almost sure. Details came fuzzy, and his mind had trouble focusing on anything in particular. The man knelt in front of him, frowning.

"Still alive?"

The words sounded distant like they came from a long way off. Or, maybe, from down a long tunnel. Hard to tell. He faded out again, and more time passed, and when he opened his eyes, the man still stood over him, talking.

"... liability. I don't want to do this but—"

All of a sudden, the man's head exploded. It just disappeared, and only sky remained in the space it had occupied. Matt felt something hot and wet splash him in the face and on the exposed skin of his hands and arms.

The bald man's body hovered there for a long moment, and then it tipped forward. Matt felt afraid it would land on him, but then a hand grabbed it on the shoulder and pushed it to the side instead.

Another face appeared overtop him: the torn face of the Indian woman. She looked down at him, horrifying and disfigured, and grinned a terrible grin. Her eyes glowed red.

"Hello again," she said.

✳✳✳

Haatim felt his world collapsing. Pain and suffering became all he knew, and he grew certain that he would drown in a sea of it. His sister gone, his father dead, and he didn't know if Abigail lived or died now either. With nothing left, he had no reason to go on living.

He fought back against the nauseating waves of depression and weaknesses, the hopelessness that Nida had forced upon him when she'd attacked his psyche. These thoughts of weakness didn't belong to him, or at the very least, weren't right. He couldn't give up. Even if things had gotten so desperate, he couldn't let the demon win.

Determined, he pushed his fears and worries down, trying to get rid of them and reclaim his mind and emotions. He needed to regain control and get back to his body, or he would lose everything.

Never had he experienced anything like this, and he didn't know how to control it. The out-of-body experience only intensified as the seconds ticked past. Every single thing felt foreign while simultaneously his own. It seemed as if Nida had hijacked his identity and left him stranded with his worries and fears used against him.

However, he could overcome. He had to. Again, he pushed back against the nether, visualizing the approach back into his body and telling himself he could do it. It felt like he had to crawl out of a hole of quicksand, but he refused to give up.

Finally, he got back in his body. Exhausted, he just lay there in the alley, panting and staring up at the sky. His heart thumped violently in his chest, and he'd never felt so grateful for life.

It felt like forever before he reclaimed his thoughts and put the fears out of his mind, but probably, it took only a couple of minutes. Haatim took a series of steadying breaths, tested his muscles, and then rolled over.

He picked himself up from the hot pavement, shaking his head and forcing away the last of the lethargic feelings.

The worst part? Not only did he lose the fight but he'd also lost his confidence. He hadn't survived his encounter with Nida: she had let him live.

She seemed long gone, and the back door to the church hung open. It looked like a fight had taken place inside, and sirens blared in the distance, headed his way.

Had Abigail come here? He didn't know. Nida had said she had business, so the man running the church must have been the last of the seven bloodlines she needed. Had Nida proven successful in getting the blood? From the look of the church, he'd guess that she had.

He staggered over to the street, and the after-effects of whatever Nida had done to him wore off.

Savin came down the road to him in his beat-up old BMW and pulled up to the curb next to him. Then he rolled down his window. A concerned expression settled on his face. "What happened?"

"I don't know," Haatim said. "Did you see anything?"

"No. They had a shooting in the market. Police closed off the entire area. Are you all right?"

"I think so. You said in the market? Did you find Matt?"

"Yes, in the market. I didn't find the priest, but I heard gunshots."

"Where?"

Savin pointed. "Over that way."

Haatim rushed around the car and climbed in. "Let's go. We need to see if we can find him."

Savin drove over to where a crowd had gathered outside one of the shopping centers. They circled what looked like a destroyed motorbike, riddled with bullet holes.

Haatim didn't see anyone else, though, and it looked like more people had gathered up ahead.

"Keep going," he said.

Savin drove on down the road, and they came to a river running through town. Unlike the previous sewage one, this looked a large and powerful river.

"What's that?"

"The Mekong River," Savin said. "It rained recently, so the water level is high."

Haatim glanced around. Another crowd had gathered off to the left, near a bridge that spanned the river. A car had parked against the railing, and a smashed bike lay on the road next to it.

"Over there." He pointed. "Get us as close to it as you can."

They drove over but only managed to go a short distance before police waved for them to stop.

"I'll be right back," Haatim said.

He got out of the car and hurried over to the sidewalk. There, he pushed through the crowd. In front of the packed spectators lay three dead bodies. One remained in the car, and he recognized it as one of the Church assassins he'd seen hunting for Abigail earlier.

Another looked like it might have been his partner, but his entire head had gotten blown away by a high caliber round. Maybe from a shotgun.

The third body, he didn't recognize, and it looked like he had also gotten shot in the face. No signs remained of Abigail or Nida in the area. However, whatever had happened ... if either of them had an involvement in *this,* then they wouldn't have gotten far.

He went back to the car and climbed in. Savin looked at him in question.

"Circle the area," Haatim said.

"We should leave here before they close it off."

"One quick circle," he said. "Then we will."

Savin put the car into gear and drove back to the main road. A lot of blocked traffic and honking ensued when service vehicles arrived and police got busy asking questions. To his credit, Savin didn't drive fast or recklessly.

They went around the area, and Haatim kept his eyes peeled but didn't see Abigail or Nida. Already, it grew darker out, and if the women had gotten away, they would hide out and prove nearly impossible to find.

"You saw the shooting?" Savin asked. "At Matt's church?"

"No."

"You were there."

"I know, but I didn't see anything."

"Why not?"

"It ..." He shook his head. "It's tough to explain."

Savin nodded. "What now?"

Haatim shook his head. "I don't know. I guess they got away."

He felt frustrated while Savin drove him back to the hotel. Once there, he thanked the man and went up to his room, where he flipped on the air conditioning.

Not until now had he felt so down on himself. It frustrated him that he had come so close to finding Abigail, but then she had slipped right through his fingers.

Worse, he had also run into Nida and realized himself wholly unprepared to face her. He had discovered that he had drastically underestimated her capabilities, and had barely lived to tell the story. The fact that she had let him go and could have destroyed him so easily ate away at him.

His phone rang, startling him. Father Paladina calling. Haatim groaned. He had missed his flight. It had slipped his mind completely.

He considered not answering, and then changed his mind. He clicked on the phone.

"Hello?" the priest said.

"They're gone," Haatim said. "Both of them."

"What happened? I received word that you didn't make your flight."

Haatim had no answer.

The priest sighed, and then said, "Damn it."

"I know. I messed up."

"Did you find Abigail?"

"No, but Nida found me."

"What happened?"

"She could have killed me." The words caught in his throat. "But she didn't."

Father Paladina sighed. "I'm sorry."

He sat silently for a moment, holding the phone to his ear. "The Church assassins are dead."

"I know," Father Paladina said. "So is Abigail."

"What?"

"One of our agents called and said she drowned in the river, and moments later, Nida killed him. When I found out you hadn't gotten on the flight, I feared the worst."

"I'm sorry."

"Frieda would have killed me. But, at least you remain safe. I will call you tomorrow with details for your flight home. This time, please make sure you get on it."

"Okay."

"Get some sleep."

Haatim hung up and lay on the bed. Though physically and mentally drained, he couldn't stop his mind from worrying. Abigail had died?

No, he refused to believe that. They'd gotten it wrong before, and they could have it wrong now.

Chapter 23

Haatim got up early the next morning, several hours before his scheduled flight. Savin should come by later in the day to drive him to the airport.

He couldn't miss this flight because if he did, he'd find himself on his own. Already, he had caused the old priest innumerable problems, and now he had to attempt to make amends.

Haatim would leave Cambodia in complete disgrace, having failed utterly to locate Abigail or free his sister from the demon possessing her. She remained in there, he felt convinced, trapped by the demon, but he hadn't managed to rescue or help her at all.

It had turned into a wasted trip, and Nida had what she'd gone searching for. Matt's blood gave the last key, and now she had all seven. He had no idea what would happen now, but they had failed as much as they could have in trying to stop her.

Upset and frustrated, he couldn't just wait in his hotel room for Savin to come by, and he had several hours to kill. To that end, he decided to go for a walk to clear his head. Absently, he walked down the street and toward the market, not sure why, but he just needed to go *somewhere*.

Haatim put one leg in front of the other, not noticing pedestrians or cars, and focused only internally. He felt deeply troubled by everything that had happened and unable to understand where he had gone so wrong.

How he had fallen so short.

Nida shouldn't have been here at all. And, at the least, when he'd heard she'd arrived in the area, he should have left. But he hadn't. When she'd confronted him, he should have gotten out of there, but again, he hadn't. His arrogance and self-righteousness appalled him.

In his delusion, he'd believed he could dismiss the demon back to hell and save his sister. He had thought he could end it all now, just dispel the demon, using the power that Father Paladina had taught him. After all, he'd used it in Raven's Peak and again at Vatican City, and Father Paladina had proven to him that he could do it on command.

However, he'd found out that he couldn't do anything. Not when it counted.

He had faced his sister but proven entirely unsuccessful in saving her. To make things even worse, he hadn't done one single thing to help Nida. He'd shown himself too weak.

He kept walking, utterly absorbed in his self-pity and doubt.

Had Raven's Peak just happened as a fluke? Just some silly accident? He remembered how he'd felt at that moment, walking through the factory and the hail of dangerous tools in the air. He recalled the demon in the basement and how he'd destroyed it. He had banished it to hell, but only a weak demon, barely an infant compared to the one inside Nida.

He'd thought he could save his sister's life. He *knew* how to use the power. And yet, it hadn't worked.

Not only that, but the demon had crushed him utterly and taken control over his soul. The feeling of getting dominated had faded, but it remained present in the back of his mind. The fear that he would never get strong enough to save her consumed him.

It also meant that he would never take on Nida in a straightforward confrontation. He had barely survived this encounter, and opening himself up like that again would not only prove risky, it would be suicidal. For sure, she wouldn't allow him to walk away a second time.

These thoughts swirled around his head as he walked. His legs ached, but he kept going. Soon, he found himself back at the market, and then he continued past and toward the bridge where they had found the wrecked vehicles the previous day. All signs of a struggle had gone, except for a few rust-colored patches that could only have come from blood.

All signs of the conflict had disappeared. Wiped away.

Haatim walked along the river's edge, heading toward the outskirts of the city and following the water downstream. He should turn back to meet up with Savin but dreaded the idea of returning. And he dreaded leaving Phnom Penh without finding Abigail. She remained here. The Church thought her dead, but he knew in his heart that she lived. She had to.

Nida might remain here, too. She could lay in wait, out there somewhere, watching and preparing to attack him once more. The thought gave him chills, but he did his best to bury it down deep and not think about it.

Resolute, he kept going, lost in his thoughts, until finally, he found himself well outside the city proper. It shocked him, feeling as if he'd just come out of a dream. Never in his entire life had he felt so sore and fatigued, and it hit him all at once that he had walked for a long, long time.

Several hours had passed, and he stood a long way from the airport. Definitely, he would arrive late for his flight.

No, he realized, not late. When he checked his phone, he saw that he had missed it completely.

Not again. He had gotten so distracted that he hadn't even noticed just how long he'd stayed out here. His phone also showed that he had multiple missed calls, the first from Savin, and the next several from Father Paladina. The ringer remained on, so how had he missed the sound?

He shook his head and let out a deep sigh. Great, on top of everything, now he would have to beg forgiveness again and see if Father Paladina could reschedule the flight.

At the river, a few-dozen meters to his right, something caught his attention. At the shore, something rested there, ebbing in the shallow current. From this distance, he couldn't identify it, but it looked like a bundle. A large bundle that had washed up out of the river.

He walked over to it, frowning, and then his eyes went wide.

Abigail.

✳✳✳

"What do you mean?"

"It's her." Haatim knelt over Abigail and held the phone up to his ear with his shoulder. Frieda waited on the other end of the line, sleepy in the middle of the night back in Ohio. "She's injured."

"Alive?"

"Barely," he said. "Her stomach's cut open, and she got shot in the hip, but she's still breathing."

"Can you get her to a doctor?"

"I don't know."

"How did you find her?"

"I don't know. I went out walking and ... it feels like something led me here. I didn't even realize where I'd come until I saw her on the ground. I missed my flight, though, so Father Paladina will get furious with me again. I shall have to call Savin for a ride."

"Who?"

"My translator and driver. He's helped me."

Frieda stayed silent for a moment. "Don't."

"Don't what?"

"Call him," she said. "Father Paladina knows who he is, right?"

"Yes."

"I received a call from Father Paladina a short while ago. He said that two of their own had gotten killed."

"I know. I saw them. I think Abigail killed one and Nida the second."

"Yes," Frieda said. "Before the second one died, he told the Church that he'd taken care of Abigail."

"That's what Father Paladina told me. He thinks her dead."

"And we need to keep it that way."

"What?"

"Father Paladina, though a good man, can't find out that Abigail lives, or he'll have no choice but to report it."

"They'll find out, eventually."

"Not today, and certainly not because of us."

Haatim fell silent, and then said, "Okay."

"The Church knows that Nida killed their assassin, so all of their energy has fallen on catching her right now. We *cannot* let them know that Abigail survived the fight."

"Then, what do I do?"

"Take care of her. Make sure she stays okay."

"She's still bleeding. I have no idea what to do."

"Try to find a local clinic and get her help, but whatever you do, don't let Father Paladina know, or anyone associated with the Church."

"What do I tell him?"

"Don't tell him anything. I'll talk to him and let him know I made other arrangements. Just don't take his calls."

Haatim frowned down at the phone. "Okay. I'll do my best. But, if Abigail gets worse, I'll call Savin for help."

"Haatim, this is important."

"So is this. I won't let Abigail die."

"If you tell the Church that she lives, you might as well just kill her yourself."

Haatim stayed silent.

"Keep her alive, Haatim," Frieda said, finally. "I'll set up travel plans to get you both out of Cambodia. Just wait for my call."

"What should I do until then?"

Frieda took a while to reply, "Pray."

"Great advice."

"I'm on my way to meet up with Dominick and Mitchell. I'll be in touch."

✳✳✳

It took Haatim almost an hour of searching around the area to find someone who spoke English, and then another hour for them to find a medical professional who could help Abigail.

In the end, it cost him all the money he had in his wallet—about eighty bucks—to get a doctor to look at Abigail and patch up her wounds. A small price to pay, though, and he would have given anything to keep her safe.

The fact that the wounds didn't seem as bad as he'd first thought gave him encouragement. Though deep, they didn't turn out as wide as they might have. The wound on her hip didn't even look that bad at all, in fact, and had barely taken a grazing hit.

The doctor seemed encouraged as well and seemed to think she would make a full recovery after a few weeks. He bandaged her up, gave Haatim medicine to give her over the next few days, and advised him to keep her injuries dry and replace the bandages daily.

Then, Haatim found a place for them to wait, in the home of the man who spoke English. There, he just sat around. How long would it take for Frieda to call him back?

Abigail remained unconscious through it all, though her breathing had deepened from when he'd found her. With her wet and dirty from the river, he spent some time with a bucket and rag cleaning and drying her.

Frieda called him a few hours after he had settled in and informed him that she had found him transportation. A boat a few hours south of his location would take them to Thailand.

From there, they would get on a flight out of Southeast Asia and to England, and from there to the United States. She had arranged everything, including setting up a hire car for him from the nearby rental agency.

The friendly man he'd stayed with gave him a ride over to pick up the car and helped him load Abigail into the backseat. Haatim dreaded the idea of driving on the Cambodian roads with the other wild drivers, but right now, that seemed like his best option.

Father Paladina called several more times, but Haatim didn't answer. He had no charger with him and, after a while, his phone ran out of power. He drove straight through, occasionally checking to make sure Abigail continued breathing and stayed comfortable.

By the time he arrived at the docks, night had fallen, and he felt exhausted. The man who waited for him with the boat didn't speak any English but helped get Abigail loaded safely. After only a short wait, they got on their way. Haatim thought to try calling Frieda once more but changed his mind.

He fell asleep during the trip and awoke sometime later. The boatman stood poking him on the shoulder. They had docked, and the sun made its slow ascent. Though tired and sore and barely able to walk, they didn't have a lot of time to stop and rest.

Together, they unloaded Abigail and set her on the ground. Haatim assumed they had reached Thailand now, but found it impossible to tell. The dock itself seemed little more than an empty shook in the woods near a dirt road.

Frieda had said someone would wait here for him, but no one came into sight. The man with the boat spoke quickly to Haatim and then took off, guiding his boat away and leaving them stranded.

He spent the time by checking over and replacing Abigail's bandages. The wounds on her stomach had started to heal, and the shot to her side had almost gone.

Whatever had happened to her in childhood must allow her to mend faster. No way could she do this well in normal circumstances. These wounds should have taken weeks to close, but already looked like little more than deep cuts. She still hadn't woken, but her breathing came easy, and she seemed in hardly any pain.

It took almost four hours for a car to show up. It felt like mosquitos had eaten him alive, and he spent most of his time swatting them away from him and Abigail. He could hardly believe that so many of them could exist, and he must have given a delicious treat considering how fervently they attacked his flesh.

The car—with yet another driver that didn't speak English—finally pulled up to the dock, and wordlessly, a man helped him load Abigail into the backseat. They then drove through the countryside to an airport. A small two-seater plane waited for them. Dirty and old, it scared the hell out of Haatim, but he didn't see any alternatives.

They loaded Abigail inside and took off. The same man who'd driven them here also flew the plane. After only a short jaunt, they landed at a larger international airport.

By the time they touched down, Abigail had woken but remained groggy. This came as a relief for him because he felt exhausted and had run out of the energy to keep carrying her. Haatim helped guide her through the customs lines and to their waiting area. Once they got ready to board their last flight to England and safety, he allowed himself to relax and feel a little more comfortable.

Almost asleep, something touched his neck. He shifted away and opened his eyes. Abigail traced the bruise lines from the chain injury. She still looked disoriented and groggy. "What happened?"

He'd forgotten about the marks on his neck and had left his scarf in Cambodia. When he settled back, Abigail rested her head on his shoulder.

"It happened in Vatican City," he said. "Father Paladina tricked me into facing a demon and ..."

Haatim glanced over and realized that Abigail had fallen asleep already. He chuckled to himself and shook his head. Now that he could relax, he realized how happy he felt. After how terribly the last few days had gone in Cambodia, just knowing Abigail remained alive and safe meant everything to him. He loved having her head resting on his shoulder.

Content, he let her sleep until they had to board, and then helped her onto the plane, where she promptly fell asleep once more. Then they got on their way to Frieda and Dominick back in the States.

Chapter 24

"Are you sure about this?" Nervous, Mitchell paced back and forth across the front room of his shop. "I mean, do you feel sure that we should do it this way? She can get kind of ... angry."

Dominick, seated behind the register, watched Mitchell pace and struggle to hide his annoyance. He had asked the man to sit down and relax at least four times already, but it made no difference. Mitchell remained too nervous and anxious to sit still, and the waiting had gotten to him.

In all honesty, Dominick couldn't blame him, as the waiting had gotten to him as well. After what had happened at the Reinfer estate and everything else going on, he had a hard time keeping his cool.

Frieda now ran at about a day late in getting to them. Something had happened to Haatim, which had slowed her progress while she tried to get that sorted, but she should arrive at any minute.

Part of him worried that she knew they planned to confront her as soon as she arrived at Mitchell's shop, but at the same time, that seemed a crazy idea. How could she possibly have them sussed? He hadn't even known himself until he got back here from the Reinfer place.

Nervous as hell, he felt more than a little apprehensive about what would happen when Frieda arrived. They would ambush her with questions about her past and ask for the truth of recent events. She had lied to him, and he worried that she might have known something about the huge monster that had attacked at the estate.

"I mean, how we will even know if she tells the truth or not? She's a good liar. An amazing liar, even."

"Mitchell."

"Come on; you telling me that it doesn't have you worried?"

"Of course I'm worried. But, just ask yourself, can you remember the last time that worrying about something helped you fix it? We just need to stay patient. She'll get here."

"But what if it all turns out true? What if she *is* working with the cult?"

"It won't."

"But what if it *does?*"

Dominick gave him a look, making it clear he wouldn't discuss that possibility. Mitchell threw up his hands in frustration and resumed pacing.

Dominick still struggled to wrap his mind around what they had discovered and the ramifications of what Mitchell had told him about Frieda and Arthur. Even with what he'd told Mitchell, he remained terrified: if even part of it held any merit ...

He couldn't fathom how Frieda would withhold something like this from him. From everyone. Did anyone else on the Council know about their origins, or had she kept them all in the dark, too? He had believed that events in Switzerland had occurred because of Aram Malhotra, but could it have related back to Frieda and what she and Arthur had gotten involved in?

He didn't know.

Didn't know if he wanted to know.

For sure, he hated the idea of confronting Frieda, but it had to be done.

"Are you sure we want to do this?"

"I'm sure," Dominick said. "We can't continue to work with Frieda until we know the truth."

"Yeah, but what if it's *all* true? What if she *did* collude with The Ninth Circle?"

"Collude?"

"Work with, then." Mitchell waved his hand.

"I know what collude means. Just wondering why you chose that word."

"If she *is* an enemy, what do we do?"

"We'll cross that bridge if we come to it."

"But what if we do?"

"Then we'll deal with it."

"But it would mean that everything we thought about the Council has turned out a lie. It would mean that we've helped the wrong side."

Dominick sighed. "Let's not jump to conclusions. Frieda deserves the opportunity to explain herself."

Mitchell frowned, still pacing. "Are you armed?"

Dominick's eyes widened. "Excuse me?"

"You have a gun, right? You know, in case ..."

Dominick stared at him, narrowing his eyes. "In case what?"

Mitchell hesitated. "We don't know how she'll react when we confront her. I just want to make sure we've prepared."

"So, you think we should just shoot her?"

"No. I mean, what if she—"

"No, we don't know how she'll react, do we? Like I said, let's not jump to any conclusions."

Even as he spoke the words, however, he couldn't help but think seriously about what Mitchell had said. He couldn't suppress a subconscious urge to tap his leg where he'd strapped his pistol, feeling the gun as it rested against his leg. The weight of it comforted.

He had another holdout pistol in a holster wrapped around his calf; his backup piece. He hoped—prayed—he wouldn't need either, but honestly, had no idea what might happen.

"Should I lock the door?"

"Why?"

"In case people try to come in."

"We put up the 'closed' sign. That should prove enough."

"But still, what happens if someone just walks in?"

"Who'll do that?"

"I don't know. I mean, I have customers. Even a few regulars."

"I've never seen a single customer here."

"I mean, not a *lot* of them or anything, but I do have *some*."

He trailed off at the sound of a car door closing. It echoed to them from outside. Mitchell stopped, mid-stride, and then rushed over to the front glass window. He peered out, and then backed away slowly. "She's here."

"Okay."

"She's coming. What do we do?"

"Calm down." Dominick rose from his seat. "Don't overreact. Take some deep breaths and relax. Everything will work out fine."

Did he say that for Mitchell or himself?

A few seconds later, the front door of the shop opened. Frieda strode in, carrying a bag and moving with purpose. She took a few hesitant steps into the room, and then saw Mitchell and Dominick waiting for her. After a glance between the two of them, she frowned. "You already know? Did Haatim call you guys?"

"Know what?"

"About Abigail. She's alive. The Church got it wrong, but she's hurt. Nida found the last bloodline and has everything she needs to complete the ritual."

Mitchell and Dominick exchanged a glance.

"But that's not what you have those expressions for, is it?" she asked. "What's wrong? What's going on?"

The two men exchanged another glance, and then Dominick cleared his throat. "Frieda. We need to talk."

✳✳✳

Calm, Frieda walked to the front of the room and set her bag on the counter next to Dominick. She looked at him, her expression mixed apprehension and worry. Two looks he had rarely seen on her face in the entire time he'd known her.

She argued, trying to misdirect, "We don't have time for this. Haatim is on his way here with Abigail. Nida has a good lead on us, and we don't even know where she's going."

"Frieda ..."

"Whatever you have to say to me, it can wait. It *has* to wait. They should get here in less than twelve hours, which means we have that much time to figure out what we should do next."

"I know, but this is important."

"What could possibly have more importance than dealing with Nida and stopping all of this before anyone else gets hurt? Now, come on; we need to get everything ready and—"

"Did the Council create Surgat?"

"What? Ridiculous. Did Mitchell tell you that nonsense? One of his crazy conspiracy theories?"

Dominick took a deep breath. "Did you perform a ritual on Abigail?"

Frieda froze, body tensing. The expression on her face showed utter shock and disbelief, mixed in with a hint of shame.

Dominick had his answer.

Without thinking, he slid his pistol free of the holster and held it at his side. Though he didn't aim it at her, the threat came loud and clear. His hand trembled, and beads of sweat formed on his forehead.

"Do you serve them? Do you work for the Ninth Circle, now?"

"What? No, of course not. You know I don't."

"Do I? Do I know anything about you anymore?" He turned toward Mitchell and nodded. "Show her."

Mitchell pulled out the stack of papers that Abigail had brought to him a few weeks earlier and set them on the counter. Frieda looked at them, and her face fell when she recognized them.

"He kept them," she mumbled, shaking her head. "I begged Arthur to destroy those."

"Arthur helped you with the ritual," Dominick said. "Mitchell told me everything. The leaders of The Ninth Circle formed the Council, and *we* created Surgat originally. The Council bound one of their own to the demon. One of *our* own."

"It isn't that simple," Frieda said, speaking slowly. "Please, put down the gun."

Dominick ignored her. "It's all right there in the text. The historical account. The *real* history of the Council and the Order. We're the cult we fight against."

"*Were*," Frieda said. "Not anymore. Yes, the original Council created Surgat, and yes, we did come from a sect of the Ninth Circle. My forebears helped bring Surgat into existence through a ritual, but they also stopped him and locked him away in his hellish prison. They realized their mistake and the error of their ways."

"Or they simply got caught and begged forgiveness."

"We stopped Surgat."

"Out of necessity."

"Maybe. I wasn't there. But I do know that the Church let us live and gave us purpose."

"The Church forgave you?"

"They didn't forgive us. They didn't kill us either. They murdered every cultist they could find that didn't help them stop Surgat and spared our forebears. The seven that remained formed into the Council. It proved, depending on how you look at it, either a penance or a reward."

"Why have I never heard any of this before?"

"Almost no one knows of it," Frieda said. "Dominick, could you please put the gun away?"

He hesitated, and then he slid his weapon back into his holster.

Frieda let out a deep breath when it disappeared and rubbed her face. "Thank you."

"Where do these papers come from?"

"That copy of the text is one of the final surviving pieces of our legacy that tells the whole story. The Catholic Church considers it too dangerous to let out of the archives, but my family had a copy. My father said it gave a reminder and that we should never forget. We spent centuries trying to escape that legacy, and gradually, the Church trusted us more and more. We found a way we could serve them, and they helped disguise our truth."

Dominick shook his head. "Insane. Then it's all true: our legacy comes from the very cult we actively hunt."

She sighed. "That makes the whole reason the Church kept those original seven alive. They'd worked in The Ninth Circle; they knew how the cult operated, and the Church could use them as a weapon against them. For years, the original Council hunted down their friends and allies, and that's how the Hunters formed. The Ninth Circle hates us for betraying them as much as we hate them."

Dominick stayed silent for a long time, digesting all the information. "How could you keep this from us?"

"My father taught the whole history to me, and he told me it made the great shame of my family that we helped bring such evil into this world. Surgat killed hundreds of innocent people before my forebears stopped him. He said that our duty had become to wash the stain clean from our legacy, but that it remained a legacy for me alone."

"The Council didn't know?"

"They knew none of this. Even Jill Reinfer had no idea of the legacy of our ancestors. Her father did, but he never passed it on to his daughter. He didn't trust her with the information."

"For good reason."

She nodded. "She would have used it against us."

"So, what happens now?"

"Nothing has changed," Frieda said. "We still have to stop Nida. The only difference is that now you know the true stake of this."

As she said it, she looked over at Mitchell. He stood as still as a statue, bug-eyed with a concerned look on his face, and shocked by all of this.

Dominick felt conflicted. Though Frieda had lied and kept things from him, he'd known her most of his life, and she'd never lied without good reason, and everything she said sounded reasonable. It still hurt that she'd withheld it, but he understood her reasons.

Even regarding Abigail, he couldn't blame Frieda for wanting to save her life. After all of this, he didn't know whether he would have done the same thing or not.

Part of him remained unsure if he could trust her, but he couldn't stay in two minds about this. Either he would have to trust that they worked on the same side, or he would need to turn his back on her completely.

In the end, it came down to knowing Frieda as a person. She might not have told him everything, but he knew her heart, and Frieda had the heart of a good woman.

He would have to trust her.

"Both of you know the full truth, now," Frieda said.

"This ... this ..." Mitchell shook his head. "Holy hell."

"You said Haatim located Abigail?" Dominick asked.

"Yes. He's bringing her here."

"How did she get hurt?"

"The Church found her. They tried to murder her, and they believe themselves successful."

"Why does the Church want her dead?"

"Not just her," Frieda said. "Father Paladina warned me that they won't come after just Abigail now."

"They want us too."

"Yes. How did you know?"

"Mitchell told me. Is it true? How could it be true?"

She turned to Mitchell. "How did *you* know?"

"I have contacts," he said, stiff with defense. "Friends you don't even know about."

She looked at him, skeptical, but didn't refute his claim. "All of us. They have ordered for all of us to be killed."

✳✳✳

A moment of silence slipped past.

"What do you mean, 'all of *us*'?" Mitchell asked into the deathly quiet. "Does that ... does that include me, now, too?"

"Anyone who has an affiliation with the Council will get hunted down and killed by the Catholic Church," Frieda said.

Mitchell hesitated. "So ... is that a yes? I'm on the list?"

"Yes."

"Crap."

"Why?" Dominick asked. "Why would they do this?"

"I suppose they've decided we've outlived our usefulness. You know our history. Maybe they think we've returned to our old ways. Or maybe it's just punishment for what Aram did. He didn't only betray us but the Church as well. I don't know, but they intend to wipe the entire Council from existence and finish what Nida started."

Another moment passed. "Crap," Mitchell said again, and then rushed to the back of the store. "I need to pack."

Dominick and Frieda both ignored him. Dominick asked, "How do we get them to stop?"

"They won't."

"Even if we stop Nida?"

"In their eyes, Nida is a symptom of the disease. They intend to make deep cuts with their scalpel to protect themselves."

"Then, shouldn't we run?" Mitchell popped his head back out of the rear room of the shop. "Get the hell out of dodge and find somewhere to hide until all of this blows over?"

"The Catholic Church has existed for thousands of years," Frieda said. "And they have a long memory. This won't just 'blow over.'"

"All the more reason to find a great hiding place."

Dominick stared at Frieda. After a moment, he nodded. "Hiding isn't what we stand for," he said. "Aram created this mess for us, but we have just as much accountability as him for letting things go this far."

"True." Frieda nodded. "It doesn't end with Aram. We all hold responsibility for the decisions we've made. I, myself, have made more mistakes than I can count. I will not stop until either the demon inside Nida goes back to hell, or I do. The two of you, however, can choose for yourself. The Council has disbanded, as well as the Order of Hunters. You no longer have to accept my commands, Dominick."

He nodded. "I know."

"You can return to your husband and find somewhere safe to live if you want. I have some funds I can acquire for you to help you start over, and with new identities, you could disappear and begin a new life. The Church doesn't see you as a priority for elimination, so they might forget about you after a few years and just let you go."

"A tempting offer," Dominick said. "But I'll have to decline, with all due respect. Nida remains too dangerous, and from everything I've heard, Surgat is much worse. If the Church has too much arrogance to bother chasing down the real threat, then someone has to stop her before innocent people die."

"I hoped you might say that."

"I wish you would have told me the truth … about all of this. But, I understand your reasons. I'll stay in this until the end."

Frieda turned and glanced over at Mitchell.

"How much money are we talking about?" Mitchell rubbed his chin. "Do you have enough for *me* to retire and live comfortably, or …?"

Frieda frowned. "Mitchell."

"Just kidding," he said. "I promised Arthur I would look after Abigail after he'd gone, and what kind of brother would I make if I let down my deceased sibling? I'm not sure how much help I can offer, but I'll stick with you guys until the end."

Frieda nodded, and a relieved expression washed over her face. "Good. I'm glad that we've got that settled."

"So, this is happening for real?" Dominick asked. "We'll try and stop Nida?"

"Yes. As soon as we find out where she went to, we'll need to move. Now, we don't have a lot of time before Haatim and Abigail get here, so let's get to work."

Chapter 25

*H*aatim.

The word hit him like a tornado, popping up in the middle of nowhere. It ripped through his mind, and an intense feeling of confusion hit him when he tried to understand.

One second he lay unconscious, and the next he had become fully aware but unable to comprehend events. The last thing he remembered, he'd stepped onto the plane in England with Abigail to start the last leg of his journey to the United States, but no more than that.

He didn't feel like he rode on a plane right now, though, or anywhere else for that matter. Just a floating emptiness, like a dream but unlike any dream he had ever experienced before. It felt too real, too precise.

Haatim.

His arms pinned in place, an unconscionable weight rested across his body and kept him still. Paralyzed, it felt like he floated on a bed of salt water, resting atop it yet unable to sink inside.

Haatim.

His sister's voice: not the one controlled by the demon but rather the one he'd known and loved growing up. The sweet little girl who had always teased and made fun of him. At first, he thought it a memory, something from their past, but then he realized it came from the here and now.

Rather, the words came from right next to him. As though she whispered into his ear, but he couldn't turn his head to see her in the emptiness.

Her voice sounded like the little girl he'd looked after before she had gotten sick. Always giggling, happy, and full of life. She remained out there somewhere, calling to him, far out in the darkness of the ether, and he could hear the fear in her voice.

The sensation seemed less like she said words, though, and more as if they passed through him like a feeling. Haatim couldn't wrap his mind around what had just happened and only knew that it *continued* to happen. His sister had called out to him, and she'd tried to reach him.

Come find me.

Her voice sounded weak, barely audible. He didn't know her location, or even his right now. Did he remain on the plane, or somewhere else? He didn't know. It all blended, and reality no longer made any sense. Haatim couldn't focus on anything except that his sister was in trouble, and he had to save her.

Save her?

The thought felt muddied and heavy. Wrong, somehow. He didn't need to try to save her; he needed to try to stop her, right? She'd become the enemy, the evil demon trying to wreak havoc on the world. She had murdered the entire Council and countless other innocent people.

His sister had gone, died, and whatever inhabited her body had turned her into something else entirely, right?

Right?

Please, come.

What if she *hadn't* gone, after all? What if he had gotten it right all along, and his sister did need help? Unfortunately, he couldn't help her. He had tried and failed.

But, what if the real Nida remained inside there, trapped and suffocating under the weight of the demon? Haatim felt paralyzed, unable to move, but perhaps that gave a reflection of what Nida felt somewhere out in the world as she passed emotions to him.

If that proved the case, then he had to try and rescue her. Damn the risk. Damn his weakness. He wouldn't give up until she became free or he died. Haatim couldn't leave his sister under the control of the demon.

He couldn't just abandon her. But, even if that proved the case, how could he possibly save her? She could remain anywhere out in the world by now.

No, not anywhere.

Raven's Peak.

The demon had gone back. He knew that with one hundred percent certainty, even though he had no idea *how* he knew it. The feeling came clear and blinding in the dark ether, and he knew it as right.

Haatim, I don't have much time.

He tried calling back, *I'm coming.* But something else intruded. Not only his sister had a presence now.

He could feel the demon, and it loomed in all its fury.

Haatim tried to push back, to break free of whatever held him in place, but it proved of no use. He felt helpless and weak, pathetic and broken. His sister felt this way too, trapped inside her body with the demon.

And now it had come for him.

He struggled, crying out and feeling as if in the midst of drowning. He suffocated. He couldn't breathe.

And the demon got closer.

It reached out to him.

✳✳✳

A tap on his shoulder jerked him awake. The sudden glaring light in his face made him blink and cover his face, and it took him a second to realize he could move.

He could move.

The relief of that knowledge overwhelmed him, and he let out a somewhat delirious chuckle while his body relaxed. It took a moment to orient himself, and he saw that he remained on the flight to John Glenn International Airport. He had simply fallen asleep and dreamed.

Several of the nearby passengers sat staring at him, confused expressions on their faces. A sheen of sweat covered him, and all his muscles felt sore and tight like they had all clenched simultaneously. He relaxed and leaned back in his seat, still breathing hard but bringing himself under control.

"You okay?"

The voice caught him off guard. Abigail occupied the window seat next to him. She had a concerned look on her face as she studied him. At least she looked healthy now, completely awake and healed after her recent injuries.

It brought relief to see her doing so well but also a shock. She barely seemed like she'd gotten hurt less than two days ago to the point of nearly dying. If he hadn't watched her experience that injury in Cambodia personally, he wouldn't have believed it had ever happened.

She had slept for the last several days, waking up only long enough to eat before passing out once more. This made for the first time he had seen her wide awake and coherent since the injury.

"Yeah," he said. "I'm okay, but I should ask you that question. How do you feel?"

"Better." She shook her head and tapped her side. "It hardly hurts anymore."

"How's that possible? You almost died."

Abigail let out a sigh. "I know. I think it comes down to whatever the cult did to me. I've healed super quickly, and I feel ... different. Are you sure you feel all right? You talked in your sleep."

"What did I say?"

"It sounded like gibberish, but you called for your sister. You seemed terrified. Did you have a nightmare?"

He hesitated, and then said, "I don't know."

"What do you mean?"

"It felt so real. I've had nightmares before, but this seemed something different. More vivid. And I felt fully present in it. It had me paralyzed but awake and somewhere else."

"Your mind will paralyze you while you sleep," Abigail said. "It happens to me, too."

He shook his head. "Not like this. This ... I sensed something else out there, too. Like I wasn't alone in my head."

She tilted her head. "What do you mean?"

"I felt the demon. The one controlling Nida. And, I felt Nida, too."

"Alive?"

"Yes. Or, at least, part of her."

Abigail frowned. "You could feel the demon?"

"I ..." Haatim felt unsure how to explain. "I think I bridged a connection between the demon and myself back in Cambodia. A telepathic bond, and I guess it remains open. The demon seemed surprised to find it active."

"How did you do that?"

"In Raven's Peak, when I walked across the floor of the factory and nothing could hit me, it felt like that, only I can control it a little bit better. Father Paladina helped me."

Abigail sat in silence, and then said, "I haven't heard that name in a long time."

"You knew him?"

"An old friend of Arthur's."

"That echoes what Frieda told me. He seems like a good guy."

Abigail chewed her bottom lip. "Sometimes."

Haatim waited for her to elaborate, but she didn't. Instead, she asked, "Where are we going?"

"Ohio. Dominick and Frieda are already out there waiting for us."

"Us? They know about me?"

"I told them. You didn't want me to?"

She didn't respond immediately. "I don't know."

"Why didn't you tell us you lived after the train? Why didn't ... why didn't you tell me?"

"It's complicated."

"Complicated? How? We thought you'd died. You let *me* think you'd died."

"Abigail *did* die," she said. "Whatever happened to me, I'm not the same person."

"Yes, you are."

"No, I'm not, Haatim. Whatever happened to me, it changed me in ways you can't even imagine, and I can't control it. I ... didn't want to hurt any of you, so I kept going after Nida."

He frowned. "I get it, but, you still should have told me."

"Maybe," she said.

"You went to Cambodia following Nida?"

Abigail nodded. "Yes. I chased her out there but didn't know what she planned, and then I realized she'd gone after Matt Walker."

"You don't know why?"

She shook her head. "I thought that maybe if I got hold of him first, I could use him as leverage to stop her plan. But then I worked out that the Church had come after me, which made things considerably more difficult. She forced my hand, though, when she went after him."

"She needed his blood," Haatim said.

"Why?"

"A ritual to summon a demon here. The one that keeps Arthur in hell."

Abigail scrunched up her face into a frown.

"What?" he asked. "You know something?"

"No," she said. "I just ... never mind."

"Anyway, she plans to collect blood from the seven bloodlines that locked away Surgat."

"Surgat the demon?"

"Long story," Haatim said. "Basically, he's the evil entity that Nida wants to let loose with a ritual, and she needs the blood of the original Council members for it."

"But, you said to summon him here?"

"Yes."

She had that same look on her face like she knew more than she let on. Haatim thought to push the issue but changed his mind. He remained grateful just to have Abigail back, alive and in one piece, and didn't want to jeopardize that by pushing her for information. If it proved something important, she would tell him.

"So that explains why she tried to get Matt," Abigail said. "I saw what she wanted and thought I could keep him safe. Did you see what happened to him?"

Haatim sighed. "Dead."

Abigail echoed his sigh. "Damn it."

"He made for the last of the bloodlines Nida needs. Now she has all seven and can release Surgat."

"Then, how do we stop her?"

"I have no idea," Haatim said. "But, I do know where she went."

"Where?"

"Raven's Peak," he said.

The dream/nightmare had faded in his memory, but that detail remained as vivid as when he'd first felt it. Without a doubt, he knew that the demon controlling his sister had gone to somewhere in Raven's Peak.

"Why there?"

"I have no idea," he said. "And I don't know *how* I know that she went out there, but she did."

Abigail nodded, and he could see a look of concern hidden just under the surface.

"You think you reached out for the demon mentally?" she asked.

"Or my sister. Or, maybe, she reached out to me. I don't know, exactly."

"Let's say you did create a connection. Do you think that the demon reached out to you and not the other way around?"

Haatim sat in silent contemplation for a moment. "You mean trying to manipulate me?"

"It knew you would want to hear from your sister, so maybe, it just gave you what you wanted."

"You reckon that, maybe, Nida did call me at all?"

"I'm just saying that, perhaps, it knew that you wanted to get that message."

"Maybe," he said, despite believing that his sister remained alive. The demon could manipulate quite a few things, but when it came to that, he felt certain that Nida still lived in there. "We know where the demon plans to perform the ritual, so whether we trap it or not, we still need to go."

"I know." Abigail leaned back in her chair and looked out through the window. "I just wanted to make sure you didn't get your hopes up."

Haatim nodded. "I can see no other way."

Chapter 26

Mitchell's shop looked the same as Abigail remembered from a few weeks earlier. From the first time that she'd even known Mitchell existed—something that both Frieda and Arthur had kept from her for her entire life.

A few weeks? Had no more time than that passed? It felt like a lifetime ago when she'd first set foot in this building. Then, she'd only begun to experience the changes within and remained blissfully unaware of the turn her life was about to take.

Everything that had happened to her made a sick kind of sense now, especially after speaking with Haatim during the flight. He had no idea about how close he had come to the truth, brushing up against it without ever actually seeing it. Everything he'd told her was true, except for one crucial detail, and one that clicked into place as she remembered the most horrible moment of her life, strapped to the table while The Ninth Circle performed their horrible ritual upon her.

Haatim glanced at her, and then pushed open the door. He went inside, and she followed him into the dark storefront. Frieda talked from over near the register on the far side of the shop, but she stopped when they entered. All three of them—Dominick, Frieda, and Mitchell—turned to face her.

"Abi," Dominick said, rushing over and wrapping her up in a huge hug. "Thank God you're all right."

Frieda nodded at her, and then turned back to the stack of papers set out in front of them on the counter. She never had seemed one for shows of affection, and Abigail could appreciate that. Abigail didn't like them either.

She extricated herself from Dominick's hug and walked to the counter. There, she turned, instead, to the papers they stood looking at to try and find out what they discussed. It looked like the copied documents she had pulled from Arthur's home before driving out here and confronting Mitchell. Pictures lay scattered in as well.

She felt eyes on her and glanced over. Mitchell stood and stared at her, but he didn't say anything. His expression appeared unreadable, and she found it difficult to tell if it made him glad to see her or not. Abigail glanced up at him, and he turned away.

The store looked dim, though every light glowed. One picture, in particular, caught her attention. Grainy, it looked like a still from a security camera and showed a tall and thin gray monster with talons at the ends of its arms. It stood in a richly decorated hallway.

"What is that?"

"No clue," Dominick said. "I ran across one in Pennsylvania. Barely made it out with my head still attached."

"I believe it's a demon," Frieda said.

"Here?" Abigail asked.

"Nida must have summoned it."

"Holy hell," Haatim said breathlessly, looking at the picture. "That thing is what nightmares are made of. I can't believe it's real."

Abigail could hardly believe it either, but she realized that it could certainly prove possible. She thought back to the train and the fire demon that had nearly killed her, and all at once, knew better than to underestimate Nida.

"What are the rest of these?" she asked.

"Rituals," Frieda said. "And spells. Anything we might be able to use to help us locate Nida."

"Actually," Haatim said, setting down his little travel bag and stepping up next to Abigail. "That won't be necessary. I know where the demon went. And my sister."

Frieda and Dominick exchanged a glance. "What?"

"Raven's Peak," Haatim said. "Nida—the real Nida—reached out to me, and I managed to pinpoint her location."

Everyone fell silent.

Then Frieda said in gentle tones, "Haatim, Nida has gone."

"You said the same thing about Abigail. You gave up on her, too. Remember?"

Frieda didn't have a good response, looking instead at the papers in front of her.

"I know you all think that," Haatim said. "But when I went to Cambodia, I created a connection to her and the demon. It could have killed me but didn't, and now I know its location, or at least, where it plans on going."

"Do you think it just baited you?" Dominick asked, his suspicion evident on his face.

"Yes." Abigail nodded at Haatim and put her hand on his shoulder. "We feel certain it set a trap, but that doesn't change anything. You ... we still have to deal with her."

Frieda gawped at her, and Abigail met her gaze. A moment passed in silence, neither of them blinking, and then Frieda nodded. Her expression grew solemn, but her eyes filled with sadness.

"You think she told Haatim about this intentionally so that we would know where to go?" Dominick shook his head. "Why would she bother? She has everything she needs to complete the ritual."

"Not quite," Frieda said. "She still needs one thing."

"What?"

"Not important. We don't have a lot of time, and we need to get moving. Dominick, get the car ready and fill up the tank. We'll go to Arthur's house to gather up any weapons he might have stashed there. Haatim, you'll come with us to help bring it all back. Abigail and Mitchell, you will stay here and get prepared for the trip. We need to be on the road in a half-hour at the latest."

✳✳✳

Abigail waited until Dominick and Haatim had left the shop to go fill up the car's gas tank before confronting Frieda. She cornered her in the back room and closed the door. Mitchell had gone out front, where he puttered around and moved things around the store nervously, so she made sure to lock the door.

"You knew," she said, turning to face Frieda.

"I did," Frieda said, frowning and with a guilty look on her face. "I knew when you were a little girl, the day Arthur first rescued you."

"All of this ... my entire life built up to this, didn't it?"

"I have always felt afraid that this day might come, just not something like this. Arthur interrupted the ritual, and since that moment, The Ninth Circle has wanted, desperately, to complete it. We wanted to make you strong, to prepare you, in case."

"Why didn't you tell me?"

"What would I have to tell?" Frieda asked. "We got a longer reprieve than I expected, but things have happened faster than anticipated. I never imagined Aram would be the weak link that they would exploit to get to you, and I hadn't prepared for *this*."

"What happens now?"

"I don't know," Frieda said, sitting on the ugly red couch. "I thought Arthur would be here when this happened. I thought we would face it together. These events got set into motion back in Raven's Peak. Arthur gave his life to buy us a little bit of time, but now we have our backs up against the wall."

"Did the Council know the truth about me?"

Frieda shook her head. "They built their version of events in their minds, but if the Council or the Catholic Church had known the truth, then no way could Arthur or I have kept you safe."

"I'm the key."

"Yes. You are the vessel."

Abigail stayed silent for a long moment. "You should have killed me."

"Never." Frieda shook her head, and then walked over to Abigail and put a hand on her shoulder, gently touching her cheek. "I swore to Arthur that I would do everything in my power to keep you alive and safe, and I will honor that to my last moments."

"So many people have died."

"None of that happened because of you. You might make the end game for the cult, but *our* failure and the greed of the Council members gave them the tools to do any of this. We failed, not you."

"If you had killed me when you should have, then no one would have any reason to come after me or do any of this. None of this would have happened."

"*This* might not have happened, but something else would have. The only difference would be that you would have died, and the world would have become a worse place for it. If Aram hadn't sold us out, none of this would have happened. If his daughter hadn't died, he wouldn't have sold us out. If his daughter hadn't been born, she wouldn't have died tragically. We cannot live life always looking back at the choices we've made. My choice, as well as Arthur's, was to keep you safe, no matter the personal cost, and I would make that choice again a million times over."

Abigail sighed. "And yet, here we are. Nida wants *me*. Only me."

"Yes."

"If I kill myself now, then there remains no ritual for her to finish."

"If we stop her, then it all ends."

"*You* have to stop her, but I cannot become a part of that. I cannot risk her using me to harm anyone else."

"We will stop her together."

"We tried that. I can't risk her becoming successful with unleashing Surgat."

"I know," Frieda said. "I created a backup plan."

"What?"

Frieda slid two vials out of her pocket. "Poison. The deadliest strains on the planet for both humans as well as demons. Enough to kill you and send Surgat back to hell twenty times over."

Abigail looked at the vials, a sinking feeling in her stomach. "Injected?"

Frieda nodded. "This will solve all of our problems *if* it comes to that. Not before. Arthur sacrificed too much to keep you safe to let you end this without a fight, as did I. Promise me that you won't use it unless it proves completely necessary."

Abigail lied, "I promise."

No way would she walk into this dangerous situation and risk the lives of her closest friends and companions if another solution to end this existed, but she wouldn't admit that to Frieda.

Frieda handed her one of the vials. "I'll hang onto the other one, just in case."

Abigail took it gently and stared at it. The greenish-blue liquid looked thick and syrupy.

Frieda turned to walk away, hesitated, and then glanced back. "I love you, Abigail," she said, stepping in and giving her a quick hug. Then she turned and rushed outside. Dominick and Haatim had returned, and Frieda went out to meet them and go to Arthur's home. They would be gone for a short while before preparing for the final showdown in Raven's Peak.

By that time, everything would be over for Abigail. She waited a few minutes until they'd left, and then found a syringe and drew the poison out of the vial.

All of this would end now. Countless people would die if Frieda tried and failed to stop Nida, and Abigail simply could not risk that. They might not understand, but it offered the best way.

✳✳✳

Abigail sat on Mitchell's couch, building up her courage to plunge the needle into her skin, when the man himself came into the back room, searching for her. Quickly, she tucked the syringe out of sight and under her leg, hiding it from view, and leaned back into the couch just as he came in, pretending like she sat bandaging up her side where the assassin had stabbed her.

He had a look of sadness on his face while he surveyed her from the doorway. The same as Haatim, and she hated that she'd let both of them down. She had wanted to reach out to both of them once she got safe, but part of her had known it a bad idea. Every passing day made it harder and harder to maintain control of herself against Surgat's onslaught, and she feared that she might lose control totally.

When that happened, anyone around her would end up at risk, and the thought of hurting anyone close terrified her. So, instead, she'd picked up Nida's trail and pursued her all the way to Cambodia.

Abigail wrapped the clean bandage tight around her midsection. Should she even bother bandaging it at all anymore? It had healed at a prodigious rate and would barely leave a scar within just hours.

Only yesterday it had made for a long and bloody gash with torn internal organs, and yet today had become nothing more than a minor scar that seeped small amounts of blood.

She could hardly believe it: her wounds should have killed her, and yet she had a modest amount of pain and almost full mobility once again.

She might have considered it a gift had she not known from whence the healing came. This proved a side effect of the horrible ritual that they had performed over her as a little girl. It made something that she had wanted to escape, but now, never would.

"How is it?" Mitchell paused in the doorway and stared at her, awaiting her permission to enter the room. "How does the pain feel?"

"Fine." Abigail nodded toward the beanbag chair opposite. She didn't particularly want to talk to him, but any distraction felt nice just now. The idea of taking her life filled her with terror, and even though she knew she had to do it, she still found it difficult. "Almost completely healed. It probably won't even leave a scar."

"Hard to believe," he said, taking the offered seat. "Truly a miracle."

"Not the word I would use to describe it."

"Dominick told me you'd died."

"I might as well have done."

"You know I'll always be here for you, should you ever need anything."

She sighed, pulling her shirt down again. "Do we need to talk about this?

I get it; everyone feels upset with me, but I had my reasons for keeping it a secret."

"We all just care about you."

"I know. Is that what you came to say?"

He frowned. "No. I mean, yes, but that isn't all: you asked me to look into those texts before you left."

"Dominick told me what you found," she said. "About the Council and the cult. Frieda filled me in on the rest. I know, now, that we got founded out of The Ninth Circle and that the Church wants us hunted down because they think we betrayed them."

"A sordid history, to be sure. But that's not what I meant."

She scrunched up her nose. "Huh?"

"You asked me to look for ways to help you," he said. "To deal with your situation ... condition. Whatever."

That wouldn't do her any good now. Her "condition" had become much worse than Mitchell could ever imagine, and she had no way of fixing it aside from injecting the poison into her veins.

"Did you find anything to help?" she asked, regardless.

"No."

She sighed. "I didn't expect you would. It's all right, though, because I've come to terms with—"

"But I found something else," Mitchell said. "I didn't find anything that can reverse or fix *your* situation, but I found something even more important."

"What?"

"I think I found a way to save Arthur."

Chapter 27

The air sucked out of Abigail's lungs, and the world spun. "*What?*"

"I think I know what Nida plans to do for this ritual. The blood could create a portal and open up a passage to the other side. Once Surgat comes through, he can maintain the portal on his own and bring his demon army through."

"And?"

"Probably, they hold Arthur in the same place the demonic army will come through."

"What?"

"When Nida summons Surgat and the rest of his demon horde, Arthur could—theoretically—come back here with them."

"He could come back?"

"In a sense. He would, essentially, get remade by the same ritual that creates bodies for the demonic army. Reformed. I don't know how to describe it, but it forms a part of what the ritual does. The main problem arises in making sure that Arthur knows how to make the trip."

Excitement coursed through Abigail. All thoughts of taking her life vanished. This changed everything.

After everything that had happened and how helpless she had felt these last few weeks, the idea of getting Arthur back struck her as incredible.

For the first time in as long as she could remember, she felt a glimmer of hope.

She glanced up. A concerned expression had settled on Mitchell's face. "What? What's wrong?"

"The thing is," he said, speaking slowly. "For this to work, we have to let Nida complete the ritual. She has to make the portal and unleash Surgat for this to happen at all."

Um. Right. That put a damper on things. Abigail provided the vessel that Surgat needed, which meant she would need to allow him to take her over for Arthur to come back. That put her back to square one because she couldn't let him come through.

Unless ...

Frieda had said the poison would kill both her and Surgat. If she could, somehow, bring Arthur through and then use the poison on herself, then she would manage to save his life and still keep Surgat from hurting anyone else.

Not a perfect plan, but just maybe it could work.

"If we open this portal, it means letting all of the demons that Surgat plans to bring with him come too. Hell on Earth."

Mitchell nodded. "And even if it proves successful, there's no saying that Arthur could make the trip. I mean, it's just a theory. An idea I had. Arthur might have become too broken in his private hell even to make the trip through the portal."

"Arthur has strength enough."

"Even if so, it won't prove easy."

"Nothing ever does."

"Maybe it would be better if we didn't do this," Mitchell said, deflating and talking himself out of it. "If we just let bygones be bygones and don't try to bring Arthur through. I mean, the idea of letting Surgat back into the world seems a little insane the more I think about it."

Abigail let out a small sigh. She stood and went to the door. Dominick, Frieda, and Haatim shouldn't get back for a couple of hours, but she still wanted to make sure that they didn't overhear her.

She closed the door gently, and then went back to the couch.

Mitchell sat watching her, a confused expression on his face. "What? What is it?"

"You got it wrong. Nida doesn't want to bring Surgat back into the world."

"She doesn't?"

"No," Abigail said. "I'm already here."

Mitchell almost fell out of his beanbag chair when he tried to stand up so quickly. It would have seemed comical if the situation hadn't become so dire. He had a look of utter terror on his face while he backed toward the wall and away from her.

"You ...?"

"Yeah," she said, still sitting and relaxing. "But, not how you think. Or, at least, not yet. I'm the vessel for his passage to Earth."

Mitchell glanced between her and the door, as though sizing up whether or not he should make a run for it.

"I won't murder you, Mitchell."

He had that guilty look on his face like a dog caught peeing on the carpet. "I know."

"I realized it when Haatim saved me, and it makes sense. The Ninth Circle performed the ritual on me when I was a little girl but didn't complete it. Arthur stopped them before they could finish unleashing Surgat, and so only part of him has reached here. The rest remains back in hell, waiting for the opportunity to cross over."

"So, that's what has corrupted you all this time?"

Abigail nodded. "But, I'm still the same person as a few minutes ago. At least, for now."

He blew out a breath and sat once more. "What a relief. What do you mean, 'for now'?"

"Nida doesn't want to summon Surgat alone. She plans to unleash him inside me. I confronted him once before, and I know how much power he has."

"What do you mean?"

"In the park when I stayed with Sara before the Council locked me up, I think I opened up a bridge connecting his two selves, and he nearly crushed me. He *knew* me, and something about the way that connection got set up scared him. Like we stood on equal playing fields, or that I knew something about him that he didn't want me to find out. I can't be sure. When Nida summons him with the blood, though, it will prove different, and I won't stand a chance."

"How do you know?"

"I just do," she said. "That's why the Church wants to kill me, too. I make a key, and they know it. With me dead, then Nida has no chance of fulfilling the ritual because she won't have Surgat's vessel."

"Holy hell." Mitchell shook his head. "Does Frieda know?"

"Yes," Abigail said. "But no one else does."

"We need to tell them."

"No," she said firmly. "We can't tell anyone, especially not Haatim."

"What? Why not?"

"Because he would never understand."

"Understand what?"

"Why I have to kill myself."

✳✳✳

"*What?*"

Abigail held up the needle full of poison. "That's why I stayed in here. This poison can overcome my regenerative abilities and end my life, and once I inject it, all of this will end. Once I die, no ritual will remain for Nida to finish."

"Can't you just kill the demon and get it out of you?"

She shook her head. "That's the thing, we both occupy the same body. We can't kill one without the other. I can't control the thing inside me. It's changed me, and still tries to *become* me, and Nida will give it the power to finish the job and scrub me out of existence."

"But, still, can't we separate the two of you and get it out?"

"There is no 'getting it out,'" Abigail said. "It *is* me. We remain bound together the same way in which the demon got bound to the original cultist at the birth of the Council. There is no removing or controlling it. We can't just exorcise this out of me. This is me, and the only way to finish it is to kill me."

Mitchell stayed silent for a long time. "There has to be something else we can do."

"No. I had intended to use the poison on myself, but now, I know that I need to complete one more task before I can take it."

"What?"

"Save Arthur."

✳✳✳

Abigail made Mitchell swear that he wouldn't inform the others about anything she had told him. Reluctantly, he agreed, and when they arrived back at the shop, he kept his word. Maybe, she had gone too far by telling him, but it had eaten her up not having anyone in which to confide.

She still had the poison ready but felt willing to wait until after she saved Arthur before using it. The thought that she might manage to rescue him made it easier to imagine taking her life, which felt a little ironic.

It would make for her one last act of penance for everything else that she had done and the way she had ruined his life. She could, at least, give it back. Abigail should take the poison now but couldn't bring herself to do it. If there remained even a slight chance of bringing Arthur back, then she had to take it.

If Haatim had it right about the demon going to Raven's Peak, then everything would come full circle. It felt almost poetic. The demon knew that, too, and toyed with them. It recognized that she lay on the verge of losing control over herself and giving in to the demonic essence inside her, and with a little nudge, it would push her over the edge.

The only way this could end came from killing herself. However, she felt afraid to die. Consciously, she could understand that it made the only way to stop this demon from consuming her very existence, but that didn't lessen the sense of dread it instilled.

Arthur's religion claimed that suicide would damn her soul to hell, but believed that she'd gotten on that track already. After everything she'd done, she doubted an alternative ending to all of this existed for her.

And, to be perfectly honest, she felt unsure that she believed in hell anyway. She believed in evil and supernatural creatures but not in one particular religion's hell. If killing herself proved the only way to stop Surgat, then she would do it.

But, she would do it after freeing Arthur from the demon's clutches.

They finished packing everything and getting ready for the trip. The mood of the group grew somber, and everyone seemed on edge. Abigail didn't make for the only one dealing with a heavy burden. It pained her to know that all of this had happened because of her, even if not all her fault.

"You ready?" Dominick asked, loading the last of the supplies into the car.

"Yep."

"Me, too," Mitchell said.

Dominick shook his head. "You should stay here. In case something happens to us. You'll need to get ready to warn the Church if we fail."

Mitchell frowned, but he didn't object. "All right."

Abigail felt glad Mitchell wouldn't go with them. He had never made much of a fighter, and they had no idea what they would walk into. If things went sideways, it made it better knowing that at least one of them would survive to walk away from all of this. She gave him a hug, said her goodbyes, and then climbed into the car.

They got on the road a few minutes later, driving south from Mitchell's shop. They would head into the mountains and to the small town of Raven's Peak. Everyone sat silent and distracted, feeling the burdensome weight of what would happen imminently.

They had a couple of shotguns, a rifle, and holy water, which might help them in dealing with Nida, but they all felt that it wouldn't give them enough.

None of them, she realized, thought that they would live through this.

Chapter 28

Haatim leaned against the window as they drove down the freeway. Frieda and Dominick sat in the backseat, so quiet that he glanced over to check on them and make sure they hadn't fallen asleep. He couldn't even imagine sleeping right now, and it had felt like a weight hung over his head ever since they'd started the trip.

Abigail drove and hadn't said anything since they had left Mitchell's shop a few hours earlier. She remained even quieter than usual and stared forward, eyes on the road and thoughts a million kilometers away.

What did she think about? He would have given anything to get a glimpse into her mind to see what worried her so much. She seemed even more somber than when they had flown back to Ohio from Cambodia. What had happened at the shop to make her so distant and withdrawn?

"You okay?"

She blinked. "Yeah."

"Just worn down?" he said.

Abigail nodded. "Yeah. Rough couple of days."

"Tell me about it," he said. "When this is all over, I think everyone will need a good and long vacation."

She sat silent for a moment. "Yeah," she said, finally.

He could tell that she felt unconvinced, but she didn't offer anything further.

"Looks like it's going to rain," he said, after a while.

"Yep."

He took that as the end of the conversation and leaned back in the passenger seat. Apprehensive about everything happening, he had no idea what they would find in Raven's Peak. Though still the middle of the day, it had grown dark enough with thick cloud cover outside that it could have been the middle of the night. The clouds hadn't opened up, yet, but when they did, it would bring a storm to remember.

Never in his life had the weather so perfectly matched his mood as right now. He had tried reaching out mentally for his sister again, but it didn't prove of any use. Whatever had happened to connect them, it had either gone or only made for something he could do subconsciously.

Still, it showed that she remained out there, fighting for her life against the demon that had overtaken her. He felt ready to do everything in his power to save his sister.

"You know that she's gone, right?" Abigail broke the silence. It seemed as though she had read his mind. She glanced over at him with a concerned look on her face. "You won't bring her back."

He could see the concern there, and the worry, and it gnawed at him. "You don't know that."

"I do," she said. "I *got* possessed, and it gave me a horrible experience, but I stayed alive. When they took over your sister's body, she'd gone already."

"Maybe they brought her back to life when the demon came."

"It doesn't work like that."

"You don't *know* how it all works," he said more harshly than intended. "No one does. What we try to do, the world we live in ... we don't have hard and fast rules for any of this."

Abigail glanced at him. "Yes, we do," she said. "The rule is: if you live this life long enough, this world *will* destroy you."

He blew out a breath. "I'm telling you, Nida *is* still in there. I'll save her. I failed once. I won't fail again."

"We need to *stop* her, Haatim," Abigail said. "I won't allow you to jeopardize what we need to do."

"I won't," he said. "But, I won't abandon Nida either."

"She's gone. The demon just wants to manipulate you."

"Do you trust me?"

"Yes."

"Then trust me when I tell you she's out there."

"Even if so, what's to say you can save her? You told me before that you confronted the demon in Cambodia and didn't stand a chance."

"That happened before I *knew* she lived. I can reach Nida and bring her back; I just need another chance."

Abigail glanced at him again. "All right," she said.

He could tell that she remained unconvinced but figured that offered the best he would get out of her. He worried that she, Dominick, or Frieda might try to kill Nida without giving him the chance to save her.

To be honest, though, he didn't feel that confident of what would happen either. He could still remember when the demon had dominated him and used him as a plaything. Part of him believed that if he did get the opportunity to redeem himself, he would simply fail once more.

Maybe it would work out better if they killed her. He didn't want to admit it, but maybe they all had it right.

✳✳✳

They drove into Raven's Peak slowly, looking around in awe at the city. It lay empty and silent throughout, completely abandoned by all of the townsfolk in the preceding months.

It reminded Haatim of the smaller version of the town out in the woods where he'd gone with Abigail. Now, this one had become a ghost town as well, forgotten by time and abandoned by the world. Though considerably larger and more modern, it would face the same fate.

Already, after only a few months of abandonment, it had fallen into disrepair. Grass and weeds pushed up through the streets and sidewalks in various places, and it showed signs of decay and rot.

The day remained cloudy and overcast, and without any streetlamps or building lights, everything lurked in shadow. It proved windier than he would have liked, as well.

He recalled those short hours he'd spent here with Abigail, which felt so long ago. So much had happened since then, and his entire world had altered.

"Where did everyone go?" he asked in awe, looking at the city from the passenger seat. The headlamps would light up a section of the city, and then it would fade back into nothing when they moved on by.

"I don't know," Abigail said. "It feels so empty."

"Evacuated," Frieda said from the back seat. "On the Church's orders."

Haatim had focused so tightly on the city that he'd nearly forgotten she sat back there. He jumped a little at the sound of her voice, and then forced himself to relax.

He glanced at her in the rear-view mirror; she seemed broken down with an unreadable expression on her face. She hadn't slept much since everything had set into motion, and Haatim could tell that all of this had gotten to her.

Dominick, on the other hand, slumped fast asleep, leaning his head on Frieda's shoulder and snoring softly. He could snooze through anything. She reached over and gave him a gentle shake, waking him. He let out a snort and blinked open his eyes. Then he yawned. "We're here?"

No one responded, just kept looking out of the windows. He rubbed his face and coughed. "Guess so."

"Everyone here moved?" Haatim cast his disbelieving gaze around once more.

"The Catholic Church bought out their properties with the assistance of the US government, forcing everyone out. Imminent domain where necessary. After what happened here, though, not that many holdouts wanted to stay. Don't worry: they got paid generously for their property."

"So, now it's just a forgotten town."

"One of a few out in the world. More than you would think, actually. Crazier things happen all the time. And making a remote town in the middle of the mountains disappear isn't that difficult with the right motivation and resources."

They drove up the road along the main thoroughfare. Haatim saw the bar and shop they'd stopped in, as well as other buildings that he remembered that looked empty and forgotten.

All of them stood abandoned and boarded up. They kept driving until they reached the far side of town and the small FedEx office he and Abigail had hidden in during the first attack on the city. His old car still sat smashed up against the brick wall, riddled with bullets.

He'd almost forgotten that beat-up old Junker, and just seeing it brought back innumerable memories.

"I see the Church left things how you found them." He pointed at the car.

"Why wouldn't they?" Frieda glanced at him. "The plan was to let things settle down for about ten years before considering whether or not to try and rebuild the town."

"I guess that won't happen now."

Frieda stayed silent for a few seconds. "No, probably not."

"You sure this is the right place?" Abigail asked. "It doesn't seem like anyone came here."

"Yep. Definitely the place we're supposed to be," Haatim said. "I haven't managed to contact my sister or the demon again since the flight, but she's out here somewhere."

"This place is important to her," Frieda said.

"Not just her," Abigail said. "She'll do it at the old church in the woods. The one where I killed Arthur."

"You didn't kill him."

Abigail didn't respond. Instead, she put the car into gear and headed down the road that led to the campgrounds, where they'd gotten attacked when driving back into Raven's Peak. Haatim still felt the sheer and brutal terror of the moment, getting shot at and attacked.

A police car and shots had come out of the fog. He couldn't help but look around, half-expecting something to jump out at them and swarm the vehicle. However, nothing happened, and they soon reached the outside of the city and drove into the forest.

"How long will the ritual take?" he asked.

"I don't know," Frieda said. "This is all new for me. The ritual I performed with Arthur all those years ago took nearly five hours, and I would imagine this one will take longer. I can't be certain."

What Frieda didn't say, possibly for Haatim's sake, was that they might have come too late already. They had no way of telling what Nida would need for the ritual, or if she had completed it. They might have walked into a trap just to face their deaths.

But they'd run out of alternatives, and this offered the only way for them to go. They had exhausted every avenue open and had no choice but to continue forward. As Winston Churchill once said, "If you're going through hell, keep going."

The trees flitted past, and the sky continued to darken. Still, it didn't rain. Haatim would almost have preferred if it had. He couldn't help but think that the weather gave an ominous sign of things to come.

It proved a sobering realization to know that they might die out here, and even worse to know that they might all perish without accomplishing anything.

Did he sit okay with that or not? They had to try and stop Nida, though. That would prove nearly impossible with such a dangerous and unpredictable foe.

"So many memories," Abigail whispered beside him. He couldn't tell if she spoke to him, or if it had just slipped out.

"I know."

To come back here brought a painful reminder of when he'd first come to the town. He remembered facing the demon and dealing with impossible situations. He also recalled the feeling of pure *rightness* when he had faced the demon. For sure, something had happened, and God had reached through him to get rid of Belphegor. He had helped save Abigail and the town.

Now, he prayed he would find that strength once more and save his sister. He had failed once: he couldn't afford to fail again.

Chapter 29

The road appeared completely quiet as they drove toward the old campgrounds an hour outside of Raven's Peak. It held a strong sense of déjà vu for Abigail and her first trip out here with Haatim.

Except that hadn't been her first trip. She had come out here before under the control of the demon that took Arthur from her. The Council had lied to her and withheld information, letting her think she'd never visited here before when she'd come with Haatim.

The possession had made for the single worst experience of her life. She had understood what happened to her but had no control over her body. Until that moment, she had never known what it felt like being helpless, and it became the worst thing she could imagine happening.

Now, though, this seemed so much worse.

When the demon had taken possession of her so long ago, something else had taken control and suffocated her. It had prepared to bring Surgat into the world, but Arthur had stopped it. She couldn't control herself against its outside influence and couldn't fight it off, but at least something *else* had done it to her.

This time, the influence didn't come from outside but from her. She could sense that *her* identity kept trying to take over and seize power. They'd become one and the same. She didn't have to fight back against an unknown enemy but to try to crush the tide of her anger and hatred.

She'd never imagined she could lose control of herself, but each day, it grew worse and more chaotic. Harder to control like holding sand in her hands. It proved physically demanding just trying to keep from giving in to her inner nature.

What Haatim had said about her not being inherently evil ... she prayed it came true. Part of her—a large part—doubted it, though, and after this ended, things would have to change. So many people had suffered already because of her. Too many.

She would make sure no one else got hurt due to her.

"Why here?" Haatim shook his head. "Why would she come back here for the ritual?"

"Second guessing yourself?"

"No. Trying to understand."

"Any number of reasons," Frieda said. "Hubris, maybe. Nida has, essentially, invited us in to witness the rebirth of Surgat, which means she doesn't think we can stop it from happening. We've gotten separated from all our allies, including the Church, our funding, and any resources we might have to stop her. She came here to further rub our noses in our defeat."

"So, this is a victory lap?"

Frieda didn't respond immediately, but eventually said, "Yes."

"What will the Church do after this?"

"If we win?"

"If we don't."

"I don't know," she said, shaking her head. "Our ties have severed, and they blame us for all of this. Honestly, I can't even blame them. Most likely, they will send in a few of their other assets to deal with this threat if Surgat gets unleashed, but probably not until too late when many people have died already."

"Then, I guess, we better not lose."

This time, Frieda didn't respond. They drove in silence the rest of the way to the old rental cabins. The gravel crunched under their tires when they drove up to the first wooden cabin.

The students had stayed in this one on vacation when Abigail and Haatim had arrived so many months ago. She had only just met Haatim and didn't yet know if she could trust him. Now, though, she thought of him as one of her closest friends and someone she could trust implicitly.

Maybe she should tell him everything? No. If he knew, he would try to stop her, and that would just make all of this that much more difficult. She knew what she had to do, and the longer he went without knowing, the easier this would become.

She pulled the car to a stop in front of the cabin and glanced into the rearview mirror. "What now?"

"Now, we walk."

"Do we have a plan to stop her?" Dominick asked. "Or do we just walk blindly into her trap?"

"I don't have a good plan," Frieda said. "I wish I did, but I have no idea what will work."

"So, improvise?" Dominick grinned. "My favorite."

They all climbed out of the car. Abigail moved to the trunk and popped it open. They had a bag full of weapons tucked inside, including her hand crossbow and darts, Arthur's sword, and a few miscellaneous pistols and rifles. She picked up the sword, grateful to see it again.

"It suits you," Frieda said, standing beside her and watching her. "Arthur would have wanted you to have it."

A twinge hit Abigail in her chest, and then she slung the blade over her shoulder. If everything went according to plan, she could give it back to him.

The boot also held a decanter of holy water and some vials, a pair of curved knives, and her bible that Arthur had gifted to her so long ago. She rubbed her hand across the surface of the book, feeling its texture, but decided to leave it behind. The realization that she would never feel it again pained her, but she hoped that when she saved Arthur, he might find it and keep it to remember her by.

In her pocket, she felt the syringe that Frieda had given to her. Surgat might know that they'd come, but for certain, he wouldn't have prepared for that. She only had to hold out long enough to inject it.

If Mitchell had it right, then when the ritual got underway, she would have a small window of time to bring forth Arthur—a sort of resurrection into bodily form. If it managed to work, then it would come down to blind luck about whether or not Arthur would even accept the ritual and come back through with the demon.

And, on top of that, it all assumed that Nida would prove successful in summoning Surgat from his resting place in hell to begin with. Not exactly the ideal outcome. If that happened, they would need to stop both her and Surgat to survive.

There seemed a lot of "ifs" in that scenario, and it didn't look too promising. That made for one of the reasons that she hadn't told anyone else about the plan. If things went wrong and it didn't look like she could bring Arthur back, then she would inject the poison and simply end it.

✳✳✳

"What do we do when we get there?" Haatim asked as they walked through the woods toward the old town hidden away there. The foliage proved minimal at this time of year, but with it so dark, it made navigating the path rather difficult.

"Scout the area," Dominick said. "We should do at least a cursory perimeter search. Make sure we don't have any surprises waiting for us when we go into the town."

"I mean once we get there," Haatim said. "How will we do this?"

"If we find her in the middle of the ritual, we should manage to slip in undetected," Frieda said. "It will keep her distracted, and all her focus will stay on that."

"What if we come upon her at a different stage?"

"We'll need a little bit of luck."

"What if that doesn't work?"

"I don't know, Haatim. Do you have any suggestions?"

"Yeah, I do. We need a distraction."

"No."

"Let me talk to her. It will give you time to get close."

"That will just give us away."

"She knows we're coming already. With luck, I can distract her long enough for you to get in and stop the ritual."

"The ceiling of the church got broken at the back," Abigail said. She remembered the layout from when she'd first come. "We could slip in through there."

"I'll stay with Haatim," Frieda said after a moment. "If you can stop the ritual, then all well and good, but if you can destroy the blood she acquired, then she won't even have the ability to restart without collecting it all once more."

"What happens if she has those ... things there?" Dominick asked. A look of genuine fear settled on his face. "The demons. The one that nearly killed me at the Reinfer estate."

"We deal with it."

"There is no 'dealing' with that thing. Single-handed, it took out a group of heavily armed soldiers and didn't even have any wounds afterward."

"Those soldiers hadn't prepared to face something like that."

"Didn't stop them from unloading full clips into it," Dominick said. "Yeah, I'm sure some panicked, but all? Do you think our weapons will do any better?"

Frieda stayed silent for a long moment. Abigail could tell that she didn't have a good argument. "One problem at a time."

They made it to the edge of the town and gazed down at it. It looked almost peaceful—like a little hamlet in the forest out away from the rest of civilization. Just looking at it made her feel like she'd walked a hundred years into the past.

The feelings of weakness and shame remained raw for Abigail. Here, the demon had possessed her. And, here, Arthur had plunged the dagger into his heart to save her. Had he known even then the demon's end game? That it wanted to resurrect Surgat? So many memories and unanswered questions remained tied to this place.

Most probably, the demon inside Nida had brought them out here for that reason. It would use her emotions and fear to weaken and manipulate her.

However, she didn't plan on letting it succeed and had an ace in the hole that gave her strength. As she had lost Arthur here, it seemed only fitting that here would also make the place she brought him back.

"Do a sweep," Frieda said softly, looking at Dominick. "When we approach, we need to make sure we have left any surprises behind us."

Dominick nodded and slipped off through the trees to the west. He moved gracefully and with little noise, and after only a few seconds, had disappeared into the dark forest and out of her sightline.

Frieda turned to Haatim. "You sure about this? Talking to her could prove dangerous."

"I'm sure."

"Don't trust her," Frieda said. "The demon will lie and manipulate you, but you cannot let it get inside your head."

"I know." He hadn't told Frieda about what had happened in Cambodia, which surprised Abigail. Already, he'd confronted the demon and lost, but if he didn't want to tell Frieda, then Abigail wouldn't spill his secret. "I'll just distract her and get her out of the building, and you guys can take care of the rest."

Clearly, Frieda didn't like the plan, but she did nod her assent. "I'll stay nearby just in case. If you need help, shout."

"How about I scream instead? I'm better at that."

Frieda ignored him. Instead, she turned to Abigail. "Are you okay?"

Abigail took a deep breath, and then nodded. "Fine."

"Are you ready?" Frieda arched an eyebrow. "What we talked about in the shop?"

Abigail understood what she meant and tapped the syringe at her side. The weight of the situation still pressed down on her, and the idea that these would make her last moments on Earth terrified her. However, she felt at peace with her choices and accepted her fate. "Ready."

Frieda had the other syringe, just in case. If the ritual got enacted, and she couldn't inject herself, then Frieda would use it on her to stop her from getting overcome by Surgat.

That, in Frieda's mind, Abigail knew, would be a last resort. Abigail hadn't told her about her plan to bring back Arthur, or the inevitability that she would end up forced to inject the poison, and she didn't intend to.

Dominick returned a moment later, a concerned expression on his face.

"What is it?" Abigail asked. "Did you find something?"

"No," he said. "Nothing at all. The town seems completely and eerily silent."

"Do you think we came to the wrong place?"

He shook his head. "I can *feel* it here. The wrongness of it. Something horrible is happening, and definitely, we reached the right place."

Abigail sighed. "All right, then. Let's go."

Chapter 30

Dominick slipped through the town, slow and quiet, and listened for any sound of movement around the area. They didn't know where, or if, Nida might have posted guards but wanted to stay ready for anything. They planned to start the fight on their terms, and every second that Nida didn't know they'd come here increased their advantage.

Raven's Peak felt like a dead place, lacking even the sounds of nature they might have expected. No birds chirping, crickets, or the rustling of nature. Even the wind fell silent. It had an unnatural feel to it that made the hair on Dominick's neck stand up. This place had something wrong about it like it had become unreal, and the closer they came to the church, the worse the feeling became.

He had been in a lot of deadly situations and faced powerful foes in his life, but this brought a whole new level from anything he had seen before. Nida represented an evil a lot older and more dangerous than the normal creatures he dealt with on a regular basis and sent back to hell.

To make matters worse, he remained distracted by the flurry of information that had bombarded him over the last few days. It proved hard to focus his mind when he kept thinking through the ramifications of what Frieda had admitted to him. Nothing was as it seemed, and it felt like his world had flipped on end.

To find out that the Council had formed out of The Ninth Circle after they'd betrayed one of their own just seemed unthinkable. No wonder the Church had always looked unfavorably upon them for all these years.

After so much time spent working to repent from the horrible things they had done and the evil creature they'd released into the world, it would all end this way. He had no doubt that the Council had gone forever, crushed by the betrayal of Aram Arison and their hubris. There would be no rebuilding from this.

Nida prepared to unleash a terrible creature back into the world, the Church had disavowed them, and basically everyone who used to consider them allies now considered them enemies.

All in all, it had become a fairly upending week in Dominick's life.

Yet, in addition to feeling terrified that they might walk to their deaths at any moment, he also felt proud that they planned to try to stop them. It didn't matter what the Council used to do, or from where they came. What mattered came down to what they did now and the choices they made.

They might fail or fall short of stopping Nida and this threat, but at least they had the willingness to risk it all and see this through to the end.

They made it to the old church, and Abigail waved for him to stop moving and stay silent. At first, he couldn't hear anything, but after a second, he made out some noise. From inside, came sounds of faint chanting, which spilled out.

As Abigail had mentioned, the roof had collapsed partly and now rotted away on this side of the church. It wouldn't give them a problem to get in, he realized, but getting in without tearing off a chunk of the wall accidentally? It looked flimsy and old, and if he put pressure on the wrong section, it just might collapse.

Abigail glanced at him, and then climbed the back wall. Haatim should have made his way to the front door right about now, and they needed to get in position to attack or help should things not go according to plan.

Dominick watched Abigail climb to the roof and then lean over the edge to look into the room. She glanced back at him, and using her hands, signaled that ten people occupied the room.

The look on her face, though, made it clear that they weren't all human. She held up two fingers, and he scrunched up his nose. *Two of what?*

To climb up there with her would make a bad idea. Abigail weighed a lot less than he did, and he didn't think the building would support his weight as easily. Instead, he moved around the side of the church, staying close to the wall and scanning the area. He found a window he could use as a point of ingress and glanced inside.

Seven robed figures stood in a circle in the center of the room, all focused on a central point, but they didn't stand alone. Nida stood there as well, walking around the robed cultists with her hands folded behind her back. The robed figures chanted at a low level, and their words filled the air with a quiet and barely audible hum.

Then, he saw the other two that Abigail had indicated and felt a moment of panic. In opposite corners of the room, perfectly still, stood demons like the one he'd faced in Pennsylvania.

Not one. Two of them.

Both of them stood frozen in place, staring straight ahead like statues. Dominick ducked out of sight, fighting the urge to turn around and head away from here. Within seconds, he'd grown sweaty and bit down his panic.

Never in his life had he faced something so horrible or deadly, nor something that had so quickly bested him in a fight. He'd barely survived his last encounter and only by sheer luck, and he hadn't come close to even hurting the thing, let alone killing it.

And now he faced two.

He fought back his fear, reminding himself that he had to do this and that no other way had presented itself. They had to destroy the blood, interrupt the ritual, and then get the hell out of here.

Sure. It sounded so easy when he put it that way.

He waited, out of sight next to the window, for something to happen.

He didn't have to wait long.

✳✳✳

"Nida," Haatim called out while he walked up to the front entrance of the church. However, in his terror, the word came out weak and pathetic, barely a whisper. He cleared his throat, took a steadying breath, and called louder, "Nida! I know you're in there. Come out and face me."

A few seconds passed, and then movement came from inside the church. The door opened, and his sister walked out onto the front steps.

Or, at least, a creature loosely resembling Nida. It no longer looked anything like his sister. The broken body looked like it had begun to fall apart, and the skin sagged and had turned pale and sickly. It appeared considerably worse than when he'd faced her only a few days ago in Cambodia.

The skin around one of her eyes had rotted and fallen off, leaving only part of the flesh behind to hold the eye in the socket. Whether they eye even worked anymore or not, he couldn't begin to guess.

Nor did he want to. To see her like that gave enough to cause his hand to shake and him to second guess everything he did here. The realization hit him like a bolt of lightning—no way could he save his sister, not anymore.

The demon had broken down her body, and the effect only intensified over time. It wouldn't take long before nothing remained. Nida's face had torn and rotted as the demon pushed her body to the limits and beyond.

After everything he had gone through, it all came to nothing.

He had nothing left to save.

Abigail and Frieda had gotten it right, though he felt certain they also had it wrong. Nida—the real Nida—*did* remain trapped in there somewhere, and in pain. He might not save her, but destroying this demon would, at least, give her the rest she deserved.

The demon stood at the top of the short staircase, sizing up Haatim, her expression unreadable.

"I wasn't sure if you would come," the demon said, standing atop the porch and looking down at Haatim as he approached. "Dear brother, I felt afraid you might have lost your will to fight when last we met."

Haatim stopped at the bottom of the stairs, about six meters from the demon. "I'm sorry, Nida. I can't help you," he whispered, speaking to himself rather than her. "But I can still stop *you*."

"What? I couldn't hear you through your pathetic simpering."

"I will end you before you can complete the ritual."

"Dear brother, if I thought you could stop me, I never would have invited you here. You remember this place, don't you? Back where it all began. I watched you even then, you know. I'm the one who sent the cultists after you in Arizona to turn you to my cause. I'd hoped you would join me, become my ally in this endeavor. After all, once you found out what our father had done, how could you possibly support him?"

"I would never join you."

"You will in time. That's the beauty of it, Haatim. We have all the time in the world. You won't join your sister, though. Instead, you will *replace* her as my vessel. And, now that I know what I can get out of *you*, you will bring me to ever new heights in the Master's regime. But that's neither here nor there. We have other matters to attend to. Where is she? The woman who took you from me. Where is Abigail?"

"Not here. I came alone."

"You don't expect me to believe that, do you?"

"Why would I bring her here? I came here for Nida, and because we have unfinished business."

"Why? Because Nida reached out to you?" The demon laughed. "You're even dumber than I thought. *I* reached out to you, using her memories. If your pest of a sister came back with me from hell, I would have crushed her long ago."

"You lie."

"I do? What would be the point? Don't you see? I've won already."

"No, you haven't. I will destroy you, and then I will stop your ritual from happening."

"Go ahead and try." The demon took a step toward him, calling his bluff. "Attack me again like you did in Cambodia. Open yourself up and let me inside. I won't prove as gentle this time."

Haatim took a self-conscious step back and winced.

The demon smiled at him. "What? Not quite as brave as you thought? Don't worry; no shame in it. I have always known you as a sniveling coward, just like I know you lied about Abigail not coming with you. She wouldn't stay away, not when I dangled such a tempting carrot in front of her."

Haatim took another hesitant step back. "What?"

"Oh, she didn't tell you? She came here because she thinks she can rescue Arthur. She actually thinks she can bring him back. So predictable."

Haatim shook his head. "You're lying."

"Dear Haatim, I told you. I have no *reason* to lie. I've won this fight already. It's over simply because you came. Now, I have everything I need, and it will take only moments until the Master arrives. I know that Abigail came here because I gave her that idea."

"What?"

"Well, not me, precisely; though, Mitchell has proven quite useful these last few weeks."

Shock ran through Haatim's system. If Mitchell worked for Nida, then she knew everything that would happen.

All their plans.

A cold chill ran down his spine. That meant that Nida knew *everything*.

"You still have time." Nida took a step toward him. "Time for you to join the correct side. Bend your knee and swear fealty to me, and I will spare you for now. Join me and help us bring this world to heel."

Haatim ignored the demon, pushing the words out of his head and refusing to focus on them. Instead, he thought of his sister, trying to remember the beautiful young woman she had been before all of this had happened. Before the demon, before her sickness. She had seemed so vibrant, so full of life. He tried to picture that version of his sister, the glowing woman so full of life.

He couldn't do it, though. He couldn't remember. All he saw now was a husk. A puppet under the control of this evil entity.

"I'm sorry, Nida," he whispered, swinging his arm from behind his back. He had a pistol ready. "I love you."

He pulled the trigger, but Nida had moved already. Had danced away from him and back into the church. She disappeared around the door and out of sight.

Haatim watched her disappear and cursed. Hopefully, he'd bought Abigail and Dominick enough time to climb in through the back of the roof, but he couldn't know for certain. He wouldn't wait around, though. Instead, he rushed up the stairs and burst into the building behind Nida.

A group of robed cultists stood gathered in a circle, chanting, with a pool of blood lying at their feet in a basin. Nida stood in the center, looking back at him with a grin on her face.

Two horrible-looking creatures flanked the room in opposite corners. They appeared humanoid demonic creatures but looked like aliens with sharp talons on their fingers and sunken faces. Their eye sockets stared, empty except for a small smoldering light.

Those must be the creatures Dominick had spoken of, but Dominick's descriptions didn't do them justice. They looked considerably more horrible than he could have imagined. Dominick had described them as un-killable war machines, but Haatim realized them as something even worse.

One turned to face Haatim, eyes boring into him. It twisted its arms, slicing its talons through the air, and then walked toward him.

"Uh-oh." Haatim stumbled back toward the door behind him.

The creature let out a horrid piercing screech and took a sudden bounding leap toward him, landing only a few meters away.

Haatim turned and ran.

Chapter 31

Haatim ran as fast as he could away from the church and the gray demon chasing him, dodging overgrown sections and struggling to breathe.

Unsure what the hell had just gone on or what those creatures might be, he did know they would prove too much for him to handle alone. More importantly, he had no idea how they would stop them, if even possible.

Though he still held onto his gun, it felt woefully inadequate for such a situation. He sucked in breaths of air, trying to get his body under control, and kept running. Dominick had taught him how to control his fear; though nothing he had taught him seemed to apply to a situation like this.

Actually coming here, facing creatures he couldn't understand and that shouldn't exist, didn't seem like something a breathing exercise would fix.

Haatim could feel it pursuing him while he weaved through the old and decrepit buildings. He ducked around tight corners and small passageways, hoping to create some distance from the demon, but it ran quickly. It didn't seem too adept at handling sharp corners, but on a straightaway, it moved much faster than he could and made up the ground.

He tried to control himself and remember the other situation in his life where he'd faced something terrible and remained unafraid. In Raven's Peak, when he faced down the demon that tried to kill Abigail, he hadn't experienced much fear at all. Belphegor had possessed a small child and wreaked unimaginable havoc on the nearby factory, but even then, Haatim hadn't experienced trepidation like this.

Of course, he'd also had divine help and confidence. Now, however, every fiber in his being threatened to lock up in terror, and he saw through tunnel vision from lack of oxygen to his brain.

He'd fought down his fear back then because he'd *known* he would overcome that threat and win the day. However, Nida had shown him his weakness and mortality back in Cambodia. He didn't have any of that same confidence in himself anymore.

Simply fighting back his fear wouldn't work, and he couldn't keep running away. Eventually, the monster would catch him. Haatim needed another strategy. He ducked around a building and put his back to the wall, out of the creature's sight.

There, he closed his eyes and focused purely on his terror, pushing all other thoughts out of his mind. Though the creature continued to come after him, he couldn't stand up against it if he couldn't get his mind under control.

To that end, he forced the image of the creature out of his thoughts as well, but with less success. He couldn't get its spindly body, talons, jagged teeth, and hollow eyes out of his mind. Determined, he focused on relaxing and regaining control of his raging emotions, and eventually, reclaimed his thoughts. Instead of a giant gray monster, he pictured it as a human, just a big ugly human with claws.

A terrible shriek ripped through the air, maybe ten meters behind him. It sounded raw, visceral, and wholly inhuman. So much for imagining it as just a man. Haatim's eyes popped open, and it felt like the scream had cut through his skin and gone directly for his heart. All of his fear came back in a wild rush, and he stood breathless once more.

Haatim let out a sobbing sound, gritted his teeth, and then took off running again. He didn't go far, though, before he decided he needed to try something else. With steeled resolve, he waited until the creature stepped into sight behind him, between two buildings.

It noticed him standing there and froze in place. The way it simply stopped moving looked unnatural and wrong, and unlike anything he'd ever seen before. The creature stood perfectly still, just watching him. He fired off three rounds from his pistol. The first one went wide, over the monster's shoulder, but the next two thudded cleanly into the torso. They blasted it, staggering the creature, and Haatim let out an exclamation of joy. It stumbled back a step, and for a second, he thought he had hurt it.

Then, it shrieked again. This time, the sound came louder and angrier, and he had to cover his ears with his hands. The creature stood up straight, eyes boring into Haatim, and then charged forward once more.

"Uh-oh," Haatim yelped.

He tried to duck back, but the creature came too fast. It lunged forward, only a meter away, and Haatim couldn't avoid its talons as they came swinging down at him.

Suddenly, an enormous explosive crack sounded next to his ear. He jerked away from it, falling to the ground and crying out in pain.

Then he rolled, pushing himself up. Frieda stood where he just had. She held a ten-gauge shotgun, which she'd just fired at the creature, barrel still smoking.

The creature lay on the ground a few meters back, unmoving and with smoke pouring off its body. It looked like the shot had blasted it a fair ways.

Shaky, Haatim climbed to his feet, still clutching his ringing ear and checking to see if it bled.

"Blessed salt pellets," Frieda said, pumping the gun and chambering another round.

"What did you say?" He turned his head so that his other ear faced her.

"Never mind."

"Is it dead?" he asked.

The body on the ground twitched. They watched as it picked itself up again. Frieda fired once more, blasting it to the ground, but after only seconds, it continued climbing to a standing position.

"Apparently not."

"What do we do now?" Haatim asked.

She glanced sideways at him, "Run."

✳✳✳

Dominick hoped that Haatim remained all right. He'd seen him come into the church—against the plan—and then sprint back out with one of the demons in tow. Frieda had joined him out there, but the kid had gotten into trouble.

However, he couldn't worry about that just now. He had a job to do, and at least one of the monster demons had come out of the church now. He glanced over at Abigail, waving to get her attention, but she didn't even look at him. She had a worried look on her face, and looked distant and lost in her thoughts.

This made for the perfectly wrong time for her to lose focus. They didn't have a lot of leeway to get this taken care of, and he couldn't wait around for her to get ready. He sighed in frustration, drew his pistol, and then stepped away from the church.

He ran toward the window and dove, gliding nimbly through the opening and landing inside the building. After a roll, he came up firing.

His first shot, he aimed at Nida, but she ducked and slipped behind the cultists. They moved quickly, forming a wall in front of her, blocking her from Dominick like a human shield wall. That didn't bother him, though. He fired into the group, and one-by-one, they fell to the ground. However, as one fell, another would move to stand between Dominick and Nida, keeping her protected.

He tried circling the group to get a clear shot, but it proved of no use. He kept firing until his clip emptied, and by the time he'd done, a pile of bodies lay in the center of the room, pooling blood. And still, he hadn't managed to get a clear shot at Nida.

His target came out from behind the pile of dying cultists, grinning at him. Thus far, the other monster in the corner hadn't moved, awaiting her command.

"Dominick. I feared you wouldn't make it."

"Wouldn't miss this."

"Of course not. And where, might I ask, is Abigail?"

Before he could stop himself, he glanced up to the roof where Abigail hid. She still looked distracted, barely even seeming to notice the fight happening below.

Nida followed his gaze, and her smile widened. "Ah, there you are!"

She gestured, shattering the roof beneath Abigail with a telekinetic blast. Abigail fell but landed on her feet about two meters to Dominick's right.

"Welcome," Nida said. "After I lost you in Cambodia, I felt afraid you would become difficult to track down. It pleases me that you remained willing to come here to me."

Abigail shook her head, and her eyes glowed red. "You're wrong."

"About what?"

"Arthur. I can bring him back."

Nida made a tsking sound. "I'm sorry, love, but you can't. He's trapped in hell and has no escape. All of that about him coming through the portal? I made it up."

"I *will* save him."

"No," Nida said. "You will *join* him."

She reached a hand out, into the air, and then made a clenching motion. Abigail staggered, letting out a gasping sound and falling to her knees. She clutched at her throat, eyes wide and mouth open.

Dominick ejected the clip, slid another one out of his coat pocket, and jammed it in place. He chambered another round and came up firing—the entire maneuver taking less than two seconds.

Nida's arm flashed, her other hand coming up, and Dominick watched in horror as the bullets stopped in mid-air, hovering in between them. He'd only fired off three rounds when he realized they didn't have any effect.

They held there for about four seconds before falling to the ground.

"I apologize, but I am both out of time and patience for you." Nida swung her hand through the air, and all of a sudden, Dominick found himself airborne. He smashed into and through the wall of the church, flying another ten meters through the air before crashing hard to the ground outside.

He let out a groan and rolled over, staggering to his feet. His entire body ached, but he had somehow managed to keep his grip on his pistol.

He looked back at the church. The second monster came out after him, knocking the rest of the wall out of its way and waving its talons in the air. It stopped in the open hole in the wall and let out a shriek.

"You've got to be kidding me."

✳✳✳

The monster came charging out of the church at him, waving its talons and bending over as it ran. Though fast, they seemed awkward creatures, and it had its head mostly down as it came, making it difficult for it to see.

Or, Dominick realized, maybe it did it for another reason. What if the creature didn't protect its face by accident, but rather, did so on purpose?

He fired off a few quick shots, aiming for the head. The body loomed large and easy to hit, but the face didn't offer that big a target at all. Normally, he wouldn't have made that the first target he aimed for; however, shooting it anywhere else on the body had little or no effect.

He missed with the first shot. The second one ricocheted off the creature's face, and he groaned in frustration, setting his stance and sighting in. The creature stood only a few meters away now, and he would only get one more try.

The third proved the charm: he hit the monster squarely in the left eye.

It staggered to the side, off-balance, and let out a piercing scream. This time, however, it came from pain, and Dominick breathed a sigh of relief when he discovered he could hurt the thing. If it could get hurt, then it could also get killed.

He turned the creature's hesitation into a chance to back away and create some distance. Somehow, the monster managed to keep its feet and continue running forward, but it moved more slowly now, more cautiously, and used its talons to block its face.

"Aim for the eyes," he called to no one in particular. He doubted Haatim or Frieda could hear him on the opposite side of the church, but he still felt the need to say it if only so he didn't feel so alone.

He continued to backpedal away from the creature, sighting in and taking his time to aim. When the monster blocked its face, it couldn't see him either, so he expected that it would try to wave its hands around and peer through to track him.

Dominick timed it, waited, and then pulled the trigger. This time, his bullet ripped into the other eye, blinding the creature. It screamed again and charged forward wildly, waving its talons at anything and everything it could. Without eyes, though, it couldn't aim at him, but rather, at where he had stood.

He sidestepped, shifting quietly, and then ducked under a wild swing. The creature kept going, rushing past him and continuing further into the town. It stopped about five meters on, freezing into place in the eerie way it did, becoming a statue once more. It stood listening for him. He held perfectly still, refusing even to breathe.

All at once, the creature screamed again, spun in circles, and tilted its head, still listening for him. He didn't know how well it could hear, and so he moved slowly, backing up toward the church and getting distance from it.

It continued to spin, searching for him, and then a loud gunshot echoed from the other side of the church. The thing spun in that direction, hissed, and then took off charging after the sound.

Dominick waited until it got out of sight, and then let out the breath he'd held. He rushed back to the church, which crumbled as more of it got destroyed.

He came to the hole that his body had created. However, he didn't go inside. Instead, he peered in. Abigail knelt on the ground, though she no longer clutched her throat.

Nida stood over her and rubbed her hair. Abigail had her arms crossed over her chest and rocked back and forth, eyes closed. Streaks of liquid ran down her face and clothes, and it looked like blood. He couldn't tell if it came from her, though, or something else.

He had no idea what he witnessed, but he wouldn't let Nida finish whatever she stood doing to Abigail. He stepped up into the room and fired; this time, catching Nida off-guard.

The bullet thudded into her leg, staggering her, and she turned and hissed at Dominick. He fired again, but she dove to the side and landed on all fours, scrambling out of the front door.

He moved to follow, but then Abigail let out a gasping whimper. Instead, he rushed over to her and put an arm around her shoulder, steadying her. The blood didn't belong to her. It looked as if Nida had poured it over her head. Where it touched her bare skin, it sizzled and let off steam.

"Abigail? What happened? What's going on?"

No response. He held her for a second, having no clue what Nida had done to her and unsure what he could do to help. At a loss, he rubbed off the blood, starting with her face and arms. It clung, however, and seemed almost like it had absorbed into her skin.

"Hang on, Abigail," he said. "Just hang on."

✳✳✳

"We need to split up," Frieda said, running alongside Haatim as they dodged around what looked like an old store in the center of town. Part of the building had collapsed when the ground gave way beneath it.

"What?" he asked. "No, no, I don't like that plan."

He felt short of breath and exhausted from running, and it seemed as though they'd gone for hours. Though he knew that only a couple of minutes had passed, it felt so much worse than that.

"One of us needs to get back and help Abigail and Dominick against Nida. This thing can't chase both of us."

"Which one will it chase?"

"Me," Frieda said. "I'll lead it away and buy you some time. Get to Abigail and get her out of here. We made a mistake and never should have brought her here."

"What? Why?"

Frieda didn't respond. She stopped and turned around, facing back toward the monster chasing them. Then she raised the shotgun against her shoulder, waiting for the creature to approach.

It became hesitant, though; it knew the danger that the gun posed to it now, and so tried to dodge out of the roadway. Frieda had readied for that, however, and timed her shot until the thing tried to dodge around her. She swung the gun and sidestepped, pulling the trigger only a meter from the creature.

The shot hit it full in the chest, and it went flying, landing in a heap about four meters back. It lay still for a second, and then twitched and let out a pained scream. Haatim watched in horror while it lifted its smoking body from the ground.

"Go!" Frieda yelled at him, pumping another round into the chamber and circling to the side of the creature. "I've got this."

Haatim didn't need telling twice. He turned and ran, ducking behind a building and heading back to the church. Another gunshot blasted behind him, and he glanced over his shoulder. The roadway lay empty, and the monster didn't chase him. It remained wholly focused on the person hurting it.

He rushed around the corner of an old home and stepped out into the clearing in front of the church. Nida staggered into the clearing away from the edifice. She had her hands in the air and focused on the doorway, and looked like she limped a lot worse than normal.

When he stepped into the clearing, he saw the front of the church collapse, blocking the main entrance. It took him a second to realize that Nida had caused it to happen, using the demon's telekinetic abilities.

The roof shook and broke apart, and a second later, it all fell, obliterating the doorway. Nida seemed hurt badly, and he watched while she turned toward him and half-ran, half-hopped, trying to get away from the church.

Haatim didn't think, only reacted. The gun in his hand came up, and he pulled the trigger, releasing a round into his sister's chest. A look of surprise creased the demon's face, mixed in with fear.

She stopped cold, still wearing a look of shock, and then sank to the ground.

✳✳✳

Frieda got down to two rounds in her shotgun. Once she ran out of salt shot, she would only have her pistol, vial of holy water, and a prayer.

The salt pellets caused damage to the demon but didn't prove enough to stop it outright, and she didn't have enough shots left to waste in trying to beat it down with simple attrition.

The vial of holy water might do some damage. If this was a pure demon—and it seemed so—then holy items would affect it even more than they would a possessed demon. She could pour it on the beast, and had no doubt that it would do significant damage, but enough to kill it? Probably not, but still.

Then she felt the syringe of poison in her pocket. The mundane poisons wouldn't harm the demon, made for the human body, but she'd mixed in herbs and ground poisons that *would* harm the beast. Holy and blessed herbs and things unnatural to them.

She had mixed enough to kill Surgat, so surely, they would prove enough to also take down this brute. Maybe those would work and finish the job where the salt hadn't managed to.

She hated the idea of wasting the poison because she might need it for Abigail, but she'd run out of options. Her pistol wouldn't do any good against the demon, and she doubted the holy water alone could kill it.

In any case, she had no more time, and the demon had made ground on her as she ran. Nerves steadied, she chambered a round and then spun.

All or nothing.

The demon loped several steps behind her, shrieking wildly and swinging its talons as it approached. Those talons looked huge, close up.

She aimed for the creature's midsection and pulled the trigger. The shot echoed through the forest and blasted the demon back several steps. This time, she didn't hesitate, chambering another round and closing in on it while it tried to find its feet.

Frieda held her next shot until she got close to the demon's head. The pellets ripped in and blasted the skull back at an odd angle, all but ripping off the head and tearing away chunks of the outer cartilage.

The entire face sizzled where the salt bore into it, but it still didn't prove enough to kill it. Now, she'd run out of shotgun rounds.

She dropped the shotgun to the ground and slipped the vial of holy water free with one hand. With her other, she grabbed the syringe of poison and pulled it from her pocket.

With a firm grip, she flipped the top from the holy water vial and poured it over the demon's exposed face. It burned where it touched, and the creature shrieked anew.

Then, Frieda jammed the needle into the soft skin under the armor, deep into the soft flesh beneath, and managed to push the poison into place, but the demon thrashed wildly as it stood there. It hit her, hard, with one arm and sliced her across the leg with one if its talons, drawing a deep gash and knocking her away.

She flew black, hitting the ground with force. Though stunned, she rolled to her feet and backpedaled, almost tripping when she tried to put weight on her injured leg. The demon got up, thrashing and flailing in pain and anger as it charged at her. Frieda rolled and scrambled, trying to create separation from the creature, and fell onto her side. The thought that the poison hadn't worked terrified her.

All of a sudden, the demon stopped, maybe two meters away, and stood statue-still. A moment passed while she kept sliding backward on her butt, and then the beast let out a piercing howl that forced her to cover her ears.

It staggered to the left and fell over, writhing on the ground in apparent agony. In disbelief, Frieda watched while its body disintegrated in front of her and turned into a disgusting black-and-red ooze on the forest floor.

The demon kept swinging its arms and trying to pull itself out of the ooze, but after only a few seconds, it got consumed completely, leaving behind only a stain on the ground.

For a few seconds, she hesitated, trying to get her body back under control. Finally, she steeled her nerves and picked herself up. The leg hurt quite a bit, but after a quick test, she found that she could put weight on it and keep moving.

Everything had fallen quiet now, and she didn't know what had happened. Had the fight finished? Did they win?

She didn't know. A rustling sound reached her, and she stopped moving. Off to her left, the other of the creatures stood in the woods a ways off.

When she set eyes on it, she almost let out a gasp. Only by a slim margin had she managed to take down the first one, and no way could she survive another encounter.

After a moment, though, it dawned on her that it wasn't looking for her or its mate. It stood listening, moving its head from side to side. Its eyes had gone, and it looked as if someone had shot them out.

After a few terrifying moments, the demon took off. It ran away from her, deeper into the forest and away from town. Thankful for small favors, she let out a sigh and headed toward the center of town.

She needed to get to the church and find out what had happened.

Chapter 32

H aatim held the pistol in trembling hands, looking down at the body of his sister as she clutched the wound in her chest. If the bullet hadn't hit her heart, it had come extremely close and done considerable damage. The expression on the demon's face, though, he hadn't expected.

Fear.

It had realized that no hope remained of salvaging his sister's corpse and it would soon die. When the body could no longer harbor it, then it would have no choice but to return home to its hellish existence.

It felt fear. The thing rolled onto its side, letting out little gasping noises, and tried to crawl away. It went slowly, scrabbling at the dirt with its free hand and pulling itself along the ground, a few centimeters at a time.

There seemed something visceral about that moment in time that stopped Haatim cold. The smell of gunpowder, and the knowledge that he had pulled the trigger. He could rationalize his sudden action because it *wasn't* his sister anymore, and he had to stop her to keep her from hurting his friends or getting away. However, that didn't change the subconscious feeling he had that he'd shot Nida.

He'd shot his sister.

"Stop," he said, his voice barely a whisper. "Don't make me shoot you again."

The demon chuckled, but then wound up coughing instead. "You think you've won."

"We stopped your ritual," he said. "It's over."

"You think this was about a ritual?" she asked. "After all this time, you still believe you understand what's going on."

"You wanted to bring back Surgat. We know your plan, and it's over. The ritual didn't complete. It's over."

"The ritual? A mere misdirection," Nida said, coughing. She rolled over to look up at Haatim. "A charade I used to bring you here because I knew that it would bring *her* here."

A sickening feeling filled the pit of his stomach. "What?"

"Don't you get it, Haatim? The ritual finished years ago. Surgat has come here already. Twenty years ago."

The words floored Haatim, and the gun slipped out of his hand and fell to the ground. He looked at the ruins of the collapsed church, and his heart skipped a beat. "Abigail."

Nida groaned and smiled, her mouth full of blood, which dripped down her chin. "Now, you understand. We began the ritual twenty years ago. I just came here to finish it, and Abigail gave me the last piece I needed. All I had to do was wake her with the blood."

✳✳✳

Abigail pushed back against the suffocating mental weight holding her down to the floor of the church, but already, she knew the fight as hopeless after only seconds. It felt like when the other demon had possessed her nearly a year ago, only this time so much worse.

There would be no controlling this demon: she wouldn't manage to fight back against it and try to bring Arthur through. That had proven a lie to bring her out here, a trick, and she had fallen for it completely. The only thing left of the ritual was to bring Surgat to life with the blood of the seven, which Nida had poured over her head.

And Surgat had truly awakened.

It lay inside of her, and she could feel the changes happening to her body while it took control. It evolved her, creating something new. Bit by bit, she became something else.

Where the blood touched her skin, it sizzled and boiled, and she understood that Surgat changed her on a fundamental level. The same as the changes she had experienced up to this point, becoming stronger and faster and less in control, but so much more.

"You need to fight it, Abigail," Dominick said, holding onto her. "Control it. Whatever's happening to you, I know you can beat this."

The words seemed meaningless, and Abigail pushed them out of her mind. Dominick had no idea, and his juvenile belief that things would turn out okay wouldn't help her at all. Of course, she couldn't fight Surgat. No way could she overcome something like this in a straight-up brawl.

No, only one way remained to end this.

A moment later, another presence stepped up next to her. Frieda. She glanced up and saw the look of extreme sadness and fear on Frieda's face.

"What happened?" Frieda asked.

"I don't know," Dominick said. "I found her like this."

"Nida completed the ritual."

"You mean ...?"

Frieda ignored him, focusing all of her attention on Abigail. "Push it back down, Abigail. You can't let it take over because when it does, *you* will be lost forever."

"I can't," she muttered, but the words barely sounded human anymore. Already, her throat had changed. Inside there, now, something else grew. A heaviness entered her voice like someone spoke with her.

Her body convulsed and made jarring movements every couple of seconds, though without any pain. Everything felt dull like heavy drugs had numbed her body.

"You have to fight this. Arthur prepared you for this. He worked toward this moment his entire life. He knew you would have the strength to handle this."

"What are you talking about?" Dominick asked, confusion evident in his voice.

Fried continued to ignore him. "Fight, Abigail. Don't give up. You can overcome this."

She could hear Frieda's words, but they sounded far away like she spoke on the other side of a closed door. Abigail pushed and struggled against the weight of the demon that crushed her existence, and she grew desperate. She didn't know how much longer she could hold onto her body.

The longer the struggle went on, the more difficult it became for her to maintain the fight. Exhausted, she weakened as they struggled against one another, but her opponent proved unyielding. It didn't get tired, didn't wear down, or lose focus. It just ... was.

She couldn't win.

Her body convulsed faster, and she let out gasping sounds, doing her best to hold the demon at bay but giving up centimeter by centimeter. Abigail retreated further into herself against the pain and nothingness of it all. She had no idea how to reverse the tide and fight back.

"Abigail," Frieda said, though this time it came out in barely a whisper. Despair laced her mentor's voice. Frieda's faith in her had diminished. "Please, Abigail. You can do this. Don't give up."

They both knew the outcome, however. Abigail only delayed the inevitable.

✳✳✳

Frieda watched with growing desperation as Abigail's body twitched and convulsed. It felt like one of the worst moments of her entire life, watching Abigail struggle with a burden that remained hers alone to bear. She wished she could help, that she could take this away from her, but she couldn't.

What had gone wrong? The cultists all lay dead around her, and their blood drenched the floor of the church. The ritual should have ended, and yet here Abigail knelt, struggling against Surgat's onslaught. How had this happened?

She must have missed something.

Realization crept in that she'd run out of options. Frieda had prayed that this encounter could turn out differently, but Nida and the cult would never stop hunting after Abigail if they didn't confront them now. Part of her had feared that things might end like this.

Perhaps, she should have simply killed Abigail back in the shop instead of putting her through this pain.

The devastation of what she had to do wracked her entire body, and she could hardly imagine going through with it. Abigail seemed like a daughter to her, and killing her would feel akin to killing a part of herself.

However, she could see no other way. A tear streamed down her cheek, and angry, she brushed it away. Arthur had dreaded this ever happening and had given everything to keep Abigail safe. They had both hoped this moment would never come to pass. Every choice and mistake she'd made revolved around this.

Yet, she had failed.

A sheen of sweat covered Abigail's skin, and her eyes fell in and out of focus. Frieda felt an emotional helplessness, a deep well of sorrow within her soul that threatened to swallow and drown her.

Abigail would lose the fight.

All of a sudden, Abigail's eyes came into sharp focus, and she looked up at Frieda, a terrified expression on her young face. She reached into one of her pockets and eased out the syringe of poison with a shaking hand.

Abigail had almost merged completely with the demon and battled for her very life. This poison would end her suffering.

✳✳✳

Abigail's grip on reality weakened as the demonic side of her fought for control. It tried to take over and knew that Frieda and Dominick stood there. It wanted to kill them and taste their flesh.

No, she realized in horror: *she* wanted to kill them. The demon shredded her very existence, destroying her identity and removing her from reality. It wanted to claim this shared body as its own and had prepared for this fight for a long time.

Part of her—a growing part—simply wanted to give up and allow herself to die. It would feel easier, less painful, and had become inevitable. She might as well give up now instead of delaying the thing bound to happen

Those thoughts hadn't come from herself. They'd arisen from the other presence, the one trying to seize control of her body. It wanted to convince her that it had already and that she should give up. It wanted to trick her into surrendering.

Which meant ...

She still might have a chance.

She thought back to their encounter in the park when she'd first faced-off against Surgat. He had feared something, as though she might remember something or knew something about him that would prove bad for it. That meant she had a weapon she could use against it. The only problem was that she didn't know what that weapon might be.

Without it, she didn't stand a chance. Abigail pushed back with all her might, taking a different tactic to try and buy some time. She envisioned them as separate entities, each trying to take control, and rather than just trying to retain control over her body, she pushed against the demonic presence too. Though a part of her, it didn't seem a part to which she had to relinquish control.

Her body moved against her commands, but that didn't bother her as much this time. Now, she had a plan, a goal, and something on which to focus. The demon felt afraid because it knew that, at the end of this struggle, only one of them would continue to exist. And the thought that she might win terrified it.

That gave her confidence and renewed hope.

The struggle remained far from over, however, and it would take a long and arduous battle for her to survive. She only prayed that the demon wouldn't manage to outlast her.

It went on for what felt like forever, and Abigail still had no idea what weapon she might use against the demon. She had it but couldn't imagine what it might be, and her panic made her desperate.

And, now, the demon had control of her body. Each second that slipped past, the closer it came to having complete control and doing whatever it wanted. She felt exhausted and weak and had no more options.

It had finished.

✳✳✳

Frieda couldn't allow Surgat back into the world, but the thought of using the poison on Abigail ripped her heart to shreds. Arthur had given his life to protect her, and she couldn't imagine allowing all of his work to get lost in these final moments.

She took the syringe.

"Do it," Abigail said, convulsing. "Please."

"Do what?" Dominick asked, glancing back and forth between the two women. Realization dawned on him, and he grabbed Frieda's arm. "No, no, no. Frieda, you can't!"

Tears streamed freely down Frieda's face now. She reached down and rubbed Abigail's cheek.

"Do it," Abigail said again, shaking in pain. "End it."

"I'm sorry," Frieda said.

She stuck in the needle, pushed down the plunger, and pushed the poison into Abigail's neck.

✳✳✳

Abigail had imagined that the poison might feel painful. After all, it was designed not only to kill her but to do enough damage that she could never recover. However, she had never envisaged the sheer level of pain it could inflict upon her when Frieda pushed it into her system.

It seemed like knives of ice pumping through her veins, and all her muscles clenched painfully at the exact same time. She could feel the pain now, no longer numb to what went on, and every synapse fired in alarm as agony coursed through her body.

Her only consolation came from the fact that the poison hurt the demon just as much as it did her. The evil within strained, and the pressure on her lessened, as the poison did its deadly work.

Time passed, what felt like a lifetime but, doubtless, only seconds, and then everything slipped away. The world made less sense, and nothing seemed to matter. The pain never let up; Abigail could simply feel everything in her body shutting down as the poison washed over and through her. She felt as if she floated on water, drifting away from reality, and everything turned to black.

The demon clung on, trying to retain control of her body, but now, both of them had lost. Her body died faster than it could heal and became hostile to Surgat as well as Abigail, and the poison inside her brought the demon nearer death. It had nowhere safe to retreat.

She crawled inward, fleeing from the pain and the agony of it all, and locked herself away. Until they both died, she would just have to wait it out. It would only take a matter of time. Her body twitched, though not as much now that she'd gone into shutdown. Everything drew toward the end, and soon, it would all be over.

✳✳✳

Haatim looked at his dying sister, who lay on the dirt and grass outside the partially demolished church. The demon still tried to crawl away, but Nida's body had weakened and wouldn't last much longer.

Every possible emotion flooded through him, from heartache to despair to unimaginable levels of loss. He had watched his sister die once already, and even though nothing remained but the demon, it hurt nearly as badly.

He knelt next to her and reached out. "I'm sorry, Nida," he said.

"Nida isn't here."

"I know she is. I'm sorry it had to end like this. You deserved so much more. You deserved a full life, to grow old and be happy. I'm sorry that we failed you; that I failed you. Please, forgive me."

"You are weak, Haatim. Weak and pathetic. Your sister knows it. You know it. I know it." The demon gasped as it dragged itself across the ground. "When I return to hell, I'll take your sister with me."

"You can't do that."

"Oh, I can and will. Your father put her here with me, and I sure as hell will not let her go. Your only prize here today comes from knowing that your sister will spend eternity with me because of *you*."

"You will not take her."

"We are both dying, and I *am* taking her."

"No." He reached out and placed his hand on Nida's forehead. "*You* shall go to hell, but not her."

"You can't stop me. I defeated you once; I'll do it again."

"Maybe." Haatim closed his eyes. "Perhaps, you will, but you sure as hell won't take my sister."

With a deep and steadying breath, he bridged the connection between himself and the demon.

The effect proved instantaneous, and the demon lashed out at him as soon as the connection formed. Ready to fight, it knew this made the only chance it would have to survive. It attempted to force its way inside Haatim's body to dominate him, fleeing from his sister's broken sack of flesh to take over his. He could feel the demon's glee when it thought it had tricked him.

However, the evil creature had done just what Haatim had expected it to do. The sheer brutal weight of the demon pressed down on him, trying to suffocate him, but instead of attempting to crush the beast like last time, he focused on misdirecting its energy.

The demonic presence washed over him, but he refused to allow it to enter his body. He held his eyes closed, keeping up a steady barrier of essence and energy against which the demon crashed. It reared back and crashed again, trying to burst through and seize control, but Haatim held it at bay.

His theory worked along the lines that the demon could exist outside of a host body, but not for long. It needed a safe harbor to protect itself lest it get dragged back to hell by its nature. If he had it right, then he had an edge: he didn't need to crush or banish it but simply to wear it down.

A few seconds passed with the demon trying to break down his barrier, and sweat beaded on Haatim's face while his concentration waned. How long could he hold up the barrier? The fear that his theory would prove wrong crept over him.

However, it turned out that he didn't have to hold on for long for it to get proven correct. The hits became weaker and weaker as the demon wore down, and he could sense the realization setting in for the beast that it couldn't defeat Haatim like this. It could beat Haatim in a straight-up fight, but he didn't plan to give it one.

Then the demon gave up and prepared to return to Nida's body to regroup. It sought the safety the body allowed, even as it died. If it made it back, then it would fulfill its promise and drag Nida to hell.

Haatim focused all of his energy into one final push and reached out mentally toward his sister, forming a similar barrier around her body to block the demon from reentering.

The effect brought disorientation and confusion, as though he'd somehow fractured his mind into a million little pieces. The demon crashed against the two barriers and mentally cried out in rage and frustration, but Haatim could no longer sense the demon itself. Only its rage and fear as he blocked it from the two bodies.

The hits came rapidly, and each time, his concentration wavered while the disorientation intensified. He started to lose focus of where he was or what was happening, and only clung to the fragile reality by telling himself he couldn't abandon his sister.

Then, suddenly, it stopped. No more hits, no anger, nothing.

A trick? Did the demon want to get him to lower his guard? Whatever, he couldn't hold up the barriers for much longer. Sweat poured down his face, and he trembled from weakness as his mind fell apart and fragmented. Trick or not, he was done.

With a pained sigh, he dropped the barriers. It seemed as if his mind snapped back into place with a rubber band, and the weakness and nausea washed over him in heavy waves. He leaned to the side and vomited, and his eyes became blurry and unfocused.

The disorienting effect lasted a full minute before, finally, he regained control over himself. Then he looked down and saw his sister lying on the ground in front of him. She remained alive, but barely, and occupied her body alone.

The demonic presence had vanished. It left behind barely any trace. It had gotten dragged back to hell, he realized with relief. It had gone.

Nida breathed softly and watched him, holding a hand over her chest. Her expression one of calm even as she lay dying.

"Nida!"

He wanted to lean down and hug her but felt terrified to move her or do anything that might inflict more damage.

"Haatim," she said, then coughed. "It's good to see you."

"Nida. I ..."

He had no idea how to explain. What could he say? So much had happened, so many things had gone wrong; where could he even start?

She held up her hand to stop him. "I knew everything that happened," she said. "The entire time."

"Don't talk." Haatim tried to use his hands to staunch the bleeding.

It was her. The real her. After all this time, here she lay in front of him, alive and present.

And dying.

Tears streamed down his face when the realization of what that meant sunk in. After all this time, trying to rescue his sister and save her from this fight, now he had to watch her die all over again.

"We can fix this." He reached down and grabbed her hand. "We can get you to a hospital, and they can save you."

Nida closed her eyes, gasping and slipping away. When she opened them, he saw not only resignation and understanding there but also contentment. "It's over," she said. "Thank you."

"Nida. No."

"I love you, dear brother."

Then she closed her eyes again. He held her in his arms, crying, as another few moments slipped past.

And then she stopped breathing, and had gone forever.

✳✳✳

Abigail's body went still. Her eyes stayed open but looked vacant, and blood ran down her face and chin. She lay perfectly still, leaning back against Frieda, and stopped breathing. Frieda let out a gasp of sheer emotion. It had finished.

"What did you do?" Dominick asked, pulling back and staring at Frieda with a look of disbelief, which anger soon replaced. "What the *hell* did you just do?"

"Dominick, there wasn't—"

"You killed her. How could you?"

"I tried to save her—"

"After everything we've been through, how could you do this to her? To us? To all of us! God damn it, Frieda."

"I didn't have a choice. She knew that."

"I don't believe you. There is always a better way to—"

Suddenly, it felt like a brick wall had hit Frieda in the stomach, and she went flying backward. She hit one of the old wooden pews and collapsed to the ground in a pile of broken wood.

A cloud of dust hung in the air, and when it cleared, she saw Dominick lying on the far side of the room. He appeared unconscious, and his mouth hung open.

Dazed, and disoriented, she staggered back to her feet and tried to figure out what had happened.

Abigail stood in the center of the room, face locked in an expression of rage and agony. She still convulsed, eyes barely focused, but Frieda knew in that instant that they'd lost all hope.

The poison hadn't killed the demon, only hurt it, but that didn't offer the worst part: Only Surgat remained. In obvious pain, it tried to push the poison out of Abigail's system, and this left the demon distracted and disoriented. Frieda knew, though, that if the poison didn't kill it, then not much time would elapse before it had made a full recovery.

Abigail opened her mouth, and a guttural roar poured out. She reached down and retrieved Arthur's sword from the ground, but then dropped it with a sudden hissing noise. Where the metal touched her flesh, it burned.

Frieda drew her pistol and fired, but the demon moved too quickly, running to the side and diving out through the hole in the wall.

Chapter 33

Haatim heard a sound and glanced behind him. Abigail came flying out of the wrecked church. Only one wall still stood, which looked on the verge of collapsing too, as the structural integrity of the building broke down.

"Abigail!" he shouted, but she didn't even turn over to look at him. Then Abigail disappeared, sprinting through the forest and back in the direction of Raven's Peak. She moved fast with unnaturally long strides. For sure, something had gone wrong.

He stood, exhaustion washing over him and making him wobble. Then he attempted to give chase. It proved of no use, though, and even if she hadn't run much faster than normal, he never could have caught up. He'd ended up too broken from his recent exertion even to try.

He felt a chill when a gust of wind whistled past. More movement came from behind. Dominick and Frieda came out of the church and headed toward him, climbing over the rubble of the building. Frieda supported Dominick, holding him under the shoulder, and in her other hand, she carried Arthur's sword.

"Why do you have that?" Haatim asked.

"The demon left it." Frieda nodded toward the forest. "I think that touching it caused the creature pain."

"Is that normal?"

"Not that I know of." She held up the sword and looked at it.

Dominick clutched his head, and blood ran down his face, and he appeared dazed.

Frieda noticed the body on the ground, and her face fell. "Nida."

Haatim closed his eyes. "Gone."

"I'm sorry."

"It's Okay. The demon didn't get her. What the hell happened?" Haatim asked.

Dominick looked at him, at a complete loss for words.

The expression on Frieda's face, though, shifted to one of despair. "It didn't work."

"What didn't work?"

"The thing she injected into Abigail." Dominick shook his head and jerked free of Frieda's support. He wheeled around on her. "What the hell was it? What did you inject her with?"

"Poison," Frieda said. "It should have killed her."

"It *what*?" Haatim felt shocked and confused and more than a little hurt at the idea. He took a few steps toward Frieda. "What the hell?"

"The idea didn't only come from me," Frieda said, backing away slowly and holding up her hands. "Haatim, I promise you, we had no other way. Abigail knew that. She appreciated the risks, and this offered the only chance we had."

"The only chance to what? Kill her?" Haatim said. "What the hell happened to saving her? This is insane."

"It meant the only way to stop Surgat."

"He got inside her." Haatim nodded. "Nida told me as much, but you still had no right to try and kill her."

"We couldn't let Surgat out into the world." Frieda pleaded with her eyes. "Please, you have to understand."

"Oh, I understand. You felt willing to kill Abigail to stop the demon. Well, did it stop him?" Haatim gestured toward where Abigail had disappeared. "Does that look like the demon got dealt with?"

"Haatim."

"You convinced her that killing herself had become *necessary* to try and deal with a demon that *your* family helped to create? And, you didn't even tell *us* what you planned to do. What the hell? Do Dominick and I matter to you at all? What, did you think that we wouldn't notice she'd died suddenly?"

"Abigail didn't want me to tell you," she said, a defeated look on her face. "Either of you. She made me promise. She thought that if you knew, you would try and stop her."

"That's because we would have," Dominick said. "Because that is a ridiculous plan. You knew that this could happen and still brought Abigail out here?"

"She had full awareness of the risks. We decided it better to confront the demon on our terms than to run and hide. We couldn't wait this out because the cult would never have given up."

"You mean *you* decided."

"*We*. Abigail planned it as much as I did."

"And she's *certainly* in her right mind. You brought her here and served her up on a platter for Surgat."

"Not that simple. It should never have come to this."

"Well, it did."

"I wanted to stop the ritual and save her before this could ever happen. The poison remained her last resort. I don't understand why it didn't work. It should have."

"It didn't, and thank God," Haatim said. "You tried to murder her."

"She knew the risks and still chose to face the demon."

"Only because she thought she could save Arthur," Haatim said.

Frieda froze. "What?"

"Nida told me that Abigail came for that reason alone. Mitchell lied to her and said it would be possible to use Surgat to bring back Arthur. He worked with Nida the entire time."

Frieda shook her head. "No. Not possible."

"Well, it happened. He played us. All of us. And now, Abigail has gone."

Frieda stood silent for a long time. "This isn't productive," she said, finally. "I understand that you both feel furious with me, and I'm sorry for misleading you, but right now, we have bigger problems. We had no other plan that could stop Surgat, and it failed."

"You thought poison would work?" Haatim asked. "I watched her recover from having her stomach torn and a gunshot to her hip in a matter of days."

"*This* poison should have worked," Frieda said. "And it almost did."

"Then, why didn't it?"

She shook her head. "I don't know. You said Mitchell worked with Nida. Maybe he found out about the poison and warned her."

"How?"

"I don't know. In any case, it doesn't change the facts or how desperate our situation has become."

"No, it doesn't. Now we have a pissed-off super-demon and no real weapons," Dominick said.

"So, what do we do?" Haatim looked from one to the other.

"I don't know," Frieda said. "I think it headed somewhere to enact the second part of its plan."

"What's that?"

"A summoning," Frieda said. "It will create a portal."

"A portal. Why? I thought they didn't need a portal to bring Surgat here."

"Not for Surgat." Frieda pursed her lips, and then said, "For the rest of his demon army."

✳✳✳

They jogged back to the car, moving silently through the woods and pushing a brutal pace to get back as fast as possible. Though all in a hurry, Haatim doubted that any of them had any clue what they should do next.

Lost in his thoughts, he tried to come to terms with everything that had happened. None of it made sense, and he felt more hurt by what Abigail had done to him than he cared to admit.

He had talked about what would happen after this ended, fishing for information and trying to instill hope for a possible future. She hadn't even proven willing to tell him that she planned to take her life if things didn't work out. Nor had she told him that she had become the vessel that Surgat intended to use upon his resurgence into the world.

She had lied to his face, letting him think that things could work out and have a happy ending. Did she not tell him because she didn't trust him? Or because she wanted to protect him?

Did it even matter?

Whatever, she had kept something huge and life-altering from him, and that hurt. He'd thought he'd broken through her shell and found the woman beneath, but now he didn't believe he could trust anything as far as Abigail was concerned.

Or Frieda, for that matter. She had withheld so much from them these last few weeks and months. Her secrets ran deep and went back decades. Anyone that good at keeping secrets always had an agenda.

Part of him—a fairly large part—just wanted out. This life had gotten thrust upon him, and his only consolation to the screwed-up-ness of everything came from thinking he could trust his new friends. Abigail, Frieda, and Dominick provided the bedrocks upon which he built his new world, and now, two of them had shattered. Could he still trust Dominick?

Did he even feel willing to try?

He didn't know. As soon as this all finished, he would need to do some serious soul searching and decide how he wanted to spend the rest of his life.

They made it to the waiting car, and all climbed inside without a word. Each of them absorbed in their thoughts and dealing with the somber situation on their own. Dominick drove, and they soon got back on the road and headed toward Raven's Peak.

It had begun to rain, only a light sprinkling, and it grew colder. The day darkened as storm clouds continued to settle in above them, and before long, it would pour down. He leaned his head against the cold window, still exhausted from his encounter with Nida's demon but recovering somewhat.

However, as he sat there, he realized that not everything he understood about the situation added up.

"Something bothers me," he said, sitting up again and rubbing his face. He spoke directly to Frieda in the passenger seat. "How long have you known?"

"About what?"

"About Surgat and Abigail. When did you know she provided the vessel?"

Frieda sat in silence for a moment. He assumed she sat there trying to decide whether or not to lie. At this point, he just expected her to withhold the truth.

Finally, Frieda admitted, "Since she was a little girl. Arthur found her, and I came in after to try and determine what they'd attempted to do. When I realized, I felt horrified. They didn't have the blood, but since she was so young, they thought they could do the ritual without it. I couldn't believe they would do something like that to a child."

"It didn't work?"

"Arthur interrupted their ritual, but not before they had managed to do significant damage to her. I knew the correct thing to do was tell the Council and the Church."

"But you didn't?"

"They would have killed her without a moment's hesitation, and I couldn't do that to Arthur. He had just lost his entire family, and saving this young girl had great importance for him. I had to choose between my position on the Council and the man I loved."

"And you chose Arthur?"

"I chose both of them. It didn't take long before I loved Abigail almost as much as Arthur. By then, I'd committed and would do anything to protect her."

"Did Arthur know?"

"Not for a long time," Frieda said. "I prayed that I had gotten it wrong and made a mistake, and for years, I wondered if maybe I had. But then, when she got a few years older, she changed."

"Changed?"

"The essence of Surgat, which the ritual transferred over, struggled to assume control; though, in his weakened state, he couldn't dominate her fully. Instead, he tried to corrupt her. I thought I could solve the problem using old cult rituals if I only had enough time. I—"

"You performed the ritual on Arthur," Dominick said. "But you didn't tell him what it really was, did you?"

She shook her head. "No, I didn't tell him everything. I explained to him that it had risks involved, but I didn't tell him the whole truth. I think he still would have gone through with it, even had he known what it would do to him eventually. I thought that with enough time, I could find a way to fix both of them. I believed I would manage to remove Surgat and put things back to normal."

"And then you lost Arthur."

"Which proved bad enough. But I never counted on Aram and Mitchell working with the cult. They manipulated Aram, and they played us. If I had to guess, Aram first got guided to the cult through Mitchell with promises that they could bring back Nida. The entire time, they had *this* as their end game. They strove for this for all these years."

"That's why the Church wanted to kill Abigail."

Frieda nodded. "I never told them the full extent of Abigail's condition, but I suspect they realized what I had kept from them when the Ninth Circle went after the blood. When they understood the risk, they ordered our deaths. They assumed that if they killed Abigail before she turned into the half-demon, they could end this without unleashing him once again."

"They nearly did in Cambodia, but she survived."

"Yes. She survived. They will realize their failure soon enough, though many civilians will die before they can stop Surgat. Our mistakes ... *my* mistakes will cost the world a lot of pain."

"What makes Abigail different?" Dominick asked. "Isn't she just possessed?"

"It goes beyond that. She merged—what the Church would call integration. Or nearly so. I think Abigail remains in there for now, but when the demon finishes destroying her, it will absorb her entire existence and use it to gain power. Her soul will get consumed completely, and the demon will have full access to all its capabilities within her body."

Dominick blew out a breath. "That's why she tried to kill herself."

Frieda nodded. "Yes."

They continued down the road in silence. The rain had picked up and worsened. Beyond the storm, though, he picked up something else. At first, Haatim had a hard time understanding it ... like a feeling in the air around them. As if they had left the world behind and entered somewhere else. Some other plane of existence.

Maybe they had. It seemed impossible to tell what would happen now, and the closer they got to the city, the stronger that feeling became.

Haatim felt angry at Abigail for withholding such important information from him, but the more he thought about it, the more he realized that despair underlay the anger. The thought of losing her left him terrified, and the knowledge that she'd felt willing to take her life, even if it *did* seem the only way to stop this demon from destroying her soul and taking her completely, ate at him inside.

Haatim couldn't bear the thought of losing her yet again. He hadn't even come to terms with the idea of her death when she got lost in the mountains, or when he'd found her nearly dead in Cambodia, and this seemed so much worse. She had gotten backed into a corner with no options, and all because of the decisions and actions people made when she was only a child.

"Where do you think she went?" he asked, after a few more minutes.

"I was going to ask you that," Frieda said.

"Me?"

"You can do incredible things, Haatim. I think you can find either the demon or Abigail if you try."

He opened his mouth to say that he didn't know how, but then realized it as a lie. He knew how to reach out and search for demons, just never so far away.

Exhausted and weak, the idea of trying to tap into those powers again made him feel nauseous.

"I don't know if I can do that right now," he said, and then took a deep breath. "But I'll try."

He reached into himself, closing his eyes and focusing on his internal abilities. Instantly, heavy nausea filled him, and his body tensed. He tried to tap into the energy but couldn't find it, and it brought physical pain attempting to reach out and search the area. It felt like the world vibrated, so he stopped and opened his eyes.

"I can't do it," he said. "I can't find her."

It took him a second to realize that the shaking of the ground hadn't just happened in his head. The car *shook*. A slight tremor as though an earthquake had hit nearby. They'd reached only a kilometer or so outside of town now, and they could see it rising in the distance.

They all exchanged glances.

"It's okay," Frieda said. "I think we found her."

***

"What the hell?" Dominick yelped when the car shook. "What's happening?"

Frieda didn't answer straight away. It felt like a thrumming—constant like a nearby jackhammer shaking the pavement. They continued forward, down the road, and the town grew larger while the rain pattered against the windshield and roof. As they went, the rumbling intensified.

"It seems like it comes from over that way." Haatim pointed up ahead. "Near the center of town."

"Yeah, but what the hell *is* it?" Dominick stared through the rain-lashed windscreen.

"I don't know," Frieda said, finally. "But I think we're about to find out."

Chapter 34

Abigail had no idea of her location.

She found herself sitting on the edge of a bed in a dark bedroom but couldn't remember ever coming into the room or sitting down. It seemed like she'd just appeared there all of a sudden.

A single window broke the monotony of the wall on one side of the room, and a door stood closed on the opposite side. She stood and walked over to the window, and then realized that everything outside looked hazy and out of focus. She couldn't even see the ground or trees clearly. Abigail could see just enough to tell that she didn't occupy the ground floor of whatever building she stood in.

The room felt vaguely familiar like she had come here before; however, she couldn't place it from memory. The bed held stains in various places, and the sheets looked torn and frayed. The old and musty walls showed chipped paint and holes where the wood had rotted.

The memory of this place didn't come only from externals, though. A vague undercurrent of fear ran through her entire body. It filled her with dread and a sense of weakness that she couldn't explain.

Dread of what? Abigail didn't know.

The last thing she remembered was standing out in the woods with Frieda, Dominick, and Haatim and trying to stop Nida. She couldn't remember what had happened, or if they'd stopped the ritual.

Had they lost?

Had she died?

"How did I get here?" she asked aloud, shaking her head. Not expecting an answer, she felt completely caught off-guard when she received one.

"I found you here."

With a yelp, she jumped to the side, but almost instantly, nostalgia replaced her fear. The voice shot pangs of emotion through her body.

Arthur's voice.

The emotional outburst she felt at that moment caused her to sob with both longing and joy.

She spun and saw Arthur leaning against the doorframe of the room. She hadn't even heard it open and suspected that, in fact, it hadn't. It had simply ... changed.

He stood watching her with his arms folded across his broad chest. He looked younger than she remembered, maybe late twenties or early thirties, and appeared a lot healthier than he had later on in his life.

Arthur must have looked like that when he'd first found her, and before he had sacrificed everything to try and save her life from Surgat. This must come from before he'd given up his life to protect her from herself.

"Arthur!" Abigail rushed across the room and threw herself into his arms. He caught her and pulled her close, hugging her back. She squeezed him for a long moment before pushing him back. "This must be a dream."

It didn't feel like a dream, though; she could feel his warmth and smell his sandalwood cologne. He felt real and complete, not some figment of her imagination. And, she couldn't even remember this version of him when she pictured Arthur in her mind. Had she conjured it in her mind?

"Hey, Abi." He put a hand on her shoulder and smiled down at her. "It's been a long time."

✳✳✳

"Is this real?"

"What do you think?"

She hesitated. "I don't think so," she said, at last. "If it were, I would at least understand how I got here, wouldn't I? We'd gone to Raven's Peak to fight Nida. That's the last thing I remember, but I don't remember if we won or lost or how I got here."

"What *do* you remember?"

"I remember ..." Abigail took a step back from Arthur.

He watched her, a curious expression on his face.

"I remember blood," Abigail whispered.

"Blood?"

"Lots of it. Oceans of it. It seemed like I drowned in it."

"Oh?"

She could recall the sensation when Nida had poured the blood on her forehead. It had felt like she'd gotten dunked into a river of the stuff—thick and coppery and overwhelming her senses.

However, it didn't make a complete memory and came more like a sensation of something she had experienced. Abigail couldn't put her thumb on it to nail it down. The details remained fuzzy and incoherent.

She shook her head. "I can't explain it."

"What else do you remember?"

"Dominick," she said. "Standing over me. And Frieda. She ..."

"She what?"

The memory came like a bolt of lightning: the needle injected into her neck, the poison pumping through her veins.

"She killed me."

"Did she?"

"Am I dead?"

"Are you?"

Abigail frowned. "You aren't a lot of help."

Arthur smiled back at her, but this time, he didn't respond verbally.

She let out a sigh and rubbed her forehead. "What did you mean when you said that you found me here?" she asked. "Found me when? Do you mean with the cult?"

"Yes. I found you here when you were a little girl. Not this room, exactly, but rather, this place."

"You never told me about when you rescued me," she said. "I asked you about it many times when I was little, but you always refused to tell me."

"The real Arthur never saw this room. He once told you that he wondered where they'd kept you, but you said you didn't remember."

"I didn't," she said. "I don't."

"Don't you?"

She hesitated. "Where are we?"

"An old manor in the woods, long abandoned and crumbling to ruins. You don't know where it is in the world, but you remember this place. Frieda told you that they kept you here for weeks, torturing you to break your spirit and prepare you for some ritual."

She shook her head. "I don't recall any of this."

"That's what you think."

"It's true."

"That's the salvation of childhood: the ability to forget the worst things that happen to us. The memories stay here, though, only locked away."

"Locked away?"

"Yes. This is as close as I could bring you without doing damage to your psyche. You must experience the rest on your own."

"What?"

"The memories feel painful. If I immerse you into them, and you reject them, then all is lost. You must, consciously, bring yourself into them."

Abigail looked around the room once more, though now, she could remember it better. She recalled the hours spent here wishing she could escape but feeling too terrified even to try. They kept her here and fed her, but they almost never talked to her.

"They kept me here when they weren't torturing me."

"Don't focus on the torture, Abigail. It isn't what we're after."

"Then, what do we want?"

"That day when Arthur saved you. It is important that you try to remember everything that happened."

"Why?"

"Because it can help you. You need to think back to that day when they performed the ritual on you. It happened during the ceremony, and you've buried that moment the deepest."

"What do you mean? Why would that moment feel worse than the torture?"

"Because the demon came into you then. You need to find the name of the demon when they summoned him."

"Surgat."

"*We* gave it that name, but that was not the demon's true name. Even The Ninth Circle never knew it, and because of that, couldn't control it when first they summoned it into this world."

"Then, how on Earth would I know the demon's true name?"

"Because the demon told you," Arthur said. "When it first entered you for the merger. They wanted to use a little girl for that reason. You would have proven easier for the demon to control. It told you."

"What do you mean? When did it tell me?"

"When you invited it in."

"I didn't invite it."

"They scared and manipulated you."

"No. I would remember."

"Don't focus on that. It's a minor detail. You must focus, instead, on the moment and find the name."

"I can't."

"Focus, Abigail. The memory remains there, and all you have to do is bring yourself into it and experience it. You will learn the demon's name, which terrifies it."

"Because it would give me power over it," she said. That gave her the reason that the demon had felt terrified when she came with Sara: it feared she would remember. "Which means I can beat it."

"Not without the name. We've come close to that memory, and you just need to tap into it."

"But, I don't remember *any* of this."

"It is all right here. Just try."

She blew out a breath. "Okay."

Abigail tried to think back to that day, or even that time in her life. It felt like such a long time ago, and the memories appeared muddled. Faint, they jumbled together.

They'd strapped her to a table; robes and pale faces; candles, incense, and chanting; nothing about the memory felt concrete enough to grasp onto. The emotions had vividness, even if the memories didn't, and after only a few seconds of straining, she gasped for air and nearly had a panic attack.

As a little girl, she'd blocked these memories, and trying to access them now invoked the primal fear she'd originally associated with them. She'd convinced herself that the memories had no reality, and it felt hard to believe any of that had actually happened to her. They seemed more like memories of something she'd seen on TV than an actual thing in her life.

"Focus, Abigail."

"It won't do any good," she said, gasping and walking back to the bed. She fought to control her racing heart. "I can't do it."

"You *need* to access those memories. I can't do it for you."

"But, you *are* me."

"In a sense, but not completely. You created me to help, but I can't do anything that you cannot do yourself. This gives us the only chance we have to stop Surgat and survive this."

"So, I'm basically just having a conversation with myself."

The echo of Arthur didn't reply.

"Great," she muttered. "I hid those memories for a reason."

The memories brought her back to when she was just a scared and broken little girl before Arthur had found her.

The moment when Arthur rescued her had become the moment when she considered her life to have begun. Everything before that didn't matter; it was just *before*.

Arthur taught her how to get strong, how to fight, and how to protect herself. He showed her how to forget about the terrible things that had happened to her and to use the emotions from those events to make her strong.

It scared her that accessing those memories would bring it all back. Everything she had done, all the trials she had overcome: it would all be lost. She would get brought back to the crying and timid little girl, strapped to the table all those years ago.

"I can't," she said. "I can't remember anything from those months, let alone that day."

"The memories are *there*."

"But I can't access them."

"Think, Abigail. This is important."

"I know, but I don't *remember*. I must have blocked it out or destroyed them."

"You hid them, but you can find it again. You can still access it, but you need to focus."

"How do you know about them, and I don't?"

"Because I am a fragment of *you*."

A sinister thought crossed her mind. What if this were the demon, disguised and trying to bring her back to that moment for its own reasons? What if it planned to use that moment to weaken her so that it could assume control? Had it told her the name for real, or was this all a distraction?

What if this all turned out as nothing more than a trick, and it used Arthur to distract her and break her will?

"Why did you come here?"

"To help you," the visage of Arthur replied.

"You aren't the real Arthur. What are you, really?"

"Your memory of Arthur."

"No. I don't remember Arthur looking like this. If I imagined you, then you would look different. I don't recall this version of him."

"Yes, you do. He looked like this when he came to rescue you. This is as close as I can bring you to that moment in time, which makes this a fitting image to display."

"The demon has access to my memories. It could use you to trick me."

"It has access to your body," the echo of Arthur said. "However, you remain in control of your memories."

She hesitated. "My body? What's it doing?"

"I don't know," the echo said. "I only exist in your memories. You brought me here because *you* know the importance of this memory."

Abigail didn't know if that held truth or not. She didn't know if the demon would need her to access the memory, or if what the echo of Arthur said would prove accurate, and she also didn't know how to verify it.

Unable to remember if she'd ever known the name of the demon, she couldn't know whether or not it spoke true. However, she did remember its fear when she'd come with Sara, and it came from something she *knew* and could use against it. But, did that give enough to trust this version of Arthur and search out these memories?

Basically, she felt stuck with an impossible decision. Trust the visage of Arthur and try to find the demon's name, or ignore it and try to fight back against the creature in another way.

It came down to the realization that she didn't have any other choice. If she left this memory without a weapon she could use against the demon, then she would, essentially, have given up. The beast would destroy her within moments. Only a fluke of the poison had hidden her away and given her a chance at all.

No, when she thought about it, she had no real choice but to trust the echo of Arthur.

Essentially, she had to trust in herself.

Abigail took a steadying breath. "What do I need to do?"

"You need to go into that memory. That offers the only chance you have of surviving this."

Chapter 35

"You ready?" Dominick asked.

Haatim couldn't think of anything in his life that he felt less ready for than what they were about to do. Dominick pulled the car to a stop, and the shaking grew worse. The day had darkened even further, and that sense of otherworldliness had intensified. It barely felt like they remained on Earth, and more like they had transported to somewhere *other*.

A place between.

Redness glowed up ahead of them, about a block down the street and to the west of their current position. The town felt less like a ghost town and more like a sleeping beast now. That red glow appeared quite ominous and seemed to form the central point of the vibration.

He could *feel* the presence of evil from that glow—like a hungry animal waiting for its moment to burst through from the other side and come forth into this realm.

"Haatim?" Dominick said. "Hey, Earth to Haatim."

Haatim glanced over, startled. "What?"

"I asked if you're ready to do this. We don't have a lot of time, and we all need to stay focused."

He took a deep breath and lied, "Ready."

"All right."

All three of them climbed out of the vehicle. Broken sections of the pavement showed huge cracks from the violent vibrations. They stood near the epicenter of it now, and it ripped apart the entire city. Haatim found it difficult to keep his feet, and the motion made him sick to his stomach.

Or, maybe, that came from the situation. He couldn't tell for sure. They circled to the trunk, and Dominick popped it open. Frieda looked as out of sorts in this situation as Haatim. For the first time since he'd met her, she appeared dirty and disheveled, covered in mud and dirt and without any of her usual grace or poise. To see her like that didn't give him any confidence.

"Here." Dominick handed him a shotgun and pistol. "Don't waste your ammunition. We don't have a lot left."

"What the hell will we do?"

"End this."

"How?"

Dominick picked up a shotgun and chambered a round. "I don't know."

"We need to kill Abigail," Frieda said. "We won't have another chance."

"And how in the world do you plan to do that? She has Surgat running the show now, plus he's about to bring in a demon army. What chance do we have?"

Frieda pulled a pistol out of the trunk. Then, with her free hand, she picked up Arthur's sword.

"How's your leg?" Dominick asked.

They had patched up her cut back in the woods before going to the car, but already, it had bled through. "Do you need to stay behind?"

"No, I'm fine."

The sword looked a beautiful weapon, and Haatim could appreciate the quality of the blade without knowing much about such things. The metal itself held intricate carvings.

"The demon didn't keep the sword?" he asked.

"It tried to," Frieda said. "But, this thing still has some tricks up its sleeve. It hurt the demon just grabbing the hilt, and I hope that the sharp end does even better."

"Do you think we stand a chance?"

"A small one," she said. "Or, at least, we do if we find Abigail in there."

"If we do, then we need to get her out."

"That possibility has gone," Frieda said, shaking her head in sadness. "But, she might give us an opening."

"What do you mean?"

"If she can distract the demon, she might give us the opportunity to kill them both."

"No."

"It's the only way we can end this."

"I have a better idea. Let me talk to her."

"Haatim."

"I can reach her. I know I can, and I can help her like I helped Nida."

"You said yourself that you've become too weak after saving Nida from the demon. Besides, I doubt you could do anything to this demon even if at your full strength."

Though she didn't mean it as offensive, the words stung anyway. However, she had it right, no matter how much he wished she hadn't. Haatim had barely survived his last encounter with a demon, and in his weakened state, it would prove suicide to open up a link to Surgat.

But, he couldn't just abandon Abigail. He had lost his sister to this demon and would be damned before he let it take Abigail without trying to get her back.

Nevertheless, he didn't object further to Frieda's plan because neither Dominick nor Frieda would side with him. They both believed saving Abigail had become a lost cause and, right now, the only thing that mattered was destroying Surgat.

Instead, he acquiesced, "Okay. You're right."

Frieda nodded. "No demons have come through yet, but the portal must be nearing completion. Once it is done, Surgat will bring through allies and slaves."

"Like the demons we fought in the woods?"

"Not likely. Those have far more power and rarity than most of his army. However, whatever he does bring, he'll have a lot of them."

"That's encouraging," Dominick said.

"How do we stop Surgat from completing the portal?"

"We need to knock the energy off balance. Redirect it, somehow."

"How do we do that?"

"I don't know," Frieda said. "Surgat won't have full access to all of his abilities until he destroys Abigail completely, but he still makes for an incredibly formidable opponent. We must stay cautious."

"What do you mean?"

"Don't underestimate the demon, and don't believe anything Abigail says. She is helpless now, and the demon has control. It will try to use your relationship with her against you. You cannot trust it."

"But, Abigail remains in there." Haatim frowned. "You said so yourself. What if she needs our help?"

"She's trapped and has no control."

Haatim looked away. "Fine. Ready?"

"Haatim, promise me that no matter what the demon says, you won't listen."

He hesitated for a second. "Okay," he said, finally. "I promise."

Frieda didn't look convinced. "Haatim."

"We need to go." He fussed with his weapon. "You said yourself that we need to hurry before he completes the portal."

"Yeah. We don't have time for this," Dominick said. "I'm sorry, Haatim; I'm with Frieda on this. I've seen demons try to manipulate before and know their capabilities."

"You both sound so sure, but still admit that you have no way to know. This is totally new territory. Nothing like this has ever happened to any of us. What if we've just condemned her to death?"

Dominick shook his head. "Haatim."

"Fine. I promise I won't listen to the demon. But, if Abigail *is* still in there, I'll try and save her." He didn't wait for them to respond, just walked toward the red glow.

They'd neared to less than a hundred meters from it now, and he couldn't shake that feeling that they moved further into some different world as they went closer. The laws of this universe no longer seemed to apply.

He hadn't gotten it wrong when he'd called it new territory. This presented something entirely new.

It seemed as if they'd passed into some place *between*, not on Earth anymore, but also not in hell. Not quite, at least. The wind had stopped blowing, and the city had a surreal feel to it. Even the clouds barely moved anymore. It had stopped raining, but the storm looked far from over.

"Abandon all hope, ye who enter here," he muttered under his breath.

"What?" Dominick asked.

"Nothing."

"Shoot first," Frieda said, though she didn't seem to direct the statement at anyone in particular. Haatim felt fairly certain that she'd spoken more to herself as much as them. "Don't try to figure out what it is or understand it. If you see something you can't explain, just kill it."

"Keep your wits about you," Dominick said. "Whatever happens, don't allow yourself to get tricked."

This statement, Haatim knew, did get directed at him. He ignored them both, holding his shotgun and preparing himself for the fight to come.

He reached the edge of the storefront one street removed from the red glow. The thrumming came from here, and it caused the ground to shake violently with unsteady tremors.

It felt like the earth would rip apart at any second and swallow them; although, energy from the red glow seemed to hold it together. Energy filled the entire area, and it felt like a living creature.

A living evil creature.

"I'll circle around and flank her," Dominick said.

"Okay." Haatim nodded.

Dominick slipped off, disappearing around the building and down a back alley. Haatim watched him go, and then glanced at Frieda.

They waited a few moments for Dominick to circle, and then Frieda nodded and hefted the sword. "It's time."

Haatim nodded. "All right. Here we go."

He stepped around the corner, raised the shotgun, and headed toward the red glow.

✳✳✳

Abigail stood in the center of the street, directly inside the red glow and facing toward them. Haatim thought to try and hide close to the building, and then changed his mind. The demon knew they'd come and waited for them, a wide smile on its face.

Streams of red energy swirled in the air, circling and flowing in arcs and leaving behind trails that emitted a soft light before fading away. These created the glow that surrounded her body.

It looked magical but had an ominous feel that caused Haatim's heart to skip a beat. The energy streams felt unnatural and evil and meant that whatever the demon had initiated, it had almost finished. Before long, the portal would complete, and demons would come forth.

"I'm glad you all could make it," the demon called out, clapping its hands. "You came just in time."

Frieda and Haatim exchanged a glance, each one waiting for the other to engage the beast. They both looked for the other's cue, and both felt afraid to initiate.

"We have only just begun," the demon said. "And it is *so* nice to have an audience. After I finish flaying the flesh from your skin, the true fun will begin."

The two moved closer to the thing in the road, fanning out to flank the enemy. They went slowly, struggling to keep their feet when the ground rolled and rocked. It looked like the demon stood at the epicenter, and the ground there didn't shake at all.

Haatim raised his shotgun, but still stood too far away to feel confident he wouldn't just waste shells. With only a few rounds, he didn't want to fire without the certainty that he could hit the demon.

To their left stood the abandoned city hall building, and on the right, lay the storefronts of a couple of ransacked shops. Dominick would come from the right, but Haatim didn't know his precise location. Instead, he focused on the demon, wanting to keep its attention so that it wouldn't see Dominick coming.

"I banished your ally. The one that possessed my sister," Haatim said.

The demon shrugged. "A temporary setback. She served her purpose. I might have destroyed her, anyway, if only to diminish her ego and keep her from conspiring against me. If anything, you did me a favor."

Haatim glanced over at Frieda, taking his lead from her. She stood watching the beast, sword held ready and with a hesitant look on her face.

"Frieda?"

She glanced over at him. "Let's do this."

"Yes. Let's," the demon said.

Then movement came from behind the demon. Dominick stepped out of hiding. He came out, gun blazing, and fired several shots at its back.

The demon neither moved nor flinched. Maybe Dominick's shots had missed. Then, soft thudding noises sounded when the bullets tumbled off the demon's back and to the ground, bouncing across the uneven pavement.

Time seemed to stop, and Haatim saw the horrified expression on Dominick's face. Slowly, the demon turned to face him.

The back of Abigail's shirt showed several holes—little circles in her clothing. The bullets hadn't missed but flattened against the demon's skin.

"Uh-oh." Dominick took a step back toward the alley. "So not good."

He echoed Haatim's thoughts.

Abigail smiled. "My turn."

✳✳✳

Dominick ducked into the alleyway just as something smashed into the ground where he'd stood. He glanced back. A car lay on its side in the mouth of the alley.

And another one flew through the air, arcing down at him. He dove to the side just as it landed and missed him by only a meter, and then he kept going.

He ran, heading deeper into the alley and trying to create distance between himself and the demon. His pistol useless, he felt sure his shotgun wouldn't do much better, which meant that he didn't have any other options to bring down Abigail/Surgat.

But, at least he could distract her and keep her busy while Frieda and Dominick tried to find a way to close the portal.

An enormous crashing sounded. The wall in front of him, to his left, collapsed. It came down like an avalanche, crumbling into huge stones.

Dominick dove forward into a roll, ducking behind an abandoned dumpster and narrowly avoiding the hail of rocks. A few clipped him, painfully, but then he got past it. The dumpster took the brunt of the impact.

From that vantage point, he glanced back. Calmly, Abigail walked down the alley. Her eyes glowed red, and she looked quite peaceful. The ground shook beneath her feet, but she remained steady while she walked.

"Almost a thousand years locked in that hell," the demon called. "I will pay everyone responsible back in full."

"Hate to tell you," Dominick shouted back, and then fired his pistol at her face. Hopefully, this one would have better luck. The bullet hit her in the forehead, flattened, and then fell to the ground. She didn't even flinch. Dominick let out a groan, and then said, "Everyone responsible for what happened to you died a long time since."

"Then, you three will suffice, for now."

Dominick turned and sprinted, heading away from the demon and deeper into the city. Then he circled back, not wanting to get too far from his friends, and watched out for the red glow, which he hoped and prayed would disappear because it would mean the demons wouldn't come.

"Come on," he said to himself. "Close that damn portal."

✳✳✳

"What do we do now?" Haatim asked after Abigail and Dominick had disappeared deeper into the city.

"I don't know," Frieda said. "I wish I did."

"We need to close the portal, right?"

She hesitated, and then said, "Right. Yeah."

"Any ideas?"

"Not yet."

Abigail had chased Dominick down the alley and away from the glowing red swirling stuff, which meant that either Surgat had made a mistake, and they would have the chance to disable the portal, or that he had supreme confidence that they couldn't close it.

Most likely, it came down to the latter reason.

Frieda edged toward the ritual spot, moving cautiously and examining it. Haatim walked with her, scanning over the area and trying to wrap his mind around it all.

"Is it just me, or did the ring just get bigger? It looks almost like it's about to open."

Frieda glanced at him, and then looked back at the rift. "Haatim." Slowly, she backed up.

"What?"

"Run."

Chapter 36

"The demon will find you in here," the echo of Arthur said. He still stood in the doorway, but his expression had gradually shifted to worry, and he looked around. "Already, you can feel it clawing through your mind. It *will* find us."

Abigail knew the specter spoke the truth. The walls had thinned and become transparent in the room she had created in her mind. It all felt less real, and she could sense Surgat searching for her. The demon seemed distracted, though, which she hoped meant that her friends remained alive.

Either way, she couldn't hide forever.

"How long until it finds me?"

"Hard to tell. The demon can sense you, and it scans through your memories, looking for this last piece of you. Once you've gone, it will have full access to its abilities."

"So, when it finds me, it will destroy me?"

"That depends," Arthur said. "On whether or not you know its true name."

"I *don't,* though."

"Names hold power. They give identity. This version of you right here makes *your* identity. It is how you associate your existence. If you remove this piece, then the body will still function, but it won't be *you* any longer. Your wants and desires will disappear, leaving only need. For a demon like Surgat, it works much the same. Once you can pin down the demon and see it for what it is, at its most basic, then you will have power over it."

"It controls me out there, doesn't it? Surgat's using me to hurt my friends."

"Most probably. That's the only reason it hasn't found you yet and remains the only thing giving you this chance."

She had prayed that, maybe, the demon didn't have full control of her body. She had hoped that, maybe, it wouldn't manage to control her until she had gone completely, but that hadn't become the case. It had never seemed a reasonable hope. When she had forfeited control over herself in the church, the demon had taken hold of the reins.

"So, I do have a chance?"

"Yes."

"How do I stop it, then?"

"You need the name. You have it locked away in that memory."

"There has to be another way. That isn't an option. What else can I do?"

There came a sudden rumbling sound, which shook the entire room. It came from the door as if a battering ram had just slammed it. Abigail froze in place. The walls phased in and out, and only blackness lay beyond the façade. Blackness and a form of raw hate that represented the demon.

It had found her.

"You're out of time, Abi."

"I don't *know* the name!"

"You do."

"It isn't here. If the demon told me its name, I forgot it."

"You didn't forget; you just have to find it."

"How?"

"You need to enter the memory."

Another crash shook the room. The demon tried to break into the memory.

"Focus on that moment," Arthur's visage said. "You know the memory you need to go into. The table. The ritual. You have no other way."

Still, Abigail hesitated. "You said that memory might prove too much for me. What happens if ... what happens if I get lost in it?"

"While possible, you don't have any alternatives."

The demon crashed into the door once more. Then everything faded out for a second. One moment, she sat in the room, and the next, she floated in a void, just a thought in the nether. The sensation only lasted for a second, and then things went back to normal, but that second nearly crippled her.

That, and worse, waited for her if the demon made it into the memory.

"I know you're in there!" a guttural voice called from outside. It sounded like her voice, only distorted and nasal and with a lot of extra bass. "Come out, come out, wherever you are!"

The echo of Arthur turned to her. "No more delays. Now or never."

Abigail took a steadying breath and nodded. "All right."

She thought back to that day, strapped down to the table. It had become the worst day of her life, but she would have to confront it if she wanted to defeat Surgat. Though scared, she brought the memory to life, conjuring and turning it into a reality.

With a steadying breath, Abigail stepped into the past.

✳✳✳

"What was that?" Haatim tilted his head in confusion.

"What was what?" Frieda stood staring at the red glow, trying to figure out what they should do. She waved her hand forward through the eerie light, but it had no effect.

"That crashing noise," Haatim said. "It sounded like ..." He couldn't explain it, and now, second-guessed whether he'd heard anything or not. Had it happened for real? Or only something in his head?

Frieda looked sideways at him. "What're you talking about?"

"You didn't hear it?"

She shook her head. "No."

He hesitated. It had sounded like something heavy crashing into a wooden wall, but he didn't know from what direction it had come. It sounded intense and vivid, as though it had happened right next to him, but no buildings stood close enough to justify such a noise.

Perhaps it hadn't happened here at all. Or, rather, not this version of *here*.

He shook his head to clear his thoughts and focus his mind.

Frieda remained focused on the energy, not paying attention to him. He opened his mouth to warn her that he meant to try something reckless, maybe stupid, and then he heard that crashing sound again. Only, this time, he could also sense Abigail's "room" and what the demon wanted.

Abigail.

"Here goes nothing," he whispered.

He reached out with his mind.

The instantaneous effect felt like nothing he'd experienced before when using his newfound abilities. This time, instead of reaching out and touching something, it seemed rather like he'd stepped outside his body and crossed over. All at once, he found himself free from his corporeal body, and the effect disoriented him.

The scenery changed, and the world seemed to slip out from underneath him. One second, he stood on the street next to Frieda in Raven's Peak, and the next, he went someplace that he didn't recognize.

He appeared in what looked like a small bedroom, though broken down with age and wear. All the furniture looked brown and rotten, and a disgusting bed lay in the center of the room, covered with hastily discarded blankets. It all had an unreal feel to it. Like looking at an incomplete painting. And, from somewhere, he heard chanting.

"Abigail?" he muttered, though not intentionally. The word just slipped out, but as soon as he said it aloud, he knew he'd done the right thing. This place belonged to Abigail; he just had no idea how. Each and every thing here felt fake, except he knew it as hers.

Hers? Her what? Memory? Dream? He had no idea. And, still, the sentiment felt true. She had been here only moments earlier.

"Where the hell am I?"

He stepped around, trying to find a way out of the room. The place had a door, which he walked toward. He reached out to touch the door handle, and his hand slipped right through it. He couldn't grasp the metal, and when his hand passed through it, the entire door became less real for a second. Then it solidified once more.

A crashing sounded, and the entire room shook, which startled him. The walls faded in and out of focus for a few seconds, and when Haatim looked down at himself, he could see that his incorporeal body did the same thing.

A moment passed, and things returned to normal.

"This isn't real," he said aloud, more to steady himself than anything else.

He looked around the room once more, but it held nothing else. Haatim had come to the wrong place. Abigail had moved on.

With his eyes closed, he focused on Abigail. He could sense the area around him, which extended beyond the room. Tense, he reached out, trying to get his bearings in the void.

Just outside the walls of this faux room, a presence filled with power and hatred dwarfed the creature that had, until recently, occupied his sister. It came from Surgat. Haatim could sense the demon through the barrier of the wall, but felt certain that Surgat didn't know of his presence.

Also, he could feel Abigail, though he had no idea where she'd gone. Outside this room, it felt like a swirling nightmare of confused energy and chaos, and impossible to pierce or understand.

She remained out there somewhere, he knew. He just had no idea of where.

✳✳✳

Abigail focused on the memories of the day that Arthur had found and rescued her from the cult. Mistakenly, she'd believed them lost, but they had only hidden. These memories, she had buried deep within her mind, locked away and forgotten.

As soon as she conjured them in her mind, a wave of nausea and confusion washed over her. The emotion of those memories made the first thing she experienced, and she realized she would need to push through that to find the memory itself. Determined, she gritted her teeth, closed her eyes, and stepped through.

Suddenly, everything shifted. She stood in another room now, lying on a hard wooden table. This one felt dank and smelled musty and damp, like rotten wood and decay. Lit candles surrounded her on the table in a circular pattern, filling the room with a faint glow, but she could see no other lights.

Abigail tried to sit up, but something bound her wrists and ankles. Though all just a memory, the bindings felt sturdy and rigid and real. They gave her almost no room to move and chafed her skin.

Pain and worry flooded into her, but she bit back the fears. They had brought her here to perform the ritual. She remembered it all, could see and feel the room, and it felt like she'd become a scared little girl all over again.

"I can't do this." Abigail pulled at the bindings. "I need to get out of here."

"You have to confront this." The echo of Arthur stood near the table, frowning down at her. It gave her relief when she saw him, but only a small amount. The image of him looked less real here, distorted and hollow.

"It happened here," he said.

"I know." She struggled to control her breathing. Then, with her eyes closed, she said, "I remember this place."

"The place is inconsequential. You need to remember the demon's name."

"I *know*."

People chanted in the background. She didn't recognize the words, but the voices formed into a steady hum that seemed to ripple through her body. Abigail trembled. The ropes tightened. The walls came closer too, collapsing in on her.

"Abigail, relax. You need to relax."

"I can't do this," she cried out, shaking and jerking her arms. The ropes remained unyielding, and she let out a little gasp. "I can't."

"You have to."

"No, I need to get out of here." She strained against the ropes and cried. The emotions came like a tidal wave, and she felt on the verge of a panic attack. Not since being a little girl had she experienced panic like this, right after she'd escaped from the cult. This, though, seemed so much worse.

"It isn't real."

"It is," she gasped. "It is *real*."

"No, Abigail. Only memories."

Each passing second, the dial of her fears turned up another ten notches.

The dagger. She could see the dagger hovering in the air over her body, ready to strike. It hung there, poised above her, and then it entered her flesh. It cut, tore, and pierced. Abigail writhed on the table, trying to get free, but the ropes only grew tighter and tighter, cutting off her circulation.

"Get me out of here!" she shouted, straining against the ropes, but it made no difference. The air thinned, the walls closed in, and she couldn't think straight. She needed to escape, but the ropes grew ever tighter.

"You need to relax," the echo of Arthur said.

"No! No, get me out of here."

"Abigail."

The voice caught her off-guard, stopping her cold, and she opened her eyes.

Haatim stood at the side of the table, looking down at her with a scared expression, next to the echo of Arthur, but neither of them seemed to know of the other's presence.

The sight of him flooded her with relief, but concern riddled the feeling.

"Haatim! Are you real?"

"What?"

"No, you must be just another creation of my mind."

"A *what* of your mind? I'm real. It's me."

Abigail frowned. Was this a trick? "How did you get here?"

"I have no idea. I just ... I heard you screaming and sort of ... latched on, I suppose. I tried to come to you and, suddenly, I ended up here."

"I mean, how did you get *here* in my memories at all?"

He stared at her helplessly and shrugged. "No idea. Are you okay?"

"No. Please, untie me."

"No!" the echo of Arthur shouted. "The memory must stay clean. No interruptions, or you won't experience it properly."

Abigail hesitated, as Haatim reached over to unfasten the bindings on her wrists.

"No, wait," she said.

"What?"

"Don't untie me. Not yet."

"What do you mean?"

"You can't ... you can't see the fake Arthur?"

He looked around, frowning. "No. It's just us in here."

Which meant he couldn't see the cultists either. "I need to see this memory through to the end," she said. "You can't let me up yet."

He frowned. "All right. What can I do?"

"Please, just stay with me."

He grabbed her hand, and where he touched her skin, it tingled with energy, which spread throughout her body, giving her strength and courage.

"Always."

She breathed a sigh of relief and closed her eyes. "Thank you."

"I will never leave you," Haatim said.

Another crash shook the room. Surgat had found her in this new location and still tried to force his way into her mind. She'd run out of time and would need to return to the memory as soon as possible to find Surgat's real name.

"It's over," the demon shouted from behind the door. "You've lost."

A wave of energy washed over her, pressing her back to the table. It felt like a wall of wind, and everything shook for a full five seconds.

When it had passed, they could hear the demon laughing from outside the memory. A horrible grating sound.

Haatim looked over at the door, wearing a terrified expression. "What was that?"

"You felt it, too?"

"Yeah." He nodded and gulped. "I think ... I think the portal just opened. We should hurry."

Chapter 37

Dominick kept moving down alleys and side streets, weaving through buildings but making sure not to get too far from his friends. Slowly, he worked his way back toward Frieda and Haatim.

The demon chasing him in Abigail's body moved at almost a lackadaisical pace. Occasionally, it lashed out at him, throwing a car or building, but the attacks seemed distracted and more to keep him moving than anything else.

It didn't focus on him, which gave him newfound hope. Probably, the demon had engaged in an internal fight with Abigail to maintain control of the body. Of course, Dominick didn't know if he led the demon on a wild goose chase, or if it did the same to him.

A few seconds later, he got his answer.

The ground still shook, but suddenly, the tremors intensified, causing Dominick to lose his balance and stagger to the ground. He scuffed his knees and hands on the rough pavement and fought to regain his footing.

A second later, a pulsating wave of energy came from the reddish glow. It felt almost as if a bomb had gone off, and the wave knocked him a meter back and onto his butt.

The wave of energy ended as abruptly as it came, leaving him dazed and disoriented. The ground shook but less so than a moment before. He stood and looked around. New cracks and rifts had opened in the ground everywhere around him.

Dominick walked over to one and peered inside, shocked at just how big and deep it seemed. He couldn't see a bottom, only an endless pit leading down into the Earth below. Not natural.

Then a creature came bursting out of the darkness of the rift. Dominick stumbled back with a yelp and jerked free his gun. The creature flew past him and up into the air, and Dominick sucked in his breath.

It appeared similar to a golem one might find decorating a gothic church, though considerably more horrible than any he'd ever seen. It had talons and a beak and wings that spanned at least three meters. The entire creature looked like it weighed at least five kilograms, and if he had to guess, it was made of stone or pavement.

The worst part was that it moved so fast. It let out a groaning sound and dove at him, flying in with its talons outstretched. He dove backward, narrowly avoiding the claws, and then rolled to his feet just as the creature came after him again. It looked like it should have moved slowly, considering how bulky and cumbersome it appeared, but that didn't prove the case.

He raised his gun, dodging another flyby attack, and then shot at the golem. The bullet ripped a chunk out of its midsection, but it seemed more like he'd shot a brick wall than something made of flesh or scales. Suddenly, a hole opened in the center of the golem where the bullet had passed through, and light shined from the other side.

He fired again, and then ducked when the creature swooped in at him once more. This shot hit it squarely in the chest, and another hole appeared, but if the creature even noticed that sections of it had chipped away, it didn't let on. The golem let out a grinding roar and came at him again.

Dominick ducked, and then dove to the side, having no clue how to take down something like this. No field manuals detailed how to handle a situation like this, and he needed a different plan.

Like shooting a wall, his bullets had no trouble penetrating. Where the bullets entered, holes appeared, and cracks splintered from those holes. Maybe he could do enough structural damage to the creature's body to break it down.

Worth a shot. He fired again and again until his clip emptied, dancing away from the creature whenever it came close. He filled it with holes, trying to pattern the shots to link the fractures.

It moved slower as he shot more holes into it, and it wobbled as it flew toward him. It didn't seem to experience pain, but he had weakened it. Holes riddled the creature now, and chunks of its body had gone missing, carved off by the bullets.

Dominick's final shot went through the midsection, linking up a network of small holes. At first, nothing happened, but then came a loud cracking sound. Its midsection fell away. The lower half of its body tumbled to the ground, crumpling to stone and sending up a cloud of dust.

The creature flew to the side clumsily, having difficulty remaining in flight without the counter-balance. It stumbled into a building and fell to the ground, letting out a rumbling sound when it tried to pick itself up.

Dominick loaded another clip into his gun and walked toward the creature. He stopped about a meter way, and then fired into its head. Each shot carved off a section until the head became little more than a stub on top of the body, which disintegrated, sinking to the ground in a pile.

Dominick took a step back, eyeing the pile of broken fragments. He looked around. The demon possessing Abigail had gone. It must have slipped away during the fight, assuming the golem would take care of him.

It pleased him that the demon had guessed wrong. He smiled, kicking at the pile of dust.

"That didn't seem so bad."

From behind, came a roaring blast. Dominick spun, startled. More creatures erupted from the rifts in the earth.

A steady roaring accompanied the exodus. More golems flew out of the rift, as well as smaller flying demons that looked like giant, scaly bats.

Dozens—maybe hundreds—of them came. Followed by other demons, which crawled out, some looking like giant fiery dogs, and others like horribly demonic spiders. He even saw a few of the demons he'd faced in Pennsylvania and again out at the church.

Smoke poured from the rifts in fetid clouds, rising into the sky, and more demons hovered in those clouds, tiny ones little more than mosquitoes, flying in groups. He counted at least a few dozen golems in those first seconds, and they circled in the air, searching for prey.

It had taken him two clips to drop the first one, and he had one clip left. "Uh-oh."

Dominick turned and sprinted down the street, heading back toward the red glow where Frieda and Haatim had hidden out. With just fifteen shots left, he had to make them count.

Two of the little bat-like creatures came swooping in at him. He ducked beneath one and raised his pistol and fired at another. The bullet hit it right in the chest, and it disappeared into a cloud of smoke and ash.

Dominick grimaced in satisfaction. At least those ones wouldn't give much of a threat. His victory proved short-lived, however, when he looked and saw hundreds more flying out of the rifts.

The other bat-thing kept coming at him, baring its razor teeth and trying to bite. He swatted at it, knocking it away, and ran on. Not wanting to waste the bullets, he refrained from shooting the thing.

At a sprint, he rounded the final corner of a building and dashed to the red portal and Frieda.

They'd gone. Frantic, he searched around for them. Each second that passed, more demons came pouring out of the ground and flew into the sky, and in other places, demons dragged themselves out of the cracks and onto the earth. There had to be hundreds in this area, and they came out all through the town.

Before long, they would get overrun.

"Dominick!" Frieda shouted from a nearby building. It looked like an old antique store with a glass front, though mostly cleared out when the town evacuated.

He rushed over and found her hiding inside, protecting an unconscious Haatim.

"What happened?"

"I don't know," she said, worry evident in her voice. "He seemed fine one moment, and then he just collapsed. I dragged him in here but can't wake him."

"What was he doing?"

"I *don't* know. Look out!"

More of the demon creatures came swooping down at the front of the shop. Dominick stepped outside, raised his pistol, and fired twice. Two more little creatures exploded into puffs of smoke.

"What the hell are those?" he asked.

"Demons," Frieda said.

"What kind?"

"No idea."

"At least they aren't hard to take down. I thought Surgat planned to bring an army."

"He does," Frieda said. "Those are the fodder."

"Why haven't they attacked us in force?"

"They will. They're awaiting his command."

✳✳✳

Abigail looked at Haatim, "I'll start the memory."

The presence of Surgat surrounded the room they occupied and attempted to break in. Each time it attacked the memory, she grew a bit weaker. They wouldn't have much time before it made it through her barrier. "Stay with me."

"I'm right here."

She squeezed Haatim's hand, clasping him for relief. "Here goes nothing."

As soon as she grasped the memory of laying strapped to the table as a little girl, she brought herself back to that time. The fear and weakness returned, just as sharp as ever. Panic flooded through her entire body, and she thrashed about, trying to break free.

Haatim disappeared from view, but she could still feel his hand and his warmth. She clung to it like a beacon, using it to steady herself.

The echo of Arthur remained there next to her table, though he looked less real now. As Surgat tried to break into the dream, the echo of Arthur weakened.

She also weakened and didn't have much time.

The only other person in the room, the cult leader, looked a bald and disfigured man with scars on his face. Though he seemed out of focus right now, she remembered some of what he used to look like. Ugly and cruel, just seeing him over her brought back all her fear of him.

"Calm," Arthur said. "You need to stay calm."

She took deep and steadying breaths, fighting down the panic attack and bottling it away. It felt difficult, but Abigail managed to slow her heart rate and regain control over the situation.

"It all happened here," Arthur said. "Here, Surgat told you his true name."

"I don't remember," Abigail said once more, but that proved a lie, she realized.

She hadn't remembered *any* of this before today because she'd buried it in her subconscious. She had locked it away with that part of her identity that wanted to pretend like none of this had ever happened.

Her life started the day Arthur rescued her. This just made *the before* of her existence. That had become the lie she told herself to pretend she had more strength than she did. No demonic ritual, no cult, nothing had happened before Arthur pulled her out of that hell where she got tortured and abused.

Except, she knew, it had.

A lot had come before Arthur.

✳✳✳

Abigail remembered the cult leader, distinctly, as a man who took great pleasure from hurting others. As she thought of him, his features came into sharp focus. He smelt terrible like rotten meat. Whenever they met, he barely spoke and always treated her with rough cruelty.

He acted as the petty tyrant of the cult, demanding obedience and hurting his followers whenever they stepped out of line. Even then, he would make up reasons to punish them for his pleasure. Their obedience to him became complete.

This man had brought her into this room and tied her to the table. He had whispered things to her, telling her it would be all right and that this would make her better. She had felt too terrified to say anything and simply gone along with it.

He'd carried a knife, she recalled, but never touched her with it. She had thought, originally, that he would use it to murder her in some ritualistic fashion, but that proved wrong. It remained symbolic and meaningful but never got used to harm her in any way. The cult leader had held onto it lovingly.

Then a startling realization hit her. Nida had used that same knife since she'd acquired it from the caves below Raven's Peak. How had it gotten there? Had they planned for her to go to Raven's Peak even so many years ago?

The memory continued forward: the rest of the cultists had come filing in only after she got tied down. They hadn't spoken, but rather, came into the room like ghosts.

They surrounded her table, blocking out the rest of the area and practically suffocating her when they stood so close. The shadows of their hoods hid their faces, but she could remember their eyes: some filled with hate, others with lust, as they surveyed the little black girl strapped to the table before them. She had felt so scared in this moment that she had nearly blacked out.

The memory struggled to consume her and bring her back to those feelings. But, now an adult, she no longer remained the helpless child strapped to this table. She had trained to fight. Had learned how to hunt down and kill demons.

Instead of struggling against the memory, she let it wash over her. The thudding sound as the demon tried to break in continued, but sounded distant now, less clear. The echo of Arthur had gone, too, but she didn't care: she no longer needed him because she had found the willingness to accept that this only made a part of her, and didn't represent the whole.

Arthur—the real Arthur—wouldn't show up in the memory for a long time, and not until the worst parts had come to pass.

The ritual began slowly. By the time the cultists stood chanting, the candles had burned down to almost nothing. Hours had passed with Abigail unable to move or get up from the table.

She remembered almost humorously how badly she'd needed to pee, and how she'd focused on that pain to distract her from what happened around her. No breaks had occurred, and she'd felt afraid she would wet herself while strapped down.

It left her exhausted, she recalled, feeling terrified for so long but with nothing happening. Her muscles tensed, and sweat coated her, yet everything remained still. She'd wondered if, maybe, this just gave another way to torture her.

When they'd started chanting, however, everything had changed.

$$* * *$$

The memory grew in intensity and power when the cultists chanted. This came close to that moment, that horrible moment that she dreaded more than anything else in the world.

She squeezed Haatim's hand for strength. They had called forth the demon, summoned it to this world with only one purpose in mind. She went back there now, fully immersed in that moment, and the experience felt the same as she'd had as a little girl.

It built to a slow pressure inside her forehead, an aching headache that pulsed and throbbed and made her cry out in pain and disorientation. She broke out into a cold sweat as soon as the chanting started, and it made her sick to her stomach.

She'd never remembered this happening, and she understood that this made the pivotal moment that she had blocked out. When she'd told Frieda and the Council about her time spent with The Ninth Circle, this had never come up. The headache had a strong sense to it of *something* else. Not human and like nothing she'd ever experienced.

She could feel *him* inside the swell of pain. Surgat. The demonic presence wormed its way into her existence, filling her but waiting patiently for his moment. He didn't possess her, not like she'd experienced in Raven's Peak when the demon took complete control of her body and dominated her. No, this seemed more of a bonding, a gentle caress while he filtered in, meshing their identities. She had thought it would feel a struggle like she faced today as the demon tried to dominate and destroy her.

Instead, the demon almost attempted to seduce her, like a predator might a young child. Only a little girl, she'd stood no chance at repelling him. The memory disgusted her, and her mind rebelled.

"Focus," the echo of Arthur said. "Focus your mind."

She did. Abigail didn't want to remember this, didn't want to believe that this had ever happened to her, but knew that it had. If she didn't get what she came for out of this memory, then it would happen again, only this time she

272

would find no way to survive it.

The demon had slipped inside her, promising to protect and take care of her for her entire life. It promised that they would stay together forever, and that it could save her from the wretched life she'd had before. And she only had to say yes to their joining.

It had asked for her to invite it in.

Chapter 38

Haatim stood over Abigail in the small room where he'd found her. It looked like an underground cavern lit by candlelight, though he could see no candles anywhere. The room remained empty except for himself, and Abigail lying on a large wooden table.

She had to confront something inside her memories, but wherever she had gone, it proved somewhere that he could not go. He felt alone in this space, and it felt less real and tangible now that she had disappeared mentally.

He had nothing to do except clutch her hand and pray that she would make it. Fear filled her wide-open eyes, and she saw nothing through them. Wherever she'd gone, the place brought something that had truly terrified her.

In this place, he didn't belong. It had seemed as though he had stepped outside himself, and he could feel his spirit weakening while the seconds ticked past. He realized, as he waited alone in the room, that the longer he stayed out of his body, then the more difficult he would find it to go back.

How long had he been here? Time didn't make sense in this realm, and it felt like he hovered somewhere between Surgat's hell and his world. To be honest, he didn't know if he would manage to go back to his body now because he had no clue how to go about doing so.

He remained stuck in the chaos that the demon and Abigail had created, and should leave right now and attempt to get back to the safety of his flesh.

"Hurry up, Abigail," he said, clenching his teeth. He couldn't leave Abigail until he knew that she'd reached safety, but that didn't mean he wanted her to take her time. His hand grew cold where she held it like her skin had become ice. It seemed almost as though she siphoned off his energy.

A scary thought: he'd barely noticed it at first, but now it felt like a dull and cold ache in his hand, climbing his wrist and into his forearm. It further weakened him, draining what little strength he had left.

He would tolerate the pain as long as Abigail needed him. To distract himself, he looked at the area around him. Not at the objects in the room, though, but rather at what lay past it. He found that when he focused, he could see through the walls and into the world around them.

Off in the distance, warmth poured out of an area of pure reddish-light that could only be the portal. Surgat had opened it, and now, brought forth demons.

Every few seconds, he could sense another presence in the area when something climbed out of hell and made its way to the surface. He could sense the portal as an object of pure evil, abstract and powerful.

The breach let through demons, he realized, and a lot of them. They didn't seem to have any sense that he stood here, flitting right past and disappearing as they entered his world. He could still sense them once they got up there, but it proved more difficult. Once they got outside this realm, they spread out, as though this made a funnel through which they entered the Earth realm.

He hoped his friends remained all right. Dominick and Frieda fought up there alone, facing this horde. Haatim didn't know how long they would manage to survive, and suspected that things would only get worse once Abigail had finished her fight with the demon.

No matter which way that fight ended.

He closed his eyes and thought about that energy portal. If he could block the breach, then he could stop the flood of demons and end whatever Surgat tried to do. It wouldn't solve all their problems, but it would make a sizable step in the right direction.

The only problem? ... He had no idea how to go about closing the thing.

Frieda had said something about knocking the energy off balance, but it sounded like a guess as much as anything else. She knew nothing about this realm, or his abilities, and wouldn't prove of any help with this.

Still, it made a good a guess and something he felt willing to try. At least, he would attempt it once Abigail had finished with whatever she did inside of that memory.

✳✳✳

The demon pressed in on Abigail, merging with her identity and becoming one inside her. She could feel every single part of it as though it happened right now, even though it had happened a long time ago. Surgat had entered her and lain dormant, waiting for the ritual to wake him and give him the strength to overcome the weak and fragile little girl.

The moment had arrived. The moment when the demon had created the bond with her. It didn't make for a one-way connection, and as Surgat stepped into her existence, so too, did she step into its. That was, after all, why they'd chosen a child; she felt too afraid to fight back and would prove easier for the demon to dominate.

In her memory, she pushed past the demonic entity. It whispered in her mind, offering soothing words to calm her heart. She pushed back her hatred of the situation, her anger at herself for letting it in, and forced herself just to embrace the moment.

Embrace the demon and listen to its words.

The little girl that she had been, on the other hand, gave in. She listened to the soothing words and became unwilling to fight back, retreating into herself and cowering from the presence. The demon, triumphant, realized that it had dominated her, and that the time had come for the final part of its merge.

That had become the part that hadn't happened; the part when Arthur had shown up and freed her. The little girl she had been didn't know that Arthur would come. She'd believed herself alone in the world, uncared for and abandoned.

That little girl in the memory didn't want to remember any of this and tried to push out the adult version of her. It attempted to push her away and stop the memory. She had hidden this for a reason, to protect and save her from the pain.

But Abigail couldn't stop now. She'd come so close, moments from truly understanding what had happened to her, and needed to see this through to the end, to experience every moment of it, no matter how horrible.

Outside the memory, she clenched down on Haatim's hand, using him to steady her. She waited, focusing on the moment, and listened.

The demon whispered in her ear, offering lies and promised to calm her. Abigail ignored it all, listening as hard as she could for the one thing she truly needed.

Finally, the demon spoke its name.

✳✳✳

Abigail's eyes popped open, and she took a few steadying breaths. She still lay on the table, but no longer tied down. Haatim remained standing next to the table, though he looked considerably worse than when she'd gone into the memory. Other than him, the cult room appeared empty.

"I have it," she exclaimed. "I have the demon's name."

"What? Really? That's amazing! So, it's over?"

She hesitated. "Not quite."

"What do you mean?"

She closed her eyes and focused, willing the table away. Her fear gone, she felt more in control of herself. When she opened her eyes, she stood next to Haatim. He had a shocked look on his face while he looked around, realizing that everything had changed all of a sudden.

"That's ... disorienting."

"Sorry."

He stepped in and wrapped her in a tight hug, and just like when she'd touched his hand, warmth flowed out of him and into her. It filled her with confidence in herself and a belief that she could overcome this. They could all survive this.

However, she checked her elation: this remained far from over, and they hadn't won yet. The demon still lingered outside, banging against the walls and trying to break in, but she felt revitalized now that she had the demon's true name.

It had given the name to the little girl as a way to unite them, assuming that once the ritual completed, and he'd dominated her, then Surgat would no longer be exposed and vulnerable. It knew the deadliness if that name got used against it, and so had fought so hard to keep it from her.

Now, though, she had it. That single piece of information would change the fight utterly.

"The name gives me power over the demon," Abigail said. "But I can't use it to send Surgat home like I could with a normal demon."

"What? Why not?"

"The demon *is* me, Haatim. The ritual The Ninth Circle performed on me bound us together, and I invited the demon in."

He shook his head. "So, just uninvite him."

"It isn't that simple. Our fates have become intertwined. When Surgat returns to hell, I go with him."

"So, what do we do?"

"I need to confront the demon. I have a weapon now, which gives me a chance, but it won't prove easy and brings no guarantee that I can do this. If I lose ..."

"What?" Haatim paled.

"If I can't win the fight, then I have to use the name to kill him."

"But you just said that will kill you, too."

Abigail didn't reply.

"No." He shook his head. "No, I won't allow you to do that. I just got you *back* for like the fiftieth time. I shan't let you go."

"I don't intend to lose," she said. "But I won't let him stay in control and use me to hurt more people."

He stayed silent for a moment, and then nodded. "How can I help?"

"You have already. You helped me get his name, and it gives me a chance I would never have had otherwise. I have to do this on my own, though. You won't stand a chance against Surgat."

"What if you tell me his name, too? I can help."

"It doesn't work like that. The name is more like a feeling. An idea. It isn't something I can repeat aloud. Just knowing it gives me power, but I can't pass it on."

Haatim hesitated, and then said, "I can still help."

"I won't risk losing you. You should go back and find the others. Help them, and you'll help me, too."

"No." Again, he shook his head. "I love you. I refuse to leave you."

Abigail stepped forward, wrapped Haatim in a tight hug, and pulled him close. "I know."

She forced the memory away, pushing outside of it and heading straight for Surgat. She did it suddenly, forcing herself away and blocking him from following her.

She left Haatim there in the memory, standing in the empty room, and headed off to confront Surgat.

✳✳✳

One second, Abigail stood there, and the next, she had gone. Just gone. Haatim had no idea where she went, or how, and now he stood alone in the empty underground room. The walls around him disintegrated, lost their partial reality, now that Abigail had left behind the memory.

Mentally, he reached out, scanning for her in the surrounding area, but couldn't find her. She had gone somewhere else, another realm perhaps, to fight Surgat. He had no idea how even to start searching.

Nor, he realized, did he even have the strength left to make the effort. He felt exhausted, and doing even the smallest things now seemed overwhelming. Abigail had gone to face the demon and intended to do it alone.

Even if it meant he would die, he should be with her. If he could help her overcome this, then knowing that she would reach safety would give enough solace for him. He didn't know what kind of help he could offer, but at least he could try to do *something*. It would feel better than just not knowing what went on.

With a groan of frustration, he squeezed shut his eyes. He should retreat to his body now. The more tired he grew, then the more the corporeal connection slipped away, but he couldn't leave just yet. Not without trying his hand at closing the portal, at least.

Mentally, he focused on the portal, willing himself next to it, and when he opened his eyes, he stood right beside it. The laws of normal physics didn't apply here, and moving proved as simple as thinking.

He shifted to the side when more demons came hurtling out of the portal. They didn't even seem to notice him as they rushed out. He watched them transition from balls of hate-filled energy into half-formed creatures as they went, and then they would disappear, crossing over to the world above.

Another demon for his friends to face alone. What did Frieda and Dominick have to deal with? A lot of demons had poured out of the portal, and he hoped his friends remained okay.

Did he stand up there next to them, a vacant and empty shell, or had he fallen to the ground when he left behind his body? With any luck, he hadn't hit his head or anything.

Would he even know if something like that had happened to his body? Maybe, he'd died already and would have no body to which to return.

Haatim forced those worries away, having no good answer for any of them. It didn't seem worth his time thinking about it if he couldn't do anything to fix it. Right now, he had to focus only on the portal.

He scanned it over: basically, just a ring of tightly-bound energy emitting a swirling red glow. It almost felt like he and the ring were underwater, floating on the currents of the sea.

However, it proved different than that, and even though he had the sensation of floating, it felt numb and empty without any sensory input—like getting stuck in a sensory deprivation tank, and the closer he got to the portal, the worse it got.

Physically, he couldn't touch the portal, so instead, he tried to reach out mentally and *push*. It wobbled, but the action of pushing it drained him.

"All right," he said, the words echoing only in his head. "Let's do this."

He reached out again, and this time, instead of just pushing the portal, he mentally redirected the energy and pulled it closed. A few seconds passed, and he wondered if he hadn't just wasted his time and the last of his energy.

Nothing happened, at first, except that a wave of exhausted nausea washed over him again. If he could have puked, he would have, but instead, he just felt disoriented and confused. Suddenly, though, something changed. The portal didn't move, exactly, but he'd done something.

A long moment passed, and then the silver ring collapsed in on itself as if in slow motion. It seemed as if someone had grabbed hold of the drawstrings of an open bag and tightened it up.

Haatim felt a moment of triumph as he watched the portal shrink. "Yes!"

The euphoria ended, though, when he glanced through the portal itself. He could see into the hell-scape from whence the demons came. It looked like an endless dark tunnel, full of green ichor on the walls and no light at all. He could see into Surgat's hell, though not visually: rather, mentally, like touch.

He could feel inside the place, though. He could feel a trapped human in there, covered in ichor and completely lost to time and sensation. He could feel Arthur.

Chapter 39

Somewhere in there, Arthur lived. It took Haatim a second to pinpoint him, but he could feel his spirit a ways inside. He felt empty, vacuous, but not dead. Or, at least, not eliminated and destroyed.

He stuck out in the tunnel, being the only non-demonic energy, and once Haatim located him, it proved easy to lock on. Though he sensed no bodily form on that side of the portal, only energy, Haatim *knew* it as Arthur despite never having met the man before.

There he was.

Abigail had made it her life's mission to bring him back since the day he had met her. It consumed her, knowing that he stayed trapped down here, lost in Surgat's hell and tortured for crimes he had committed.

Though not her fault, convincing her of that proved an impossible task. The only reason she had come out here to Raven's Peak to face Nida was because the demon had tricked her into believing she could rescue her mentor from hell.

A thing she had no capability of doing, which the demon knew.

But ...

Maybe *he* could.

Haatim hesitated, watching the silver ring close in on itself. He had, maybe, fifteen seconds before it sealed completely and his only chance to cross over disappeared.

Perhaps, he should stop the portal from closing and give himself more time. In the next instant, however, he made the decision not to. If he even managed to stop it from closing, then no way could he start the process again. He'd gotten too drained and couldn't risk letting the portal remain open.

Which meant that crossing over to Surgat's hell offered only a fool's errand. He could go back now and find his body and forget about this. Abigail didn't know he had spotted Arthur, and he didn't need to tell her.

In fact, he shouldn't say a word. It would just hurt her and open old wounds. This impossible situation brought a much greater risk than he should, reasonably, undertake to try and save the life of a man he had never met.

No, he should just go back to his body, forget about ever spotting Arthur, and omit this part of his story if he ever again set eyes on Abigail.

Right, of course he couldn't.

It didn't matter about Abigail and what she would think of him. It mattered more about himself. Haatim believed that he knew himself as a person and imagined himself as the kind of person who would risk his life to save people. However, he'd never thought that he would get that opportunity, but part of the identity he had created for himself rested on that kind of person.

If he left now, he didn't know if he would ever reconcile the identity he'd assigned for himself with the reality he faced down here. He felt terrified of crossing through the portal, and it would mean risking his life to save someone he'd only heard about in stories, but he knew it as the right thing to do.

Even if neither of them made it out, it would remain the right thing to do.

Resolved, he steadied himself and then dove through the portal, heading for the essence and soul of Arthur Vangeest.

✳✳✳

"We're losing him," Frieda shouted.

"What do you mean?" Dominick glanced back at Frieda in the center of the antique shop. They had stood here for only a few minutes since the portal had opened to allow demons to cross over into their world, but already, things looked hopeless. The streets and skies had filled with thousands of demons, and more came through every second.

They still hadn't attacked in force, which meant Abigail still fought back against Surgat; but, occasionally, a few wandered close enough that Dominick had no choice but to engage them. It continued to rain, and the odd blast of lightning and thunder struck in the distance.

"I don't know," she said. "He just keeps gasping for air."

"What happened?"

"I don't know. One second, he seemed fine, and then this."

"Is he breathing?"

"Barely."

"Then barely has to be enough."

Dominick leaned against the doorframe, checking over what remained of their weapons. He had two shotguns with five shells between them, his pistol had gotten down to two rounds, and Frieda had a full clip in her gun. After that, though, they would get reduced to knives and fists.

He could bottleneck the door to their building and keep the demons at bay when they attacked, but it had a glass front window that would prove easy to break through whenever the demons decided to swarm them.

Whenever that happened, they'd be dead. They couldn't last for more than a few seconds against a concerted attack.

Nor could they see Abigail any longer. She had disappeared from view amidst the demons; although, the last he had seen of her, she'd stood perfectly still. Her eyes had remained open, and whatever battle she fought, it happened inside her. He prayed that Abigail would win out in the end but had begun to lose hope.

Worse, the demons grew anxious. They might attack without waiting for

Surgat's commands. Several of the dog-like demons paced out in front of the store, about ten meters away, and watched him.

"That's the least of our problems," Dominick called back. "We're outnumbered and surrounded, and I can't even get a clear shot on Abigail. Not that I could do anything to her, but this looks hopeless."

One of the rock golems came swooping down all of a sudden, flying in straight at Dominick. He stepped outside, raising one of his shotguns, and lined up a shot. He waited until the demon came close enough that he could reach up and touch its talons.

Then he fired, exploding the chest and head. The bullet did significant damage, and the demon disintegrated into dust and small stones in midair. A shower of dust hit Dominick a few seconds later as it fell.

Once the dirt cloud had cleared, he spotted a couple of the little bat-like demons flying at him as well. He drew his pistol, lined up his shots carefully, and pulled the trigger.

That spent the last of his bullets, and all three of the ugly little bats burst into puffs of smoke. It felt a little bit rewarding to see them explode like that, banished back to hell. His happiness soon curbed, however, when he looked back at the sky and saw the enormous clouds of demons circling overhead.

"What are they doing?" Dominick stepped back into the building to reload and reset.

"Testing our defenses," Frieda said. "And waiting for their commands."

"From Surgat?"

Frieda nodded. "Abigail must still be fighting back."

"Do you think she can win out?"

This time, Frieda didn't reply.

"What do we do?" Dominick asked. "We can't stay here. When they swarm us, we're done."

"I know. We have to wait." Frieda turned back to Haatim. He still lay gasping. She touched his cheek. "He's cold."

Dominick knelt next to her. "Wait for what?" He frowned. "Frieda, we can't win. We need to get out of here while we still can."

"We can't leave Haatim."

"I can carry him. We *need* to go, or we'll never get out of here."

She smiled at him sadly and shook her head. "That ship has sailed. I'm sorry I brought you here, Dominick. They have us trapped and surrounded, and when Surgat decides the time to end us has arrived, we won't stand a chance."

Dominick fell silent, frowning, and then said, "So, we have no chance?"

"Not if Abigail loses."

"Then, what do we do?"

"I don't know." Frieda looked up at him. "Do you pray?"

Chapter 40

O nce Haatim reached the other side of the portal, something shifted in the realm he'd come to. On his side of the portal, it had seemed as though he floated in the air in a black void, freely able to move around but a touch disoriented. On this side, however, it felt considerably more horrible.

The pervasive sense of otherworldliness intensified dramatically, and everything felt wrong. It felt like he was drowning, but instead of water, it had the substance of a heavy tar weighing him down. The green ichor on the walls clung to him, trying to blot out his soul. He couldn't wipe it away, and it felt suffocating.

Haatim could sense himself on both sides of the silver ring simultaneously. Only his essence had crossed over, and the link to his body in the real world had weakened. This world seemed like a living creature, and wherever he'd come, it would prove reluctant to let him leave.

However, he couldn't worry about that right now. Arthur remained over here, trapped beneath the green ichor somewhere up ahead. Haatim moved toward Arthur down the hallway.

Outside the portal, he could move with only a thought and cover any distance simply by willing it. In here, on the other hand, it felt like he'd had heavy weights strapped to his ankles to weigh him down. It reminded him of slogging his way through mud, and each step proved harder to take than the last.

By the time he made it across to Arthur, the disgusting green ichor covered him. His body no longer remained tangible, yet the stuff still managed to stick and hold onto him. Where it touched, he felt cold and empty, as if it drained his life force. Similar to when Abigail had touched him, only much worse. The stuff had buried Arthur totally, and digging him out wouldn't give any fun.

A glance back showed that the silver ring had almost closed. That gave his only chance of escape; though, by now, it looked a million kilometers away. Neither time nor distance seemed to work the same way here as they did outside, and so he had no idea how long it would take for the portal to close.

He turned back to Arthur, steeling himself for what he would have to do. Then he reached down and scooped at the ichor.

It felt like sticking his hands into a bucket of frozen ice; only ice wouldn't have proven nearly cold enough. This seemed more like liquid nitrogen, and the pain almost blinded him. Not normal cold, though, as rather than going numb to the pain, it only grew more intense.

Within seconds, his mind screamed for him to stop, but he refused. He pushed down the pain and kept scooping, getting as much of the stuff off Arthur's soul as he could.

"Wake up." Haatim reached out and touched the identity of Arthur, which seemed less like a humanoid spirit and more like a golden blob, vaguely humanlike though completely disembodied. When he touched it, the blob quivered. "We don't have much time. You have to wake up."

Nothing happened. Arthur didn't budge, and the spiritual entity didn't change. Too weak, Haatim realized. Too drained by the ichor and his time spent in this place.

Maybe nothing remained to wake. It was possible that Arthur had stayed here for too long and that he had nothing left of his humanity.

Haatim couldn't think like that, though. He had to believe that something remained, and that it would take only a small nudge to bring back the powerful man. One last time, he glanced back. Only a small ring of the portal showed. Mere moments made the difference between them escaping or getting trapped here for good.

Here, in Surgat's hell, where the Council had trapped him, and where spending an eternity wouldn't prove any fun. It sapped him, drained him, and ate away at his soul.

Haatim steeled his resolve, and then turned back to Arthur. Now or never.

"Come on! You need to get up. We need to get out of here."

He could sense understanding from Arthur, but also weakness. The man sat broken, barely conscious, and unable to focus on anything outside himself.

Haatim remembered when Abigail had touched him, and it had seemed like she siphoned his energy. Perhaps, he could do something similar here, like feeding Arthur to bring him back to consciousness.

He reached out and touched the golden globe of energy. Focused, he pushed essence out of himself and directed it into Arthur. There didn't seem much left. After everything that had happened today, he now ran on empty.

The effect happened in an instant, and the globe shivered under Haatim's touch as the essence poured into it. Though it weakened him, the idea that it strengthened Arthur emboldened him.

However, to wake the globe and give Arthur the strength to get out of here, he would need a lot more energy.

Maybe more than Haatim could give. If he failed, they would both get trapped here.

With the portal so near to closing, Haatim felt unsure of whether he could escape now even if he fled this very instant. The place had a hold on him, and he'd weakened. It would take everything in his power to get out. The thought of spending the rest of eternity trapped here in this place terrified him.

"Last chance," he whispered.

But, he couldn't go. Not without Arthur. If he abandoned him now, he would condemn the man to spending the rest of eternity trapped here. He

286

wouldn't be able to live with himself.

With a final push, he turned back and bridged the connection to Arthur, feeding energy into the orb. His essence revitalized Arthur, and the man came back and reclaimed his identity. It happened slowly, though. Oh so slowly.

It felt like the world closed in on Haatim. He remembered speaking to Father Paladina and how his gift wasn't endless. At a certain point, it switched over to tapping into his soul, and now, he'd made that switch. It ate away at him, siphoning off parts of his existence, but he couldn't stop. Arthur had nearly come back.

He only needed a little bit more.

The weakness overtook him, and he wouldn't manage to make an exit from this realm now. Not anymore. He couldn't possibly escape, not when he'd given too much of himself to Arthur, and so, he had doomed himself to getting stuck here for eternity.

Though, maybe, Arthur could still get out. Haatim pushed harder, forcing every drop of life essence he could out of himself and into Arthur. More fully now, the man came to life.

And then reality went out of focus.

✳✳✳

What is happening?

The thought came as a surprise when it flitted through Arthur's mind. From where had it come? Why had it come? He hadn't had a conscious thought in what felt like ages.

Arthur hadn't even realized what it felt like to no longer think until he'd lost the ability to do so. He'd lived in a sad and dark emptiness, which took from him every time he tried to reclaim his reality.

As a consequence, he had closed himself off to that world, refusing to let his torturers harm him any further. He had retreated into himself and locked himself away, accepting that he would never escape from this realm and that no reason existed for him to allow himself to think anymore.

And yet, here Arthur sat.

It felt like waking from the longest and most painful nightmare he'd ever experienced but so much worse than that. Surgat and his pet demons had rebuilt and broken him on a constant basis before tiring of him.

Eventually, they had forgotten him and left him to his own devices, which almost proved worse. The green ooze filling the place had sapped his strength and left him constantly cold and vulnerable.

He ignored all of that, focusing only on the tangible details of what happened right then, and tried to understand what had changed to wake him. Arthur felt strong, stronger than he had since coming to this place.

Something had happened, he realized. Most of the demonic horde had gone, and what remained shivered with excitement when they prepared to leave too. He could sense them and their hatred and lust. They didn't even seem to notice him anymore.

Then he noticed the orb floating next to him. The light of energy represented an entity like himself, but this one looked completely different. It shined with a purer light than his, but it had also almost extinguished.

Arthur didn't recognize it, and could only sense that it didn't belong here. Was it a person? An outsider? How did it get here? Had this woken him? It seemed a likely possibility, but why?

Then the silver ring in the distance caught his attention. A portal to the other world. His world. He could see through it to light beyond, his home. The ring had almost closed and would disappear in only seconds. The demonic army flitted through that breach, one by one, and headed to the world above. As he sat there, he could also sense the demons beyond the portal, flying in that world and answering Surgat's call, and other things, too. More people. Frieda, and Dominick.

Then, he sensed *her*.

Abigail.

She lived, out there in the world above, but battled for her life. This moment, he had dreaded and prayed would never come to pass when he might lose more than just the sweet girl he had raised like a daughter.

He couldn't worry about anything else right now. No, he had to get out of here, find Abigail, and escape this hell before any of the demons realized he had awoken.

To that end, Arthur propelled himself toward the hole, grabbing the husk of white light at his feet, and raced forward. Though moving through here felt torturous, nearly impossible, he had learned how to navigate it through his years spent down here.

It would be a close call. The portal had almost shut, and it would make a tight fit to get out into the world above. He moved as fast as he could, pushing through the ooze and toward the surface.

Almost there.

Arthur pushed, scrambled, and dove through the portal just before it sealed. The green ooze covering him, and the husk of the person he carried, didn't go through the portal, but peeled off and stayed behind. Whatever they were, they couldn't exist up here.

Suddenly, everything felt softer, and Arthur's soul rejoiced. The world lightened and made more sense. His soul washed clean in the light of his world, and he felt only joy.

However, it proved short-lived. He could also feel his friends up here, battling for their lives. The person who'd woken him thinned, and it wouldn't take long for it to break down completely and evaporate. He needed to find the body it belonged to and return it home.

Arthur had an awareness of Abigail here, too, but couldn't see her. No matter where he searched, he couldn't locate her in this realm. Frustrated, he hunted instead for Frieda and Dominick. He found them in one of the buildings up above, fighting against the demons.

Another body lay up there with them. Did this soul belong to it? Arthur raced for the surface, gliding away from the portal. Things continued to change as his identity shifted and took form.

His body grew tangible, and the closer he got to the surface, the more real he became. Reality shifted, and the world became more real, until he felt like himself once more. Arthur pushed the soul into the waiting body, and then started his final trek between this realm and his own.

Chapter 41

Dominick stood in the doorway of the old antique shop, trying to hold the army of demons at bay. They pressed closer. It wouldn't take long before they breached the shop, with or without Surgat's orders.

Two of the little bats came flying in. He fired his pistol, dropping the approaching demon, but when he pulled the trigger again, it clicked.

Empty.

"Frieda!" he shouted, spinning.

She knelt further inside the building, guarding Haatim and watching the backroom entrance of the shop. So far, nothing had tried coming in from that direction, but he didn't know how long their luck would hold.

She grabbed her pistol from the floor and tossed it at him. That meant he had only the bullets in this gun, two shotgun shells, and then his knife.

Not encouraging.

Deftly, he caught it and spun just as another group of demons charged in. He ducked down and slid the knife out of his boot. One of the bats reached him. Dominick dodged and dove to the side, coming up and stabbing with his blade.

It sank deep into the demon's chest, and the creature let out a screeching sound before exploding in a puff. The other demons reached just a few steps away. One, a hellhound, looked ugly, and fire wreathed it. The other seemed a spiderlike demon with way too many eyes.

He backpedaled into the shop, dodging a bite from the dog, and then fired into the face of the spider-demon. The bullet struck it in the head just as it leaped at him.

Dominick dove into a roll and came up firing, putting two more bullets into the thing's head. It collapsed to the ground, slowly disintegrating while still reaching its long ugly arms up at him.

The hellhound rushed through the disintegrating spider, which turned out to be a mistake. The spider legs latched onto it, grabbing hold with a death grip, and pulled it down toward the ooze even as it broke apart.

The hellhound tried to pull free but couldn't. The head of the spider shot up and latched its mandibles onto the hellhound's neck. The beast let out a whimper, shaking and trying to pull free, but Dominick watched in horror as they both got dragged back to hell.

So much for loyalty.

He rushed past the ooze, careful not to step too close to it, and checked the door. The other demons stayed back, circling the place but not approaching.

With a sigh of relief, he checked his magazine. Four shots left.

Suddenly, another wave of energy erupted from the ground in front of him. It swelled and washed over them like a burst of wind. It knocked him back, and he stumbled, hitting hard against the wall.

"What the hell was that?"

"I think the portal closed," Frieda said. "Thank God. No more demons can escape."

"Fat lot of good that will do us." Dominick laughed, stepping back to the doorway and raising his pistol. "Have you looked at the sky recently? Thousands have come here already."

"But no more," Frieda said. "Small victories."

Dominick sighted in and pulled the trigger, careful with each shot. Each time a demon got too close, he put a bullet in it. However, for each one he dropped, two more appeared in the crowd, watching the building and waiting to attack.

The street no longer shook or vibrated, which made it easier to take down the demons, but once he ran out of ammo, he would need a new plan. He dropped a demon with each shot, but it wouldn't prove enough. They came too fast, and when enough of them grouped up, they would attempt to come in.

Finally, the pistol clicked. He'd run out of rounds. With the weapon now useless, he dropped it and picked up the shotgun. Two left, and he couldn't afford to waste them. It would only take a few seconds for the demons to realize he had run out of ammunition, at which point, they would be completely out of time. He backed up into the building to stand next to Frieda and Haatim.

"Ready to fight?" he asked.

"Always." Frieda stood, grabbed Arthur's sword, and swung it through the air to loosen her arm.

"Good. Let's take down as many of these suckers as we can."

A coughing sound reached Dominick, and he glanced down. Haatim lay on the ground, clutching his throat and letting out a violent hacking noise.

"Hey, it looks like—"

The front glass window of the antique shop burst open, and little shards of glass flew everywhere. Two demons charged in. A hellhound, wreathed in its supernatural fire, came through first, and then another of those annoying stone golems.

"Crap!"

Dominick staggered back, firing and dropping the golem with a headshot. It exploded into a cloud of dust and rubble, and he pumped another round into the chamber.

Shotgun raised, he sighted at the hellhound, but it leaped to the side. He pulled the trigger, but only managed to clip it. With a curse of frustration, he dropped the gun to the ground.

No more rounds.

The dog circled, growling, and prepared to pounce. The shot had slowed it, but it hadn't fallen out of the fight yet. Dominick drew his blade once more and fell into a fighting stance, standing between it and Frieda. Behind the dog,

292

out on the streets, hundreds of demons had gathered. Emboldened, they approached the broken window.

"Not a great day to die," Frieda said from behind.

He didn't turn to look at her, staying focused on the dog. "As good a day as any."

The hound approached slowly, sizing him up, and hunched to attack. Dominick lunged forward just as the hound pounced, raising his blade and shifting his body to avoid the brunt of the hellhound's bite. It might get him, but his blade would sink into its chest. Dominick tensed, ready to feel the weight of the hound as it collapsed into him.

Yet, neither hit landed.

Instead, something appeared to the side, materializing and forming in the room between him and the hound. As it did, a fist lashed out and hit the dog, knocking it flying into the wall. Dominick hesitated, having no idea what had just happened.

The thing materialized. A panting and naked man stood there, facing away from him, arm outstretched. He had punched the hellhound.

"What the hell?"

The man turned around. Frieda gasped in shock. Dominick did a double take, amazed when he recognized the man in front of him.

"Arthur?"

He smiled. "Good to be back."

✳✳✳

"How did you ...? What were you ...? What the hell is going on?"

Arthur didn't get a chance to answer before they heard a loud roar outside. Suddenly, the army of demons came charging in, recognizing Arthur. Their fury seemed to outweigh their discretion, and they didn't wait for orders anymore.

"Another time," Arthur said. "Looks like we have work to do."

Dominick turned to face them, stepping into position just as they approached. He dodged an attack from one of the golems, and then stabbed one of the flying things. Luckily, in the cramped quarters, the flying demons had trouble maneuvering.

One exploded in a puff of smoke, the heat scalding Dominick's hand.

"Do you guys have any guns? Let me help."

"No guns," Dominick called out. "We ran out of ammo."

"You didn't bring enough?"

"Apparently not."

"I swear, I'm gone for a few months, and everything goes to hell."

Dominick couldn't help himself; he burst out laughing. "You have *no* idea."

"No guns," Frieda said. "But I do have something better."

Arthur turned around, and Frieda held out his sword. He took it gingerly, the weight settling into his hand and giving him strength. Dominick could see the look on his face shift to one of confidence when he held the blade aloft.

"It's been too long." Arthur turned to face the door and the approaching horde. "Time to get some payback."

He charged alongside Dominick, swinging his sword and cutting down another bat-like beast. He swiped again, his attack cutting through two of the flying golems in one swing. Both collapsed to the ground, kicking up dust into the air.

"Just like old times?" he asked Dominick, cutting down another demon.

Dominick faced off against another hellhound. "If we had times like these," he said. "I would have quit long ago."

Arthur laughed. "Touché."

They fought in sync, stepping around each other and blocking the front entrance of the shop. Frieda stood behind them, ready to assist if needed and making sure none of the demons made it past the two men to encircle them.

Any demon that came close, Arthur's sword sliced. It amazed Dominick at how graceful the man looked. He'd only seen him fight a few times, but watching him in action seemed awe-inspiring. The sword moved as an extension of his arm.

They might actually have a chance. That thought didn't last long, however. Dominick glanced past the approaching demons to the street outside. Larger demons lurked out there, including at least five of the type he had faced in Pennsylvania and a few more that looked even bigger and more horrible. They just waited, watching patiently.

The creatures wanted to wear them down. Their trio fought only the fodder, and killing them had no effect on the main army. Eventually, they would grow weary, and the stronger demons would step in to finish them.

Despite their best efforts, they only delayed the inevitable.

"Where's Abigail?" Arthur asked during a lull in the fight. He stood panting and looked tired, but for now, they still held up. "I felt her here somewhere but out of my reach."

Dominick didn't answer right away. He couldn't think of anything good to tell Arthur about the situation that wouldn't cause the man to worry. Instead, he exchanged a glance with Frieda, hoping she might explain. However, she looked just as helpless as he felt.

"Is she okay?" Arthur glanced between the two of them. "What aren't you telling me?"

"No," Dominick said, finally. "She's not all right. She did this."

✳✳✳

Frieda felt the strongest conflicting feelings of her life, a mix of hope and sadness, as she watched Arthur and Dominick battle next to the broken window. She had accepted that she would die here, but that came before Arthur had shown up, and now the thought of losing him all over again filled her with dread.

Elated to have him back, just seeing him standing there left her breathless, but knowing that they would all die here like this terrified her. At least, he wouldn't die in hell, but rather with his sword in his hand.

How had he returned? How had he escaped the clutches of Surgat's hell? He looked like the Arthur she remembered and even had the same scars on his body that she had traced with her fingertips those many years ago.

Lost in thought, trying to come to terms with the idea that Arthur had come back, she heard a coughing sound behind her. Haatim lay there with his eyes open. He appeared completely disoriented as if he couldn't get a grasp on his surroundings.

"Haatim." Frieda bent and grabbed his hand. "Are you okay?"

He blinked. "I don't know."

"You look like hell."

He chuckled, and then coughed. "It hurts to laugh. My head hurts. Everything hurts."

"Did you find Abigail?" Frieda asked. "Is she still alive?"

After a pause, Haatim nodded. "Yes."

Frieda let out a sigh. "Thank God."

Haatim shook his head. "Alive for now."

Chapter 42

Abigail found herself in a vast empty space, no longer surrounding herself with memories to make it seem more real. She couldn't afford to expend the effort to create scenery for them. Instead, she would need all her focus for the demon if she stood any chance of coming out of this alive.

As soon as she lowered her mental barriers to keep Surgat at bay, the demon's ugly presence locked onto her. It came hurtling out of nowhere and enveloped her. It had the effect of dropping her into an endless ocean of freezing cold water, and she entered a fight for her life.

Surgat attacked and manipulated, trying to scrub her out of existence and claim the body for its own. Its raw hatred contained mixed-in euphoria. It grew certain that it had won the fight, and now that she had nowhere left to run, it would take only a matter of time.

And it had it right; or, at least, it would have done under normal circumstances. Abigail couldn't possibly go toe-to-toe with the demon in a battle of wills. The creature just had to destroy this last little bit of the previous occupant, and the body would belong to it. The integration would have completed.

But she couldn't allow that to happen.

She had an ace up her sleeve.

Abigail waited until the demon pressed in on her and their identities intertwined, and then she focused on the last memory she'd visited, strapped down to the table. With her eyes closed, she let the demon come inside, and then brought out the name.

She spoke the demon's name.

Not aloud, but powerfully and with utter surety that she *knew* the demon. She knew the true and abstract existence it occupied and had the power to will it out of existence. Here, it acted as a weapon, emboldening her and giving her strength as it weakened the demon. It represented the very essence of the creature and took away its power.

Everything stopped all at once, the demon quivering in horror when it realized the implications.

She could destroy him.

"I know your name," she said. "I know the real *you.*"

"*You know nothing.*"

"I know that you have no power over me," she said. "Not anymore."

"*You think that you can defeat me?*"

Abigail could feel its rage, as well as its fear. Then it came at her again, attacking even more furiously than before.

Abigail felt stronger now, more in control of the situation, but the fight remained far from over. The only difference now was that now they stood on equal footing.

✲✲✲

"More are coming," Dominick said, trying to catch his breath. Arthur glanced over toward the broken window. More demons gathered outside, and the larger ones looked about to enter the fray.

His arms ached from swinging the sword, and his feet throbbed where the broken glass had cut into his bare skin. Each step he took left a bloody trail on the floor, but he didn't mind the pain. Loved it, in fact, and let it wash over him. Just feeling the pain brought joy because that meant he could feel *something*. So much time had passed since he'd experienced any senses at all.

Arthur looked out at the approaching demons. Many of them he knew personally. Knew how dangerous those ones were, and even with his sword in hand, the Hunters wouldn't stand up long against them when they attacked.

The trio had bottlenecked the demons to the window with decent effectiveness, but as they became wearier, it would become more and more difficult to hold them at bay.

Worse still, the ground of the shop had split apart under their feet. He stepped back, avoiding one such rift, and turned to face Frieda. "What's going on?"

"The portal created the rifts," Frieda said. "But it has closed now."

"What does that mean?"

Frieda hesitated, chewing her lips, and then said, "The ground will collapse like a giant sinkhole."

"That sounds bad," Dominick said. "Is that bad?"

Neither of them responded.

Across the street, the town hall building crumbled as entire sections fell into the rifts. It made a shuddering roar as it fell apart and disappeared into the world below.

"We need to move," Frieda said. "It won't take long before this building falls too."

"What about Abigail?" Arthur asked. "Where is she?"

"We don't know," Dominick said. "But it's over. There is no going back."

Arthur didn't want to believe that. Even if the demon had taken control of her, no way could she have *gone, gone.*

Right?

"No, she can't."

"It's over." Frieda stood behind them and helped the other man to his feet. "We lost, Arthur. I'm sorry. Abigail has gone. If we don't try to leave right now, we'll go too. The portal closing gave us a chance, and we can't afford to miss it."

Arthur didn't have a good response but knew in his heart that Frieda had called it right. Even if Abigail overcame the demon, if they didn't leave immediately, then they would die regardless. He felt fine with dying, and in fact, had experienced death for a long time already, but he didn't want the other three to share the same fate fighting for a lost cause.

Arthur nodded his agreement. "We should go and, at least, make the attempt."

"We can leave out the back. Our car is parked nearby."

They edged toward the back of the shop, attacking any demon that came close, and moved in a line. The door, though locked, proved no obstacle for Dominick, who broke it open with the hilt of his knife.

The street behind the shop stood empty, which came as a relief. Frieda and the other man—Arthur assumed that was the man who had saved him—headed out toward the car. She half-carried the guy as they went, and he seemed thoroughly rundown and beat up. Arthur didn't know if he was a new Hunter or someone else, but he felt grateful that the man stood with them.

Behind them, the demonic horde moved into the shop, making a lot of noise as they went. Arthur waited until Dominick got outside before following. He pushed the door closed and ran over to the car.

"Let's go." Dominick ran toward the car and climbed into the driver's seat. He turned on the engine, bringing the car to life. Arthur jumped into the passenger seat, and Frieda climbed into the back.

The other man, however, hesitated before getting in, glancing behind.

"What is it, Haatim?" Frieda asked.

"Abigail."

Arthur followed his gaze but couldn't see anything. Only the demonic horde. "I don't see her."

Haatim shook his head. "Neither do I, but I can sense her. Abigail needs our help."

Just hearing her name filled Arthur with raw emotion that he hadn't experienced in what felt like forever. His adrenaline rush had worn off now, and things had settled, and so he only just started to understand how much he had lost. Those years in prison and his time in hell, it seemed like multiple lifetimes away from his daughter.

"Abigail," Arthur whispered.

"Haatim, come on!" Frieda shouted.

"She needs our help," Haatim said.

"We can't help her anymore. We can't do anything. It's over. We need to get out of here."

Haatim stood firm. "No," he said. "There is nothing *you* can do."

✳✳✳

Abigail fought for her life. The void surrounded them, a vast and incomprehensible emptiness for their final showdown. It all came down to this moment. She had nowhere to run anymore, no chance to retreat and regroup. This was it, and she fought like a cornered animal who understood that survival depended on this instant.

The demon saw that the end had come, too. Whoever won this showdown would gain control of Abigail's body. Even though she knew its name and had power over it, the beast refused to give up. It thrashed and struck at her, trying to break her will with brute force.

It felt like their fight went on for hours, but time had no meaning in this place. It probably lasted mere seconds, or maybe no time at all. They simply floated in this place of unreality.

At first, it seemed as if they fought evenly matched. She pushed against the demon, and it pushed back against her, and nothing changed. They both fought to break through the other's defense and crush their will, and nothing concrete happened. However, finally, they each recognized a pattern in the fight.

The demon had more strength.

Slowly, and though only a centimeter at a time, they both realized that Abigail faltered. Inexorably, it crushed her, demoralized her, and it would only prove a matter of time before the demon won complete control and wiped her out.

Simply coming to that realization made the fight that much more desperate for Abigail. She would lose, which made continuing the fight at all significantly more difficult. Only delaying the inevitable, no matter how hard she tried to convince herself, she couldn't win.

The demon gloated and redoubled its efforts. It wouldn't take long now before it had consumed her soul.

Chapter 43

"We need to go," Frieda grabbed Haatim's arm and tried to draw him back into the car. "It's over."

He refused to believe that; it couldn't end like this. Somewhere in the horde of demons, he could feel Abigail. She trembled with weakness. The fight raged inside her, like two titans battling for survival where one of them would, eventually, get destroyed. They clashed against one another for control and domination.

He could also sense that Abigail stood on the losing end.

"She's still in there." He pulled his arm loose and took a step toward the demons. The ground shook underfoot, but not from the portal. Now, the cracks in the pavement expanded, and the entire town neared collapse. It became difficult to keep his balance while the rifts collapsed in on themselves. "She needs my help."

"She's gone," Frieda said. "It's over; we need to go. Before it's too late."

"We can't leave her!"

"She's right," Arthur said, with heaviness in his voice, and eyes full of pain. "Abigail has gone."

Frieda grabbed his arm once more and dragged him toward the car. Haatim glanced behind. Dominick sat in the driver's seat, frowning at him. He didn't say anything, but Haatim could tell by his eyes that he, too, had given up.

He didn't have any hope. He believed, like Frieda and Arthur, that Abigail had become lost to them. They all believed that the demon had control now and that the integration had completed. They couldn't imagine a way in which they might help her, and they remained right that it had come time to leave.

Not for him, though. He refused to accept that Abigail would lose this fight and her identity. Though this could only stay as her fight, he wouldn't let her face it alone. He could help her, if only by offering support and encouragement. After everything that had happened, everything they had been through, it *couldn't* end this way.

It wouldn't.

Haatim jerked free once more and rushed forward, running to the throng of demons and Abigail. Frieda called something behind him, stepping out of the vehicle and trying to follow.

"Go," he shouted. "Leave me."

He recited a sutra chant, something that had always made him feel calm and relaxed, and focused on the words. Haatim drew strength from them, using them to focus what remained of his energy and tapping deep into his reserves. The chant made him feel stronger.

The rift expanded, and the ground tore asunder as the Earth weakened and collapsed. It acted as a giant sinkhole, and everything fell into it. Already, jagged cracks had split apart and now widened and expanded. At this rate, in no time at all, it would have swallowed the entire town.

Haatim rushed toward the demons, and they parted before him. They fled from him, climbing over each other to get away, and the ones that proved too slow disintegrated when they reached about a meter from him. They let out cries of pain and lost their hold on this world, collapsing to the ground.

Coldness stole over him, but he couldn't stop. Determined, he continued to force his way through the horde. They closed in behind him, cutting him off from his friends. As soon as his barrier fell, they would attack and rip him to shreds.

That didn't stop him, though, and he kept going, pushing to the center. Abigail stood right in the middle of it all, near one of the rifts. Her open eyes glowed red, and her face bore a mask of pain and rage.

Haatim stumbled toward her, not sure of his plan. He doubted he could drag her away. Doubted he could even hold the barrier for more than few seconds. Out of ideas, he continued chanting, finishing the sutra.

Surgat wouldn't let him get close to her. Most probably, it would kill him just for trying. Still, he had to make the attempt.

A violent shudder rocked the ground, and he tripped, falling forward and landing hard on his chest. He hit his head on the pavement and lost focus on his chant. Dazed, he forced himself to sit up. The demons hadn't approached yet, still afraid, but he wouldn't manage to recreate the barrier. Once they realized it, they would eat him alive.

He stood and hurried toward Abigail. She spun, staring at him, face contorting violently.

The demon had control of her body once more. Whatever remained of Abigail had almost lost the fight and would soon get snuffed out. He could barely sense her anymore, and the internal battle wound down. Haatim would find it difficult to reach her.

However, he had to try.

"Abigail." He took a step toward her. The ground continued to shake, and he had to raise his voice. "Abigail, please. I know you're in there."

"The girl has gone," Abigail said, her voice deep and guttural. The piercing red eyes bored into him, digging through his soul. The sheer confidence and evil of the demonic presence made Haatim quiver. "This body is mine."

"Not so. I can feel her in there, fighting. Please, Abigail, I know you can hear me."

"You know nothing. Not yet, at least. Soon, though."

Abigail stood next to one of the rifts, and it went further down than the light could reach.

"I know you're in there, Abigail," Haatim said. "I don't want to speak to this demon. I want to speak to you."

It took a step toward him, and he fought down the urge to flinch.

"I told you; she's dead."

"Then, so am I. If Abigail has gone, then just kill me. You should find it easy, right? I won't even try to stop you."

The demon took another step, then hesitated midstride. A confused expression crossed Abigail's face. A flash of fear came from the demon, quickly replaced by rage.

"I knew she remained in there," Haatim whispered. "Abigail, please. If you can hear me, you *have* to fight this."

A moment passed. The ground continued to shudder. The cracks in the pavement widened. It sounded like thunder in the distance as different sections of the town fell into the rifts. They expanded near him, and all too soon, this section of the town would collapse as well.

Time had all but run out.

"You can do it, Abigail. I know you can. You can push it back."

"I can't," she said, panic in her voice. And it had become her voice once more; the demon forced aside temporarily. "Please, run, Haatim. Don't make me kill you."

"I won't go anywhere. I know you can do this. You can gain control."

"It's too much. I tried and lost. The demon has won."

"It hasn't won while you remain."

"I don't have strength enough."

"No, I refuse to believe that."

"It's inevitable," the demon said, regaining control. It took another step toward Haatim, only a few meters away. "She *will* fall to me."

"You won't fail," Haatim said, still speaking only to Abigail. "Don't listen to the demon; focus on my voice. Only on my voice."

Another step from the demon, but this one wavering. It held a knife, which looked jagged. Haatim imagined it ripping into his stomach, cutting him open. He envisioned himself, lying on the pavement and bleeding out only moments before the town collapsed, and he disappeared into the world below.

He thought to try and channel again, to call upon whatever power coursed through him to help Abigail. Maybe he could help her push back the demon.

However, something inside him knew that as untrue. For one thing, he felt too weak to channel right now. And trying it again would prove dangerous, if not deadly, to him. More importantly, it would be *wrong* to try and interfere. Whatever this battle was, he couldn't help with it. This had to remain Abigail's fight, and hers alone.

"I ... can't ... Haatim. Please, I beg you. Run!"

"No," he said, speaking softer now. "I shan't go anywhere. Either you'll win this, or the demon will kill me. You have to choose."

"Not a choice! I can't stop it. The last time Surgat came to Earth, they tried *everything* possible to control him, but nothing worked. What chance do

I have?"

"The difference between last time and this time." Haatim stepped forward and put his hand on Abigail's arm. The muscles tensed, but she didn't pull away. "You. Abigail, *you* are strong enough to handle this. When we first met, you saved my life, and you didn't even have to. You are the most amazing, selfless, and caring person I've ever come across, and if anyone can overcome this and win, you can."

The hand holding the knife moved up, shaking, and stopped an inch from Haatim's throat. He refused to move or flinch, staring straight into Abigail's eyes. They remained red, but now flecks of brown had mixed in as she tried to regain control.

A crack spread near them, only a few meters away. The ground under his feet became unsteady, soon to fall, and Haatim doubted he could get away from it even if he tried. The building to his right ripped apart, fragmenting from the foundation up to the roof, and collapsed into the nothingness below.

The crevices seemed to go on forever. He imagined falling into one of the holes and held no doubt it would take a long time for him to reach the bottom. Abigail had more strength, but they'd run out of time. He needed to *reach* her and convince her that she could do this.

"You risked your future to try and save Arthur from hell, and then you risked your life saving the people of Raven's Peak from a demonic threat that you didn't even have responsibility for. You didn't know those people. You didn't owe them anything, and yet you still felt willing to give up your life to save them."

"That doesn't make you intelligent," the demon said. "It makes you a fool."

"It makes you brave," Haatim said. "It meant you had the willingness to stand up to any threat and protect anyone no matter what the cost. It makes you a hero. You don't think you can beat this demon, but I *know* you can because you are the most selfless and courageous person I've ever met. If anyone in the world can deal with this, it's you."

"I failed once already."

"You hadn't readied for it then. This time, you have."

The eyes grew unfocused while the battle raged inside Abigail's body. Next to them, the crack came dangerously close, but Haatim didn't move. The rift had cut him off from his only avenue of escape and made it impossible to get away.

"If I have it wrong, Abigail, then just let go. Let the demon kill me. If I have it wrong, then just give up and stop fighting."

"Haatim, please, leave. I don't want to kill you."

He closed his eyes, sure that death reached for him, no matter what happened. The ground shuddered, the crevice expanded, and he had just a few centimeters of solid ground left on which to stand.

"I know," he said. "But, will you save me?"

He took a step back, to the edge of the crevice, and let go of Abigail's arm. Then, with a sad smile, he fell back into the rift.

The darkness swallowed him.

Chapter 44

Abigail watched in horror when Haatim disappeared into the crevice. It seemed like watching through a blurry window, as she remained only vaguely aware of her surroundings. Still locked in mortal combat with the demon, it tried to finish crushing her.

All of her focus on the fight flew away at that moment. Her fear and worry that she couldn't defeat Surgat took a backseat to her worry that would lose Haatim forever.

With all her strength, she lashed out and reached for him through the black void. She wouldn't let him die. Not after losing Arthur. No, she refused to lose anyone else, and least of all Haatim.

The demon roared in her mind, trying to crush and push her back. Instead of engaging it, though, she forced her way past it and disregarded Surgat totally. Abigail found reserves of strength she hadn't even known existed and focused on one simple idea ...

She wouldn't allow Haatim to die.

Angry and determined, she seized control of her body and forced the demon into submission. Then she reached toward Haatim through the darkness.

✳✳✳

Haatim didn't want to open his eyes. The air rushed around him, and raw panic hit during the interminable fall into the abyss. However, in addition to the panic, he also felt a tranquil peace wash over him. If he had to die like this, then he could accept it.

Seconds ticked past while he plummeted, and he imagined what his body would look like broken and shattered at the bottom. Would it hurt when he hit? Would he feel anything? He prayed that he would die on impact and not suffer for hours before, finally, expiring. Haatim didn't want to die alone in a hole after hours or days.

More time slipped past, and the whistling wind buffeted him as he fell.

Then, suddenly, he stopped.

At first, he believed that he'd hit the ground, though felt no pain to go along with his lack of momentum. It felt as if he lay on a bed of air, buoyed by something he couldn't explain. His eyes popped open, and a pinprick of light above led out of the rift and to the sky.

Then, he floated upward.

Confused and bewildered, he looked around. Some entity or energy pulled him toward ground level. He flew out of the hole and settled on the street only a meter away from Abigail.

His friend looked exhausted when she collapsed to the ground next to him, but very much herself. Even her eyes had reverted to the brown that he'd known from so long ago.

The eyes that he'd fallen in love with the first time he'd met her.

"Abigail?"

"I'm here," she said.

He scooped her into a tight hug and pulled her close. She shivered, cold, but he felt her hold him back. "Thank God."

She didn't respond. Slowly, they separated, and he glanced around. Haatim had forgotten about the demons, but when he looked up, he saw that most of them fled. Some ran, others flew, but they all tried to get away from them. Off to the right, the car still sat parked, and Frieda, Arthur, and Dominick stared at them with shock on their faces.

The ground continued to shake violently, and wide fissures spread all around them. The devastated city sprawled around them. Half of the buildings lay destroyed, some on fire, and utter chaos surrounded them.

"We need to go." Haatim climbed to his feet and reached out to Abigail, who took his hand, a look of confusion in her eyes.

"Is it ... over?"

"Not yet."

They ran toward the parked vehicle. Arthur threw open the door and stepped toward Abigail as she came, an expression of sheer awe on his face. He had found a coat and pair of shorts now, probably from Dominick's gear. They appeared a little small for him.

Arthur wrapped her in a big hug. "Abi!"

"I thought ... I thought I'd never see you again," she said.

"We need to go," Dominick said. "The reunion has to wait."

As if to emphasize, the ground shook even more, and then tipped sideways and sank. Quickly, they jumped into the car, and Dominick drove toward the road that led out of town.

The cracks lay all over now, expanding even further, and still, demons flew through the air. Dominick weaved around the cracks and rifts, bouncing over torn sections of pavement.

Haatim looked back at the town and wreckage. The demons scattered, disappearing into the woods and flying off into the sky. Soon, the place would have gone entirely.

"What's that?" Dominick asked.

"What?" Haatim turned to face forward. The others all sat staring ahead. Things blocked the road.

"Demons," Haatim said.

"Hundreds of them." Arthur nodded. "They've blocked the way. They don't want us to leave."

Dominick slowed, but the vibrations of the ground caught up with them. The collapse had a compounding effect, and already, this section seemed about to fall too. "We can't get through them."

"Keep driving," Abigail said. "Go faster."

"There are too many!" Dominick said, but did do as asked. He kept going, picking up speed. Behind them, the road gave way and disappeared.

"Abigail?"

"Keep going," she said.

The demons waited just in front of them, maybe fifteen meters ahead. They formed a wall to block them, claws and talons out and ready.

"Abigail?"

"Go!"

Haatim gritted his teeth and glanced over at her. They couldn't make it through the horde blocking their way, and nor could they go back. But, if she thought that their car could get through the group, then she'd turned into a crazy woman.

When he glanced at her, though, he changed his mind.

Her face looked focused, and she had her eyes closed, concentrating and barely breathing. When they reached just a few meters from the horde, she opened her eyes, and they glowed.

Except, not red anymore. Now, they glowed with a golden light, pure and beautiful.

An explosion sounded. All the demons erupted. Not into puffs of smoke or cement but into black and green ichor. It splashed all over the car, blocking the windows. Just as well they'd come to a stop.

In shocked silence, Dominick eased past the goop and pulled out of the city and onto the road. A moment passed, and then Dominick reached up and flipped on the windshield wipers. It did little in clearing away the goo, but it gave enough to keep driving.

Another ten minutes passed, still in shocked silence. When Haatim looked over at Abigail, her eyes no longer glowed. She looked sleepy, but otherwise all right. Then she glanced at him with a quizzical expression, but he couldn't think of anything to say.

Finally, Dominick said, "What the hell was that?"

No one answered. They continued in silence, heading away from Raven's Peak. After a while, rain fell and washed the disgusting entrails and ichor off the car.

Abigail laid her head on Haatim's shoulder and fell asleep. Still not speaking, they continued onward, looking to put as much distance between them and the city as possible before stopping for the night.

It took a long while for it sink in for Haatim, but when it did, he found himself smiling.

It had finished.

They lived.

Epilogue

They drove in silence for a few hours, finally stopping at a hotel a few cities away. The roads held little traffic at this time of night, and if anyone outside Raven's Peak knew what had happened, they didn't let on. It seemed too quiet.

Haatim felt exhausted in ways he'd never even imagined but also euphoric and vindicated beyond his wildest dreams. They had won; or at least, had survived. Though the town lay destroyed, and countless dangerous demons got released into the world, Abigail lived, and Arthur had come back.

Abigail lay asleep on his shoulder, but when they parked to go up to their hotel rooms, he tapped her to wake her. She yawned, looking up at him blearily, and he smiled.

"Hey," she said.

"Hey."

He helped her out of the car, and then walked her up to her room, helping her inside. She kicked off her shoes and collapsed onto the bed, falling asleep as soon as her head hit the pillow.

When he made his way back to the vehicle, he found only Frieda there. She smiled at him, and then shook her head. "Passed out?"

"As soon as she laid down."

"I can't believe ..." Frieda shook her head. "I can't believe it's over."

"Not quite," Haatim said. "What about Mitchell?"

She sobered, frowning. "We'll have to deal with it."

"If we can find him. No doubt, he'll have gone into hiding."

"We *will* find him," Frieda said. "You can count on that."

"Where did Dominick go?"

"I sent him to get clothes. For Arthur and Abigail."

Haatim laughed. "We didn't exactly pack thinking we'd win."

Frieda smiled. "No. We didn't."

Dominick returned about an hour later with a ridiculous amount of clothing. Frieda took it and put it in Abigail's and Arthur's rooms for when they awoke, and then the three of them went to the hotel dining hall and sat down to eat. Haatim wanted to shower and get cleaned up, but right now, he felt starved. He ordered two of their largest meals, including sides, and then ate all of it.

Frieda and Dominick watched him with something akin to surprise.

"What?" he asked.

"Hungry?" Dominick said.

Haatim looked down at the empty plates with a bit of embarrassment. "Yeah, maybe a little."

By the time they'd done eating, Abigail and Arthur had woken, changed their clothes, and showered, and now came down to join them. Abigail took a seat next to Haatim, smiling. She had brushed her hair and cleaned up, and he couldn't help but stare.

"What?" she asked. "Do I have something on my face?"

When she brushed at her cheek, he shook his head quickly. "No," he said. "You just ... you look beautiful."

Abigail blushed and looked at the menu, smiling ever so slightly.

Arthur leaned down before taking his seat and kissed Frieda full on the lips. That drew surprised looks from Dominick and Abigail, followed by a round of laughter. When they parted, Frieda sat there, breathless.

"I've wanted to do that for years," he said. "To hell with the Council."

Dominick cleared his throat. "About that."

Arthur frowned. "What?"

Dominick opened his mouth, and then shrugged instead. "It can wait."

They ordered their food, and everyone sat in silence, just savoring the moment and glad to be alive. Once Abigail and Arthur had finished, they headed outside and into the night air to talk away from the crowds.

They explained to Arthur what had happened since he'd gone, and about the loss of the Council and Church. Some of it shocked him, but certain parts didn't seem to surprise him as much.

Dominick asked him about his time spent in Surgat's hell, but he brushed the topic aside. Clearly, he didn't feel ready to talk about that, so they dropped the issue. Whatever had happened there, Haatim knew, it had been horrible.

"What happens now?" Haatim asked, finally. "What do we do next?"

They all glanced at each other. Arthur remained extremely quiet, lost in his thoughts and barely seemed to pay attention.

"I don't know," Frieda said. "You should leave, though."

"What?"

"The Church won't stop hunting us. All of us, but not you. Father Paladina assured me that you would stay safe as long as you cut all contact with us, but they won't stop coming after the rest of us until we all die."

"Because of me," Abigail said.

"Because of all of *this*," Frieda said. "Not just you."

"But, if I did die," Abigail said. "Then the Church wouldn't have any further reason to come after you."

"We don't know that," Frieda said. "What we *do* know is that if Haatim leaves, he can stay safe and escape from all this violence."

Haatim stood in silence for a few seconds, all eyes on him. He let the information sink in. This gave him what he'd wanted: a chance to get out of this life and away from the people who'd lied and hurt him. Ever since he'd met Abigail, his life had gone on a wild roller-coaster ride of violence and loss.

This offered his chance just to walk away like he'd planned earlier when entering Raven's Peak. He had accomplished what he'd set out to do, and Abigail had come back safe. Yes, he could leave now, never look back, and pick up his life where it left off in Arizona.

Except, he realized, that wasn't his life. Had never been his life. He had just gone through the motions, wandering in a daze. Abigail hadn't disrupted his life when she rescued him from the cult but woken him. No, he had nothing to go back to.

His life waited right here.

"No," he said. "I won't go anywhere."

"Haatim, you should seriously—"

"After everything we've gone through, after everything that happened to us, I'm staying. I can make decisions about things, and I choose this. Whatever the hell just happened back there in Raven's Peak, we let a lot of evil into the world."

"The demons," Frieda said, smiling.

"Thousands," Dominick said. "Most just left and remain out there somewhere."

Haatim said, "And it will fall to us to stop them and send those creatures back to wherever they came from. The way I see it, we're still Hunters."

They all stared at him.

Then Dominick burst out laughing. "Couldn't have said it better myself," he said. "Count me in."

"Me too," Arthur said. "We made the decisions that led to this, and the responsibility lies with us to help set things right."

"So, what, then? The Council has gone," Frieda said. "Our allies disavowed us. We have no more obligation or necessity to live that life."

"Then, we make a new one," Haatim said. "We start over. Maybe, we can convince the Church to stop hunting for us, maybe not. Either way, we have a job to do, and we can't sit around patting ourselves on the back. Our job starts now."

Everyone turned to look at Frieda, who hesitated, and then raised her hands. "All right, then. I'll make some calls."

They spent the rest of the night talking and reminiscing. One by one, they all headed up to their hotel rooms to sleep until only Haatim and Abigail remained. They sat at the picnic table in silence, enjoying the night air and each other's company.

She looked distant, thoughtful. Haatim watched her, wishing he knew what went through her head. Generally, she seemed a quiet person, keeping to herself. Haatim had thought he'd broken through her barriers, but each time he took one down, another went up in its place.

"I love you," he said.

She blinked, coming back to reality, and looked over at him. Then she opened her mouth, but he held up his hand to stop her.

"You don't need to say anything," he said. "You don't need to tell me it back or say a single word, and it will never change no matter how you feel about me."

A moment passed. "Then, why tell me?"

"Because you're leaving," he said.

Surprise flashed across her face, quickly replaced by sadness. Finally, she nodded. "How did you know?"

"Because I know you just as much as I love you. I can't stop you, and nor would I want to. I won't ask you to stay because it wouldn't be fair to you."

"I feel ... different," Abigail said. "In the town, I ..."

"You stopped me from falling in midair," Haatim said. "How?"

"I don't know." Abigail shook her head. "No one else saw it happen, but you all saw when I ..."

"... made the demons explode?" Haatim smiled.

"Yeah, but I can't explain it. I forced Surgat down and beat him, but something feels different."

"You took control. You won."

"Maybe," she said. "But it changed me."

"How so?"

"I don't know. That's what I need to find out. I need to find out for myself, or things will never go back to normal."

Haatim nodded. "I understand."

Abigail breathed a sigh of relief. "Thank you." She rose from her seat. "I should leave now before the others wake. You'll tell them for me?"

"Of course," he said. "You will come back?"

She nodded. "I will. This isn't goodbye forever. Only goodbye for now."

Haatim thought about that. "You promise?"

"With all my heart. I *will* return to you."

"I'll hold you to that," he said. "Don't make me wait too long, or I'll come looking for you."

Abigail smiled. "I know you will."

Then she stepped in close and kissed him on the corner of his mouth.

His heart skipped a beat, and he wrapped his arms around her and pulled her close. He focused on the way she felt, the smell of her skin, and the taste of her lips.

When they pulled apart, her eyes glowed that same golden color he'd seen in the car.

A flash, and then they returned to normal.

"Goodbye, Haatim."

Then, she turned and walked away from him.

"Goodbye," Haatim said.

Every fiber in his being wanted to go after her, to keep her here. But he didn't. At that moment, he knew that he loved her in a way he would never love another human being no matter how long he lived. And because he loved her, he would let her go.

He just prayed that she would come back.

End of Book III
Lincoln Cole

About the Author

Lincoln Cole is a Columbus-based author who enjoys traveling and has visited many different parts of the world, including Australia and Cambodia, but always returns home to his pugamonster, Luther, and wife. His love for writing was kindled at an early age through the works of Isaac Asimov and Stephen King, and he enjoys telling stories to anyone who will listen.

Intentionally Left Blank

Intentionally Left Blank

Intentionally Left Blank

Intentionally Left Blank

Intentionally Left Blank

Intentionally Left Blank

Intentionally Left Blank

Intentionally Left Blank

Intentionally Left Blank

9 781945 862014